D1015103

Jan 18

THREE
SIDES
OF A
HEART

stories about
love triangles

THREE SIDES OF A HEART

stories about love triangles

EDITED BY NATALIE C. PARKER

HARPER TEEN
An Imprint of HarperCollinsPublishers

Library of Congress Cataloging-in-Publication Data
Parker, Natalie C., editor.
    pages   cm.
    Three sides of a heart : stories about love triangles / edited by Natalie C. Parker.
    First edition.
    ISBN 978-0-06-2424471 (hardback)
    [1. Romance fiction, American.   2. Short stories, American.   3. Love—Fiction.
4. Short stories.]
PZ5.T4128   2017   [Fic—dc23]

Typography by Erin Fitzsimmons
17 18 19 20 21   PC/LSCH   10 9 8 7 6 5 4 3 2 1

First Edition

For my brother, A. Cajiuat Posadas,
who left beautiful stories in his wake

◄ CONTENTS ►

DEAR READER

The love triangle. The only topic more likely to spark a disagreement over Thanksgiving dinner is politics.

Whether your first encounter with the love triangle was Olivia/Viola/Orsino in Shakespeare's *Twelfth Night*, or Heathcliff/Cathy/Edgar in Brontë's *Wuthering Heights*, or James Potter/Lily Potter/Severus Snape in Rowling's Harry Potter series, it's unlikely you emerged from the experience emotionally unscathed. Perhaps you lost your heart out on the moors of England, or secretly wished the cards fell in Olivia's favor. Or perhaps you started a petition to end any and all fictional romantic entanglements involving more than two people. Love triangles can be enticingly sexy, deeply divisive, or occasionally hilarious, and the trope isn't limited to the romance genre. It appears in all kinds of fiction, from space adventures to boarding school dramas.

Young adult fiction is no exception and has become ground zero for love triangles guaranteed to cause arguments, memes, and tears alike. But within YA the trope is criticized for creating unrealistic expectations for readers, for falling into formulaic patterns, and for weakening otherwise strong female protagonists. In the wake of *The Vampire Diaries, Twilight,* and *The Hunger Games,* young adult fiction saw an abundance of the classic love triangle—one girl choosing between two boys who in some way represent different versions of the person she wants to become.

But within these pages are sixteen reimaginings of the love triangle. Some toy with the traditional, others depart dramatically, but all are an examination of what this trope has to offer. The triangles that follow challenge and interrogate the classic; they are political and inclusive and representative of every genre. Through the lens of romance, these stories pose questions about self-determination and what it means to embrace the power of choice.

It has been a pleasure and an adventure working with the authors on this collection, and it is an honor to introduce sixteen new faces of the love triangle. I hope that in them, you find something familiar, something new, and something unexpected.

Riddles in Mathematics
KATIE COTUGNO

"All right," Steven says grandly. "You walk into a room with a kerosene lamp, a candle, and a fireplace. What do you light first?"

I watch Taylor think about it. She's lying on the couch in my parents' living room, her feet up in Steven's lap. Her socks have Nordic-style reindeer prancing across the ankles. "A match," she says finally, triumphant.

My brother frowns. "How did you know that one?"

Taylor shrugs. "Child's play," she says, then grins at me. "Right, Ro?"

"Right," I agree. I'm sitting cross-legged on the carpet next to the coffee table. It's Christmas Eve, so our house is full of people: my grandparents in the dining room, my little cousins running up and down the stairs, Dean Martin crooning on the stereo about a marshmallow world. My mom's collection of ceramic Christmas trees is clustered on the side table, their tiny colored lights winking away.

"Try this one, then, smarty," Steven tells Taylor, and I get up and go into the kitchen before he can finish. Taylor's mom and our mom were the only two pregnant women on our block in 1997, meaning my brother and Taylor have been best friends since they were zygotes. There's a picture of them on the bookshelf in our family room, three years old in their bathing suits, holding hands.

Back in the kitchen, my mom is finishing the seven fishes, which is actually five fishes because she already put out shrimp cocktail and clams casino as appetizers. She is nothing if not efficient. "Do you need help?" I ask, and she looks surprised I'm offering, which makes me feel a little crummy.

"I'm set," she says, pushing her dark bobbed hair out of her eyes with her forearm. "Go tell everybody to come sit down."

I pass the message on in the dining room and out in the backyard, where my namesake, Auntie Rowena, is smoking a cigarette on the deck. She lets me have a drag and tells me she loves me—something everyone in my family has been doing lately, like I've got cancer or I'm dying, or maybe just like I've suddenly got a reason to doubt my own lovability. Grandma Cynthia keeps glancing at my shorn head like it's done her harm.

I double back to the living room, where Taylor and Steven have their heads tipped close together; they've never dated, supposedly, although they went to every formal together freshman and sophomore year. Junior year Taylor had a real boyfriend, and it made Steven so totally unbearable that when Taylor finally dumped the guy I would have been ecstatic even if I hadn't hated the idea of him almost as much as my brother did.

"Time for food," I say, glancing at Taylor again. She's wearing dark jeans and a fuzzy cardigan, her hair long and a little frizzy. In the light from the candles on the table, her skin seems to glow. All through middle school I thought I wanted to be her, look like her, and dress like her, which, as it turns out, was not what I wanted at all.

"All right," my mom calls, carrying a giant pan full of spaghetti out into the dining room. "Everybody ready?"

Christmas Day is always kind of anticlimactic in our house, just the four of us instead of last night's parade of one thousand family members. In the afternoon Steven goes to Taylor's and I hang out watching a Hitchcock marathon on the classic movie channel, my mom perched like a swallow in the armchair across the living room. My dad comes in and settles beside me, the worn leather couch dipping under his weight. "You have a good Christmas?" he asks, putting a bearlike arm around me. "You like your presents?"

I nod. I did too, buttery brown leather hiking boots like Steven's that I know my mom picked out specially, plus a sterling silver key ring with my initials engraved on it. "For car keys," my mom explained apologetically when I opened the little box, and everyone grimaced. Three days ago I failed my road test. I couldn't manage the parallel park.

North by Northwest is on now, which is my dad's favorite.

He's the movie buff in our family, but my mom's the one who got me into costuming, who taught me all about Edith Head and Irene Sharaff. I've always loved clothes. The two of us used to go shopping together constantly, back when I still dressed to copy Taylor. Every year on my birthday we'd take Metro North into the city and go look at the costume exhibit at the Met.

"Do you still want to go?" she asked this year, a worried-looking furrow between her eyebrows. "Even though . . . ?"

For a second I thought she meant even though I was going to be sixteen and maybe I was too old for it, but then I realized she meant "Even though you're gay now," like she thought that meant I wouldn't like costumes anymore, and just like that I didn't want to do anything with her at all. "No," I deadpanned, "I want to go to a Giants game," and she actually nodded earnestly before she realized I was making fun of her.

"Really, Ro," she said, frowning, but then my birthday came and went and we had a cake and all, but neither one of us has brought up the museum since then.

"You okay, Squish?" my dad asks me now, squeezing my shoulders a little. I lean into the bulk of him, looking at the tree. I waited until my parents had been back together for almost six months before I came out last summer, and even then I was kind of afraid it was going to somehow break them up again. I told my mom first, had her parrot it back to my dad for me after I was in bed that night; afterward he came into my room and turned on the desk light, crouched down next to my bed. "I wish you'd told me," he said quietly. "I'm so sorry if I made you feel like you couldn't."

Now I tilt my head onto his shoulder, look back at the TV. "Yup," I say, rubbing the side of my face against the sleeve of his sweatshirt. "I'm good."

Play rehearsals start again at noon on the day after Christmas, so I jam one of Steven's hats on my head and schlep over to school through the snowdrifts. I started borrowing his clothes way before I chopped off all my hair, his big Patagonia sweatshirts and his skinny boy-band jeans, his T-shirts that were somehow always cooler than mine. We're nearly the same height, me and Steven, all long bones and noses and hooded eyes. My mom loved it at the time, even buying me my own stash of chinos and stripy boy sweaters. "It's adorable," she said back then. She did the same thing when she was my age, I know from family photos, decking herself out in overalls and big seventies glasses. "It's such a look." She finds it less adorable now, although of course she wouldn't say that. Instead she just frowns.

Rehearsals the day after Christmas is extreme, even for our school: Thomas Jefferson High puts on three shows a year instead of two, but only the most serious theater dweebs do the middle one because it goes up in January, which means coming in over break. I've never cared. My best friend, Danielle, goes to Pompano Beach every Christmas to visit her grandma, so it's not like I'd be doing much anyway. This year she tried to convince me to come with her, like she was especially worried about leaving me on my own.

By the time I get to school I'm sweating inside my puffy coat, but my hands and feet are frozen. I yank off my gloves with my teeth and dig my keys out of my backpack. Normally juniors don't get a key to the costume shop, but there were no rising seniors last year, and so Mrs. Royce gave it to me. This year's January show is *Once Upon a Mattress*; I can hear Donnie O'Neal singing in the auditorium about how he's in love with a girl named Fred.

Mariette Chen is waiting in the hallway outside the locked costume shop, sitting on the linoleum floor with her ankles crossed in front of her. "Hi, Ro," she says, getting to her feet. Her hair hangs long and black and straight past her shoulders. She's wearing leggings and boots that go up to her knees, like a Triple Crown jockey or one of the girls from the Pony Pals.

"Hey," I tell her, and smile. I always feel a little embarrassed in front of Mariette. Last year at the cast party for *The Glass Menagerie* we kissed a little, and after that she sent me a Facebook message wanting to know if I wanted to hang out, which I never answered because I am a piece of trash and also that was the same time Taylor broke up with her boyfriend and was over at our house every day for a week.

"How was Christmas?" Mariette asks as I let us inside and flick on the lights. The costume shop is tiny, just two dinosaur sewing machines left over from home ec in the nineties and piles of whatever mismatched fabric Mrs. Royce can get on clearance at the craft store. A lot of times all we do in here is modify weird dresses or whatever that come from Forever 21 to try and make them look like they're from colonial times or the Wild West, but every once in a while I get to make something really cool.

"It was good," I tell her. "How was yours?"

Mariette smiles like she wasn't expecting me to return the question, which makes me feel like a jerk. I like her, is the thing. I wouldn't have kissed her if I didn't. She's just not—

Anyway.

"It was nice," Mariette says, launching into a play-by-play of the fight her aunts all had over a Lord & Taylor gift card, and just like that, it isn't awkward anymore. We hang out in the costume shop for the rest of the afternoon, sewing underskirts for the ladies-in-waiting, passing the measuring tape back and forth. I show her how to use the serger. After a while we dig the ancient school-issue boom box out from under a pile of cardboard crowns, but the only station coming through is local Lite FM. "Who *listens* to this stuff?" Mariette asks, laughing in disgust after the second Celine Dion song comes on.

"My mom," I say, even though it isn't true. In reality she likes the Talking Heads and Patti Smith and Joy Division, has flawless post-punk taste.

But Mariette smiles at that, shakes her head a little ruefully. "Yeah," she says. "Mine too."

"Come on," Taylor says later that night, appearing in the doorway of my bedroom and curling her delicate fingers around the jamb. I'm at my desk, supposedly writing an essay about social reformation movements in the 1850s but actually doodling trim designs for the edges of the queen's red velvet gown in the margin of my notebook. "We're going to Carvel."

My heart stutters in the second before I recover, before I

realize that of course she means my brother is coming too. "It's actively snowing," I point out, nodding at the window above my bed.

Taylor shrugs. "All the more reason to get milk shakes," she tells me, coming into the room and peering over my shoulder. "That's pretty," she says, pointing at the trim design with one gold-painted fingernail.

"Yeah?" I ask too earnestly, looking up at her. Her tangle of hair brushes my cheek.

"Mm-hmm." Taylor tips her head and smiles at me, all lip balm and one crooked incisor; then, like we both realize at once how close our faces suddenly are, she straightens up, and I look back at the computer.

"Milk shakes," I say too loudly, immediately worried I've freaked her out somehow. I click save on the computer and push my chair back. "Let's do it."

Taylor's car is a ten-year-old Jetta that smells a little like Play-Doh but mostly like the sprigs of dried lavender that dangle from the rearview mirror. "Who was sitting up here?" Steven asks as we climb inside, adjusting the passenger seat to make room for his long, spindly teenage-boy legs. He's wearing the hat I borrowed earlier and of course it looks better on him, cooler in some ineffable Steven-ish way.

Taylor rolls her eyes. "What are you, my dad?"

"No," he defends himself, still fussing. "I just take my seat very seriously."

"Oh, we know that about you," Taylor says as I slide wordlessly into the back.

"Okay," she continues, switching to her riddle voice now and curling one hand around Steven's headrest as she backs out of the driveway. "Paul is six feet tall, works as a butcher's assistant, and wears size nine shoes. What does he weigh?"

"Meat," I say without thinking.

Taylor grins at me over her shoulder. "Nice, Ro."

"She's a ringer," Steven agrees. I slump down in my seat all the way into town.

It's strangely warm inside Carvel, considering it's an ice-cream shop in December, and we peel off our layers immediately, shedding scarves and gloves like molting lizards. Steven pulls his arms out of his unzipped parka and hangs it off his head by its hood like a little kid as he tries to convince Taylor that they should buy a Fudgie the Whale cake. The air smells like vanilla sugar. "See?" Taylor says, waving me off when I try to hand her money. "Carvel is always a good idea."

She swings her arm around me as we head back out into the parking lot, a chocolate milk shake heavy in my hand. My whole body prickles through four different layers of wool, everything hot and cold at once.

"You hanging in?" she asks, and I nod. I made Steven tell her for me after I came out to my family, not that he would have kept it a secret from her either way. She hugged me for an extra-long time the next time she saw me, and we haven't said a word about it since.

I'm not sick, I think about telling her. *I'm just gay.*

"You guys hanging out here tonight?" I ask instead, as we're driving back to my parents'. I'm working hard not to sound like I care one way or the other, but still I'm hit with a stab of disappointment when Steven shakes his head.

"Nah," he says. "Gonna head over to Henry's and watch a movie—which is why," he tells Taylor, "we should have gotten a Fudgie the Whale. We would have been fucking heroes." Then, over his shoulder, "You're on your own, Squish."

"Ro could come," Taylor points out, glancing at me in the mirror. "Why don't you come?"

Because that would be pathetic, mostly. "Nah, I'm good," I say, too brightly. I wish Danielle was back from the beach. "Thanks, though."

Back on our street, the Hudson kids three doors down are having a snowball fight by porch light, yesterday's snowman slouching drunkenly to the side. "Night, Ro," Taylor says as I'm climbing out of the backseat, her fingertips catching the edge of my sleeve as she waves over her shoulder. I watch the car until the taillights disappear.

Later that night I'm watching a makeover show on the couch when there's a clatter in the kitchen. For a second I think it's thieves or murderers, but in reality it's only Steven and Taylor—Taylor dragging Steven, actually, him stumbling with his arm slung over her shoulder. Taylor looks colossally annoyed. "What happened?" I ask, setting down my late-night bowl of Lucky Charms on the coffee table.

Taylor grimaces. "Like four shots of Jäger."

"Gross."

"Pretty much." She sighs. "Are your parents home?"

I shake my head; Taylor nods grimly. She juggles Steven's limbs for a second, navigating him around the side table to get to the staircase. She only comes up to his shoulder.

"What has an eye but can't see?" he slurs cheerfully.

"A needle, Steven," I can hear Taylor saying as she drags him up the stairs. "I told you that one in second grade."

She comes back down a few minutes later, scooping her hair out from under the collar of her jacket and twisting it into a knot on the top of her head. It's so thick it stays without a rubber band or a pin or anything, like she keeps it like that through sheer force of will. "Fucking hell," she says, blowing out a breath, and I laugh.

I'm expecting her to leave, but instead she plops down on the couch beside me, pulling the bowl of Lucky Charms over and picking out the last of the marshmallows. "How was your night?" she asks. She smells like cold air and beer.

"Fine," I tell her, wishing I'd done something to make me seem like a little less of a loser. "It was mostly, you know, this." I gesture to the TV.

"I love this show," Taylor says, and we watch for a little while in silence. It's the first time we've been alone together in what feels like forever. When I glance over, her eye makeup is migrating down her face a little, a smudge of jet-black liner just above her cheekbone. I want to reach out and rub it off with my thumb.

"That's better," Taylor says, when the stylist cuts off all the dumpy woman's hair. Then she looks at me. "I like *your* hair like that," she says. "Have I said that to you already?"

I smile. "Really?" It's so short. It's nineties boy hair, is what it is, floppy in the front like Devon Sawa and razored along my neck. I explained myself like six times to the Supercuts barber, and still he asked if I was sure. "My mom cried when I did it."

Taylor's eyes widen. "Did she really?"

I nod. "Not like, big theatrics or anything. But she went into the pantry for a really long time."

"*Claudia,*" Taylor says, which is my mom's name. "Come on." She pulls one knee up onto the sofa, tucking it under her and facing me head-on. Her own hair is still up in its tieless bun, curly and witchy and magic. "Well, I think it looks great."

I wonder for the first time if she's drunk. "Really?" I ask, blatantly fishing now. "Not too much like Steven's?"

Taylor laughs. "Only if Steven was really girly looking and also maybe an elf." She plucks another few marshmallows out of the bowl, hearts and moons and rainbows, then puts her hand down on the sofa cushion, so close that for a moment our pinkies brush. She takes just long enough to pull away that for a second I let myself wonder if maybe it's on purpose. "He told me about your road test, by the way."

"Yeah," I say, sinking back into the couch with my shoulders up around my ears. "It's no big deal. I can take it again in January."

Taylor nods. "Well, I'm an expert parallel parker, for what it's worth. I could teach you."

"Really?" I look at her for a moment, all apple cheeks and long, spiky eyelashes. If I kissed her, her tongue would taste like processed sugar.

"Sure," she says, standing up quick and steady—not drunk at all, then. "Come on."

"What, right now?" I glance down at my pajamas, a huge sweatshirt of my dad's and flannel pants with holly berries on them. Every year, my mom gets us a pair to open up on Christmas Eve.

Taylor shrugs. "Why not?"

Why not. I give in, pulling on a pair of boots listing on their sides in the foyer, and we go out the front door and trudge around the side of the house. It's started to snow, fat flakes sticking in Taylor's hair. There's only one other car parked on our street, a red Volvo down in front of the Fowlers', and Taylor has me parallel park behind it half a dozen times, talking me through it with slow, precise instructions. She's a good teacher, patient, not clutching her seat belt for dear life like my mom did the whole time I was learning.

"See, you got it," she says, ignoring the fact that it took me like seven full minutes to get close to the curb. "You're better than I was, anyway. I had to take my road test four times."

I smile at that. "I remember." She was a holy terror about it for weeks, functionally incapable of taking a joke, storming around our house slamming doors in a whirl of righteous indignation and hormones. My mom, a big believer in not disciplining other people's kids, had to ask her to take it down a notch.

"Can I ask you something?" Taylor pipes up suddenly, sitting back in the passenger seat, and there is a moment in which I nod but do not breathe. "Why did we stop hanging out?"

Why did we . . . I shake my head. She's got her face tipped toward me earnestly, waiting. "We're hanging out right now," I say.

"No, I know," Taylor says, waving my words away. "But the three of us used to hang out more, didn't we?"

"Yeah," I say slowly. I think of pitching it like one of the riddles she and Steven are always telling: *What has dark hair, bony wrists, and a miserable crush on her brother's best friend and probable soul mate?* "I guess we did." We stopped right around the time Taylor finally passed her road test, actually, when she and Steven got old enough to start going to parties with booze and I got old enough to figure out that I didn't want to *be* her.

Taylor wrinkles her nose at me a little. *"Well,"* she continues, pitching her voice sort of theatrically. "There's a New Year's Eve party at Bodhi Powers's house. If Steven isn't still hungover by then, we're going to go. You should come."

I think about that for a moment, about what it would look like. "Maybe," I say finally.

Taylor nods like I've already agreed. "Good," she says, then reaches over and taps the steering wheel. "Go one more time."

Steven is indeed massively hungover the next morning. I take a perverse kind of pleasure in opening all his windows, freezing cold air whistling through the room and the bright morning sunlight reflecting off the snow outside. He groans and yanks a pillow over his face, throwing the other one at me blindly.

"Need to puke?" I ask, taking pity as he suddenly lurches toward the edge of the bed. "I can get the barf bowl."

He waves me off, rubbing a hand through his messy hair.

"Go downstairs and steal me a carb."

"They're gonna know you're messed up," I say, but I do it anyway, swiping a sweater off his floor as I go, gray with a red Fair Isle pattern around the cuffs.

"And stop stealing my shit!" Steven calls, but I'm already pulling it over my head.

Downstairs, I select a banana and an English muffin, shoving it in the toaster oven as my mom wafts through the door with the morning paper. She's probably been up for hours, running on the treadmill or sorting through the mail. Just the fact of her feels like a rebuke. "Hi there," she says, cupping the back of my prickly head and tilting it down to kiss my forehead. "Did you leave a bowl of cereal out overnight?"

Steven got drunk. "Sorry."

"It left a ring on the coffee table," my mom adds. Then: "Is that Steven's shirt?"

"Sorry," I hiss, shrugging out of her hold as the toaster oven dings. *Sorry sorry sorry.* I slam the muffin onto a plate and slather both halves with peanut butter and the fancy jam my dad always buys. It disappeared from the fridge the whole seven months my parents were separated last year, even though they were switching off who was living with us at the house. It was like my dad didn't think it was his place to buy any more. Suddenly I'm mad about that too. Suddenly I'm so mad about all of it.

My mom purses her lips. "Attitude," she says mildly, and leaves me to my fuming.

Upstairs, I plunk the plate down on Steven's desk with a bang. "I'm not lying to them if you puke and they ask me what's up," I warn, kicking at one of his socked feet.

Steven lifts the pillow off his face, looking supremely unconcerned. "What are they gonna do, ground me?"

He's right, they definitely won't. In eight months he's going off to Columbia and our mom is quietly, desperately freaking out about it, like she's feeling guilty for time lost during the separation but also, I think, like she's afraid to be left alone with just me as her kid. And just like that I'm pissed at him too now, Steven and his self-satisfaction and his early decision and his easy life, swashbuckling his way through adolescence while the rest of us founder and drown.

"You're not an only child, you know," I tell him, nastily and apropos of nothing. "I know you're the favorite or whatever, but it's not like they're gonna have an empty nest."

Steven looks at me like I'm insane. "I'm not the favorite," he says, sitting up and holding his head rather pathetically. "Mom is like, dying for you to be her friend again, you know that, right? She says it to me all the time."

I whirl on him. "She *says* it to you?" The idea of them talking about it just enrages me more, Rowena and her attitude and her *situation*. "What does she *say*?"

Steven shrugs, preternaturally calm in a way that makes me want to deck him. "I don't know, just what I said. That she misses you and wants you to like her again."

I shrug back, irate. "She's the parent, isn't she?" I snap at him. "She should try liking me first."

Steven opens his mouth, then reaches for the glass of water instead. I guess there isn't anything to say.

Steven doesn't emerge from his room until past noon, shambling downstairs still wearing yesterday's clothes. *Subtle, Steven,* I think, but true to form, my parents don't seem to notice or care. We spend the day as a family, eating Christmas leftovers and doing a giant puzzle of the Lone Cypress. I sit at the kitchen table and put the finishing touches on the queen's dress and train for *Once Upon a Mattress,* feeling like a spotlight is on me when my mom leans over my shoulder to watch. *Gay girl still likes clothes, news at eleven.*

Still: "That's beautiful, Ro," she says quietly, touching the back of my neck with one cool hand, and I have to take a big gulp of orange juice to swallow down the weird lump in my throat.

The next day I hike back out to Thomas Jefferson to sew up the design with Mariette Chen and another junior named Sarah Murray. "I love your style, Rowena," Sarah says when I slough off my coat to reveal my big striped rugby shirt, which is how I know she doesn't love it at all. "And your hair. I could never pull it off."

"Thanks," I say awkwardly, just as Mariette says, "That's dumb."

We both look at her.

"Well, it is," she says, shrugging. "No one ever says that about boys, you know? That they can't pull off short hair. They all just do."

For the first time in my breathing life, I badly want to kiss someone who is not Taylor Lavoie.

♥ ♥ ♥

Steven picks me up at five o'clock, stomping through the linoleum hallways in his Converse and puffer coat to fetch me when
I miss his text. Already he looks too old for this place. "Taylor
says you gotta come to the party on Saturday," he tells me,
instead of hello. Sarah Murray is already giving him the eyeball,
my pretty, dumb brother who never has to try.

I snap a thread between my teeth, standing up and looking
around for my coat. "Taylor says a lot of things," I tell him once
I've waved good-bye to the others, following him back down
the hallway. "Probably she just wants someone to help carry
you home when you pass out."

Steven flings himself elegantly against the push bar on the
exit door. "I think she values you for more than your upper-
body strength, Squish," he says mildly, and for the billionth
time I wonder if he knows how I feel about Taylor, the same
way I know how he does. But that would mean Taylor knows
too, so I stop wondering. "Just ask Mom and Dad, okay?"

I do; it doesn't go well. "I don't know, Ro," my mom says,
frowning. She's shredding up lettuce for a salad, lighter fare
after two days of Christmas leftovers.

"Steven is going."

"Steven is eighteen years old."

"Steven is seventeen and a half." I feel hot all up and down
my spine. The truth is, I was half-hoping she would do this—an
easy out, political cover, "Sorry, Taylor, but my mom said no."
But now that she actually has, I'm furious.

"Aw, Claud, let her go," my dad calls from the living room. It should be nice to have backup, but instead I wish he hadn't said anything it all; it still freaks me out when my parents present less than a united front on anything, even dinner reservations or what to watch on TV. It reminds me of right before the separation, of being caught in the middle: *pick a side.*

"No, it's fine," I hear myself say, high and brittle like a wheeze. "I won't go. I mean, at least if I'm here, you can make sure I'm not kissing a girl at midnight, right?"

My mom opens her mouth. *"Ro."*

"No, no, seriously," I say. "This works out for everyone. It's perfect." My voice cracks on the last word, and I hightail it out of the kitchen before I start sobbing.

I stomp upstairs to my bedroom, slamming the door so hard that my rehearsal schedule flutters down off the bulletin board. I don't bother to pick it up. After a few minutes my dad knocks on the door, pokes his head in.

"Quite the performance," he says. "You should be onstage instead of in the costume room."

I don't bite. "She hates me," I say to the ceiling. "She hates that I'm gay."

"That's not true," my dad says immediately. "Hey, uh-uh. She would run into a burning building for you, you know that."

"Do I?" I shoot back sulkily.

My dad fixes me with a Look. "Yes, Rowena," he says. "I think you do." Then he sighs. "Teenage girls are supposed to hate their mothers," he tells me after a moment. "Isn't that a thing?"

I snort, but it makes me smile. "Did you read that in a parenting book?" I ask.

My dad rolls his eyes. "Anyway, she said to say you can go to the party," he tells me, patting me on the shoulder. "If you want."

I sigh, look out the window at the pine trees. "Yeah," I tell him. "I want."

New Year's Eve, my mom orders a bunch of Chinese food for everybody, all of us camped out in front of the dried-out tree in the living room to eat and an old *Law & Order* on in the background. "Any word from Barnard?" my dad asks Taylor, while a couple of trench-coated detectives peer down at a mutilated body in Central Park.

"Leave her alone," my mom and I say at the same time, then stare at each other, surprised.

"It's okay," Taylor says, but she smiles at me like *thanks*. I feel a pleased red flush creep up my neck.

"She's a shoo-in," Steven says. "Probably didn't even need to fill out the application."

Taylor shakes her head. "We'll see," she says softly, but there's something about her tone that makes me think she knows Steven's right. The two of them are sitting side by side on the floor with their ankles crossed; without taking her eyes off the screen, Taylor reaches over and steals a forkful of lo mein out of Steven's bowl.

I look across the room at them for a moment. Then I look back at the TV. Finally I pick up my phone and scroll through until I find Mariette's number, press the button for a new text. **Hey**, I type, thumb moving quickly across the keypad before I can chicken out. **You wanna come to a New Year's party with me tonight?**

Thirty seconds later, my phone vibrates on the arm of the sofa. **Sure**, Mariette says, and I grin at the screen.

When I look up, Taylor is watching me, quizzical. "What?" she mouths, tapping the tines of her fork against her bottom lip. When I shake my head, holding up the phone kind of sheepishly, she only shrugs.

"I'm going to run home, change my clothes before we go," she announces suddenly, scrambling up off the carpet. "I'll pick you kids up in a few."

When I come downstairs later that night, my mom is lying on the couch with a library book, a balsam-scented candle flickering on the coffee table beside her. It's strange to see her in repose like that—when I think of her she's always *doing* something, sliding earrings in on her way out the door or scrubbing hard at a day-old coffee stain on the kitchen counter. It occurs to me that maybe I haven't really looked at her in a while.

"You look nice," she says, sitting up and marking her place with her index finger.

"Thanks." I'm wearing Steven's jeans and the boots she got me for Christmas; I glance down at them, then back at her. "I really do like these a lot."

"I'm glad," she says, and she sounds very careful. *It's me*, I want to tell her. *Come on, it's just me.* "Well," she says finally, lifting her book a couple of inches and dropping it back into her lap again. "Have fun tonight, okay? Be good."

"Yup," I tell her. "I will. Hey, Mom," I blurt, before I can think better of it. "Do you maybe want to go to the museum one day before school starts?"

Her eyes widen; she sets the book back down in her lap. "I'd love that," she tells me, sounding almost heartbreakingly eager. Her smile takes up the whole bottom half of her face. "I—yeah, Ro. I'd love that. Just say the word."

The party is a rager out in one of the golf course developments, where the houses are built to look like they're part of a quaint English village and the streets are named after characters from Robin Hood. I ditch my coat on Bodhi Powers's little sister's bed before going looking for Mariette. At first I think maybe she didn't come after all, but after I do a couple of laps I find her standing by the fire pit in the backyard, where a scrum of football players is feeding supermarket firewood into the flames.

"Hey," I say, bumping her gently on the shoulder. "What are you doing out here?"

"Kind of hiding?" Mariette confesses. She's wearing a red wool cap pulled down over her ears, cheeks gone pink in the cold. It's not a bad look. "I don't actually know anybody."

"You know me," I point out, and Mariette smiles. Back inside the house, we get beers and sit at the top of the basement steps, looking down at a vacuum cleaner and an overflowing Rubbermaid bin full of half-naked Barbies. Mariette is easy to talk to, about the show but also about how much we don't want school to start again and the last season of *Sherlock*; we wind up playing slaps for like twenty minutes, both of us laughing so hard at one point that Mariette almost falls down the stairs. It's a relief, chatting with a girl I'm not blindingly, unrequitedly in love with. I'm not worried about impressing her, so I can stop thinking about what I'm doing every second and just be normal. I wonder for a moment if this is how my brother and Taylor feel when they're together, if it can be like this when the feeling's mutual, and after that I try to push Taylor out of my mind once and for all.

"I'm sorry about last year," I tell Mariette suddenly. It feels important to say it before we go any further. "After the party and everything. I was a jerk."

"Oh," Mariette says, coloring a little. "No, it's okay."

"No, it's not," I say, taking a deep breath and putting my hand down on top of hers. "Can I maybe get a do-over?"

Mariette bites her lip then, gently pulls her hand away. "Rowena," she says, "I have a girlfriend."

I blink for a second. Absurdly, I almost laugh. "You do?"

"Yeah," Mariette says, shrugging. "She goes to Edgemont. She's skiing with her family over break."

"Oh," I say. I can feel my blush spilling everywhere, from my ears to the webs between my fingers, the creases behind my knees. "Oh, okay. That's totally cool. Sorry."

"No, it's fine," Mariette is saying, but now my throat is getting tight and weird anyway, which is ridiculous because I don't even want to date her, not really. I'm just embarrassed. I just feel so *lonely*. I feel like everyone on earth is paired up with somebody but me.

"I should probably go," Mariette tells me, pulling off her

hat and then putting it back on her head again, her hair going a little staticky with the motion.

"You don't have to do that," I say, even though both of us are already standing somehow, like both of our bodies are propelling us out of this encounter as quickly as possible. "It's almost midnight."

"That's okay," Mariette says. "My mom was a weirdo about me coming anyway, she thought people were going to like, drive drunk inside the house. I'll see you at the shop, though?"

"Yeah," I say, my voice fake and bright as the light-up Santa on Bodhi Powers's lawn. "Definitely."

Once Mariette is gone, I make my way through the empty kitchen, where the table is littered with tipped-over plastic cups and capless liquor bottles, something sticky and congealed pooling under a place mat. The refrigerator is papered with Christmas cards, smiling families with their arms around one another on vacations in Montauk and Vail. The clock on the stove says it's six minutes to midnight. There's no reason to feel like I'm going to cry.

Some guys from the cross-country team brought fireworks to set off after the countdown, and everyone is heading out to the fire pit to watch. I edge my way along the floral runner in the hallway, past a couple of kids from my lit class kissing by the bathroom door. I retrieve my coat from the pile on Bodhi's sister's bed, winding my thick wool scarf around my neck; other people are doing the same, bundling up for the show, and no one says a word to me. I don't even look out of place until I start heading toward the front door. Taylor and Steven are still playing chandeliers in the living room, too cool for sixteen-shot roman candles. I dart across the archway with my head down, but I'm not quite quick enough.

"You leaving?" Taylor calls, and like five people look over. I nod and give her a thumbs-up, don't worry about it, but she catches me in the front hall. "Where are you going?"

"No place," I say stupidly, then amend. "I mean, home."

"You are?" Taylor frowns. "Why, what's wrong?"

"Nothing," I tell her. "Just had enough."

"Well, you can't walk," Taylor points out. "It's way too far. You want me to drive you?"

"No thanks," I say too forcefully, yanking the front door open, but she follows me out onto the lawn anyway. She's wearing a party dress, black and sleeveless with a full skirt and golden elephants marching along all over it. It should look like something for little kids, but on Taylor it doesn't. On Taylor it looks like she knows something the rest of us don't.

"Aren't you cold?" I ask even as I'm heading for the side-walk. It is too far to walk, Taylor's right about that, but now I'm in this and I feel like I can't admit that. It occurs to me too late that I don't really have a plan.

Taylor knows it too. "Yeah, I'm freezing, Rowena," she tells me, sounding vaguely impatient.

"So then why are you out here?" I snap. "Go inside."

Taylor puts her hands on her hips like somebody's sitcom mom. "I want to make sure you're okay."

That's too much. The last thing I want is for her to feel sorry for me, to be some little kid who tagged along and now needs tending. "Can you please stop trying to big sister me?" I ask snottily. "I know you're probably going to marry my brother and everything, but can you just—you're not—"

Taylor laughs out loud, an open-throated cackle. "Marry your *brother*?" she asks. "Do people still think that? I didn't think anybody thought that since we were in, like, fourth grade." Then her face abruptly falls. "I'm not trying to big sister you. That is . . . yeah. Rowena. That is, like, the opposite of what I'm trying to do here."

Something about the way she says it, the expression on her face, stops me. "What are you trying to do, then?" I ask her, and it comes out a lot quieter than I mean.

Taylor looks at me like I'm being thick on purpose. "Rowena," she says after a too-long pause, jamming her hands in the pockets of her elephant dress. "Come on."

"You come on," I say stupidly, my heart thrumming at the back of my mouth. If I am misreading this, it's so much worse than Mariette. If I am misreading this, I might actually die right here on this lawn in the golf course development. "You never said—"

"*You* never said!" Taylor retorts, and I'm taken aback by how hurt she suddenly sounds. "I had to find out in the first place from your brother. If you wanted me to know, then—"

"Of course I wanted you to know," I blurt. "You're like, the one person who I really wanted to know, I just—"

"Okay. Okay." Taylor is taking a step closer to me now, reaching for my wrist where it's poking out of my coat. Her fingertips are very chilly. I smell dried lavender and snow. Inside the house I can hear people counting down to midnight, that rhythmic chant; Taylor tips her head and I'm honest to god 80 percent sure she's going to kiss me in the moment before the front door creaks open and Steven pokes his head out, dark hair falling into his eyes.

"What are you guys doing?" he calls. Then: *"Oh."*

Taylor laughs, and we lock gazes for a moment; I don't know whether to cry or scream. But she doesn't look annoyed, and to my surprise I find that I'm not, either. Whatever just happened here feels like a to-be-continued, a comma instead of a period. It feels like being suspended in the best part of a dream.

Steven looks at us for a moment, realization dawning on his face. The fireworks are going off in the backyard, more sound than light, but still somebody is definitely going to call the cops soon. I think of the riddle from Christmas Eve: *first, strike a match.*

"We're getting out of here," Taylor tells him, lacing her fingers through mine and squeezing tightly, bold and unmistakable. This is not a thing I am imagining here. "You coming?"

Steven peers back and forth between us for a moment. He looks, if this is even possible, both shocked and completely, *enormously* unsurprised at the situation. At the very least, he doesn't look pissed. "Whatever," he says slowly. "Sure." Then he nods at me. "You want shotgun?" he asks. His voice is so, so casual.

"Sure," I say, nodding back at him, and the three of us head for the car.

Dread South
JUSTINA IRELAND

*To the editor of the Savannah Morning News. This letter is in
response to your editorial of February 1, 1876, entitled "The
Women of the South Have No Need of Self-Defense Arts."*

*In your article you state that the nearly thirteen years since the
Undead Rising at the tragic Battle of Gettysburg have led to
unprecedented stability and that the Northern system of engaging
Negro girl Attendants as protectors should be adopted here in the
South. You go on to say that to encourage womenfolk to take up
the defense arts would only lead to destabilized families and an
increase in spinsters. This, sir, is wrong.*

*You have neglected fundamental aspects of the system. Many
unfortunate families cannot afford to contract Attendants for their
daughters. What of these poor girls, endangered by their poverty?
Shall we let them be devoured by the undead? And how can the*

women of the South depend on Negroes to keep us safe? We are
not Northerners. We know better the childlike temperament of the
colored. Every Southerner knows that Negroes do not have the
capacity to reasonably protect themselves or anyone else. . . .

Louisa Aiken, 1876

It was five miles into the city proper from Landsfall, the Aiken
family plantation, and Louisa felt every single one of them drag
by as she sat in the rider's compartment of the pony with her
mother.

Once, they would've traveled to town in a finely appointed
carriage, with coachmen and a matched set of four horses. But
that was before the restless dead stalked the woods and flatlands,
hungry for flesh. Horses were a beacon for the undead creatures
and rarely survived the encounter, so instead people traveled
in ponies, carriages pulled along by a smoke-belching, steam-
powered engine compartment. In the winter, Louisa loved
traveling in the pony, when the rider's compartment wasn't
nearly so stuffy and insufferable from the Georgia heat. But
today her mother generated enough hot air that even August
would've been hard-pressed to compete.

"Mrs. Helmsley told me that Bradley Winterbrook has
already come to call on Rebecca three times. Three! She'll be
matched by the end of March, mark my words. Why, I'm sure
if you'd just declare your intent for Ashley Ellis, he would've
come to call and you'd have a betrothal by now."

Louisa schooled her expression to blankness. Mrs. Aiken had

been the most beautiful debutante in her year, way back in 1856, her blond curls and blue eyes and perfect pearlescent skin peerless throughout the Low Country. Now the bloom of her youth and her beauty had faded into something dull and unbelievably sad, like an overblown rose with only a few petals clinging. Louisa shared her mother's looks, a fact her mother frequently brought up whenever Louisa wore a color her mother deemed "unflattering."

At seventeen, Louisa knew her own mind well enough, and her mother's criticisms always put her in a bit of a snit. The only reason Louisa had agreed to accompany her mother into town was the letter to the editor of the local newspaper tucked into her bodice, a letter that Louisa needed to post without her mother's knowledge.

Louisa pulled her attention back to the conversation within the pony. "Mother, the Ellis family's property is nothing but salt marsh. I do not want to live on a salt marsh." It was easier than pointing out the fact that Ashley Ellis had buckteeth and was overfond of groping the servant girls. The last thing she wanted was a husband who was going to put a babe in every colored girl he met.

"Well, what about Everett Hayes? He danced with you twice at the Christmas Cotillion. And he has called on your father about courting you."

"He has?" Louisa fell silent as she thought about Everett. He was the most eligible bachelor in all of Chatham County, and handsome to boot. A few years older than Louisa, he had dark wavy hair, blue eyes, and pale skin that bore the kiss of sunshine. He hadn't just danced twice with her. He'd asked her to step outside with him for a glass of punch, and while they'd been alone he'd told her she was the most beautiful girl at the entire cotillion. The admiration in his eyes had made her heart grow wings.

He hadn't kissed her, of course. That would've been entirely too forward. Even if she was reasonably sure she would have kissed him back.

That being said, his attentions hadn't stopped him from dancing with Sophie Parker, a fact that Louisa had been trying to forget even as she nurtured a secret hope that she would see Everett again. It was understandable that she hadn't, though. Travel was dangerous, and as the only son of a shipping magnate, Everett's family preferred he stay inside the safety of the city walls. Those in the city rarely traveled outside of them for fear of the undead.

The pony came to a screeching halt. Louisa fumbled for a handle while her mother yelped in dismay. "Why are we stopping?"

The window between the driver's compartment and the passenger area slid open. A dark face appeared in the space. Herman, the family coachman. "There's a pack of shamblers in the road, ma'am. I'm waiting for them to clear."

"Well, can't you just ram them?" Mrs. Aiken demanded, a quaver in her voice. The undead were a reminder of the trials and travails of the war and the failed attempt at secession. Neither was a subject Louisa's mother liked to think about. The war years had been hard on their family, leaving Mrs. Aiken's brother Louis, for whom Louisa was named, a feral, mindless monster.

Herman shook his head. "There's too many, I'm like to get the wheels mucked up with shambler if I do. Sorry, Miss Alicia. If we're lucky they'll wander off." He slid the window closed, effectively ending the conversation.

Mrs. Aiken flushed and began adjusting the button closures on her gloves. "These damned undead," she swore as she slammed back in her seat. Louisa bit back a smile. On any other occasion her mother would've corrected the help, told them forcefully what to do. But not when the restless dead were involved.

Louisa scooted closer to the tiny window to get a glimpse of the figures moving just beyond the bars. Louisa could see movement, but it was too far off to discern whether she'd known them or not. It was always quite a scandal when a family got turned. Some part of Louisa secretly hoped she'd see dark-haired Sophie Parker out there, dragging along in her familiar emerald green.

There were a few far-off pops, and the window to the driver's compartment slid open once more. "Looks like the patrol is clearing them out, ma'am. We should be moving in a bit."

"There are Federal troops out there?" Louisa asked.

"No, Miss Louisa, it's the Negro patrol. Well, here we go." The carriage lurched, and they were on their way once more.

Louisa sat back in her seat and grimaced. Negro patrols. No wonder they had had to wait so long. Federal troops would've made sure that the undead never made it to the main road to begin with. But the Federal troops were gone, headed back north thanks to President Rutherford B. Hayes and his Corrupt Bargain.

"This is why you need an Attendant, Louisa," Mrs. Aiken said, fidgeting in her seat. "We both need Attendants. I've heard no self-respecting woman in New York leaves her house without her Attendant. Can you imagine, your own Negro girl to protect you? I'm not sure why the fashion hasn't caught on here. We have more than enough Negroes milling about, shiftless as all get-out."

Louisa's lips twisted, but she said nothing. She shifted in her seat, the letter containing her thoughts crinkling as she moved.

A Negro girl to keep her safe from the undead.

Not if she had any say in the matter.

By the time they pulled into Ellis Square, Louisa was ready to be finished with the whole day, and her mother besides. After a quick stop at the health inspector's to show that they were healthy and untouched by the Undead Plague, the carriage was admitted through the city gate. As soon as the pony stopped, Louisa hurried out as quickly as she could without looking unladylike, which wasn't nearly as fast as she would've liked.

"Louisa, where are you going?" her mother called as Louisa headed down the sidewalk to the post box. Louisa ignored her.

"Louisa!" Mrs. Aiken shrieked, several feet to the rear and not at all ladylike.

Louisa turned toward her mother's call without slowing her pace, which was a mistake. One that sent her hurtling headlong into the arms of Everett Hayes.

"Miss Aiken," he said in surprise, his voice rumbling delightfully as he caught her. A spate of goose bumps sprang up under the sleeves of Louisa's dress, emanating from his hands on her arms, and her breath floundered.

"Mr. Hayes. I am so sorry. Please forgive my clumsiness."

"Already done," he said with a smile, and Louisa's mouth went hopelessly dry. The Hayes family owned a shipping business, and Everett was a skilled sailor in addition to being a gentleman. He certainly seemed steady on his feet as he gently helped Louisa regain her balance.

"Louisa! You mustn't go rushing off like that—Mr. Hayes! How lovely to see you here in the square."

Louisa stepped back, putting some distance between her pounding heart and Everett's gentle smile. He tipped his hat at Louisa's mother, even though his eyes were still on Louisa.

"It's a welcome surprise," he said.

"What are you about, Mr. Hayes?" Louisa asked, regaining her composure.

"Well, a couple of the boys down at the shipyard got bit and had to be put down, sad to say. So I'm heading over to the market to hire some help."

The market in Ellis Square was well known throughout Georgia. When Louisa was very little, Daddy had taken her to see the Negroes brought in for sale. She didn't remember much about the trip except for the dark faces, their expressions stoic, and the sugar candy her daddy had bought her for being a good girl. But that was long ago, before the War of Northern

Aggression and the dead walking, before a single bite could turn a man feral.

Negroes were no longer sold in the market. The Great Concession had ended both slavery and the Confederacy, in exchange for the assistance of Federal troops. So now the market was the place to hire extra help, both colored and white. It was said by some that the labor contracts offered to the whites looking for work were better than the wages offered Negroes, but everyone knew that Negroes were naturally inferior, so no one who mattered made much of a fuss.

Mrs. Aiken smiled and clapped her hands together. "Well, isn't this a happy coincidence. Louisa and I were headed there as well. Perhaps you'd be so kind as to accompany us?" A calculating look gleamed in her mother's eye.

Louisa's mother was scheming.

Mr. Hayes gave them a smooth bow. "It would be my pleasure, Mrs. Aiken."

Everett held out an arm to each of the ladies and they took them, the trio gliding across the square to a low-slung building with a fresh coat of paint. Mrs. Aiken kept up a lively chatter about the weather while Louisa fumed. She'd been ensnared in one of her mother's plots.

It was a short stroll to the market. Employment agents called out to passersby looking to hire help, creating a cacophony of sound.

"You need a cook? Then you must taste the preparations of Miss Jessie, best cook in the city!"

"Strong men! You need them, and aye! I've got them."

"Don't go anywhere, fine ladies, without an Attendant to see to your safety! Gentlemen, don't you want your womenfolk protected? A faithful Attendant is the thing for you! And here they are, from the finest school in all the states, Miss Preston's School of Combat for Negro Girls, in Baltimore, Maryland!"

Mrs. Aiken stopped suddenly in front of a platform, bringing Everett and Louisa to a halt as well. A short man with a florid face and a frayed stovepipe hat stood in the street, imploring passersby to look at the girls on the platform, to see their prowess and loyalty. The girls didn't look any different than the other Negro girls Louisa had seen, except for the fact that they wore incredibly sharp-looking knives and swords strapped to their bodies. Their eyes were hooded, their hair braided tight to their scalp, and they radiated an air of supreme disinterest in the whole of the goings-on in the square.

"Good sir," Mrs. Aiken called to the small man. "Your girls, they are Attendants?"

The man scuttled over, a wide smile on his face. "Oh, yes'm. Best in all of Georgia, my girls are. More dead have been harvested by these girls than all of the Federal patrols combined! And a fair price too. For one hundred dollars, you can employ one of my girls for a six-month contract."

"A hundred dollars!" Mrs. Aiken exclaimed, her gloved hands fluttering to her face like startled doves. "What exactly does one get for a hundred dollars?" she asked, trying to cover her shock.

"Why, protection, ma'am. What is that worth in these dark times?"

Mrs. Aiken and the small man went back and forth for a moment, but Louisa tuned them out. She was studying the girls, and her gaze was drawn toward one in the back. She didn't wear a dress over pantalets like most of the other Attendants on the platform. Instead, she was dressed like a man: trousers, shirt, waistcoat in a jaunty blue paisley pattern. She wore a belt, low slung on her hips, that looked as though it should carry revolvers but instead carried a pair of short swords, their edges glinting wickedly sharp in the sunlight. The girl's hair was braided in even rows, the braids ending at her shoulder blades.

Louisa's eyes met those of the girl. She tilted her head to the side, openly appraising Louisa. Louisa blinked, taken aback slightly at the colored girl's naked assessment, and when the dark-skinned girl grinned and winked, Louisa gasped audibly, loud enough to distract her mother from her conversation.

"Louisa, what is it, dear?"

"Nothing, Mother."

Louisa busied herself adjusting the ties on her coat to cover the heat rushing to her cheeks. What an impudent Negro! No wonder they were hard-pressed to secure employment.

"Personally, I think the idea of Attendants is a good one," Everett interjected, interrupting whatever Louisa's mother had been saying to the barker. "There is nothing quite so important as the safety and security of our womenfolk. Especially our most precious blossoms." He looked straight at Louisa as he said this, and she felt herself flush again.

Everett cleared his throat and turned back to the small man.

"Which is why I'm going to give Miss Aiken the gift of an Attendant."

Shock radiated through Louisa's body. "Mr. Hayes . . . ," she said, trailing off. Words failed her. The gift of an Attendant? It was much too generous.

Everett took Louisa's hands and smiled down at her. "It isn't jewels or dresses, but your safety is the most precious gift I can give you. If I'm going to court you, the world needs to know that I am going to cherish and protect you."

Something in Louisa's chest shifted, and she felt faint. It was happening so fast, and Mr. Hayes! She'd lain in bed at night and imagined what it would be like to be courted by him, but none of her imaginings had included an Attendant. It was strange . . . and yet perfectly right.

"Mr. Hayes, this is the most generous gift I have ever received."

Everett smiled wide. "Excellent." He moved off with the small man to finalize the paperwork.

"Well, that was fortuitous," Mrs. Aiken said, her finger tapping her chin as she stared off, deep in thought. Louisa glanced over at her mother.

"Why do I suspect that you had something to do with this, Mother?"

"Well, I may have mentioned to Mr. Hayes, when he came to visit your father, how you were in need of an Attendant. Louisa! You realize you're the first woman in Savannah to have one? Hildy Brenner is going to be absolutely flush with jealousy."

Uncertainty settled heavily into Louisa's middle, and suddenly her gift seemed less generous. "You talked Everett into getting me an Attendant?"

"Nonsense, darling! I did no such thing. I made a suggestion, and the boy was bright enough to pick up on it. Trust me, the ability to take a hint is a fine trait in a husband."

The men were returning, a signed document in Everett's hand and a wide smile on the face of the barker. Everett handed the paper to Louisa, while the small man whistled up to the dais. Louisa clutched the paper to her chest. "Mr. Hayes, I'm still not sure how to express my thanks."

"How about by calling me Everett?"

"Of course, and you must call me Louisa."

"Here she is," the small man said, interrupting the moment between Louisa and Everett. Louisa turned. The girl in the trousers was only a few feet away.

"Her?" Louisa said, all of the warmth and happiness from Everett's generosity melting away into irritation. "No, I don't want her. She's highly inappropriate."

The small man laughed nervously. "Oh, you can't judge a package by its wrapper, miss. Juliet's my best girl and well-mannered despite her odd attire. Your beau there said he wanted my best, and here she is."

Juliet hadn't said a word, but there was an expression on her face like she found this all to be incredibly amusing. She swept into a deep curtsy, her movements fluid like a dancer's. It would've been impressive in a dress but looked strange in trousers. "I'm pleased to make your acquaintance, miss."

Louisa's mother clapped her hands and laughed. "Well, isn't she just a hoot? Louisa darling, you are going to be the talk of the town."

The barker grinned a gap-toothed smile and rubbed his hands together. "Looks like we're all settled."

Louisa looked from Everett's apologetic smile to her mother's satisfied expression to Juliet's smirk and realized with a sinking heart that things were, in fact, quite settled.

It wasn't until they were heading back to the pony, Juliet and Mrs. Aiken's parcels in tow, that Louisa realized that she'd never even mailed her letter.

The girl was completely incorrigible.

It wasn't that she was loud or headstrong or sullen, issues Louisa knew how to handle in Negroes. It was that Juliet was perfectly well-behaved, quick to follow a request or to anticipate a need, so that Louisa could find no fault with the girl. But Louisa got the sense Juliet was playing at being the loyal servant, rather than serving loyally. It made Louisa nervous, so much that she tried to avoid the girl.

And the girl was everywhere.

No matter what Louisa was about, there was Juliet, a silent shadow, dogging her steps and watching with that half-lidded, slightly bemused expression.

The only upside to Juliet's constant presence was Everett. He stopped by once a week, sometimes twice if the roads were passable. The undead were always out and about, but as the weather warmed to spring, the creatures became even more prevalent, cluttering roads and making travel nigh on impossible. Everett's visits were chaperoned by Mrs. Aiken and Juliet, although Louisa wanted nothing more than to be alone with Everett—a completely scandalous thought, and one she did not share with anyone.

The first week in April, Everett came to call upon Louisa while Mrs. Aiken was away visiting friends. He walked in carrying a large wicker basket and wearing a smile that had Louisa setting aside her needlepoint and climbing to her feet.

"Louisa! Your father said I could find you in here. I was wondering if you'd do me the honor of accompanying me on a picnic?"

"Of course! It would be a pleasure," Louisa said, smiling up at him. Thanks to his frequent visits, Everett looked completely at ease in the Aiken family drawing room, and Louisa realized that their courtship was going quite well. At this rate, she would be married by fall. The thought brought a strange combination of joy and terror. Louisa pushed it down so that she didn't have to examine the emotion too closely.

"You look beautiful," Everett said, offering his free arm to Louisa. She was wearing a pale green silk that she'd felt undecided about, and Everett's compliment settled her mind that it was a good dress.

Louisa took Everett's arm, and the two of them went out to the Aikens' picnic pavilion, located a short distance from the house. Juliet followed along closely behind, saying nothing, and Louisa found herself irritated at the extra company. She'd thought through a hundred different ways to politely tell Everett that after nearly three months of an Attendant, she didn't wish to have the girl around any longer. But no matter how she tried to parse it out, it just sounded ungrateful, and the last thing Louisa wanted was to have her future husband think her petty.

They were nearly to the picnic pavilion, a short walk across the grounds of Landsfall, when a bloodcurdling scream came from the fields. Louisa turned to see Negroes running from the tobacco fields back to the shotgun houses in the rear of the property. She stared openmouthed as Everett grabbed the arm of a colored woman fleeing past them.

"What is going on?" he demanded, and the woman flinched as though he'd hit her.

"Begging your pardon, sir, but there's shamblers in the fields. The back fence has gone down, and shamblers are all over the place."

Juliet stepped up, her half smile replaced by a steely expression. "Where?"

The woman pointed back behind her before hurrying off. Sure enough, undead were lumbering through the fields, their swaying walk distinctive.

Juliet turned to Everett. "Please escort Miss Louisa to the pavilion, Mr. Everett."

Everett nodded. He was whiter than a christening gown, and when he laid a hand on Louisa's arm to guide her to the nearby pavilion, she detected a tremble. Louisa wasn't quite as scared, but most of her experience with the undead was from a safe distance. God only knew what Everett had been through.

Juliet took long strides toward the tobacco fields. The plants were still small, little more than seedlings, really, and Juliet was careful to step between the rows as she moved toward the undead. From her perch in the pavilion Louisa counted ten shamblers, and for a moment she felt a pang of fear for Juliet. How could she possibly take down so many of them? Walter Mattias, an old man who'd fought in the war, often told the story of the day his unit was overwhelmed by the undead. "If your odds are more than five to one, I guarantee those shamblers will be dining on your flesh. Trust me, boys, you see more than three and you're by your lonesome, you'd best turn tail. No shame in knowing when you're outmatched."

But now, here was that fool girl Juliet walking out into a field with ten—no! Eleven, *twelve* shamblers, all focused on devouring her.

Louisa sighed. Well, at least she would be finally rid of the girl.

Juliet drew the gleaming swords from their holsters. There was a moment of hesitation, and then she sprang into action.

The short sword whistled through the air in an arc, catching sunlight for a moment before it detached the head of the first undead. Louisa gasped. She'd seen shamblers put down, but she'd never seen it happen so quickly, so effectively. She didn't have time to even consider the creature's end before Juliet was on to the next one, those shining swords detaching another head, silencing the moans and groans of another undead. Juliet moved through the pack with deadly efficiency, her movements fluid, the entire act a rapid dance that left Juliet grinning wide and smeared with the black blood of the undead.

Walter Mattias was wrong. Juliet had just put down twelve shamblers in the space of a few heartbeats, and she barely looked fatigued. The girl was more than competent. She was a master.

Next to her, Everett was saying something inane about Juliet being worth her mettle. From the direction of the house came the Aiken family patrol, led by their overseer, Gregory, a blustering white man with a florid complexion and a limp from the war. All of it was secondary to Juliet standing in the tobacco field, a wide grin on her face, an angel of true death with two gleaming swords.

Something fundamental tilted in Louisa, as though she was seeing reality for the first time. This was what it meant to be a woman of the world. To know how to handle oneself and be endlessly prepared. It wasn't a husband Louisa needed; her mother was wrong as usual. It was this, the ability to defend herself against the undead. A skill she'd been denied in her endless trainings to be a good wife. Now she understood. The defense arts were everything she'd wanted.

And the girl Juliet was going to be the one to give them to her.

Once Everett had been sent on his way, a handful of houseboys accompanying him to ensure he got home safely, Louisa found Juliet outside near the well, hauling up buckets of water and dumping them over her head. For a moment Louisa paused, a curious warmth shifting low in her middle. There was something . . . appealing . . . about the way Juliet looked soaking wet, water running over her dark skin, the black blood of the undead rinsing away.

Louisa grabbed the feeling and shoved it down violently. She'd heard stories of men, and women, who developed affections for Negroes, and she had no desire to do the same. Down that path lay ruin, and that was not for Louisa. She was respectable.

Mostly.

"I want you to teach me how to do that."

Juliet paused, the bucket waist-high. "Dumping water over your head? I reckon you just pick up the bucket and dump it, miss."

"No, fighting the undead. Killing them."

Juliet laughed, a surprised bark of sound. "You don't want that, miss. Isn't proper."

"I do want that," Louisa said, and something in her voice caused Juliet to pause, to stare at her intently.

"Teaching you how to kill the dead isn't in the contract."

Louisa took a deep breath and let it out slowly. That wasn't a no. "How about I double your contract fee, give you another hundred dollars if you teach me the self-defense arts between now and when your duties are complete."

"Six months isn't enough time. I went to combat school for three years."

Louisa felt that thing, that nameless desire, begin to slip away from her grasp. "But you can teach me something in that time, right?"

Juliet stood, considering. "Yep, surely something. But a

hundred dollars' worth of something? The last thing I need is some agent of the court chasing me down because I stole from some white woman. No, miss, I don't need that at all."

"I promise that won't happen."

Juliet's mouth twisted into an ugly smile. Louisa realized Juliet was talking from experience, not a hypothetical. Louisa felt trapped, and she threw up her hands in exasperation. "I'll have my father negotiate a new contract with your agent."

"That man charges me thirty percent of each contract, so make it a hundred thirty dollars, and you got a deal. Now, if you don't mind, miss, I need to finish getting tidied up. And you need to get inside where it's safe."

Louisa nodded and moved away, toward the house. From the nearby fields came the shouts and calls of the Landsfall patrol clearing out the undead Juliet hadn't put down.

Louisa had convinced Juliet to teach her the self-defense arts. Now she just had to convince her father it was a good idea.

Two weeks later, after much cajoling and begging and even the threat of tears, Louisa's father relented and agreed to pay Juliet to train Louisa in defense.

Mrs. Aiken was quite against the idea, but the thought of undead walking Landsfall sent her to bed with a bad case of the vapors every time it was mentioned, so her objections were easily overlooked.

Louisa had not thought much on self-defense arts beyond knowing it was something she didn't have and therefore wanted. The hunger burned deep inside of her, and if it had not been for Juliet's actions the day of the picnic, that need might have gone on slumbering. But watching Juliet move, seeing her confidence, made Louisa acutely aware of her shortcomings.

Deficiencies she was determined to correct.

They worked from sunup until it was time for dinner. Juliet explained how to hold the short swords, and then watched as Louisa swung one sword to and fro. For her part, Louisa didn't complain. She'd fought hard to be allowed to train with Juliet, and she was afraid that if she said anything about her tired arms or the perspiration pooling under her corset, Juliet would stop showing her the finer points of self-defense.

As Louisa worked with Juliet, her arms became stronger and her corset looser, since loosening the ties allowed her to accomplish more of the drills that Juliet assigned. Working so closely with Juliet gave Louisa a new appreciation for her Attendant. And as Juliet taught her how to hold the swords and move with them, Louisa began to ask questions.

"Juliet, where are you from?"

"Juliet, do you have any family?"

"Juliet, where did you learn how to kill the undead?"

Louisa probed until she had the whole of Juliet's life story: born on a small plantation outside Charlotte, then to Baltimore with her mother in search of her father after the war, and eventually a student at Miss Preston's School of Combat for Negro Girls.

"I figured, if the dead were always going to be trying to kill me, I might as well kill them right back," Juliet said, a laugh in her voice. She reached out and moved Louisa's hands on the swords. The brief contact flustered Louisa, but Juliet didn't notice. "Loosen up on the handle, not too tight. You don't want to get tired too quickly. Shamblers are a persistent sort; you want to be able to outlast them."

Louisa adjusted her grip and practiced the swing again, somewhat breathless from both the training and Juliet's touch. "You are completely unlike any other Negro I've met."

Juliet laughed, the sound hollow. "Truth is, I'm just like every single other colored person on this plantation. You just ain't paying attention. Follow through on the motion, don't halt yourself on the back swing," she said, moving past her gentle rebuke so smoothly that it took Louisa a few moments to realize it had even been said.

But the words had been uttered, and Louisa mulled over Juliet's comment that evening and the next day. And every day after that. She started to take closer note of the goings-on around Landsfall, began to notice small things around her. She noticed the dismissive way her father and Everett talked about the Negroes over supper, as though they were lesser just because of an accident of birth. She saw how the colored servants would laugh and smile when they thought whites were not around. She watched how their expressions became guarded whenever Louisa or any of her family entered the room. And she noticed how a couple of the girls smiled at Juliet, a knowing smile that usually followed small touches. It would've been nothing if Louisa hadn't caught Juliet kissing one of the girls passionately before defense practice one morning, a sight that caused Louisa to blush and gave her fevered dreams that left her troubled and out of sorts.

Louisa liked training with Juliet and listening to her talk about her life before Savannah. But it wasn't the only thing she liked.

She began to appreciate entirely too much. Like the way Juliet's arms looked, the muscles straining at the material of her shirt, and how Juliet would smile at her, truly grin, when Louisa managed to complete an especially tricky series of drills. After two months of working with Juliet, Louisa felt like a different person.

A better person.

"I think I'm ready, Juliet," Louisa said one day without preamble as she turned the swords in a move Juliet called "Harvesting Wheat."

"Ready for what?"

"I want to go out and hunt the undead," Louisa said.

A frown crossed Juliet's face, but it was quickly smoothed away. "Louisa, that isn't a good idea."

Louisa let her swords fall to her side. "Why not?"

"Because you're not ready yet. I trained for a year before I even took on my first shambler, and then I still had my teacher watching to make sure I didn't get the fright. The shamblers out there are thick as mosquitoes in July. You go out, untrained and unready, and you won't stand a chance."

"Have you thought maybe I'm just better than you, Juliet?" Louisa harrumphed.

"No, I haven't, Miss Louisa," Juliet said quietly. Louisa sensed that she'd stumbled into something dangerous. It was the first time Juliet had used the honorific in front of her name in months. Her suspicions were confirmed when Juliet said, "I think that's enough for today, Miss Louisa. Mrs. Aiken told me you needed time to prepare for the trip into town."

"What do you mean, a trip into town?"

Juliet shrugged, something Louisa had never seen her do before. "I don't know anything, Miss Louisa. I just do what I'm told."

Louisa stood in the grass, searching for something to say as Juliet took back her swords, checked their edges, holstered them, and went off into the house to attend to her own business.

Louisa wasn't sure why she felt so bad about Juliet's sudden detachment, but she did. She'd done something wrong, something that had upset Juliet. Louisa didn't want her to be cross; she couldn't bear the thought of not seeing Juliet smile down at her. It made her heart clutch painfully to think that something she had done had erased that joy from Juliet's face.

She didn't know how to fix things, and she didn't know why she cared in the first place.

After washing up and donning a fresh dress, Louisa entered the foyer to find Mrs. Aiken barking at the staff as they brought trunks down the stairs. Louisa recognized her own traveling trunk, one that she hadn't used since she was small, sitting among the stacks.

"What's going on?" she asked.

Mrs. Aiken turned around and smiled brightly at Louisa. "This morning Everett came by and asked for your hand in

marriage. Engaged before the fall! Oh, Louisa, you will be the
envy of all of Savannah. Less than a year from debut to wedding.
Your father has decided we should spend the rest of the summer
in town, since it will make the festivities easier. There've been
reports of a considerable horde heading our way, so we're going
to leave this afternoon."

Louisa tried to take a deep breath, to steady herself. It was
all happening so fast. She was to be engaged. And to Everett!
But there was a horde coming toward them, and that seemed
like a matter of grave consequence. There was also the matter
of Landsfall and the staff.

"A horde, Mother? Shouldn't we stay here and secure Landsfall? That many undead doesn't sound good."

Mrs. Aiken waved away Louisa's concern. "That's exactly
why we're going to Savannah. We'll be much safer in the city,
behind the wall with the patrols." Mrs. Aiken patted Louisa's
hand. "Don't worry, we'll have your girl to see to our safety."

Mrs. Aiken moved off and began instructing a few of the
men on loading the pony. Louisa tried not to wring her hands
in worry, but abandoning Landsfall seemed like a terrible idea.
Wouldn't there be more danger from the undead in a closely
packed city, regardless of the wall?

Louisa looked over to Juliet, who was talking in a low voice
with one of the other colored girls. The girl was visibly upset,
and whatever Juliet said calmed her some. Juliet smiled down
at the girl and then pulled her in for a hug, and Louisa was surprised by a sharp stab of jealousy. She wanted Juliet to calm her
like that, to wrap her strong arms around her and make her feel

safe, the same way she had the day the undead broke through the fences of Landsfall.

Juliet released the girl, looking up to meet Louisa's gaze. Juliet raised her eyebrows in question, and it was at that moment Louisa realized she was staring, her hands clenched in fists.

Purposely looking anywhere but at Juliet, Louisa went to prepare herself for the trip to Savannah.

The trip into town was uneventful, despite Louisa's anxiety that the horde would intercept them before they made it into the city. And as the days filled with engagement dinners and wedding planning, Louisa completely forgot about both the rumored horde of undead and her spat with Juliet.

Because there was Everett.

He was solicitous, coming round to the Aiken family townhouse at least twice a day to check on Louisa, to see if there was anything she needed. He brought flowers and a warm smile, and Louisa couldn't help but think she was going to end up married to the best man in the world.

Even so, there was still a niggle of doubt in the back of her mind. It wasn't that she had any other prospects—marrying Everett was really the only acceptable thing she could do with her life. It was that she wanted something more than Everett's perfunctory kisses and gentle touches and a life of wifely duties.

But what?

And every time she asked this question, there was the image of Juliet kissing one of the Landsfall girls out behind the pavilion.

All of these emotions churned through Louisa the day the undead breached the city wall.

It came as a clanging of bells, and at first Louisa thought there was a fire. But the screams and shouts that filtered through the windows from the street quickly made clear that nothing was burning, but the city was in trouble all the same.

Juliet ran to the front door, throwing it wide and looking down the street.

"What is it?" Louisa asked, hurrying to stand next to Juliet.

"Shamblers."

They were everywhere. Men and women ran down the street in wide-eyed panic while the undead lumbered after them, arms reaching out to, more often than not, clutch empty air. The smell was terrible, a sweetly foul rot that overwhelmed and made Louisa gag. A man tripped and fell, the undead swarming him quickly, the echo of his screams fading soon after they fell on him.

But not soon enough.

Juliet closed the door and locked it, moving the huge barricade bar in place. "We need to get you out of the corset, Miss Louisa. You need to be able to breathe if you're going to run."

"What about Mother?" Mrs. Aiken had gone to Mrs. Arsbury's house for a luncheon. She was trapped out there, somewhere.

Juliet shook her head. "Our best bet is to get out of town, head down to Landsfall. Maybe get a boat and double back through one of the marshes. . . ." Juliet trailed off as she thought, her teeth capturing her full bottom lip and worrying it. Louisa felt a sudden shock as she realized that Juliet was so young, yet so much wiser than she was.

"Why don't you just call me Louisa anymore?" It was a petty thing to bring up at such a time, but she couldn't help it.

Juliet didn't miss a beat, ushering Louisa up the stairs to change. "Because for a moment I forgot you were a white woman, but then you reminded me, and I don't need for that to happen again."

Louisa didn't want to understand what Juliet meant by that, but she did. Training with Juliet had caused her to see Negroes in a different light . . . but not nearly enough, it seemed. Louisa knew it wasn't fair for someone as competent as Juliet to be trapped in a position of perpetual servitude, but that was just the way things worked, and it wasn't up to Louisa to change things.

Was it?

Louisa was full of doubts and questions, but it was a terrible time for existential crises. There was a horde quickly overrunning Savannah. It would all have to wait.

Juliet helped Louisa out of her dress and her corset, and helped her dress again in a plainer traveling dress made of cotton. They ran downstairs to find the undead pounding at the door and the windows, the metal bars the only thing keeping out the ravenous creatures. The cook, Dessa, and her two small girls were standing in the foyer, clinging to one another. Juliet went over and whispered something low to Dessa and the girls, who were crying quietly. They settled a bit, nodding at whatever Juliet said.

"Let's hope they haven't found their way down the alley,"

Juliet said. She paused to hand her swords to Louisa before pulling Mr. Aiken's cavalry sword from the war off the mantel. She
tested the edge while Louisa looked.

"What are you doing with Daddy's sword?"

"You need a weapon. Dessa is going to have to mind the
girls as we move through town, and you aren't strong enough
to take out a shambler with a single-handed weapon. So I get
to pretend to be a Confederate for a minute. More's the pity."

Louisa said nothing, and Juliet continued. "I'm taking the
lead. Louisa—" Louisa noticed the lack of honorific and smiled.
"You take the rear. We don't put down a shambler unless we
have no choice, you hear? The goal is speed, not glory."

"Shouldn't we stay here?" Louisa said, pointing to the
undead trying to claw through the windows. "The bars seem
to be holding."

"This is the leading edge of the horde, and it's already a hundred deep. Once the bulk of them get here, we'll be trapped.
Our chances are better on the move."

Juliet waited, as though she expected Louisa to argue, but
Louisa just nodded. "I'm right behind you, then."

Juliet walked toward the back of the townhouse, through
the dining room and the kitchen and out into the garden. The
yelling, the gunshots, and the rasping growls of the undead filtered in from the front of the house, but the small alley behind
the house was quieter and free of undead.

"Shamblers go after noise and movement. There's enough
shenanigans on the main road that we should be able to travel
for a while," Juliet said.

They navigated the alleys, moving away from the screams and shouts, dashing across the more exposed lanes like frightened rabbits. Once they burst out of an alley onto a small pod of three bent over a fallen woman, the wet sounds of their feeding loud. Dessa wrapped her arms around the girls while Juliet removed the heads of the undead, sticking the sword through the eye of the fallen woman so that she wouldn't rise again. Louisa watched, swallowing hard when she felt her lunch attempt to come up.

They kept moving, quickly, cautiously. After they'd gone a few blocks, the sounds faded away to normal city noise. Juliet led the group toward the river and the docks, and once they were in view, it quickly became clear that others had had the same idea.

The docks were in chaos.

People were trying to climb the boats moored to the shore while sailors pushed them away. A few people had jumped into the water to try and swim across the river, heedless of the undead that might be lurking in the depths. A man waded into the river carrying a door, and after placing it on the water he climbed aboard and began to paddle himself across the murky water. People were pushing and yelling, screaming and pleading, and Juliet looked lost as she took in the scene.

"The scare must've started a while ago," she said, gesturing to the number of people crowding the wharf. "There's no way we'll be able to hitch a ride out of here at this rate."

"Louisa!"

Louisa turned. Everett hurried toward them, his normally

healthy skin unnaturally pale. "What are you doing with those swords? Is it true? Is the city lost?"

Louisa nodded. "We need to find a boat out of here, head back to Landsfall. We'll be safe there."

Everett shook his head. "Not likely. The horde came from the south. I'm sorry, Louisa, but Landsfall may be lost."

A calm settled over Louisa. Her childhood home, gone. And what of the people, what of all the men and women and children who worked the plantation, colored and white alike? Were they also gone?

Everett gathered her up in his arms, and Louisa fell into them gratefully. "I'll protect you, my beautiful Louisa. We'll be married and I'll care for you."

"Not if we don't get across that river," Juliet said. "The horde came from the south? Then that explains why everyone is trying to swim across to Carolina. I've got kin there, if you have a boat that can get us to safety."

Everett released Louisa and looked at Juliet, Dessa, and the girls as though he was seeing them for the first time. "Just exactly who do you think you are, speaking to me that way?"

"Everett, Juliet navigated us through a city full of undead. She knows what she's doing," Louisa said, laying a hand on his arm. His face flushed.

"I'm not of the mind to put up with uppity Negroes, regardless of their use. I can protect you now that we're to be married, and these three can be on their way." Everett pushed Louisa behind him and advanced on Juliet, who once again wore the slight smile Louisa had come to know was a self-defense mechanism.

Louisa straightened, anger making her brave. No one was going to treat Juliet poorly. "I'm not going to marry you, Everett."

Everett turned back around. Louisa prepared for an argument.

That was the moment an undead Negro woman launched herself at Everett, tearing into his throat.

Dessa and her girls screamed in unison, a counterpoint to Everett's howls of pain. Louisa watched the spurt of red with wide eyes, her hands going slack and the swords tumbling from her grasp.

Juliet sprang forward, taking off the shambler's head and Everett's as well. She tucked the cavalry sword into one of her holsters and picked up the short swords Louisa had dropped.

"You hear me?" Juliet said, snapping her fingers in front of Louisa's face.

"Yes! I had a shock, I haven't been struck dumb," Louisa snapped.

Then she looked down at the ground and her now headless fiancé. Tears filled her eyes. "Oh, poor, stupid Everett. It was probably better this way."

Juliet laughed, and Louisa realized how her words must have sounded. She'd heard that people acted strangely in life-or-death situations, and she knew that she probably wasn't acting rationally.

But hearing Juliet laugh was such a welcome sound that Louisa found herself reaching out, pulling Juliet close, and planting a kiss right on her smiling lips.

Juliet leaned back in surprise. "Well now, don't start celebrating yet. We've still got to find a way out of town," she said, glancing over her shoulder at Dessa and the girls. None of them were paying attention, since the undead were starting to flood the riverfront.

"We need to run," Juliet said, pointing north along the waterfront. "If the horde came from the south, we might be able to flank them."

They began to run, quickly at first, then more sporadically as the girls developed side cramps. Louisa made the mistake of glancing over her shoulder, only to see people devoured as the horde of undead rushed into them, pinning them between the river and the fallen city. Some people ran north, like them, and others jumped into the river, drowning or swimming for the South Carolina shore.

Once they were out of sight of the undead, Juliet routed them back through the city. It was still madness, but for the most part the horde had skipped the northern part of Savannah, leaving people to evacuate if they could, and flee.

Juliet was unfazed by all of it. Every so often she would cock her head to the side, listening for some far-off sound and then stepping out smartly once again.

They walked for hours, making their way out of the city's north gates, thrown open wide to allow folks to escape, and onto the main road to Charleston with all of the other refugees. After a while on the road, Dessa saw a few of her kin, and a teary reunion stopped all traffic for a moment. She and her girls parted ways with Louisa and Juliet, Dessa taking a penny from around her neck and pressing it into Juliet's hand despite her refusal. In resignation Juliet fastened the penny around her neck, and Louisa watched them go, a hollowness opening up in her middle. Now that the immediate danger was gone, a dark despair settled over her.

Juliet caught sight of Louisa and frowned. "Hey now, what's the matter?"

"I've got no one," Louisa said, the words catching on a sob. "Landsfall is gone. Everett . . ." Louisa trailed off, Everett's last moments flashing before her eyes. "I'm all alone and wholly unprepared for this."

Juliet sighed and patted Louisa's hand awkwardly. "Aww, let's hush that fuss. You've got me. I'll make sure you get settled up nice in Charleston. And then we'll find a way to see if your family home is still standing."

Louisa hiccuped one last time. "What about California?"

Juliet stopped and crossed her arms. "What about California?"

"I heard you talking about it last week when Dessa asked you what you were planning to do now, once your contract was over." Louisa looked at the other refugees from Savannah walking on either side of the road and lowered her voice. "I want to go with you. I want to be with you." Louisa tried to put all of her feelings into her voice, to express how she hated the idea of being apart from Juliet, no matter whether it was right or not.

Juliet's expression quickly cycled through shock to anger and finally sadness. "You don't deserve to be with me," she said, and continued walking.

Louisa watched her go, her desperation draining away. Juliet was right. Louisa didn't deserve her. Not yet. But that didn't mean she couldn't change.

Running to catch up, Louisa followed after Juliet, down the road to Charleston.

Omega Ship
RAE CARSON

The first thing I know is that I'm curled up on my side, suspended in loving warmth. My body sways, adrift in a tropical ocean of blue water. No, blue gel. It coats my eyeballs—there's no need to blink—and my vision is a bluish haze. Beyond the haze is glass, the glass of my . . . window? Ceiling?

Stasis pod.

My mind snaps awake. Warm comfort flees.

I shouldn't be awake. Not while inside my pod. I try to lift my hand, but it doesn't respond. I try again. My heart pounds once, hard, as if springing to life. Then again. Then regularly.

My hand twitches. Gradually I push through the gel until my fingers reach the glass. I splay them across the undersurface. It's convex, and icy cold.

I push against it, but it won't budge.

The gel oxygenates me, protects my skin. I know this, but

I'm trapped and my lungs yearn to gasp for air and I can't stop my diaphragm from contracting.

Gel floods my chest. I choke and heave, lurching against the suspension. The pod lists left like a sinking ship. I pound at the glass—*bang, bang, bang*—as my mind shouts *wrong, wrong, wrong.*

A great lurch, and the pod and I are freefalling, spinning into a void, my hands still pressed against the glass as my diaphragm convulses helplessly with the need to scream.

We crash. Metal groans and glass shatters. My left hip is numb for a split second before agony explodes in my bones.

Too late, emergency protocols kick in and my pod releases, shooting icy stimulant through bluish goo that already drains away, free of its prison. I vomit mucus and gel, choke hard as acid burns my throat, and then finally, *finally,* I inhale cold air, real air, my first breath in years or decades or maybe even centuries.

"Hey! Can you hear me?" A male voice, coming from a throat as raw as mine. "Can you walk? We have to get out of here."

A shadow looms, extends an arm. I blink to clear my eyes, and the shape becomes a person. A beautiful young man. Broad shouldered, naked. Pale skin and blond hair slick with gel.

I reach for his offered hand, and he clasps my forearm. My left hip screams anguish as he yanks me upward.

"You took a beating when your pod fell," he says. He assesses my own naked body. His eyes are bright blue, intelligent but on the edge of panic. "Nothing broken, thanks to the stasis gel. C'mon."

The floor heaves. My hip doesn't want to support my weight, but the young man's grip on my forearm is a vise, and I keep my feet.

"The *Omega* hit atmo," he says. "We find the escape capsules, or we die."

As I stumble after him, my hip loosens, and my feet remember they're feet and begin to bear my weight without aching. We're in the starship's central hold, a massive cylindrical tower stretching so high that the ceiling is lost in shadow. The walls are full of stasis pods, thousands of them, held in brackets at a sloping angle in overlapping rows, like glass shingles. Many of the brackets are empty, their pods crashed to the floor.

As the boy leads me through the wreckage of bent steel and shattered glass and wobbly bluish gel, I catch glimpses of pale skin. Gel-wet hair. A limp hand.

"Wait!" My first word in who knows how many years. I yank my arm from his grasp. "The others! We have to help—"

"Everyone's dead," he says. His jaw clenches for a moment, and then he adds, "Everyone but us."

No. I can't be the only girl left in the universe. I can't be. "How do you know? Look at all those pods. Thousands of them. They might—"

"Something went wrong," he says. "The *Omega* went into conservation mode, cutting power to the pods one by one. Only a fraction were still powered on when she found a suitable planet—"

The ship jerks. I watch in horror as a pod six stories up slips from its brackets and missiles to the floor, explodes into glittering glass and crunching metal. Before I can turn to run, we both rise into the air a meter, float for a moment, then crash back to the glass-strewn floor, collapsing to our knees.

"Ship's grav is in and out. We have to move *now*."

I gain my feet and hobble after him. The glass is in tiny crumbles, like thick sand, and it feels odd on my feet but does not cut as we wade through bent metal and pale limbs toward a darkness in the far wall. A doorway, I hope, but it's hard to tell in the dim emergency lighting.

My knees collide with a pod. I thrust out my hand to steady myself and realize pod number 4289 is intact, the body inside still encased in blue gel. The light indicator near the control panel blinks green.

"This one's alive," I call out.

He yanks at my arm. "There's no time! Please . . ."

I don't hear what else he says, and I don't care. I push the release button, but the lid doesn't unlock. The emergency protocols didn't kick in for this one, and I have a minute, maybe seconds, before the stasis pod becomes a coffin.

"I'll leave without you!" the blond boy says.

"Then go."

The air fills with chemical smoke. Smoke means we'll be out of oxygen soon. I run my fingers along the pod's edge for the emergency lever. Each pod has one, fail-safe after fail-safe, designed to protect stasis humans in every circumstance except unforeseen planetfall. I find the latch with my middle finger, hook it, pull. The lock releases, and something hisses as stimulant is injected into the gel. The top unseals, folds away on a hinge.

Damn. It's another boy. Dark haired, Asian features. He blinks up at me, his black lashes thick with gel.

A flood of bile pours from his mouth as he chokes and coughs.

I don't know if he's fully awake, or if he'll be able to stand without absorbing the stimulant for at least a few seconds more, but the blond boy was right and we have no time, so I reach for his armpits and pull him upward.

He is slender but tall, too heavy for me to lift alone.

I turn, saying, "Hey, I need your help . . ."

But the first boy is gone. We are abandoned, and I don't blame him.

The dark-haired boy tries to speak, chokes instead.

"The ship's going down," I explain, fast and loud over the sound of atmosphere screaming against the hull. "We have to find the escape capsules. Keep an eye out for survivors on the way."

He nods and gathers his feet and supports enough of his own weight that I can half carry, half drag him to the darkness in the wall that might be a door. I glance at each shattered pod as we go, and I wish I didn't have to, because all I see are broken bodies. A very few, the ones who were alive before falling, bleed freely onto the floor. Blood coats the shattered pod glass. In the ship's emergency lighting, it seems as though we wade through a sea of shimmering rubies.

The darkness in the wall is indeed a doorway, and I almost cry from relief. I drag us left into the hallway, curve around the pod tower, open the first access hatch I see. The hatch slides easily aside, revealing a round capsule with six jump seats, face guards dangling before each seat, and the blond boy, already belted in.

"Oh, thank god," he says. "A few more seconds and I would have had to launch."

I strap the dark-haired boy into his seat and make sure his belt and harness are fastened tight, then I grab a seat of my own and buckle in.

"Ready?" the blond boy says.

I stare at the three empty seats.

"Ready," I whisper, and my voice is lost in some kind of explosion as the capsule shudders and the blond boy slams the release button.

My back presses into the seat as we are jettisoned with incredible, bone-numbing force. The two small windows grow bright with fire, then my sight goes black as we spin through it.

And suddenly we're free. My vision returns as a bright point, but gradually expands to reveal the faces of my companions. Tears stream down the blond boy's face, and I'm not sure if it's fear, relief, or too many Gs that are making him cry.

The dark-haired boy's eyes are wide, as if he's finally, truly waking up, and it's to a horror beyond his imagination.

"Look!" says the blond, wiping at his wet cheeks. "More escape capsules. We're not alone."

He's looking out one of the tiny round windows. Three other capsules fall through the mesosphere alongside us. They look like small comets, their hulls shiny with friction, heat streaming behind.

"No."

It's the dark-haired boy. The first word he's spoken since I yanked him from his pod.

"They're supply capsules only," he adds. "No windows, see?"

My heart sinks, but the blond says, "Isn't that good news? I mean, the *Omega* would only release supply capsules if it found a habitable planet, right?"

"Right," the dark-haired boy says flatly. He catches my eye, and I know exactly what he's thinking. He'd give up all those supplies for just one more person. Another girl.

The capsule begins to shudder. "Grab your face guards," I say, reaching for mine. I yank it down and place it over my nose, making sure the mouthpiece fits snug. A variant on the stasis gel coats my teeth and gums, and my head clouds with drowsiness.

Fire erupts along our hull again as the strange planet's gravity grabs our capsule and drags us into oblivion.

In spite of the parachute, the air jets, the gel sedative, and walls designed to absorb crushing shock, we land so hard it feels as though my tailbone lodges in my sternum. We spin at impossible speed. The atmosphere roars around us as we cannonball across the planet's surface. Gradually, we decelerate and come to a neck-wrenching stop.

I sit stunned for a minute, maybe longer. Our capsule came to rest so that I dangle from the ceiling, staring down at the two boys seated across from me.

"You okay up there?" says the dark-haired boy.

"Think so." I unbuckle the lap belt and reach for the chest harness.

"Wait," he says.

The blond watches mutely as the other boy extracts himself from his own harness and moves into position to help me down.

"Unbuckle now. I'll brace you." His hands wrap my waist in readiness.

I press the release and slide neatly against him. He holds me a moment, making sure I'm steady on my feet. We are skin to skin, his breath warm on my scalp, both of us still slick with stasis gel.

"Hey," says the blond boy, too sharp and loud. "Let's check out this planet the *Omega* found for us." Without waiting for a response, he punches a code into the console. My ears pop as our capsule matches the outside atmosphere and pressure. The air fills with moisture and organic sweetness, reminding me of hot summer nights on Abuela's porch, drinking her tamarind-rum punch.

The hatch slides open, and I put up a forearm against the brightness. We step gingerly on bare feet into a humid world of white sunlight and waxy, wide-leafed foliage. Jeweled insects larger than butterflies flit from plant to plant, sending probos-cises into thistly red flowers. Warm mud squishes between my toes.

The dark-haired boy says, "Welcome home."

We've set up camp using our crashed capsule as a focal point. A smoking ground scar stretches for miles behind it, but the rest of

the world is pristine and lush. Using the capsule's limited supplies, we've erected a tent and a space heater, but I'm doubtful
we'll need either. We sit around the heater for its comforting
familiarity though, eating ration bars. We have no chairs, not
even the equivalent of Earth stumps to sit on, so we've stripped
giant leaves from nearby plants to lay on the ground as a barrier
to the mud.

Every few seconds, the sky flashes as a chunk of starship
debris meteors through the atmosphere. I watched them at first;
they were so beautiful, the brightest shooting stars I've ever
seen. But then I realized I was watching a funeral for humanity's legacy. The greatest thing we ever built, still dead and gone,
no matter how brilliant its pyre.

"We have enough food and water for two months," the
dark-haired boy says.

"We need to find those supply pods," says the blond boy
around a mouthful of ration bar. "That's what we should do
first. Then we'll—"

"Hey, I have a crazy idea," I interrupt. "We could start with
names. I'm Eva Gonzales-Aldana, eighteen years old, from Ciu-
dad Juárez, Mexico."

The dark-haired boy's smile hits me in the gut. "Nice to
meet you, Eva," he says. "I'm Jesse Niyamoto. Also eighteen.
Los Angeles, California."

I smile back. "Hi, Jesse."

The blond boy swallows quickly, says, "Dirk Haas. Nine-
teen. Amsterdam."

"Hi, Dirk," Jesse and I say in unison. I take a bite of ration bar and chew. Another shooting star streaks the sky.

"I guess it's just the three of us," Dirk says. A muscle in his jaw twitches. "In all the galaxy."

"Guess so," says Jesse.

"Dirk?" I say. "You lost someone on that ship, didn't you?"

"My sister."

Only one per family, that was the rule, and we all said our forever good-byes before climbing into our stasis pods. But multiple births were expected to be a fundamental part of the culture of the new world, so they made a few exceptions.

"Your twin?" Jesse says.

Dirk's lips twitch as if he's trying not to cry. "Hers was the first pod I found. She was . . . the *Omega* cut her power long ago."

"I'm sorry," I say.

"She was in love with the adventure of it," he says. "Couldn't wait to have children. Always wanted to be a mom."

Suddenly they're both staring at me. All of me. My breasts, my belly, the mound of hair between my legs. I pull my knees to my chest and wrap my arms around them.

I thought I had lost my shame over nudity. We're used to being naked. We trained naked, entered our stasis pods naked. Two years prior to launch, when we realized Asteroid Holly-Krause's impact would destroy the Earth nine months sooner than originally calculated, we had to speed up our manufacturing timetable. That meant steel-frame stasis pods instead of titanium, bulky freeze-dried rations instead of food paste, and many other shortcuts. It made the *Omega* too heavy.

Some bright-eyed engineer realized we could lose fifteen thousand pounds of launch weight simply by eliminating our clothing. Humanity didn't *need* clothing, she argued. Not in the right environment. In the end, it was either lose the clothes, or eliminate the arts and culture track. We voted to get naked.

"Okay," Dirk says, wiping his eyes. "Someone needs to address the elephant on the alien planet."

Jesse frowns, wrenching his gaze from my skin.

Dirk presses on. "So I'll just go ahead and say it: we need to start making babies."

The ration bar is dirt in my mouth.

Within me is enough genetic diversity to restart the human race. My ovaries contain several hundred thousand oocytes, transplanted from women all around the world. I signed a contract saying I would bear at least two children on the new planet. All of us girls who won the New Hope Lottery did, whether we wanted children or not.

But now that I'm the only human woman left in the universe, my two contracted children won't be enough. I'll have to get pregnant and stay pregnant until I die.

"Eva should have children by both of us," Dirk says. "Just to be safe."

"She doesn't need to," Jesse points out. "She could restart humanity with just one of us." Dirk is about to protest when Jesse puts up a hand and adds, "But you're right. Having children by both of us would be best."

I force myself to swallow my bite of ration bar.

"I know this is awkward and inconvenient to talk about,"

Dirk says, "but it's important to establish right away that she shouldn't mate with both of us at the same time. We need to keep the bloodlines clear. Make sure our offspring doesn't mate with each other. There'll be no way to determine the father by looking at the kids. We'll have to keep track."

Finally I find my voice. "I'm right here, you know. And maybe I don't want to pop out a baby every nine months—"

"This isn't about you," Dirk says. "It's about the human race. We thought the *Omega* would be the vessel of our salvation, but it's not. It's your body, Eva."

I open my mouth, close it.

"Let's give it a few days," Jesse says gently. "We just got here. We've all been through something terrible. Let's make this camp comfortable, use the test kits on the soil and atmosphere, try to find those supply capsules. Then we'll talk again."

Dirk frowns. "We can't put this off for long."

A shadow blocks the sun, cooling the air on my skin. I look up and find a massive winged creature soaring overhead, long flight feathers trailing like a jet stream. There's so much about this new world to learn, and what we don't know might kill us a lot faster than infertility.

Jesse and I push through the alien jungle. Earlier, Dirk climbed what passes for a tree and spotted another ground scar, made by one of the supply capsules. "Follow the moons," he said. "I'll do soil testing while you're gone."

A break in the canopy of leaves frames them perfectly. The smallest moon hangs heavy and full, the texturing of its surface like the skin of an old man. The larger one sits behind it, dwarfing its smaller sister. It's only a quarter full, its outline hazed. How big must it be to appear so huge and yet so far away? Monstrous. Planet sized. If there's an ocean on this world, it might take us generations to understand its tides.

I stare at Jesse's back as we hike. He is tall and slender but wiry with muscle. Beneath his taut waist, his glutes and hamstrings contract with each graceful step, and I can't help but wonder if the conspiracy theorists were right, that the New Hope Lottery wasn't a lottery at all. There were some basic requirements to enter, of course—younger than twenty, certified physically fit, less than 5 percent observable epigenetic degradation, levels of testosterone and dopamine sufficient to produce high libido. But looking at Jesse and Dirk, it's easy to believe the lottery was rigged to select humanity's most beautiful specimens.

Jesse stops suddenly, and I almost collide with him.

He turns. "Eva, I need to thank you," he says.

"Why?"

"For saving my life." His dark eyes are very close. He's a whole head taller than I am. My forehead would fit perfectly in the crook of his neck. "I would have died on the starship if you hadn't yanked me from the pod. You got me moving before I was even aware what was going on."

If I shifted the smallest bit, I could kiss him. "Oh. Well, you're welcome."

He continues through the jungle, and I follow.

"To be honest," I say to his back, "I was kind of hoping you'd be a girl."

He spins around. "You like girls?" The disappointment in his face makes me smile.

"I like men."

"Oh. Okay. Good."

"Not that it matters. Everyone had to sign the procreation contract, right? It's just that I was hoping I wouldn't be the only baby factory left in the galaxy."

His eyes drift to my breasts, but he snaps them back to my face. "Sure, that makes sense."

"Hey, I think we're there," I say, pointing beyond him. Something metallic glints each time the breeze rustles the trees.

We run toward it, shoving leaves and branches aside, and we break into a field of wrecked vegetation and smoking ground. The capsule is hugged up against a massive boulder, scarred but intact, its hull lights still blinking.

Jesse reaches for the release panel.

"Careful," I warn. "It might be too hot to touch."

He tests the air temperature with his palm. "I think it's okay." He enters the key code, and a small panel swings open. Jesse clasps the latch inside and gives a great tug and twist. Air hisses as the door lifts and slides sideways.

"Eureka," Jesse says.

It's jammed with stuff. Food rations, water purification pumps, solar energy packs, and four white chests, each emblazoned with a bright red cross.

"Medical supplies," I say.

Jesse brightens. "Check this out." He grabs an orange plastic case. He opens it to reveal a shiny silver handgun, an anti-projectile vest, a set of handcuffs, and multiple syringes, all set in cushiony Styrofoam-like material. "Sheriff's kit."

But as he stares at the kit, his face becomes morose and his chest and shoulders deflate like a dying balloon.

"What's wrong?"

"I was law enforcement track. I loved it. The physical training, even the psych classes . . . I mean, I *really* loved it."

"Then you should be the one to carry that gun."

"Yeah. I guess." He closes the kit and latches it.

"What were those syringes?"

"Adrenaline, painkiller, sterilization, tranquilizer."

I stare at the case. "Sterilization?"

"In case the sociopath gene cropped up."

"Oh."

"What about you?" he asks. "Which track?"

It's my turn to be morose. "Arts and culture. I played cello." Just saying the words puts a pang in my chest. "Something I'll never do again."

"But you *really* loved it."

"I did." I had a full scholarship to the New York School of Music. Two weeks before launch, I was one of seventy recent *preparatoria* graduates selected to perform "Adagio for the Holocaust" at Carnegie Hall.

He studies me a long moment. "I bet there's a supply capsule somewhere on this world that contains a cello. The *Omega* had everything, right? I mean, we sacrificed our clothes so we could have music."

"Yeah. Maybe."

His gaze is so warm, so full of understanding, that my eyes start to sting. He adds, "Holly-Krause killed our planet, not our humanity. If there's a cello anywhere on this new world, we will find it."

Who has time for music when you live to raise an army of children? I appreciate his effort, though, so I force a smile and say, "Let's gather what we can carry and get back to Dirk."

The day will not end. Even after establishing camp, hiking miles to the supply capsule and back, and eating a meal of reconstituted split pea soup, the sun sits angled in the sky, indicating early afternoon.

"So, what next?" Jesse says, scraping at his soup cup for every last calorie.

"We need a water source," I say. "And better food. This soup is gross."

"It looks like an avocado mated with a mudslide," Jesse agrees, peering into his empty cup.

Dirk grins. "Never look at what you eat. That's the rule for interstellar travel. We should be okay for water, though, as long as we get to work on it."

"The soil is moist," I say. "So either it rains a lot, or the water table is high."

"If you two don't mind," Jesse says, "I'd like to explore the area a little. Try to find a creek or something."

"I'm not sure you should go anywhere alone," I say.

"There's been no sign of animal life," Dirk says. "Except butterfly things and those giant birds. This planet is in a very primitive evolutionary stage."

"I'll take the gun," Jesse says. "Just in case."

My vision is bleary with exhaustion, and sweat and mud coat my naked skin, making me itch. The medical supply chests contain a few sanitary wipes, but if Jesse found a creek, I could wash up for real. "Be careful," I tell him. "We'll dig a latrine while you're gone."

"Unless we hit groundwater," Dirk amends.

Jesse grabs the gun from the bright orange case and, after a quick smile in my direction, disappears into the trees.

"How long are the days on this planet, do you think?" Dirk asks, his eyes on the space Jesse just vacated.

"Longer than Earth days, that's for sure," I tell him. "I'm so tired I could die."

"Please don't," he says, with a slight smile. "Eva, I have to tell you . . ." He grabs a stick and pokes at the mud with it. "I know I behaved . . . badly. While the *Omega* was going down. You were right to look for survivors. I was wrong, and if I'd had my way, we wouldn't have found Jesse."

I'm not sure he deserves a concession, but I give him one anyway. "It was a terrifying moment."

His full lips are turned down, and he stares at the mud he's poking at like it holds all the mysteries of the universe. "I had just found my sister's body, and . . . I know that's no excuse. I was a coward. And I'm sorry."

"Apology accepted."

Relief floods his features. "Thank you." He lumbers to his feet. "Let's start digging. If I don't work on something, I'll get all mopey again." Dirk is not as tall as Jesse, and we are exactly eye to eye. His jaw is perfect, his lips curved and sensual, his neck and shoulders corded and thick. Where Jesse is fire and grace, Dirk is mass and power.

His thumb comes up toward my cheek, and I almost flinch away, but then I don't. I want him to touch me.

His caress is as gentle as butterflies' wings. "I'm glad it was you," he says softly.

"Huh?"

"Who I found in the pod, I mean. You're smart, you're kinder than I deserve, and . . ." A smile quirks his lips. "And the most beautiful girl in all the world."

It's not that funny, but a giggle bubbles from my chest anyway, and his answering snicker sets me over the edge and suddenly we're both laughing so hard we can hardly breathe.

Night has finally fallen, and I'm curled up alone in the escape capsule, wrapped in a Mylar blanket. The blanket is probably overkill in this planet's warm climate, but I like the comfort of being wrapped in something.

Jesse did not find water, but he plans to try again when the sun rises. He and Dirk share the tent tonight. Soon enough, it will be me in that tent, sharing it with whichever one I choose. I don't think I can go wrong. They both seem decent enough. Willing to work hard. Gorgeous.

Dirk was right. If we're going to save humanity, I need to get pregnant right away and have as many babies as possible while I'm young and healthy and strong. I don't know how many pregnancies a woman's body can take, but if I start now, and my body holds up, I could potentially bear twenty or more children before menopause.

Twenty children. My heart speeds up, and my skin is suddenly slick against the Mylar.

Twenty times, my body's organs will rearrange to make room for life growing inside me. Twenty times, carrying a weight against my pelvis and spine. Twenty times, stretching out the skin of my belly, my breasts, my thighs, until it hangs on me like dirty laundry. Twenty agonizingly painful labors. Twenty chances to die.

I owe it to humanity. As Dirk pointed out, my body is not my own.

I hardly know what I'm doing as I thrust the space blanket aside and clamber from the capsule. Our camp is swathed in silence. The smaller moon has set, but the larger one is high in the sky, casting plenty of light to see by.

I tiptoe through our unorganized supplies, past the tent. One of the boys breathes loudly with something that is not quite snoring.

The orange case sits beside the space heater. I open it slowly, and the hinges do not squeak. Jesse returned the gun to the case; it glints up at me, bluish in the moonlight. Beside it are the syringes.

They're all carefully labeled, leaving no doubt which is which. I uncap the one I want and hold it up to the moon, studying it for a moment, hesitating, thinking about the future.

With one swift motion, I jam the needle into my right thigh

and hit the plunger. The liquid is ice cold and stinging, and my fingers tremble so badly that I drop the empty syringe into the mud.

I grab it back, wary of the needle, wipe it up as best I can with leaves, replace it in the case, and close everything up. A laugh starts to squirm out of my chest and I have to cover my mouth with both hands. Why did I bother putting the syringe back? Jesse will realize exactly what I've done as soon as he opens the case.

What *have* I done?

Slowly I make my way back to the capsule. Maybe it's the irrevocableness of it all, but my heart slows to normal, and it feels as though a weight lifts from my shoulder. I belong to me again.

I curl up in my Mylar nest and sleep like a baby.

All three of us are awake well before the dawn. Maybe, years from now, we'll adjust to the new planet's rotation and learn how to sleep fourteen hours straight. But not today.

After a quick breakfast of freeze-dried beef Stroganoff, Jesse says, "Going to look for water again. I'll head east this time."

"I'll go with you," I say, popping to my feet. I woke this morning overcome with the desire to explore. Does this world have oceans? Mountains? It can't all be dense and tropical like this Eden. I want waterfalls and flowers. Deserts and ice caps. I want a closer look at those glorious flying creatures. I want to see everything.

"Okay by me," Jesse says. "Dirk, if you're going to be here

alone, you should keep the gun."

"Agreed," Dirk says. "That should be a rule. Whoever is alone gets the gun."

I glance at the orange case. The empty syringe inside seems to scream at me.

The boys will figure out what I've done soon enough. No doubt they'll hate me for it. I just hope they come around over time, once they realize we're all we'll ever have.

"Be careful," Dirk says.

"We will," I say. "Back soon." And I give Dirk a slow, deliberate smile that is full of promise. He catches his breath.

The giant quarter moon guides us as Jesse and I hike through the jungle. The ground here is rockier, less muddy, and my feet become scraped and sore. They'll toughen soon enough. Like fingertips against cello strings. Human skin is remarkable that way.

Dirk's and my latrine yielded no groundwater, which is fine. It means we're not likely to contaminate a water source with our waste. It also means we need to find a creek. Or better yet, a nice, clear pond perfect for bathing.

And it's like I've summoned it with a thought, because we push through a giant fernlike plant and nearly trip over a perfect pool of rippling, moonlit water.

Jesse draws in a breath. "Have you ever seen anything so beautiful?" He crouches toward it.

"We don't know what's living in there," I warn.

"Just testing the water." He pulls something from his carry pack. Dips it into the water. Holds it up to the moon.

"And?" I prompt.

"Perfect pH," he says, grinning. "Nothing toxic. A few organic compounds from the surrounding vegetation, some microbial life."

"Then we should purify it before drinking," I say.

"Yes, but . . ." His grin becomes as bright as a sun. "We can still go swimming." With that, he drops his pack to the ground and plunges into the water.

He's under for several seconds. My heart is in my throat by the time he breaks the surface, black hair streaming against his temples, skin glossy with water. He stands waist-deep. "It's cool and shallow," he says. "Come on in!"

He doesn't have to tell me twice. I shuck my pack and step in after him, mud squishing pleasantly between my toes. I dunk once to rinse off yesterday's grime. For a split second, it feels like I'm back in my stasis pod, floating in beautiful nothingness.

I surface and slick back my hair, then I open my eyes to find Jesse watching me, lips slightly parted. His gaze roves down to my belly and up again, comes to rest on my breasts.

"Jesse," I whisper.

"Eva," he says. He doesn't bother to hide what he's staring at. I stare right back, admiring his lean muscle, his trim waist. But I hesitate to close the distance between us because I'm not sure it's me he wants. Maybe he wants the utility of me. Maybe he wants to be the father of the new humanity. Maybe he'll hate the real Eva.

I breathe deep and stand tall, enjoying the feel of his gaze on my skin. My life—humanity's life—is going to be short, a blip on the universe's timeline, and I want it to be filled with moments to savor. There's no time to waste.

So I just come out and say it: "I want you." For now. For tonight.

One swift movement brings him into my space. His hands slip around my waist, glide down to my rear, where he cups me tight, hitching me against him. Water sloshes around us.

My arms go around his neck, and I lift my face to take in his gaze; it's hungry and filled with wonder. The skin of his chest is warm against mine. "Thank you," he says, "for choosing me."

A laugh bubbles from my throat before I can stop it, because if Dirk were here instead, it would make no difference. "I'm not choosing you," I say. "I'm choosing me." And I press my lips to his.

La Revancha del Tango
RENÉE AHDIEH

The gray cab lurches to the side of the empty street. It hits the curb with a whimper and a bang, blasting a cloud of dark exhaust into my open window. Through the smoke, I catch a glimpse of my eyes in the sideview, watering, real classylike. Think Ingrid Bergman in *Casablanca*, but not as picturesque. Or as blonde.

"Uh . . . ¿Cuánto cuesta?" I fumble through the wad of sticky bills in my palm, pausing to mop the sweat from my brow.

Without a glance in my direction, the cabbie flicks the meter screen toward me so I can see the amount, a cigarette dangling from his lips.

Good one, Maya. Numbers are universal. I count out the pesos with care, a grin plastered across my face. If I were in a more cooperative mood, I'd probably take the time to arrange the bills sunny-side up, for my cabbie's singular enjoyment.

But I'm not exactly in a cooperative mood. I can't wait to find a shower and a bed.

I shove some money at him and mutter "Thanks," like a well-bred American girl. He snorts and says something under his breath, cigarette ash crumbling all over his jacket. As soon as I lug my rolling suitcase from the cab's rusty trunk, he hauls ass off the sidewalk, popping a wheelie in the process.

That is one gangster cabbie. I almost want to take back the many times I silently cursed him on our drive from Ministro Pistarini International Airport.

Almost.

Now where is this effing hostel with the black cat?

I scan down a dark side street of Buenos Aires.

Eh. I'm not going to lie; it's not exactly what I pictured.

The sidewalks are lined in nondescript tan buildings, checkerboarded by dirty windows and air-conditioning units. Condensation drips from a slew of humming underbellies, staining the walls brown like a bad Jackson Pollock painting.

It smells of gutter and sweat, with a tinge of salt.

Gritting my teeth, I proceed down the sidewalk, putting an extra cumbia skip in my step, for good measure. The heel of my sneaker splashes in gutter water, and I cringe as the oily spray soaks through the cuff of my jeans.

#perfection.

While on my flight from Miami to Buenos Aires, I read a magazine article about the disappointment tourists feel when faced with the sad reality that their final destination isn't the paradise they anticipated. The author of the article had taken a trip to see the pyramids at Giza and was pissed when he realized the city—with all its noise and pollution and *normalness*—was only a few blocks away from the pyramids.

I know I'm not quite in the same position right now.

But a part of me feels that way.

It vaguely reminds me of the way I felt the morning my father died in the hospital last year, after his car accident. Like I'm waiting for something terrible to descend on me. Some terrible yawning darkness that's just lying in wait in the nearby alley, ready to crush away all chance at happiness.

I push aside the sensation before it takes hold and force myself to smile as I continue walking across the cracked cement. After wandering aimlessly for a few minutes, I pause to rummage through my carry-on, then yank out my guidebook.

Black cat, black cat, black cat.

I skim over a sea of small text—blind promises of cheap steak and chimichurri. I catch myself almost snickering, which is kind of weird to do when you're alone. Like, what are the chances a girl who snickers to herself has a well-intentioned bone in her body?

All I can think about is why I have yet to hear a whisper of life around me. I know it's a ridiculous thought, but where the heck are all the people? It's barely dinnertime. Where is the tango? By now, shouldn't I be bathed in its dulcet tones, caught on some lambent street corner, whiling away the night with some tango god?

I really should throw out this guidebook.

Finally, at the very end of the street, I see a tiny neon sign of a black cat. The word HOSTEL glows back at me, with all the menace of a B-horror flick. As I walk closer, the sign starts to snarl, zip-zapping like a squirrel with a nervous disorder.

A hostile hostel.

Fitting for a girl who snickers.

I push open a creaking door covered in layers of simultaneously shining and peeling paint. "Hola, me llamo Maya. Yo—"

"Yes. We received your messages," a bored-looking boy drones from behind the desk in lightly accented English. "Give me your passport and sign in here."

Though the skinny dude has it coming, I dig his Alabama Shakes T-shirt too much to get smart with him. Not now, at least. He points me down the hall to the common room, and then jerks his thumb to the left, where the girls' rooms and bathrooms are located.

"Choose an empty bunk bed. Here's a key to a locker." The boy inhales as he turns over a rusty ring of iron and brass. "You should not lose it."

"Grrrracias," I trill back, my grin purposefully smarmy.

He narrows his eyes. "¿De donde sos?"

"What?" I blink, lost. That's what I get for trying to be a smart-ass.

"I'm sorry. I thought maybe you might be from Peru. Or Mexico?" His eyes cut again, as if his vision is degenerating in hyperspeed. "Where exactly are you from?"

Not this again. For the eleventy billionth time in my rather short life. "The United States."

"I know." His thick brows inch up as he taps my passport. "I mean, where is it your family is from?"

And I thought Argentina was supposed to be progressive. Which would mean my "mocha" skin and "almond" eyes belong here.

Or . . . not.

I sniff, sporting the kind of disdain that transcends culture. "My family's from India."

The boy nods. "Enjoy yourself in Buenos Aires." He says "Aires" in a way I hope to master one day, even if only to make other people feel as uncultured as I feel right now.

Too bad the boy has such good taste in music.

I trudge down a hall reminiscent of Number Twelve Grimmauld Place, its crown molding stained black and its tiled floor fraying at the edges. The wheels of my suitcase catch on every lip in the floor as I make my way to the girls' side of the hostel and dump my backpack onto the first available bunk I see. Once I peel off my Duke sweatshirt, I get a good whiff of the airplane and desperation that's been clinging to my skin for the last eighteen hours.

Holy shit. I need a shower.

My clothes are sandwiched to one side of my suitcase, as though they could smell my anguish all the way from the luggage bay. I tug free a pair of skinny jeans, some underthings, and a navy tank top before grabbing the rest of my toiletries and jamming my bags in a locker.

After a weak shower, I get dressed and decide to take a look in the common room, just to see who the black cat dragged in.

The room's furnishings are a strange hodgepodge of sofas and barstools from the seventies. Everything is set as a backdrop for an old, polished wooden cabinet with scuffed edges, clearly meant to serve as a makeshift bar. Perched at its center is a big, clear . . . *thing* . . . with a silver tap. It's filled with a purple concoction drifting around bits of pale miscellany.

Yeah. I'm not drinking that. It looks like fairies drowned in it.

There are several people lounging around, drinking fairy killer from chipped mugs and murky water glasses.

"Look oo we got eeyah," barks a young guy with dark-rimmed glasses and a beard he really should reconsider. It's almost like he's trying to fool the world into thinking he's older and wiser by sporting a beard worthy of a wizard. His lanky form is sprawled across the arms of a beaten Barcalounger.

He reminds me of my least favorite cousin. The one who got drunk at my father's funeral and hurled all over my mother's rhododendrons, all before announcing to the world that my grandmother never liked my father anyway.

Funerals are the best. Add my family to that mix? *Amazing.*

When the young guy with the glasses tries to flag me down once more, I disregard him. It's too early in the night for a boy wizard. Especially of the British hipster variety.

Clearly not one to be ignored, the boy flings an arm into my path. "Oi!" A hand waves wildly in front of my face.

I side-eye him. "Is that accent for real, or are you embellishing?"

He grins nice and slow, like the Cheshire cat. "Real saucy,

ain't you?" His lips twitch, making the ends of his auburn beard dance. If this dude starts lecturing me about free trade coffee or Proust, I can't be held responsible for what happens next.

"Definitely embellishing." I'm barely able to catch my grin.

"No," another boy, with green eyes and tousled hair, to my left, interjects. "He's not embellishing. He's always like that." His features curl upward wryly. "At least, he's been like that for the last two days."

This guy seems normal. He's sitting on the right part of the chair. Not smirking like a fictional character.

Not sporting a beard that would be the envy of Gandalf.

"I'm Maya." I lean over and shake the hand of the normal guy. The cute one.

"Dustin."

"The name's Blake." The ginger wizard pops to his feet and shoves his right hand in my face. Again. He's surprisingly agile, for an oaf.

"Yeah." I take his hand and shake it once, my motions as clipped as my tone. "Maya."

The mouth twitches again. "Maya from where?"

"North Carolina."

"I'm from Jersey." Dustin shoves his hands in the back pockets of his jeans, his broad shoulders rolling forward with the motion. "Just finished freshman year at Rutgers. You?"

"Starting Duke in the fall."

His gaze is dubious first. Then the edges of his lips slide into a frown. "You just finished high school? And you're here alone?"

"I'm not alone," I say with unblinking solemnity. "God is with me." My palm presses against my heart.

Dustin clears his throat and looks away, a flush rising up his neck.

Blake doesn't miss a beat. He laughs loudly and claps a large hand on my shoulder. Catching myself on a stumble, I send a pointed look his way. One of my patented Maya Patel glares.

Still Blake doesn't flinch.

Possibly the first boy outside my family to not flinch at a patented Maya Patel glare.

With a grin at Dustin, I clarify. "I finished high school two weeks ago. As a graduation gift, my family sent me on a trip to Machu Picchu, which is something I've been dying to do since I was twelve. My older brother works for the U.S. embassy in Brazil, and he's meeting me here tomorrow morning so we can go to Peru together. So technically I'm only alone for seventeen hours, which is one whole hour less than the legal drinking age in Argentina. And yes, I did look that up before I flew here."

In response, Dustin laughs, and I can feel him starting to relax again.

Blake watches us as we talk. I can feel his dark-rimmed eyes roving over my face.

It's sad how much it unnerves me.

"Did I hear you right when you said you were going to Duke?" Dustin teases, oblivious to my silent struggle.

"Yeah."

His mouth falls open with horror, but I can tell it's good-natured. "Damn."

"Be original." I return a teasing look of my own. "Everyone hates Duke." My lips pucker to one side. "Wait . . . don't tell me. You just *love* Carolina. Inexplicably."

He laughs again, and it crinkles the corners of his eyes. "Guilty as charged." We both smile at each other. Aside from the bad bedhead, Dustin really is cute.

Just not my type.

"What the feck are you two going on about?" Blake interrupts.

"Basketball," we both reply in unison, then laugh again, like a clip from some sort of cheeseball commercial.

"Lovely." Blake takes a long swig of fairy killer.

"What *is* that?" I can't help but ask, my curiosity winning out.

He takes full advantage of the opportunity and steps closer. Just on the edge of too close. If Blake thinks I'm going to back down, he's wrong. I'm small, but I pack a mean punch. "Well, love," he begins, "it's got to be the worst bloody sangria I've ever had in my life. But it has alcohol in it, and I'll suck a cotton swab dry, so . . ." He laughs at his own joke.

I can't help it. I snicker.

Dammit.

"Did you just snicker?" Blake says.

I sniff. "So?"

"Do it again."

"No. I also won't dance like a monkey for you, either."

"Well, shit. There go my winnings for the evening."

Dustin shakes his head, amused. "And he was planning to

use them to buy drinks at the club."

"I suppose you'll have to go without me," Blake says.

"What club?" I ask, my shoulder brushing against his arm. Refusing to move aside.

"It's some Latin dance club." Dustin's light green eyes warm invitingly. "A bunch of us are going tonight. You should come."

The groan that escapes my lips is wretched. Melodramatic. My favorite kind.

I need to sleep. I have only three days in Buenos Aires before I leave for Machu Picchu, and I need to squeeze every last drop out of my guidebook. The cheap steak. The chimichurri. The . . .

Why am I even playing?

He had me at Latin dance. As a recovering salsera, I'll take any chance to eight-count my way across any room. It isn't really my fault. My best friend, Cristina, has been entirely to blame, since the moment she first taught me how to salsa four years ago. Cristina may have inherited her addiction in her Puerto Rican blood.

But I acquired mine.

What can I say?

Machu Picchu isn't the only reason I wanted to go to South America as my graduation present.

"I'm in," I say, my smile growing wider by the moment. "Can I go like this?" I flourish my right hand from my head to my toes—my best impersonation of a bad beauty queen.

"Uh?" Dustin's face is GIF-worthy.

"Who am I kidding?" I point at Blake's russet beard. "If he

can go like that, I can totally go like this."

Blake grins. "Quite saucy. I rather like it."

Though Dustin doesn't say it, it's clear from the warmth in his expression that he wouldn't leave my smart mouth behind either.

Too bad he looked away earlier. The flincher.

Over the course of the next half hour, we wait for everyone to gather in the common room. Instead of partaking in any fairy killer—and flouting the legal drinking age of eighteen all at once—I opt for a can of nondescript soda, thinking it's my safest course of action. You know, just in case I run into any angry sprites bent on avenging their drowned brethren.

Soon a mixed party of eight travelers gathers in a warm-ish Buenos Aires night, just beneath the zip-zapping black cat outside. The chill in the air hasn't descended yet, but I can tell it's imminent. The last breath of wind carries the brisk scent of the cold. Argentina lies below the equator, and the seasons here play out in reverse. Just as we're about to jump into summer, they're fading past fall.

We hail a few cabs, and I'm pleased to discover that no one expects me to display my impressive Spanglish skills. My pitiful attempts to speak Spanish aren't even remotely necessary, not in this group. Half of them speak the language as though they were born to it.

Thank god for Europeans, or else Dustin and I would have been four-letter-worded in a bad way.

Our caravan of cabs winds its way to yet another side street of Buenos Aires. I glance out the windows, taking in everything around me. At least this street has the grace to sport streetlamps. Curling wrought iron casts ominous shadows across the cement. Pools of sepia light the sidewalks, almost like a daguerreotype. Each of the glowing lamps is encircled in a gauzy haze of white. It brings to mind days of old.

I love it. Everything about it is sexy, in that wonderfully sinister sort of way.

The cabs grind to a halt before an avenue teeming with smiling pedestrians. Filled with incessant peals of laughter. Through it all, I can hear the music pulsing from outside the nearby club.

Eddie Santiago. One of my favorites.

Who knows, Argentina might win me over after all.

After we stand in line to flash our respective IDs at a comically stern pair of bouncers, we make our way into the thumping interior.

Whenever I travel anywhere, I always find it interesting how there appears to be this requisite formula for nightclubs. Like a universal checklist sent out to all proprietors of these establishments, delivered in every conceivable language:

Flashing lights to blind them.

Pounding beats to grind them.

And in the darkness, bind them.

I know, I know. I need to stop it with the Tolkien . . . and the book references in general. People have told me.

The Eddie Santiago song ends by the time we make it onto the dance floor. Marc Anthony picks up where Eddie left off. "Aguanile."

I frown. Bring Eddie back. Slow salsa songs are the best.

When I least expect it, Blake sidles up to me, his long arms crossed. I'm dismayed to realize I'm comforted by the nearness of him. The smell of dryer sheets and worn leather are rising from his linen shirt. "You look brassed off. Good and proper." He keeps his gaze focused forward.

"I'm fine." I shrug, then mime his pose, staring straight ahead. "I just liked that other song more. Eddie Santiago's a classic."

His head turns toward mine. "You listen to salsa music?"

"So?"

"Right. Pardon my curiosity."

I exhale in a huff. "I'm sorry." I look his way, remorse beginning to soften my expression.

"You should be." His eyes twinkle. "You and your god."

Before I can stop them, my lips press together. I'm trying too hard not to laugh. "Where are you from?"

"England." Again he grins like the Cheshire cat, and it's too obnoxious for words.

"No shit, Sherlock." I bare my teeth back at him. "Where in England?"

"Oxford."

That . . . gives me pause. "Oxford, like the town? Or the school."

A quiet laugh. "I believe they're one and the same, love."

I blow a puff of air into my black bangs.

Strike two, Maya.

I turn toward him, full-on. "Well, pardon me, my good sir. What do you study?"

"English literature. What about you?" He pivots in place to face me. He's nearly a foot taller than I am, and his cheeks are ruddy. I can't tell if it's from the pulsing heat of the club or from . . . something else. "Have you decided what you're going to study yet?"

My eyes cut in half. Honestly, I'm trying to take the crazy beard and the insane sparkle in his green eyes seriously.

"English literature."

"Well, bugger me." Blake grins.

Meanwhile, the dance floor has cleared, and a strange new chord of music begins to emanate from the massive speakers perched high in every corner. A hush descends . . .

Then a white spot slices through the darkness, shining in the center of the scuffed wood floor.

A girl around my age *struts*—really there's no other word for it—into the silver beam of light. She's dressed in backless black silk with a slit cut all the way up her slim right thigh. Her shoulders circle slowly as she takes position, her right toe pointed, her chin held high. A mass of dark curls falls down her back, and her crimson-stained lips pucker suggestively.

The young man who meets her under the spotlight is nothing short of spectacular. Even though his body isn't a boy's—every muscle in his arms and chest ripples under the thin material of his shirt—his face is determinedly set. His smile is just too perfect to be a smirk. His slicked-back hair should be cheesy, but against his tanned skin, chiseled features, and broad shoulders, it's the touch of Old World that he desperately needs. The touch that elevates him above the standing of a mere arrogant boy.

That, and his beautifully wicked smile. His crisp white shirt is open at the throat, and his black pants are cut to perfection.

The tango god of my PG-13 dreams.

My jaw hangs low, low, low.

Blake starts to laugh.

The music cuts in. The bandoneóns count out the beat. The drums thud softly.

And the girl dips to the floor, dragging her left foot in a slow semicircle across the wood to begin the tango. The boy spins her in a lazy arc and then brings her up onto his chest.

She slides . . .

. . . down his body.

They mirror each other's motions in perfect unison. To an unhurried beat. To a pair of Spanish guitars and a languid piano. Twisting, turning, dipping . . . gliding.

It's beautiful. So elegant.

So fucking sexy.

The boy spins her in place with a single crisp flick of his wrist. She faces him. He catches the girl behind the right knee and lets her fall back almost to the floor, her curls dusting across the scuffed wood.

Then he pulls her across the scratched surface and she comes out of the dip, one hand on the side of his face. He meets her there, to finish the tango with a careful slide of their joined hands. The music fades, a note lingering from the double bass.

For a breathless moment, the entire club is still.

The stillness is swallowed by cheers. Men and women of all

ages whistle their approval.

And I'm stuck there, dumbfounded. Motionless.

Needless to say, my dreams are no longer PG-13.

"You're drooling, Maya," Blake teases.

I'm rudely shaken from my fantasy. "Shut up, Gandalf."

"Gandalf?" His eyes go wide.

"Well, somebody should tell you." I try my best to peer down my nose at him, which is pretty difficult, since he's so much taller. "That beard is the worst."

"Actually, now that you've likened me to one of the Istari, I think I'll keep it forever."

Again, I'm forced to look him in the eye. "The *Istari*?" Disbelief flares in my voice.

"That's what they're called, love," he condescends. "If you'd read the books instead of just watching the films, you'd—"

My eyes practically bug from my skull. "I read the books! My senior exit project was on *The Silmarillion*, you Oxford swine! I bet you—"

Mickey Taveras blasts from the speakers, cutting off the rest of my perfectly premeditated retort.

Indignation humming through the air, I march onto the dance floor to the sound of the salsa drums blasting from the speakers.

What a prick!

Who cares what he thinks anyway? I look around for Flinching Dustin, and find him sitting at a small table by the bar, deep in conversation with one of the Swedish girls who came to the club with us.

I face him once more, his eyebrows waggle in playful jest.

Then he rolls his shoulders back and forth, his tongue wedged between his teeth. It's disturbingly sexy, in an awkward sort of way.

I can't help it. Unabashed laughter spills from my lips, way too loudly.

When the song ends, I'm almost sorry.

Until another hand taps me on the shoulder.

It belongs to the tango god. The one of the crisp white shirt and the perfectly sly smile.

Holy shit.

Argentina, we are going to be good, good *friends.*

My heart slams in my chest as the tango god grins at me. Then he asks a question in heartbreakingly beautiful Spanish. I shake my head and point at my mouth, as though it's to blame for my inability to speak. He laughs, and it's just as gorgeous as everything else on him. Like honey and smoke.

He still holds out a palm, insisting.

Who cares that we can't understand each other? Love transcends language. Transcends culture. Transcends—

"You should dance with him," Blake says quietly.

Startled from the fairy tale weaving through my mind, I glance at Blake. The fuzzy dreamscape clears.

Sharpening into focus.

Standing before me is a boy who doesn't flinch. A boy who isn't a dream.

A boy who surprises me with his truth.

I hesitate. "But . . ."

Blake's features soften. "I'll wait for you over there."

"You will?" I say softly.

"Of course." He nudges me. "Let him sweep you off your feet. But only for a little while." Blake leans in close, his breath brushing the shell of my ear, sending a shiver down my spine. "Then let me show him how it's really done."

With a knowing smile, I take the tango god's hand.

As I look back, Blake smiles at me.

There is no trace of the Cheshire cat in it.

And I'm whirled into another dance.

With the possibility of something more over my shoulder.

Cass, An, and Dra
NATALIE C. PARKER

My futures are snaking threads that tangle through my present, my past. Mom tells Pia and me to mark the paths we choose so that we keep our memories in line with the reality we've lived.

She says, "Your great-aunt's mind forked like a river and she lived two lives—one that was real, one that was only real in her mind. Those forks split again and again and again until she didn't know who she was anymore."

When we ask how that's possible, her response is, "Just because we choose one future doesn't mean the other one is forgotten."

It's a short story, but it has long fingers that have curled over my shoulders and around my throat since the first time I heard it. I must always know which future I choose and which I don't, or my mind will wander away from me.

There are only ever two possible futures. They appear before me like a question: this or that? This has been true since the snakelike voices first whispered in my ear. *Choose, Cass, choose.* They do not care which way I choose, only that I do.

It's like this.

An sits at the edge of the river, her white sandals flung on the sidewalk behind us, her legs hooked over the edge of the embankment. We are at the farthest end of the public path, away from the playground and open green. The only people who pass by are joggers and cyclists and teens like us, looking for a spot to call their own. We should not be hanging ourselves over the concrete barricade between the path and the river. It's dangerous, not safe; risky behavior. The river here is fast and deep, but this is what An and I are—we are risk and challenge, we are the person the other constantly seeks to impress.

The day is as warm as Puget Sound summers get. The sky is clear for miles, and the river is flush with glacier melt. School is out and whatever hours we haven't committed to working our asses off for cold, hard cash, we spend together.

With her hands pressed to the embankment behind her, An dips her body down until the bottom edges of her shorts darken with water. The river spills up her warm brown thighs. She laughs, tosses her bright smile up to where I sit with legs crossed, shoes on. I am not impressed, and she knows it.

"Cass," she says, pulling herself out of the river and onto the concrete beside me. "Let's go to the bridge. Let's jump."

I look down the river from where we sit. The bridge is half

a mile away and more than a hundred yards up. We've talked about jumping for two years, since we were fifteen and the senior class shut down the bridge with a midnight party on the eve of graduation. Nobody jumped. The river there is rocky, though not shallow. The water is dark and tempting, and An and I decided jumping would be the kind of adventure that made us legendary: Cass and An, the kids who did what everyone else was too scared to.

Choose, Cass, choose.

If I say yes.

We'll grab our bicycles from where we threw them in the grass and fly down the path. The summer sun will dog us all the way, warming our backs. My legs have always been stronger than An's. Even so, I'll be sweaty and breathless when we arrive. She'll kiss me—salt and raspberry lips stealing the little breath I'll have caught.

"Don't think about it," she'll say. "Just do it."

The river will race beneath us. My skin will prickle with sweat. We should not be doing this, but once we're there, there's no going back. We'll wait until the cars have cleared before we climb to the other side of the fence.

The drop will look steeper without the protection of the fence. I'll feel dizzy and alive in a way that is paralyzing and unlike anything I've felt before.

I know that is how I'll feel. The future doesn't come with sensation. It comes with facts. These are the things that will happen if I say yes. I only *know* the future, I don't *feel* it.

An will take one of my hands in hers. Our palms slick and hot and unsteady.

"Don't forget to scream," I'll say.

Then we jump. The world will rush by and it hurts—oh, I *know* it will hurt—when we hit the water. There is blood and a few tears and we'll laugh even as the cold river sweeps us away.

If I say no.

An's frown will be as pretty as any other part of her. I'll lean forward and kiss her—river brine and raspberry lips stealing my breath.

She'll pull away and try one more time. "Please. I'm bored."

"Not today," I'll answer. "But I have a better idea."

We'll grab our bicycles from where we threw them in the grass and pedal to our secret spot. The air will be cooler beneath the bridge, the shadows closer. We know exactly how to slip between the scratching brambles of the blackberry bushes to the chilly space beneath.

An will kiss me, the river will splash and rush and I'll kiss her back. She'll take one of my hands in hers. Our palms slick and hot and unsteady, but we've been there before. I know exactly how that will feel. The future can't hide it from me.

It all flashes through my mind in an instant. Like memories, they arrive fully formed. I know them as well as I know things that have actually happened, both paths as alive as if I've lived them. They fit snugly in my mind next to memories of what I ate for breakfast and the time I broke my arm jumping on (or off, rather) the trampoline behind An's house. And that's the way it always is. I remember every future I've never lived, so sometimes choosing one over the other seems irrelevant. Why bother if I'll have both from this moment on? But Mom's story of my great-aunt haunts every choice I meet. So I choose the brightest of the two, because that's the moment I'll remember.

It doesn't matter that I know what happens on either path. What matters is the experience. It's not *knowing* I'll survive, it's *feeling* the fall.

I say yes. We jump.

I decided long ago that I would always choose An. No matter what the future offered me, An was both relentlessly steady and perfectly unpredictable. I can't control the futures I'll see, but I can control my path through them. An is my guiding light, the compass that points true north through countless futures, and the force that will keep my mind steady.

We became best friends when we were just kids. Probably because the others in our grade weren't born with the risk bone, but instead with the survival bone, the think-of-the-consequences bone. Or maybe we were too obsessed with each other to let anyone else get close. Whatever the reason, our transition from friends to best friends to something so much more was as natural as a growth spurt.

If I know nothing else, I know that my future will always include An. When the future says, "Here is another fork in the road, that way includes no An," I say, "Then I choose this way." When An says, "Let's go to U Dub and study theater," I say, "Okay."

♥ ♥ ♥

An calls on a Friday night. There's a party—there's always a party—and even though we are not the partying sort, she wants to go. This one will be different, she promises. It's not in town. Not even close. It's in so-and-so's backyard, well, sort of their backyard. It's in a lot next to so-and-so's backyard that's just been cleared for a new house, and it's on the edge of a hill that overlooks the Cascade Mountains. It'll be glorious, she promises. Mountains in the moonlight, a bonfire, and music, and someone's bringing Jell-O shots.

An pleads and teases. It's our last summer as kids, she says. It'll never be the same, she says. She dares me to wear that top she loves so much. It's soft and nips in oh so slightly at the waist in a way that makes me look more like a girl. An loves it. I don't, but I'd wear it for her. I can imagine the smell of smoke, the gentle kiss of the night air against my cheeks. I will lose my head, dance until all I am is the beat of the bass, then lean into An's arms and dissolve like paper in water.

In my mind, it's nice. I think I'll say yes.

But before I can answer her, I hear the snakes whisper in my ears. *Choose, Cass, choose.*

If I say yes.

The party will be everything An promised. It'll be in a clearing that overlooks the mountains, the bonfire will be roaring, the stars will embody every diamond cliché I can think of. There will be dancing and shrieking and making out. I'll wear the shirt An loves, but ground myself in cargo pants and boots.

As usual, I'll be a walking paradox that no one knows what to do with. No one except An. She'll guide me into the dance, and I'll catch the flash of her bright lips and the gloss of her dense brown curls in the firelight as she hops and twirls and tips her head to the sky. She'll touch my waist, I'll tug at my shirt and convince myself it fits, but ultimately, there will be something about the crowd I just can't sink into.

I'll slip out of the bobbing throng of bodies and find a spot at the edge of the clearing. I'll lean against a pine tree, checking first for sap, and then I'll wait for An to get her fill. I'm always envious of her ability not to care. Of course, it's easier for her. I've always been unable to lose myself like she does, and instead I'll lurk at the edge of the party where I can watch without being seen.

That's when I'll spot a figure directly across the clearing, leaning against a pine tree in much the same way I am. They're disinterested in the party, but as soon as we lock eyes, I know that disinterest doesn't translate to me.

The figure will move, push away from the tree and walk toward me with so much purpose, I'll feel—I mean, I *know* I'll feel—pinned in place, an iridescent beetle held still by the light pressure of a single finger. In the inconsistent cut of firelight, I won't see more than the hip-length leather jacket, the confident stride, the flash of black hair against golden skin.

They'll stop two feet from me, and I'll be breathless.

"What's your name?" I'll ask.

"You don't know?" Their voice will slip against my skin like satin.

"I don't know you," I'll say in protest.

Leaning in, they'll pause half in, half out of the firelight so that one eye is utterly black, the other a prism of brown and tan and ocher rings. "I know you."

This is the trouble with going to a big school. There's no way for me to know everyone. Though our town isn't huge, the students roll in from the surrounding foothills and townships to make ours one of the largest student bodies on the Olympic Peninsula. It's the sort of thing they tell us at assembly. I don't naturally know that kind of thing. I don't naturally care about that kind of thing. What I do naturally know—in the way of future memories, that is—is that the name of this person standing before me is Dra.

There's a piece of conversation that I'll blitz out of for a moment, because one second I'm staring at the way those bare lips make beautiful shapes out of moonlight and the next, I hear it, "Dra."

"Dra," I'll repeat, the A so long it fades in a breath.

"You were paying attention." Again, that voice knocks against my ribs, *knock-knock-knock* like it anticipates a welcome.

"I'm always paying attention," I'll snap, but there's something about this person that keeps any true irritation at bay. Maybe it's that they're brazen or beautiful or maybe it's that they're completely, 100 percent unknown.

"Are you? I would like your very close attention."

Their eyes on my lips. My heart in my mouth. I'll want—I mean, I *know* I'll want—this. And I don't know which of us moves first, but in the space of a gasp, we are together. Our kiss will be lips, tongues, teeth. It'll be rushed and long and sure.

When we part, I'll know she's seen us. An. I'll know that even while that kiss was creating something new, it was destroying something old, and I'll feel—I don't need to imagine this—like I have jumped off a bridge and there is no river beneath to catch me.

If I say no.

It doesn't really matter, does it? I say no. We fight, and I can't tell An that the reason I don't want to go is that I'm afraid of what I'll do, so my reason is a flat-out lie, which I hate, but lying to her now is better than the alternative.

"I had a vision," Pia—who is three years younger than me and thinks she's thirty years wiser—says, standing in my doorway.

"I'm busy," I answer.

She glances scornfully at my pile of laundry and mostly empty duffel on the floor. I find it incredibly challenging to pack for short time frames like the road trip An and I are about to take to visit the Oregon Shakespeare Festival. I have to start days in advance. Let my packed duffel sit for a while and see how I feel about it in the morning. No matter what I do, my luggage will end up containing options and possibilities and what-ifs. I try to limit that as much as possible, so I pack in a bag the size of a Corgi. So it's not really a lie. I *am* busy.

"Uh-huh," Pia says. "Well, I'm supposed to come and talk to you or you're going to do something hella stupid."

"I don't have time for this, Pia."

Instead of answering, she pulls a strand of hair between her fingers and begins to twirl it, looping it in and out of knots. Our hair is the same dark brown, but against her paler beige skin it looks almost black. Her eyes rest on me, stubborn and unaffected.

"Stand there if you want." We say it at the same time. Her voice mimicking the irritation in my tone.

I suck my teeth to keep from cursing—Dad really hates it when we curse inside the house. I do my best to save my foul language for people who appreciate it, but damn. Pia had a vision.

This is the trouble with clairvoyance. It runs in the family, which means Pia figured out early that she could use it to her advantage. She's always been like this. Teasing futures to get what she wants out of the present moment. I find futures troubling enough without adding those I've only imagined. But this isn't one of those cases, and she knows it.

"So, what is it?" I ask.

She says, "An hasn't called you today. What did you do?"

"Shut up, Pia," I say.

"I know what you did. And you could fix all of this shit if you'd just tell her the truth." She leans in my doorway while I fold T-shirts, jeans, underwear into my duffel bag.

Pia has been telling her friends that she can see the future for years. She says she doesn't have time for lies and deception, but I know what would have happened if I told An the truth. It's not a future I want.

"It won't work. Maybe it works for you, but it won't work for me. She won't believe me."

"You don't *know* that. You're always assuming the one future is a permanent future, and it doesn't work like that!" she insists.

We've had this discussion. We've had it a dozen times, but she will never understand because she's never had anyone look her dead in the eye and call her "crazy," "freak," "demon."

"I saw it in a vision," I say, my voice cutting.

"Bullshit. You saw it in *a* future and you decided it was the only one," she says, but she sits on the ground next to me and starts pairing my socks, eyes judging every item of clothing I pack. "Are you really taking that white button-up?"

And just on her heels, the snakelike whispers creep into my ear. *Choose, Cass, choose.*

If I take the white button-up.

An and I will get into town, the one and only Ashland, Oregon, early enough to find dinner before the play. We'll pick a diner called All's Well That Eats Well and order hamburgers and fries and milk shakes. An's eyes will shine with delight as she slides a bare foot up the inside of my calf and teases my thigh.

She'll tease just a little too far, and I'll drop blood-bright ketchup down the center of my bone-white shirt.

We'll be forced to scarf the rest of our dinner and race back to the hotel so I can change before the show, only we'll take just a second too long and by the time we reach the theater, we'll be forced to wait for intermission to find our seats.

The frown won't show on An's face, but it'll be there in her eyes.

If I leave the white button-up.

We'll still get to town in time for dinner, but we won't actually get dinner. I'll take a minute too long deciding between a black short-sleeved Henley that's nice no matter what Pia thinks, and a navy button-up with an overly long tail, and by the time we leave the hotel there's no time for dinner. We'll get to the theater early, spend too much money on too-little snacks at intermission, and An will have to stifle her laughter when my stomach roars into a silent theater.

It's embarrassing, but also a no-brainer.

These are the kinds of futures I like. They don't matter in the long run, I barely remember them when the moment has passed, but they're useful in small ways.

I turn to Pia. "No, actually. The button-up stays here."

She nods, pleased. And there's no reason for me to tell her my decision had nothing to do with her, so I don't.

All I can think about is Dra. It isn't right. An and I have plans. We've been making plans since we met. Everything has been leading up to this moment when she and I would be freed from our loving but limiting families and strike out into the world on adventures of our own. We applied to the same colleges and mapped out a future of morning classes and weekend road trips and a year abroad somewhere with seasons. That was me determining my own future. With An.

But I cannot erase this future—the unchosen future in which I made a bad choice and kissed Dra—from my mind.

I cannot unremember the kiss. I cannot unknow that if I'd gone to that party, I'd have fallen hard and fast and even if it was only for a moment, it would have been a lasting one. I didn't do it, but I would have.

I'm not even sure that if given another chance, I wouldn't do the same damn thing.

And An has no idea.

An is still upset about the party when we pack the car later. Not for the reasons she should be, of course. She has no idea that I harbor a traitorous soul. She still assumes I'm a loner killjoy who thinks I'm too good for the unimaginative horde we've endured in school all our lives. Lucky for me, she's wrong. And lucky for me, she's not great at holding on to anger. By the time we've snapped our seat belts and waved good-bye to my mom and Pia, An is smiling that full-of-bite-and-mirth smile. All past hurts forgotten.

It's road-trip time. The Oregon Shakespeare Festival is putting on *Much Ado About Nothing* and *Hamlet* and we're excited as hell to be going. For a while, I was worried *Macbeth* would rear its ugly head in the season lineup and we'd have to change our plans. (I love the Bard with nearly all of my heart, but there's no space in it for that wretched play full of wretched prophecies and wretched futures.) But luck was on my side, and when the season was announced, we had our tickets in minutes—third row, center.

It's a four-hour drive down Interstate 5. Seven hours for just me and An. Four hours away from the future I can't forget. We stop for burgers and slushies and take pictures of our tongues—hers is electric blue, mine hyper red. We kiss with cold lips, sing to music so loud it obliterates our voices, and twist our fingers together over the gearshift of my vintage Chevy Caprice Classic. All of it makes the ride too short, and we're pulling into the aggressively charming town of Ashland before we know it.

This is high season for the festival, and the streets are packed. Cars pressed end to end, pedestrians aimlessly wandering between them, street performers cutting here and there like agreeable predators—it all combines to create a perfectly romantic tableau.

An says, "Though this be madness, yet there is method in 't."

I laugh and answer, "Thanks, Polonius."

We have just enough time to unload at our faux-Tudor, truly rundown hotel—where I have trouble deciding between a black Henley and a blue button-up—and prepare to walk the half mile to the theater before the show starts. An looks incredible in her skirt and blousy top—the hint of curves brushing the fabric without revealing themselves completely, her brown skin illuminated by bold colors.

Guilt is sharp in my ribs. Pia is right. I should tell An everything. She is the surest, truest thing about my life, and she should know why I am occasionally irrational and strange, why choosing her sometimes will make her angry.

I should tell her. I will tell her.

It's time to go. She extends her hand to me, and the snake-like voices whisper. *Choose, Cass, choose.*

♥ ♥ ♥

If I tell her.

I'll take her hand in mine, which is sweaty and seems to pulse with my heart. I don't have the benefit of having rehearsed this conversation, because I never anticipated a future in which I'd have to have it. I'll open with the expected "An, there's something I need to tell you," and it won't get any better from there. I'll use phrases like "I see the future" and "Sometimes I have to choose" and "I know how this sounds."

It'll be a horrible, awkward conversation I'd rather forget. Confusing, since it hasn't actually happened yet. But there it will be. My truth presented to An in agonizing clarity.

I'll watch her grapple with all I've said. Her eyes will cut away from me to the tickets on the table.

"We should probably just go," she'll say. "And talk about this later."

Then the future moves swiftly, and suddenly months have passed. We're in college. We'll take morning classes and weekend road trips, but it's not how I imagined it would be. An believes me now, I'll be sure of it, but it makes her nervous in a way I know I'll feel every single day.

One morning, as we stand in line for lattes, mist rising from the forested hills around Western Washington University, she'll say, "You have that look again. What did you see?" Before I open my mouth to answer, I'll know she won't trust what I say.

The future slides again. More months have passed, and it's summer. An stands at the edge of a great canyon. The sun is setting against the rocks, igniting and dampening them row by sedimentary row. It'll be one of the most beautiful things

I've ever seen. An will smile. This is the kind of adventure we always wanted to have, this is exactly what our future should look like.

But when An turns and her warm brown eyes land on me, her smile will fade away. We won't share that moment at all. We'll just be there at the same time.

If I don't tell her.

I won't take her hand. Instead, I'll kiss her. I won't care that I'm ruining her lipstick. She won't either. I'll pull her into my arms, thread my fingers through her hair, and inhale the sweet jasmine scent of her. We'll kiss until our lips are warm and bare, until our cheeks and necks shimmer with the sunset smear of our makeup. We'll kiss until An pulls away and, laughing, says, "We really should go, Cass."

The show will be incredible. It's *Hamlet*, so literally anything is possible, even an Ophelia who makes me think about the play differently than ever before. Obviously, that's what will happen.

Ophelia will come on stage as you'd expect—sweet little dress, hair in curls, her mouth and eyes perfectly outlined. She is beautiful, and for a moment I'll forget to listen, because it's my eyes that feel hungriest.

The next time she'll be on stage, she won't be she. S/he'll come out in sleek pants and a bloused top, hair slicked beneath a cap that shadows his eyes, features undefined and startlingly sharp. He'll move differently, speak differently, *breathe* differently, and suddenly Hamlet's impending retreat from the reality everyone else adheres to will be unnerving and accurate. This is an Ophelia unwilling to conform to the demands of society, an

Ophelia who floats seamlessly between genders, their desire the only fixed point about them. It will be one of the most powerful things I've ever seen.

And all I'll be able to think about is Dra. The person I've never met except in the future.

An will sit beside me, comfortable and challenging, a sure path into the future. We can continue as we always have. But in my mind, it'll be the unknown promise of Dra I can't let go of, the unreal memory of that kiss and the exciting way thinking about Dra keeps my mind from settling in one space for too long.

An will squeeze my hand and I'll feel guilt knuckle into my rib cage like a gun where I should feel love. An will be there with me, but I'll be in a distant, unrealized future.

I freeze, desperate for a third choice. But there is no time. An's hand waits for mine. I take it. I don't tell her.

I've always known my path through the future was An, and so I've never feared it, but now I worry that every decision I make will bring the snakelike whispers to my ears. I worry that my next choice won't include An. I worry that I won't *want* to choose An.

The summer ends, and cloud cover moves in like a rock wall. Life between summers here is damp and withholding. Atmospheric, my mom says. Enigmatic, Pia says. Anemic, I say.

The school year starts, and it turns out the biggest difference between high school and college is that I have to get myself up in the mornings and can't rely on Pia's shrieking cat alarm to do the job.

Once more the snakelike whispers tease me with a future of Dra. I'm simply walking between classes when the wind hisses in my ears. *Choose, Cass, choose.*

I go to my next class.

Everything will happen as it should, except I'll trip going downstairs and crash to the landing below. My jeans will tear, my skin will break, and I'll shed a tear no one was ever meant to see. It will be horrible and painful and horrible.

I skip my next class.

I'll get halfway there when I spot Dra, crossing my path with a bag slung across their shoulders, clearly on their way to class. I'll feel the dread—the thrill—of knowing this is also their school and I'll never turn another corner safely again. It is impossible not to stare at the figure of Dra, long lines with confounding combinations of sharp angles and smooth curves. In the corners of their mouth, I see a girl I'd like to kiss. But in the sweep of their hair, a boy I'd like to caress. They are both of these simultaneously and I find the fluidity of them intoxicating.

Realizing I've stared too long, I'll start to change directions, but in that very same moment, Dra straightens as though they've forgotten something and suddenly shifts course.

There's no stopping it once it starts—our eyes will meet, Dra's mouth will curl into a confident, knowing smile, my heart will hammer and swirl like a storm. I won't move from where I stand when Dra approaches. I'll barely hear when that satin voice says, "My name's Dra." I'll barely hear when my own answers, "Cass."

I won't understand it—I don't understand it—but when Dra asks if I'd like to grab a cup of tea or coffee or whatever it is my tongue prefers to taste—"You don't have to tell me now"—I'll go.

I go to my class. I get my bruises, shed my tears, and when An asks how it happened, I tell her I was clumsy.

My schedule becomes rigid—class, rehearsal, work, homework, sleep. Though my mind spins back to Dra again and again, I leave no options for any path but the one I walk. I convince An to eat in, to study hard, to sleep over, to work out instead of go out. And it works. For a little while. But eventually she is restless, anxious, bored.

"Cass, I know school is important to you, but we have *got* to leave this campus. Let's do something!"

I hedge—there's a test, I need my scholarship, it's just a huge change—but she's unconvinced. She drops a stack of Canadian bills on the bed between us and says, "I'm crossing the border this weekend. I got directions to this beach party that happens every spring. It's only sort of a party. It's really a bunch of kids cliff jumping into freezing-ass water, and I think it sounds perfect."

The temptation sinks down through my bones. She knows I want this. She knows this kind of stupid risk is what we're made of. She knows I won't say no. And she's right. Saying no to this is saying no to us, and that will never be my choice.

The beach is like this.

There's a plateau at the top of a cliff, cleared of trees. It's sort of sandy, but not enough to warrant the term "beach," and it's littered with giant floppy ferns all the way up to the edge of a truly dizzying drop-off. The rest of the coast is just as tall, but with cliffs that billow out like skirts, hemmed by crashing waves. Here the rock wall is sheer, and just at this part of the coast it curves inward instead of out, allowing the water to pool below. That's the only reason anyone would think of jumping. That, and someone must've done it before. And clearly they have, because when I peer over the edge of the cliff, I see a few dark figures on a narrow sandy embankment that curls around the pool. There's a fire too, a beacon for future jumpers.

The clouds above mirror the smooth texture of the rock walls and they glow with a ghostly, diffused sunset. We are all paler versions of ourselves in this light. Maybe that's what makes us feel like jumping is a logical, harmless thing to do.

Maybe it is a logical, harmless thing to do. It's the not knowing that makes it real.

An and I don't know anyone here, and that's just the way we like it. There are maybe eighteen of us, maybe twenty. I've never been great at estimating a crowd. Mostly because I'm not great at being in a crowd. Too many possibilities. But this group is different. We're a collection of people who don't like crowds. I doubt there's anyone like me, afraid of futures coming out of nowhere to taunt and torment. Still, we maintain our orbits, sporadically spaced across the cliff like stars in the sky. I like it.

And then, all of a sudden, I don't.

An sits at the edge of the cliff. Her red ballet flats balance precariously from the tips of her toes, and she's smiling down at the crashing waves. The air is salt and wet and loamy earth. Her smile is the prelude to a challenge.

She leans back on her hands, butt scooting dangerously close to the edge, and she looks up at me. "I have an idea," she says.

I look down the long drop and my head feels heavy, like if I leaned just a little farther, the weight of it would pull me off balance and I would fall.

I shift back from where she sits, but I only move an inch before I'm stopped by another body.

"You really shouldn't jump," says a voice I should not—*not in this present time*—recognize. But I do. Oh, I do. I know the shape of the hand that has landed, feather light, on my waist. I know the look that waits for me in those endless brown eyes. I know the taste of those lips I've never seen in real life.

And all the feelings I knew I would feel are suddenly whispering down from my neck, fluttering in my lungs, warming in my belly.

An sits up straight, so urgently that one of her red ballet flats flies from the tips of her toes and down the cliff. It is swallowed by the dim light before it hits the water below. A trick of the light, I know, but a good one.

"You two know each other?" she asks, alert. No, alarmed.

I pull a curtain over my damn face and shake my head. "No."

But that isn't the truth. At least not for me.

I am afraid to turn around. I am afraid that seeing that smooth skin, those lithe curves, that confident stance will undo the very small amount of control I have.

Dra steps away from me and extends a hand to An. "Dra."

"Whatever," says An, but she shakes the offered hand. "Cass?"

I am frozen. The wind snaps around us, the waves sing beneath us, and I am terrified that my next move will be the wrong one. Behind me stands Dra—the person I've only ever known in my future, but who is promise and possibility and every tantalizing unknown—asking me to stay on the cliff, not to jump. In front of me is An—the person I've known nearly all my life, and who is the surest thing about it, the future I've always determined for myself, for my mind—holding out her hand, asking me to leap with her, because no matter where we go or what we do, we'll be together.

And for the first time in months, I wish the future would give me the right answer. I wait for the whisper—*Choose, Cass, choose*—to come and show me how to answer this question.

But there is nothing.

The moment is up to me.

Lessons for Beginners
JULIE MURPHY

FROM: Paul Villanueva <PaulYall@LFB.com>
TO: Ruby Mae Otto <KisserFixer@LFB.com>
SUBJECT: client inquiry
10:24 p.m.

We had a new submission on the site from a couple.
There's more you need to know about it, but are you even
down with couple lessons?

FROM: Ruby Mae Otto <KisserFixer@LFB.com>
TO: Paul Villanueva <PaulYall@LFB.com>
SUBJECT: RE: client inquiry
10:28 p.m.

Sure? I'm up to try it once. It could get weird though.

FROM: Paul Villanueva <PaulYall@LFB.com>
TO: Ruby Mae Otto <KisserFixer@LFB.com>
SUBJECT: RE: client inquiry
10:31 p.m.

Well, it's about to get weirder.

"Call Paul," I dictate to my phone, as I shake the soapsuds off my free hand.

It's not even half a ring before he answers. "Why are you switching modes of communication on me in the middle of a conversation? How am I expected to keep proper business records like this?"

I hold back a giggle as I blow bath bubbles off the tips of my kneecaps. "Paul."

"And you're in the tub," he says. "I can hear the fan running in your bathroom. You're going to drop that phone in the water and then you're going to be really screwed."

"Whatever," I say. "We're cash positive."

"We won't be for long if we rack up business expenses every time you want to take calls from your tub."

"When have I dropped my phone in bathwater?" I ask.

"Last spring. Right after you finished your final lesson with Mallory Stephens . . ." I can hear him clicking around on his computer, checking his calendar—which he merged with mine and which I haven't even looked at since Presidents' Day, almost six months ago. (I couldn't remember if the district gave us the day off school or not.) "And three days before your first session with Jacob Booth."

"Ah, yes. The slurper." That was definitely a case of doing the best I could with what Mother Nature gave me. "Well, whatever. I'm the talent."

Paul groans. Paul is not only my business partner, but also my best friend and my first client. It was three years ago, and the summer before eighth grade. I'd just experienced that classic middle school shift when not only is your body growing in weird, awkward ways, but so are your friendships. I was lonely and practically friendless and stuck at Micah Salih's thirteenth birthday party, which my grandmother had forced me to attend. (The woman would lie down on the tracks and let a train speed right over her if she thought it was the polite thing to do.)

The game was seven minutes in heaven, and I was up next, along with a new kid named Paul who'd just moved to town with his recently divorced mom. That night, Paul and I learned three life-changing truths in that closet.

1. Paul was a bad kisser.
2. I was a good one.
3. Paul was definitely gay.

After a minute or two of sloppy kissing, Paul and I began to talk—decidedly the better use of our mouths. We made a pact to tell everyone things had gotten super steamy between us, and Paul asked me to show him how to be a great kisser. The only problem was, I didn't even realize I was a great kisser until he said so. Suffice to say we spent much of eighth grade platonically making out and taking notes and making out some more until I'd cracked the science of kissing.

Monetizing my skill? That was Paul's idea, of course. Some great kissers are born. Most great kissers are made. Some of them are made by me. With careful practice and close tutelage, of course, which comes at a price.

My hands are turning into prunes, which means it's time for me to get out of the tub. And off the phone. "Okay, so come on. The couple. What's so weird about them?"

"Don't freak out."

"I'm not going to freak out."

"You're going to freak out, Rubes."

"Just tell me."

He pauses for a moment. (For dramatic effect, I'm sure.) "It's Annie Kim and Theo Simpson."

My stomach drops. "Annie? As in Annie Annie?"

"You're freaking out."

"I'm not freaking out."

"Uh-huh," he deadpans.

"Okay. Okay. Yeah. I'm freaking out."

I sit in my childhood tree house on the far edges of my grand-dad Jake's property. It's not an ideal location for kissing lessons, but it's private, and when you're in the business of neckin', that's priority numero uno.

Annie Kim sits across from me in cheer shorts and an over-sized T-shirt twisted into a knot at the small of her back. Her black bob is gathered into a half ponytail sprouting out from the top of her head like a weed. Annie is Korean American. Dumb people who don't know any better mistake her for Chinese or, even worse, "Oriental." She smells like sweat, but it's not the same kind of stench that used to radiate from my brother, Ralphie, after football practice. She holds her bedazzled cell phone up for me to see. "He should be here any minute. He's helping his dad do a sound check for tomorrow morning's service."

I nod and make no effort to mask my sigh. "I don't normally do couples." I decided that agreeing to meet with Annie and Theo was the professional thing to do. I have a reputation to uphold, and I'm not going to let sour grapes ruin that. Plus Annie offered to double my normal fee.

"And I appreciate you taking us on. You're not easy to get in touch with, ya know?" she says.

"There's a contact form on the website," I say.

"Well, it just felt like there was a lot of vetting."

"For good reason." As the setting sun behind her head burns into the trees, I plug in the twinkly lights that Granddad Jake wired through here when we were kids.

She nods. "This place looks just the same." Silence hangs there for a moment, suspended in midair. "I know this is awkward. I wouldn't have reached out if I had known that you . . . were you. Even after I found that we would be meeting you here, I didn't actually believe that it would be you waiting for us."

"Well, here we are." I've been giving kissing lessons for two years now, but my identity remains a secret from everyone except my clients. I keep their secrets, and they keep mine. Paul is my only real friend, so situations like this have never been an issue.

She nods. "I can't believe how much tinier the tree house feels." It's just small talk, I know, but I appreciate the effort. Besides, we're going to be doing things a lot more awkward than talking once Theo gets here.

I pull myself back a little farther into the corner. "Funny how things change," I tell her. The dynamic between us is stiff and awkward, but also somehow familiar. Ever since we were girls in this little tree house, I remember being so aware of how much more space I took up than Annie. For Annie to be aware, it took her a growth spurt and boobs.

After a few moments of silence while she chews on her cuticles, she shakes her head quickly. "I can't get over how weird it is to be back here."

I simply shrug. For Annie to still be sitting here, she's gotta be desperate.

Beneath us, leaves rustle as Theo takes the ladder two slats at a time. He pulls himself up and first turns to Annie. "Sorry I'm late."

Annie nods and helps him up, but the way her shoulders slope down slightly tells me that his tardiness means more to her than Theo knows.

And then he turns to me. "Ruby?" he asks. "Ruby Mae? You're the Kisser Fixer?"

I smile with my lips pursed tightly together. I get this a lot. Use whatever kind of euphemisms you want. Curvy, big-boned, junk in the trunk, heavyset, chubby. I'm the fat girl. Always have been. Not many people regard me as a romantic interest, but the proof is in the pudding and my pudding is kissing.

Theo is a classic PK—preacher's kid—and the kind of guy who always wins. It could be anything from a game of wall ball to a radio contest. The guy's just lucky. But you can't exactly fault him for it, because he's nice and charming. Or at least he's good at pretending to be. Theo shuts the trapdoor behind him and takes Annie's hand. "So give it to us easy, doc," he says in a mock serious voice.

Annie swats at his leg. "He tries to make jokes of everything."

Theo grunts. "Well, this is sort of a joke, anyway."

I close my eyes, and breathe in deeply through my nose. "No one is forcing you to be here, but you should know: I don't do refunds."

Theo huffs. "Let's get this over with."

"Most people remember their first kiss more vividly than the first time they had sex."

"Well, we haven't ever had sex," Annie says.

Theo's lips press into a thin line.

I scoot on my butt, inching myself closer to them, so that our knees are touching and we form the shape of a triangle. "I'm going to kiss each of you. Think of it as a physical, like a check-in to see where we are. This will allow me to evaluate your strengths and weaknesses." Up here, this is my domain. I may be quiet at school, and a little lost in my small Oklahoma town, but up here in this tree house, I'm in charge.

Theo turns to Annie. "You're okay with kissing a girl?"

"Baby," she says, taking his hand.

"I'm not complaining. As long as you're not making it a

habit." His smile is goofy, but his tone is serious. "I'll go first," Theo says, like that somehow makes him brave.

I close my eyes again, and force myself to erase every pretense, and to think of Theo as a blank slate. I open my eyes and see his grin has been exchanged for terror. I can see all the questions there on his face. *Is this technically cheating? Am I actually going to kiss a fat girl? What if I really am a bad kisser? What if I get a boner?*

"It's okay," I tell him. "Use your whole body."

His fingers dig a little too deep into my soft waistline, and he places his heavy hand on my shoulder in an oh-buddy, oh-pal kind of way. And then there's his mouth. His mouth opens so wide that I can only assume his plan is to devour me whole, starting with my dental records.

Poor Annie, a voice in my head screeches. I push the thought of her aside and concentrate on Theo's every move. The clumsy but too-eager hands. The wet, wide-open mouth that reminds me of one of those nonpredatory fish that just float through the ocean with their lips in an O, catching whatever meals dare float through their path. But something about his meaty hands is aggressive and territorial.

But then he pushes a little farther, and his hands are too heavy and too persistent. He tries to dominate me with his lips and tongue, and I can't tell if this is just business as normal for him or some kind of psychological bullshit. Some people see auras. I don't know if I buy all that, but if Theo's kissing had an aura, it would be an angry purplish bruise.

I press against his chest, tapping out, and he pulls back a

moment too late with a grin on his lips.

"Okay."

"That's all you've got?" he asks. "Okay?"

I've done this enough times to know that me unloading a laundry list of all the ways he's a horrible kisser won't get either Theo or Annie anywhere, but still, I have to bite my tongue.

I turn to Annie. "You ready?" I almost wish I could brush my teeth in between the two to cleanse my palate.

She leans in. And then pulls back, hesitating.

I smile easily. A part of me wants to reach out and comfort her and pretend that middle school never happened. Seeing her so unsure of herself . . . it's nothing like her. "This is your show. Just do it how you normally do. Close your eyes and pretend I'm Theo if you have to."

She leans in again but doesn't close her eyes until her lips meet mine. In every movement, she is tentative and then abrupt. Like, someone self-possessed enough to know what they want to say, but lacking the vocabulary to actually follow through. It's the opposite of the Annie I grew up with—the girl who saw the world in black and white or yes and no.

And yet, I sink into her. Something about the way she extends herself for just a moment and then pulls back makes me want to reach out and grab her. I break my own rule and kiss her back just a little. Encouraging her just a little. Just a little.

It's hard not to remember all the history this tree house holds for us. I almost wish our friendship had ended with some final fight or with a bang so that I could neatly wrap that chapter of my life up and stow it away. But Annie drifted out of my world in an uneven way that could only be blamed on us growing in two separate directions.

Theo clears his throat, and Annie pulls back, startled. But Theo doesn't startle me. Not at all. Something about him makes me defiant. And something about her reopens a wound that never healed.

My gaze drifts back and forth between them for a moment. I've never had to mediate between two people like this before. And on top of that, two people I have such clear feelings toward. I shake my head, forcing out every thought that begins with the word "I."

"You're both speaking two different languages," I finally say. "Annie, you're waiting for the kiss to come to you. And Theo . . . you're . . . well . . . you're overcompensating for that."

She reaches for her backpack. "I—can I take notes?"

I bite my lip to stop myself from smiling. "Of course."

The sky outside is dark now, and with my twinkly stars lighting the tree house, and against my better judgment, I help bridge the gap between Annie and Theo as I teach them a language they can both understand.

That night, as I'm standing in my bathroom, long after Gram and Granddad have gone to bed, I coat my lips in a pricey organic lip scrub that I bought online with my Lessons for Beginners money. An investment, I told myself. A business expense. (One that I've managed not to tell Paul about.)

Every time I so much as blink, it's Annie I see draped against the backs of my eyelids. Sitting in my tree house in her cheer shorts and spiky ponytail.

My phone rings, and I start the bathtub so Gram can't hear me.

"Hello?"

"Don't hello me," says Paul's voice on the other end of the line. "How'd it go?"

I sigh into the receiver. Paul is visiting his dad in Tulsa, and I would do anything to have him here with me tonight. Gram won't admit that Paul's gay, but she does let him spend the night. It infuriated me at first, but Paul said that she was making a bigger effort than I could understand.

"I don't know," I tell him. "It was weird. But nothing new either. Theo is like kissing a drooling puppy who can't keep his hands to himself and might bite your face off if you take his bone away. And Annie . . ." I trail off, not ready to share the details of our kiss. "I just feel bad for her. It was weird."

"I still can't believe you kissed the preacher's kid's girlfriend in front of the preacher's kid. I want to be you when I grow up."

"Har har. How's your dad? Is he still dating Creepy Karen?"

While Paul narrates his week thus far for me, I strip down and get in the tub, since I'm already wasting all this water. I lick off my sugar scrub before biting down on my lip as I ease into the tub. For a moment, I even let myself pretend that it's Annie's teeth clenching my lip.

It's hard for me to say if I'm gay or straight or bi. I've never been in a real relationship, but I do know that I like kissing 'em both. Nobody's made my chest hiccup like Annie tonight, though. And that realization is something I don't know how to process. I don't know what it means. Maybe it's just our history together that confused everything.

But, at the end of the day, I guess it doesn't even matter what it means. She's got Theo, and kissing her is just another day on the job.

The aerosol can hisses as I coat my legs with bug spray while I wait for Theo and Annie in the tree house. We've rescheduled this second session four times, and Paul thinks I should drop them as clients altogether without a refund. But I probably won't see Annie until school starts back up again if I do that, and even then, we don't move in the same circles. Shit. I don't move in any circles at all, unless you count Paul and me. Plus, of course, I just feel plain old bad for her.

"Hello!" calls Annie's voice.

"Up here!" I answer.

I don't know what this is. A crush, maybe? But whatever it is, my heart is pounding quicker and quicker with Annie's every step up the ladder. It can't be a crush. The only thing between us is a childhood friendship that took its time fizzling out.

"Hey!" she says when her head pops through the trapdoor like a gopher.

I help pull her up and shut the door behind her. This time she's wearing a short, white, gauzy dress with long sleeves that bell out past her fingertips and are longer than the dress itself. Her long bob is curled into perfect little waves, and if I weren't so taken aback by how pretty she is, I would ask what color blush she's wearing, because her round cheeks that sit high on her face shimmer gently against the setting sun.

"Theo should be here soon," she tells me.

I nod, because my mouth is too dry to talk.

I've always considered myself to be sort of like a doctor. Your doctor sees you naked sometimes, but there's nothing sexual about it. And that's how it's always been for me too. I kiss to diagnose. Nothing more.

But right now I can barely breathe. Never mind talking.

Christ. Where is this guy?

Annie sits directly next to me so she can see the sunset too. She hesitates for a moment. "Can I ask you something?"

"Yep."

"How did you know you were a good kisser?"

"No one's ever asked me that." I think for a moment. "It was more that I could spot bad kissers. And I guess knowing every possible fault makes you hyperaware of what works. The first time I kissed someone—like, really kissed someone—it wasn't fun. It didn't feel good. And I knew that had to be wrong. So I decided to figure out why."

She shakes her head and laughs. "You really haven't changed at all. Do you remember when you debunked Austin Crout's science fair project in the third grade after he beat you for second place?"

I shrug. "He got photosynthesis all wrong."

We both laugh, and I can feel the wall between us lowering. She settles in beside me, and our legs are skin to skin.

We're silent for a moment, and I let myself close my eyes to soak in the sensation of her bare thigh against mine, because the beauty of a setting sun and the feel of our skin pressed together is too much for me to consume at once.

But I force myself to wake up from this moment. "You and Theo must be pretty serious."

She turns to me. "I like him a lot, ya know? He's funny and he's got a good family too. My mom likes him, and she doesn't even like me." Her phone buzzes, but she doesn't look away.

"Your mom liked me."

"You liked her food. Of course she liked you." Her gaze wanders outside. "But I knew there was something missing with me and Theo. He was the first person I'd ever kissed, ya know? And I just couldn't figure out how it was that he could be such a good boyfriend and such a bad kisser. Like, the minute our lips touch, all the chemistry evaporates."

"Well, it would help if he weren't trying to swallow your face."

She laughs. "I don't mean to talk bad about him. I don't. Theo is good. He's good to me. He's the kind of person who makes you think of where you're going. Not where you came from."

That stings.

Her phone buzzes again, and this time she checks it. Her whole body slumps against the wall of the tree house. "He's not coming."

I could say any number of things. *Good.* Or *I don't do refunds.* Or *You're better off without him.* Or *Maybe it's fate.* But instead I just take her hand and say, "I'm sorry."

"He thinks it's bogus." Her voice shakes a bit, like she might cry.

"Well, do you?"

She pauses for a moment. "It didn't feel bogus."

My senses are on overdrive. Blood pumping and heart pounding.

But I'm not alone. She anxiously searches my face and bites down on her lip. Her lip. Her lip. Her lip.

I tug on her hand, pulling it into my lap. I can't make the first move. I won't. If I do, I'll always wonder if the feeling was mutual.

Annie studies our entwined fingers for a long time before she pulls my hand to her lips and kisses my knuckles one by one.

If I were standing, my knees would have given out by now. She's so slow, but deliberate in a way that she wasn't during our first lesson.

She squares her shoulders to face me and pulls my hand up so that it cradles her cheek.

"Relax," I tell her, unable to let go of my teacherlike encouragements. "Go at your own pace."

She nods, and leans into me. Her lips hover a breath away from mine before crashing into me. It's slow and fast and measured and reckless.

I decide then that this is my first kiss. I'm staking my claim on this kiss with my own flag. I am the United Nations of Ruby, and this is my first official kiss, and I want to live inside of it forever.

We kiss, and we kiss. The sun sets without consulting us, and my twinkling lights glow all around the tree house, like a lighthouse in my Oklahoma woods. And we kiss.

♥ ♥ ♥

Weeks later the bright white stadium lights illuminate the Pinkerton High football field. The air around us is thick with humidity, and I don't even know how anyone could do anything more than sit perfectly still on a night like this.

When Annie left after our kiss in the tree house, it didn't occur to me that I wouldn't have any good excuse to see her for the rest of the summer. Which is why I've dragged Paul to the first football game of the season. It's been three weeks and four days since we kissed. I didn't mean to keep count, but I have and I am. Our kiss seemed like plenty of reason for her to call or text, but I guess it wasn't.

Annie cheers with the rest of the varsity squad on the track ringing the football field while Theo and his friends sit on the top row of bleachers behind us. I am hyperaware of my proximity to both of them at all times, even at school. I can feel the tension taut between the three of us like we're the Bermuda Triangle, and every moment I've spent with either of them has been forgotten by everyone except me.

Paul and I got here late, so we're stuck next to the band and have to scream to even hear each other. But I don't mind drowning in the music and just watching Annie as she shakes her pom-poms in the air and does toe touches one right after the other. Her skin is slick with sweat and the stray hairs falling from her ponytail curl at the nape of her neck. She laughs in between cheers at our mascot, a tiger in cowboy boots and a matching hat with a rudimentary understanding of gymnastics.

Something in my chest twists tight like a tourniquet. I want to make her laugh. I want to get in a fight with her so we can make up. I want to see her cry so I can kiss away her tears. I want and I want, but a silly want seems like no good reason to disrupt her whole life. And mine. These feelings have festered for weeks now, and the only good thing about it is that I'm no longer confused. I know exactly what I want.

Cymbals crash beside me, shocking me back to reality.

Paul turns and shouts in my ear, "This is boring as hell! If we get outta here, we can still catch a movie at the Grand."

The buzzer sounds for halftime, and the cheerleaders create a human tunnel with their arms and pom-poms for the football players to run through as they head back to the locker room. I nod. "Yeah, okay. Let's go. I'm gonna run to the bathroom first."

"Meet you in the parking lot," he says, and practically sprints down the stairs ahead of the crowd.

I'm slower and am left to shuffle through the herd of spectators making their way to the bathrooms and concession stands. As I wait there on the steps, Annie's eyes meet mine. She stands in line behind the rest of her squad as they wait to take the field for their halftime show.

The person behind me nudges me forward, but I don't look away. I lift my hand for a small wave.

And then she smiles. She smiles because I make her smile. A whistle blows, and she looks away quickly before filing onto the field.

While I wait in line for the bathroom, I hear the upbeat halftime music crackle over the speakers. After washing my hands,

I walk around the back of the cement building housing the bathrooms, and someone pulls me into the shadows.

"I didn't see you at school this week," Annie says.

We stand in the dark, outside the pools of light shining around the football field. The soil beneath us is soft from yesterday's rain as my feet sink farther into the mud.

"Maybe you weren't looking hard enough." I sound hurt because I am. The kiss we shared. It was more than just a kissing lesson.

Annie nods. "I didn't know what to do." She reaches for my hand, and her fingertips brush mine, before I pull back. "But I can't stop thinking about it. You. The kiss."

All I can think about in this moment is how she's with Theo. Why would I fight for her when there's nothing to fight for?

Her ponytail bounces as she shakes her head. "You were the first girl I ever kissed, okay?"

She's unsure. I get it. I was too.

"And I'm confused," she says. "But not about what you might think. It's not about"—her voice drops an octave—"kissing a girl. It's about choosing between the two of you. Because I can't have both, can I?"

My mouth goes immediately dry. "No. No, you can't."

"I like you, but Theo's trying. He really is. And I can introduce Theo to my parents. To my mom. You know how hard things always were for me and her."

"I already know your parents. And your mom."

"As a friend," she says. "They wouldn't understand if we were anything beyond . . . and I'm going to homecoming with Theo. I bought a dress, and—"

"I can buy a dress too. Or a tux, or whatever the hell." I hate that I'm trying to convince her. I've never been the type to meet others any closer than the middle. But there's something about her that makes me want to meet her wherever she is.

"Annie!" Theo's voice barks from around the corner.

She jumps a little and slips in the mud, but I catch her by the elbow.

"What's going on back here?" Theo asks as he turns the corner. "Annie, the squad is looking for you."

"I—I have to go. I have somewhere to be."

Theo's eyes focus in on my hand on Annie's arm. "Sorry it never worked out with your, uh, services this summer. Guess we didn't really need you in the end, right, Annie?"

He takes Annie's other hand and pulls her away from me. My fingers drag down the length of her arm as she leaves me. She looks back over her shoulder, and says good-bye without even a single word.

At first, I wake up every morning and pray that today is the day she chooses me. Every time a new client reaches out, I wonder if it's actually her trying to make some kind of covert contact. But days pass, and then weeks.

Soon my inbox is full of unanswered emails and all I can bear to do is float in my bathtub with my ears just below the surface of the water so that the world around me is distant and muffled.

♥ ♥ ♥

Annie's schedule and mine overlap briefly every other day, when she's leaving phys ed and I'm going.

I take my time getting changed. It's Friday, and who's ever in a hurry to sweat anyway?

As I sit with my leg hiked up on the bench, tying my shoe, a voice calls, "Hello? Ruby?"

Annie peers around the corner and approaches me slowly, like I'm a wounded animal.

"I wanted to tell you before you found out from someone else." She sits beside me, straddling the bench. "I broke up with Theo."

My foot falls to the ground. "What? Why?"

The final bell for next period rings. "Don't act like you didn't kiss him too." She sighs. "Besides, it was lots of different reasons in the end. The kissing was just the first clue."

"What about homecoming this weekend?"

"I'll probably just go and say hi to everyone and go home."

The words are spilling out of my mouth before I can stop them. "Go," I tell her. "With me. Paul will come too." *Though it might be news to him*, I think.

"Just as friends, though, right?"

It's just two words, but they're two words that make this sweet moment a little bitter. "Just friends."

Paul is our chauffeur. Or third wheel, if you ask him. No matter how many times I explain to him that this is not a date, he refuses to believe me. He wears a black button-up shirt tucked into black skinny jeans, and with a herringbone bow tie. He looks way too hip for Pinkerton, Oklahoma.

When we pick up Annie, her mom answers the door and recognizes me immediately. "Ruby Mae!" she squeals into my ear after pulling me in for a hug. "I'm so happy to see you around again. Annie needs good friends and you were always a good friend. You must come over for kimchi pancakes next Thursday, okay? Annie," she calls, "next Thursday. Don't forget!"

I nod. "Yes, ma'am."

She steps back to reveal Annie in a soft yellow chiffon strapless dress that floats just above her knees with a sweetheart neckline and an antique locket. Huddled together, we walk back down to the car where Paul is waiting.

I want to tell her she's beautiful and that I can't believe she's my date—albeit platonic.

"You look amazing," Annie tells me.

I glance down at the satin hunter-green dress Gram bought me for Christmas Eve services last year. Paul calls it my sexy secretary dress. The skirt is fitted and hugs my hips a little more than Gram expected, and the short sleeves poof up just enough to be cute. The first thing that I think to say is *Are you blind?* or *I don't feel amazing*, but instead I force myself to take the compliment. "Thank you."

Entering the dance feels like some huge moment, but it's all in my head. No one looks at us. No one knows I'm here with the girl I have a huge crush on. A few of Annie's friends swoop in and coo at her, asking her about Theo and if it's just a temporary break. But Annie is quick to shake them off. It's a small gesture, but one that's a step toward healing the wound left behind by middle school.

The three of us dance all night to loud and fast music. When the first slow song comes on, Paul is quick to disappear while Annie and I shuffle off to a dark corner to catch our breath and have some punch, which I'm sad to report is not spiked.

In the dark, we're just two silhouettes. All the baggage that makes up me and makes up Annie dissolves until all that's left is two girls—two people—in a dark corner. I take Annie's empty cup and place it on the floor alongside mine.

I pull her arms around my shoulders and wrap mine around her waist. We slow dance, like two girls on a date, because that's what we are. Paul's said it enough times that it's almost starting to feel real.

She nuzzles into my neck with her lips pressed against my pulse. We shift around in our little corner as the song plays on.

And then she's ripped away from me. It takes a moment for my eyes to realize what they're seeing.

Theo stands in front of me, and he's yanked Annie back by her hair. Her eyes are watering, and even though he's let go, she holds a hand to her head.

"Her?" he yells. "Of all people, you're leaving me for this fat piece of shit?"

He comes for me. He storms right at me and throws me against the wall. I feel my spine crushing into the brick. I become much smaller than I am.

Paul is shouting. The music stops. The slow halogen lights

above are brightening.

One. Two. Three. That's how many seconds it takes for the adrenaline of the moment to hit me.

I push back, and maybe he's not expecting it or maybe I don't know my own strength, but he rocks back on his heels and falls to the ground.

I'm surprised by myself, but not as much as he is. His jaw drops as he just lies there on the floor, completely stunned.

This isn't some barbaric display where I claim Annie as mine. I'm claiming her as her own. And I'm showing Theo—a guy who is far too used to getting everything he wants—that I bite back.

Hands and arms pull me back even though I'm not touching Theo. Miss Purdy, our vice principal, is talking at me, but all I can do is search for Annie.

She stands off to the side with Paul, still holding her head. Her lips are melted into a frown, and her perfectly curled hair is a knotted mess.

I hear "suspension" and a "zero tolerance policy concerning violence on school property" and something about calling Gram in on Monday morning.

I can feel bruises forming on my back, and when I reach back, I feel pulls and snags in my satin dress.

I look for Theo, but he's already been dragged off to the other side of the gym. I know how this will go and how it will be spun. The preacher's kid attacked by his ex-girlfriend's predatory lesbian mistake. But I know who made the first move. Who yanked Annie from me by her hair, like a dog being pulled away by her scruff.

Mr. Houghton, our campus security guard, hands me a handkerchief, even though I'm not crying, and guides me by my elbow out of the gymnasium and toward the parking lot.

"Slut!" "Dyke!" "Whore!" All names shouted at me above the constant whispers as I leave the homecoming dance. In the dark hallway, shoes clack behind me, and I glance over my shoulder to see Annie and Paul following close.

Outside by the carport, Mr. Houghton turns to me and says, "Now, Miss Purdy will be in touch with your grandmother on Monday morning, but don't you come back here on campus without permission. Don't want to start no more trouble."

I nod and offer him his bloody hanky back.

He shakes his head. "Y'all head home before things get rowdy out here."

"I'll pull the car around," says Paul. I can see in the way he looks at me that he's trying to piece together this new facet of information he's learned about me tonight. Not only am I a lover. I'm a fighter, too.

With Mr. Houghton and Paul gone, I turn to Annie. Finally. "Are you mad?"

She takes a step toward me. "I think I'm supposed to be. But no. No, not even a little bit. Not at you." Gently, she grazes my cheek with her thumb.

I grin, but dread settles into my stomach as I wonder how I might even begin to explain this to Gram. But then . . . I don't really care.

Annie kisses my cheeks, one at a time, and then my lips.

I'm hesitant at first, but Annie separates her lips with mine and doesn't shy away despite the audience spying on us through the gymnasium windows.

Paul's car idles beside us for a moment before I pull back. Annie's soft yellow dress is rumpled, and her mascara is smeared under her eyes. But she doesn't seem to mind.

"Our carriage awaits," I tell her.

The two of us sit in the backseat curled into each other like two bruised question marks as Paul drives circles around our little town and blasts the kind of music our parents don't understand.

Triangle Solo
GARTH NIX

Anwar hated, hated, *hated* triangles. His best friend Connor didn't, but he resented how Anwar always got his own way. So Connor took a stand against triangles as well, because there was no way he was going to let Anwar win out on absolutely everything.

Since Anwar and Connor were the only two percussionists in the school orchestra, every piece of music that had even the hint of a triangle part became a battleground. Anwar would refuse to play it on the grounds he hated triangles, and Connor would refuse because Anwar shouldn't always get his own way. Most of the time the triangle part would be written out or Mr. Gantz would end up playing it himself, in order to keep the peace.

Mr. Gantz was the school's music teacher and conductor of the orchestra. Or he had been, right up until a few days ago. Connor and Anwar were still adjusting to the news of Mr. Gantz's heart attack. They were used to teachers changing; most of them were on two-year contracts. They came, they went. But the only two who had always been there—like the ancient rock structures in the desert—were the principal, Commander Yaping, and Mr. Gantz. And now Mr. Gantz was gone.

"You think he'll die?" asked Connor.

"Who?" asked Anwar, idly tapping out a complicated tune on the xylophone with four hammers, two in each hand.

"Mr. Gantz. Who else are we talking about?"

"Oh, yeah. No, Essel said they got to him in time. He'll be out for a few months, though."

"Why didn't you tell me that in the first place?"

"I forgot," said Anwar, changing up his xylophone piece. He glanced at Connor and kept playing as he added, "You want to hammer out 'Dust Storm'?"

"Dust Storm with Flying Rocks" was their own joint composition, thrashed out on eight kettledrums. Mr. Gantz had described it as having "deep emotional impact without a great deal of artistry or originality" and forbidden them to play it when anyone else was in the school, even with the rehearsal room's soundproofing.

"No," said Connor. "Seems sort of disrespectful. You know, as soon as he's gone—"

"He isn't gone yet," said Anwar. "They might not even ship him out."

"Yeah, well, I don't feel like playing 'Dust Storm' anyway," said Connor.

"Duel then?"

They were about to embark upon a swordfight using timpani mallets when someone they vaguely recognized as the new and somewhat frightening deputy principal came into the room. She only came up to the boys' shoulders but had the kind of calm "don't mess with me" presence that all teachers would like to have but very few do. A fat folio of sheet music under her arm suggested she was involved in some music-related stuff.

Timpani mallets suddenly went from the en garde position to the "we were about to play something, honest" posture.

"Good morning," said the woman. She didn't smile. "I am Dr. Bethune. I didn't expect to see anyone here yet. I expect you know I'm the new deputy principal."

Connor and Anwar nodded obediently.

"I am also a music teacher and will be assuming the duties of Mr. Gantz until he recovers, including managing the school orchestra. You must be our percussionists, Anwar al-Zein and Connor Brennan?"

"Uh, yes, Dr. Bethune," chorused Connor and Anwar. Anwar pointed to himself and Connor pointed to Anwar.

"I'm Anwar."

"He's Anwar."

"Very good. I'm glad you're here early. We'll be rehearsing a new and very interesting composition this term, and there are a number of challenging passages for the percussionists. Here are your parts."

She rummaged through her folio and handed over several sheets of music. Anwar and Connor took them without great enthusiasm and began to look through the pages. Dr. Bethune wandered about the room, straightening music stands and placing the appropriate music at each chair.

Typically, Anwar was the first to spot the trouble in the percussion part.

"Solo for you here, Connor," he said, tapping the concertinaed-out music.

"What?" asked Connor suspiciously. There was no way Anwar would give up a chance to grandstand on xylophone or drums . . . his eye flicked over the music.

"Triangle? A triangle solo? Who would write a *triangle* solo?" Anwar flicked to the last sheet. There was no composer's name. Just initials.

"'K.E.' Whoever that is."

"I'm not playing it," said Connor.

"Hey, I don't do triangle," said Anwar. "You know that."

"Yeah, well, neither do I."

"Is there a problem?" asked Dr. Bethune. She was pushing the piano so it lined up more exactly with some grid in her head for how a school orchestra should be positioned. Since the piano hadn't been moved in years, the wheels turned slowly.

"There's a triangle solo," said Anwar. "Triangle. Solo. Kind of contraindicated, if you ask me."

"I don't believe the composer would be all that interested in your opinion, Anwar," said Dr. Bethune. The piano's wheels gave a little shriek of submission, and she shoved it across a few inches. "She—and I—would just like you to play it as written."

"Yeah!" exclaimed Connor, a wide smile on his face. It was

very unusual for the charming Anwar to be forced into accepting something he didn't want to do.

"One of you to play it, that is," corrected Dr. Bethune. She finished with the piano and went to the door, pausing to deliver her ultimatum. "You may decide between yourselves. If you both have such an antipathy toward triangles, you can decide randomly. Cut cards. Whatever you like. But it will be played."

"We'll work it out," said Anwar. He smiled and gave the deputy principal a cheery wave as she left.

"Yeah," said Connor, with a sideways glance at his friend. This time he was going to make sure Anwar didn't get his own way. This time . . .

They argued about it all the way to the gym. If they could have cut class to keep arguing about it, they would have. But gym was the one thing their parents always checked up on, and the school took it very seriously too. And once they were working in the machines, there was no chance to argue.

After showering, Anwar made a suggestion as they walked across the quad, just before they split up, Connor to Advanced Math and Anwar to the theater. He had been let out of a lot of classes so he could rehearse for the school play, the principal's favorite: *Planetfall*. Anwar was playing the lead, of course.

"Hey, how about we have some sort of challenge to decide who plays the triangle solo?"

"What kind of challenge?" asked Connor suspiciously.

Anwar thought for a moment. He liked to win. But he was also usually fair, Connor had to admit.

"How about longest walking on hands?"

Connor considered the suggestion. They were both pretty good at walking on their hands, thanks to one of their early teachers being so keen on all the acrobatics that were easier in the lower gravity. Anwar didn't have an obvious lead in walking on hands.

"So whoever walks the farthest on their hands doesn't have to do the triangle solo?" asked Connor.

"Yeah," said Anwar.

Connor thought some more. There had to be a catch. A loophole Anwar would exploit.

"So from a start line, we walk entirely on our hands," he said slowly. "Whoever walks the farthest, staying on their hands, without falling over, they don't have to play the triangle solo."

"Exactly," said Anwar. "When do we do the challenge?"

Connor hesitated, but it *did* seem like a fair way to resolve the triangle solo problem.

"Tomorrow morning, early. Across the quad, before anyone else gets here."

"Across and back, surely?" asked Anwar, raising both eyebrows.

"Have you been practicing?" asked Connor. "Oh man! I knew—"

"See ya, sucker!" called Anwar, racing off. Several other students loitering nearby looked at him, and then back at Connor. He shrugged and trudged off to math.

He had just gotten his head down and was trying to sort through a complex series of equations on the screen when the class was interrupted by someone coming in late. Connor didn't look up, deep in linear algebra.

"Connor?"

The voice was familiar. Connor lost his train of thought, $T(u+v)$ instantly erased by a cascade of memories reaching back to preschool. He sat up in his chair as if he'd been electrocuted, and stared wide-eyed.

It was Kallie who'd spoken. And she was standing right in front of his desk. Only it wasn't Kallie, or at least it wasn't entirely the Kallie he remembered from seventh grade, when she'd left. This was a young woman, not a girl in dirty coveralls looking no different from any boy. His best friend from the first days of school to that terrible, awful day four years before when she'd told him about her parents' irrevocable decision: their whole family was going back to Earth.

She was beautiful. He felt instantly many years younger, as if he had remained the twelve-year-old schoolboy Kallie knew before, while she had been transformed into a fully adult goddess. He struggled to overcome the feeling so he could speak.

"K-K-Kallie?"

"Yeah! I'm back!"

She leaned over and hugged him. Connor stayed rigid for a few seconds, then slowly returned the hug, just in time to make it awkward as Kallie straightened up.

"I . . . I can't believe it!" exclaimed Connor. "I mean . . . four years . . ."

They'd emailed at first, but the correspondence had died away after six months or so. They just didn't have that much to say to each other, at least not in writing, and with the lag, anything more immediate was impossible.

"I almost didn't recognize you," said Kallie, smiling. "You must be like what, one-ninety centimeters? You make the chair look small."

"One-ninety-five," said Connor. "But you know, growing up here means *up* . . . you look . . . you look good."

"Not so tall," said Kallie. She was around one-eighty centimeters, Connor thought. They'd been the same height four years before, but then she'd been in heavier gravity since then.

"Just . . . ah . . . just right," said Connor, blushing.

He was saved from more embarrassment by the intervention of Ms. Culp.

"Sorry to interrupt the reunion, but we have a lot of work to get through. Ms. Esterhazy, your modules have been set up on desk five."

"Hey, thanks," said Kallie. She smiled at Connor and went over to her desk. Everyone watched her. A new student was always exciting, but a returning student was even more special. Particularly one who looked like Kallie. And then there were the long coat and boots she was wearing. There were several people in the class, female and male, studying her clothes as intently as if they were watching a fashion parade, trying to figure out the material and cut and whether they could replicate it locally or not. Not being the most likely outcome.

Connor returned to his linear algebra, but he couldn't focus on it. He wanted to look over at Kallie, but she was behind him. There was so much he wanted to ask her . . . and Anwar would freak when he saw her . . . Kallie was almost as old a friend to

Anwar as Connor, he'd arrived in year two. . . .

Connor stopped even trying to focus on the work in front of him. Anwar would not only freak, he would turn on his full charm assault. He wouldn't be happy just being friends with Kallie, not like in the old days. She was super hot now. Anwar was between girlfriends, since Lilian had gone back to Earth with her family.

If Anwar went after Kallie, Connor would have no chance.

It was at this moment that he realized he *wanted* a chance with Kallie, for something other . . . different . . . *more* than their old friendship. It wasn't the same as before. He wasn't twelve. Kallie still liked him. She'd hugged him straight out. But did she like-like him? Had that hug been an "old friend no sex please" hug? Or had it hinted at something else?

Connor felt a melancholy shiver as he considered this. All being equal, he thought the hug had to be considered as one of the old-friend type. He was doomed already and would just have to make the best of it.

After the class, Kallie was swamped by everyone else, checking out her clothes, asking about where and what she'd been doing, marveling at her latest-model phone, even though it was basically useless given the bandwidth situation; here people only had emergency text/locator units. Connor hovered about the periphery, not wanting to push himself forward. After five minutes he gave up, waving and smiling to Kallie when a small gap momentarily presented itself between Dropal and Charleese.

Connor didn't see Kallie start to push through the gap toward him, reaching out. He was already gone, thinking depressive thoughts about how he was going to cope—or not cope—when Anwar and Kallie invariably got together, and how he was also going to lose the hand-walking challenge and have to play the triangle solo, just to add insult to injury.

He met Anwar as usual out the front of the school. Their families lived in the same outer dome, so they had to buddy up as per the rules to cross the six hundred almost-airless meters from the main dome. Before he could tell him the news, Anwar was leaping about him, excited as anything.

"Hey! Guess who's back?"

"Kallie," said Connor. "I saw her in math."

"And she has grown up!" exclaimed Anwar.

"Time passing does that."

"But who knew she would look like she does now?" enthused Anwar. "I mean, she was always super smart, super musical, and super everything else, *except* in the looks department. But talk about the whole ugly duckling thing. I mean—"

"Yeah, yeah!" interrupted Connor. "Totally out of our league, right?"

"Speak for yourself," said Anwar. He tapped his chest. "Who is the new best-looking girl in the school bound to go out with? The best-looking guy, right?"

"It isn't all about looks," said Connor. Even though he thought it might be.

"I'm going to ask her out right away," said Anwar. "Which reminds me, can I borrow fifty till next month?"

Connor sighed, took out his card, and Anwar did the transfer.

"You should ask her out too," said Anwar. They'd been best friends for so long they could interpret each other's silences. "You know, you used to play together in the preschool sandpit even before I arrived. Maybe she's kind of nostalgic, might give you a slight . . . and I mean *slight* . . . edge."

"No, it's okay," said Connor heavily. He tried to smile, but it came out more as a grimace. "You know, she's bound to get together with you or maybe Evren or someone, and I'd rather it was you."

"Evren? Muscles don't make the man."

"Maybe . . . but then he's got the way he dances and the classical good looks going as well."

"So?" said Anwar. "You've got . . . uh . . . let's see . . ."

"Thanks."

"No, seriously, what is it with the self-defeating attitude? You look fine, you just haven't grown into your face. In a couple of years, everyone might even think you're more handsome than me. If that were possible."

"It probably isn't possible," said Connor, the faint trace of a grin quirking up his mouth. Anwar had the remarkable gift of being able to cheer him up even when he was the one making Connor feel down in the first place. It was one of the reasons they stayed friends. Also, Anwar couldn't help being superior in so many ways, and he didn't—usually—flaunt it.

"Come on, let's get home. And don't practice walking on your hands too much tonight, you might hurt yourself."

"I don't need to practice," said Connor. Inside, he was grimly determined that Anwar wasn't going to win that challenge, no

matter what. His friend might get the girl, but he was also going
to play the triangle solo and look stupid in front of everyone.

Kallie and her reluctantly dragged-along-for-buddy-purposes
younger brother, Justin, called in at Connor's house that night,
even though her family was in another dome and it was somewhat risky to move around outside after sunset, when the
temperature dropped to minus forty degrees Celsius.

But Connor was out with his mom, helping her reset an
experiment on top of the nearby hill everyone called Lookout!
Mountain, from the time the balancing boulder came down; his
dad was working the night shift at the air plant; and his eleven-
year-old sister, Siobhan, forgot to mention the visitors when
Connor got back because she was totally engrossed in designing
a game that concerned space unicorns going shopping.

Connor couldn't sleep that night. He lay awake, thinking, dozing off, waking again. It wasn't the walking-on-hands
challenge, or the triangle solo, that kept troubling him. It was
Kallie. And more than that—himself. He'd just given up, and
he felt weak and useless.

Finally, about four o'clock in the morning, he got up and
went and made himself a so-called milk shake, or at least the
vat-grown supposed equivalent. Connor had never known anything else, so he didn't mind it, but all the nonnative people said
the stuff was disgusting.

His father came in from the night shift just after five thirty.
He didn't seem surprised to see Connor half asleep, sprawled
across the kitchen table.

"Early start this morning?"

"Uh, yeah," said Connor, sitting up. "Got . . . um . . . a thing to do with Anwar."

"Anything I should know about?" asked Niall Brennan. "As in, anything contrary to the safety and well-being of the colony's structures, personnel, morale . . . you know, the usual."

"Dad! We haven't done anything like that for years. And we didn't mean to make that gas, it was a byproduct—"

"I know. But there is always the danger of backsliding, and you have an odd look on your face. Kind of guilty."

"It's not guilt," mumbled Connor.

Niall sat down opposite his son, sniffed the half-drunk milk shake, and made a face.

"What is it then? Anything I can help with?"

"I don't think so," said Connor. He glanced at his dad. They'd always gotten along very well, but Connor didn't naturally confide in him. Or in his mother. Or anyone. He kept things bottled up inside.

They sat in silence for a while.

"I saw Matyas Esterhazy last night," said Niall eventually. "He's coming back to the plant as second engineer, which will be a big help to me. He was always a good guy to work with. But his really big news—which is secret until later today, so keep it to yourself—is that Chizuko's taking over as chief scientist and 2IC Colony."

"Wow!" said Connor. Chizuko was Kallie's mother. But the exclamation came out kind of feeble and restrained.

"And Kallie's come back with them," said Niall. "I thought

she might have stayed on Earth to finish school and then go to university there, but she didn't want to, Matyas told me."

There was more silence. After an internal struggle, Connor made himself look at his father.

"Yeah," he said. "Kallie's back. That's . . . that's why I'm awake and doing my impersonation of a holed atmosphere suit."

"You were always such good friends," said Niall. "What's the problem now?"

"Being friends," said Connor heavily. "I mean . . . I just . . . we've grown up, and I'd like . . . to be more than friends. But she's, she's gotten really beautiful, and Anwar wants to ask her out, and he always . . . I mean, anyone he asks, for anything, they always go along with him. . . ."

"He's got the charm, that's for sure," said Niall. "And it's not just surface deep. But relationships aren't all about charm and good looks, fortunately. Your mother and I would never have gotten together if that were the case. You should ask her about her boyfriend Robert Robinson sometime, before I—"

"Uh, no thanks, Dad. All the same."

"Yeah, well, too much information, I know. But my point is, what makes you think Kallie would prefer Anwar over you? Have *you* asked her out?"

"Uh, no," said Connor.

"You should. Maybe she'll say no, but that's better than moping around wondering what might have been, or just giving up. Ask her to something she likes. Music was always her main thing, wasn't it? There's a visiting quartet coming in on the *Triplex* next week, I forget what they're called. Invite her to that."

"Maybe I will," said Connor slowly. A thought had just risen to the surface of his otherwise misery-sodden brain.

Kallie.

Music.

The new composition for the orchestra.

The triangle solo.

Kallie knew all about the long struggle between Anwar and Connor to not play triangle.

"You look a lot better all of a sudden," said Niall. "I'd like to think it's due to the brilliance of my parental advice, but I doubt it. Is it?"

"Yeah, kind of, Dad," said Connor with a smile.

"Do I get a hug?"

"Don't push it," said Connor.

"All right. I'm going to bed. You need to talk later, feel free to wake me up."

"Thanks, Dad. I'm okay."

"All right. See you later."

Connor met Anwar at the airlock. They both gave the traditional grunt they'd developed to mean "too early to talk," got in their air suits, and cross-checked. Halfway across to the main city dome, without needing to discuss it, both paused to look up. Phobos was zipping across the lightening sky, with the much smaller Deimos trailing under it, and the bright star that was Earth apparently static below both.

"Why would you live anywhere else?" asked Anwar.

"Yeah," said Connor quietly.

They started walking again, following the lane between the safety wires, the green lights set in the path every meter giving their constant reassuring flicker. In a dust storm they would brighten a hundredfold, and Connor and Anwar would clip on the wires.

"You all ready for the challenge?"

"Yeah."

"You'd better not break a wrist just to win by default," said Anwar. "You *are* going to be playing that triangle. Even if your whole arm is in a cast."

"Yeah," said Connor.

"Vocabulary failure this morning, I see," said Anwar.

Connor didn't answer for a minute or two, until they were almost at the main airlock.

"Anwar," he said. "I'm going to ask Kallie out too."

Anwar gave him a thumbs-up and grinned, eyes bright through his helmet visor.

"That's more like it!" he exclaimed. "She might even say yes."

"You don't mind?"

It was Anwar's turn to be silent. He looked away, watching the outer airlock door swing inward.

"Yeah, I do. I mean, I don't mind you asking. I hope she says yes to me. But it's Kallie's choice. She might say no to both of us, match up with Evren like you said. Or no one. Or one of the girls."

"Right . . . ," said Connor. "I hadn't thought . . ."

"It ain't all about you," said Anwar. "Anyway, better to ask and find out rather than getting all pathetic."

"That's what my dad said."

"He's a smart man," said Anwar. "He's learned a lot from me, of course, over the years."

Connor snorted and followed his friend into the airlock.

The quad was deserted. School wouldn't start for an hour, even the early homework workshop. The lights high above in the dome were still set for dawn, so it was kind of dim. Anwar did some stretches near the principal's podium, interlaced his fingers, and flexed his hands. Connor did a little shadowboxing and shrugged his shoulders.

"Ding, ding, ting a ling ling," said Anwar. "Get used to the sound, you're going to be practicing at home a lot to get that solo down."

"Why do you hate the triangle?" asked Connor. He'd asked before, but Anwar had never given a proper answer.

"Dunno," said Anwar.

"You always say that."

"I really don't know," said Anwar. "I mean, who does?"

"I actually don't mind playing triangle," said Connor thoughtfully. "Or the sound of it."

"Then why are we doing this?" asked Anwar. "You can just take the solo."

"Because it's bad for you to always get your own way," said Connor. "I'm helping build your character."

"I'm not sure losing a challenge and ending up doing what I want you to do anyway is very character building," said Anwar.

"For me, anyway. Maybe it's good for you."

"Let's see," said Connor. "We start here? On three?"

Orchestra practice was the first lesson of the day. Anwar kept giving Connor sideways looks as they went in, because he couldn't figure out what was going on, and Connor refused to tell him.

They were the first there, as per usual. Anwar took up his xylophone mallets and absently picked out a tune.

Connor picked up a triangle and a wooden striker and began to softly play along.

"If you're doing that to annoy me, it's working," said Anwar.

"I'm just freeing up my fingers," said Connor. "That solo is going to be pretty hard to play."

"And you are going to look particularly stupid playing it," said Anwar. "But somehow I get the feeling there is something—"

Kallie came into the rehearsal room, talking to Dr. Bethune. She was wearing bright blue coveralls now, the standard school uniform, and she'd had her hair cut shorter overnight, like most people did to make the air suit helmets less annoying. Connor thought she looked even more beautiful than before and felt his hand actually shaking with nervousness, so he had to put the triangle down.

Anwar played a wrong note and dropped one of his xylophone mallets. He was staring at Kallie too—or rather, what she held in her hand.

A conductor's baton. And she had sheet music under her arm.

"Oh, I get it now," groaned Anwar. "'K.E.' I *knew* even you couldn't fall off your handstand in the first three seconds."

"Hi, guys," said Kallie, coming over. She spoke as if to both of them, but she looked directly at Connor, and she seemed to struggle a little, as if feeling something very deeply. "Dr. Bethune says you . . . neither of you . . . want to play the triangle in my new composition?"

Anwar groaned again and rested his head in his hands.

"Because I wrote it . . . I wrote it for . . ." Kallie was having trouble getting the words out.

"I'm playing the triangle solo!" blurted out Connor. He stepped closer to Kallie, looking her right in the eyes. He took a deep breath and continued. "And will you come and see the visiting quartet that's arriving on *Triplex* next week? With me. Not just friends. A date."

The last word came out a bit strangled, but Kallie didn't laugh.

"Yes," said Kallie. "Of course. Why else would I come all the way back to Mars?"

Connor got the hug right this time.

"You know, I *am* prepared to reconsider my whole 'I hate triangles' thing," said Anwar.

But Connor and Kallie didn't hear him.

Vim and Vigor
VERONICA ROTH

Edie bent over her tablet, stylus in hand, reviewing her sketch. Vigor, the super-strong heroine of the Protectors, stood on the edge of a building, her fingertips bloodied from clawing a hewn stone in half. Edie had dotted Vigor's nose and furrowed brow with freckles as an homage to the fanfiction writer whose work she was adapting into fanart.

It was almost done. She just had to get Vigor's cape to look like it was fluttering.

After the day she'd had, she was glad to have a distraction. She had been asked to prom—twice. And though her friend Arianna insisted it was a "nonblem"—a problem that wasn't really a problem, like having too much money to fit in your wallet—Edie still felt short of breath. And not in a good way.

She shaded the underside of the cape, the corner tipping up in the wind. Vigor was one of four superheroines in the

Protectors, a line of comics featuring Edie's favorite super-heroines. Vigor was half of a duo with her sister, Vim. They developed superpowers after being exposed to a radioactive explosion. Separately, Vim had boundless energy, never requiring sleep, and Vigor had super strength, but together they could summon a crackling, destructive energy they called the Charge.

Her phone buzzed against the desk. She leaned over to read the new message. Arianna, of course.

Arianna: Pros for going to prom with Evan: Good-looking, smart, good conversationalist. Cons: pretentious. Totally corrected my grammar that one time.

Edie scowled at her phone. Arianna was just trying to be helpful, but she had been hounding Edie about her decision all day. She had a point about Evan, though. Their flirtatious friendship formed around smoke breaks in the field across from the high school, during their lunch hour. He was the only person who would talk to her about the human brain for more than five minutes. But the only stories he read were about listless men who didn't care about anything or anyone, and he had asked her to prom between two puffs of a cigarette.

Edie: Well, you did use "between" instead of "among."

Arianna: Shush.

Arianna: Pros for Chris: Hot. Funny. Allegedly a good kisser. Cons: you dated him for a year, so high potential for drama.

She had loved Chris Williams once. Or at least, that was how it had seemed, in the dark in the back of his car with his hands on her, or swimming in the lake behind his house in the heat of summer. She had loved the glow of his smile against his dark skin, and the way he always opened doors for people, even if it made him late. But their relationship had been like a house with no foundation—one little storm washed it away.

Well, maybe it was more than a little storm.

It had been a heap of twisted metal and a wooden box lowered into the earth.

Edie's stylus wobbled on the tablet screen, and she swore, hurriedly erasing the stray line that ruined Vigor's cape. She had that hot, tight feeling in her throat again. She'd gotten another text, and it sat open on her desk, waiting for a response.

555-263-9888: Hey! It's Lynn. Want to go with us to see the Vim and Vigor movie tonight?

Lynn had attached a selfie, and in it she was wearing Transforma's signature purple lipstick, her lips pouted in an air kiss.

Lynn was one half of what was left of the Protectors Comics Club Edie had joined in middle school. Originally, there were four members—Edie, Kate (the founder), Lynn, and Amy—just as there were four superheroines in the Protectors—Vim, Vigor, Transforma, and Haze—so they had each taken on a superheroine name and identity. It was cool at the time.

They had been all but inseparable for four years. Then Kate, who was always full of questionable ideas, suggested they drive to the local 7-Eleven for slushies one night, even though she only had a learner's permit. It was supposed to be a twenty-minute quest for sugar, and it ended in a car crash.

Amy was gone now, her resting place marked by a simple headstone in the Serene Hills Cemetery just outside of town, with a little slot for her data next to her name. At such a young age, her "data" amounted to a few files of childhood artwork and her school records.

555-263-9888: Opening weekend! (!!!!111!)

At one time, the Protectors Comics Club had talked *incessantly* about a movie based on Vim and Vigor coming out, but it had looked unlikely until last year. Kate had even texted Edie when the movie's release date was announced, but Edie hadn't known what to say back to her. And now it was here, and she didn't know what to do—not about prom, not about Kate and Lynn, not about anything.

Deep breaths, she told herself. Her therapist had told her not to fight the anxiety when it happened, to just count her breaths and accept it. She tried that. When her heart was still racing a few minutes later, she fished around in her purse for the little tin of pills that had been prescribed for exactly this purpose. Her fingers felt clumsy, almost numb. Edie popped one of the pills in her mouth and swallowed it dry.

Then she typed a reply to Lynn.

Sure. Time and place? Gotta support the cause.

They had always talked about the Protectors like that, as more than just a bunch of comics. They were a cause, because they were stories about women being heroes, not just spunky reporters or love interests who were sacrificed to the latest villain.

After the text sent, she picked up her stylus and started to draw again.

♥ ♥ ♥

Edie waited outside the theater for Lynn and Kate, her little purse clutched close, feeling self-conscious. She spotted Kate from a distance because of her huge, baggy Protectors sweat-shirt, with the symbol of the group on the front, curved and blue. And Lynn was easy to find because she was wearing her bobbing, horned Transforma headband. Transforma could shapeshift into any animal or alien the Protectors came across, though in her "human" form she always had red horns. And purple lips.

Kate stuffed her hands into the center pocket of her sweat-shirt and gave Edie a frown as she approached. Her freckled nose scrunched a little.

"Hey," Edie said. She wondered if Kate knew that Edie still read her fanfiction. She definitely didn't know that Edie still sketched it. Would she like it, if she knew? Or would she think it was pathetic?

Edie didn't know why she still kept up with the Protectors, or with Kate's work. She didn't know why she stored all her Protectors stuff in the closet instead of tossing it. Or why it was easier to let go of Kate herself than the thing that had brought them together.

"Hi!" Lynn said, a little too cheerfully. "Well . . . shall we? We want good seats, right?"

They went in, scanning their tickets at the entrance. Con-versation was sporadic, at best. It was like they were all leaving space for a fourth party to contribute, only that fourth party wasn't there. Amy had always been critical of the comics, more so than Edie, Kate, or Lynn. Edie had thought Amy didn't even *like* them, for a long time, before she saw Amy's bedroom, and all the posters tacked to the walls there, and the stack of Protectors-themed T-shirts in Amy's closet. It was just Amy's nature to pick at things.

They settled themselves in the middle of the theater, in the middle of the row. The floor was sticky under Edie's shoes. She'd smuggled a box of candy into the theater—chocolate-covered raisins, her favorite. She buried her fingers in the box, and Kate eyed her for a second before sticking out her hand, silently asking for some. Edie provided them, automatically, her muscles remembering how to be Kate's friend even if the rest of her didn't.

"I'm excited to see how they portray the Charge," she said to Kate, across Lynn's body. Lynn was a good mediator, and she had trouble taking sides. Amy had started fights, and Lynn had smoothed them over, time and time again. But Kate and Edie weren't having a fight now, not exactly.

Edie ran her fingers over the dark red velour that covered the seats, worn where most people's legs pressed against it, and watched the little screen as she waited for Kate to respond. It was so early that the theater was playing trivia instead of coming attractions.

"I'm nervous about that," Kate said. "The budget wasn't that high for this movie. You know, because it's not a sure thing."

"Yeah, we all know lady-hero movies don't make money," Edie said, rolling her eyes. "Except, say, that Wonder Woman movie . . ."

"And *Black Widow*!" Lynn piped up, her horns bouncing on their springs.

"They're just looking at the facts," Edie said with false firmness. "Don't get so emotional about it, ladies. Are you PMSing, by the way?"

Kate laughed.

"Shh," Lynn said suddenly. "The lights are dimming."

And it all came back in a rush, that breathless feeling when all the expectations and hopes and fears formed over years were balanced on a knife's edge. When you had loved something for so long and for so many reasons that all you wanted was for that love to expand inside you.

She clenched a hand around the armrest and watched, forgetting about the chocolate-covered raisins spilling into her purse, and the tension that had driven her farther and farther away from Kate until they couldn't even speak to each other anymore, and the way Lynn chewed so loudly Edie could hardly hear the quieter lines.

She watched Vim and Vigor stumble out of uncertainty and embrace their heroism and save the city.

She watched them grow up together, then break apart, and come back together again for the sake of something greater than either of them were alone.

And in the climactic moments, where it looked like Vigor might be lost in the power of the Charge, directing it to destroy instead of to heal, she locked eyes with Kate and smiled.

"And the part where Vim was double-fisting coffee cups with all those stacks of paper around?" Kate laughed.

"Classic Vim. Can't go anywhere without making a mess,"

Edie said, almost proud, for some reason. After all, Vim had been *hers*.

"The final act was a little fast, pacing wise," Lynn said. "But I liked the rest. Wonder if it'll do well."

"Hope so," Kate said. "I really want a sequel."

"Yeah, me too," Edie said, a little wistful. By the time a sequel came out, they would all be in college, and what if she didn't find anyone to share the Protectors with there? Would she have to pretend like she was over it, like she did with Arianna?

Kate checked her phone. "It's still early. Want to go back to my place?"

"Sure," Edie agreed, though a second later she regretted it. Lynn had that look on her face, the one that said she was about to say no.

"I have to head home," Lynn said. "I didn't finish my physics homework, and it's not like I'm acing that class."

Kate gave her a knowing look that made Edie realize how little she knew about Lynn's life now. She had no idea if Kate or Lynn were acing their classes, or if either of them were dating anyone, or if they had had their first drink, their first grope, their first anything.

And Edie had already agreed to go to Kate's house. If she backed out now, it would be obvious that she didn't feel comfortable alone with Kate anymore.

"Um . . . meet you there?" she asked Kate.

"Sure," Kate said, sounding just as uncertain.

Edie couldn't help but think that everything would be easier if she could just say what was going on. *Look, you and I clearly aren't comfortable around each other without Lynn there, so maybe another time?* But that just wasn't what people did.

Edie was always running into the barriers between people, wishing they were easier to break.

Kate's house was stark and modern, pale floors and white walls and stacks of glass blocks instead of windows. When Edie got there, she walked straight to the kitchen, where she knew Kate would be, dumping popcorn into a bowl and rustling in her white refrigerator for another can of soda.

"Want one?" Kate asked her.

"No, thanks," Edie said. "Where are Dr. and Dr. Rhodes?" Her affectionate names for Kate's parents, one of whom studied brains and the other, history.

Kate's dad—the famous Dr. Russell Rhodes—had invented the Elucidation Protocol, simulated reality technology that aided in clarity of thought and decision-making for people in high-stress fields. It essentially used extensive research and psychological and sociological principles, as well as personal beliefs, to reveal the likely outcomes of particular decisions through virtual reality. He had envisioned it being used to help world leaders make decisions, but it was the legal sector that had taken to it the most. It was currently used in prisons, to rehabilitate criminals, and in crime prevention with high-risk populations.

"On a date." Kate's mouth twisted. "They do that now. They make out in the kitchen too."

Edie grinned. Her own parents slept in separate beds these

days, claiming that her mother's snores were the reason, but Edie knew that wasn't all.

"So." Kate turned her soda can around in a circle. "Did you notice the Haze cameo at the end of the movie?"

As if Edie could have missed the Haze cameo. Haze was the youngest superheroine in the Protectors, and the movie had set up her origin story, showing a teenage girl staring on from the crowd as Vim and Vigor claimed their victory over the super-villain.

"Haze" was what they had called Amy. She had been the youngest of the four of them too.

"Yeah," Edie said. "Good casting, though. That red hair."

"Remember when Amy tried to dye her hair red in her bathroom and stained the tub permanently?" Kate smiled at her soda can. "Her mom was *so mad.* . . ."

"Yeah, and it turned her highlights pink," Edie pointed out. "Which I could have told her would happen, if she had asked, but *no* . . ."

"You always were best at that kind of thing," Kate said. "I guess it makes sense you've gone pro."

Edie looked down at her clothes—nothing special, just red jeans and a blazer with a little pin on the lapel. A skull and crossbones, to match the ones on the toes of her flat shoes. But it was more stylish than Kate's baggy sweatshirt. "Are you referring to my outfit?"

"Yeah." Kate shook her head. Her freckled nose twitched. "Sorry, I . . . I think it's cool, that you know about all that stuff. I still remember the day my mom presented me with a hairbrush instead of a comb, like 'Oh, I guess this might be easier for you.'"

Kate's mother had a short, practical haircut, and the most makeup Edie had seen her wear was a dab of concealer under her eyes. But Kate's hair was wavy and thick, frizzing close to the scalp so it glowed when light shone through it, and she had the kind of long, curled eyelashes other people pined over. No need for mascara.

"I remember that too," Edie said. "We were fourteen, and the comb just broke in your hair."

She laughed, and so did Kate, and that was how they ended up in Kate's bathroom, with her mom's old cosmetics spread over the counter and Kate perched on a stool with Edie standing in front of her, talking to her about eyeliner.

After giving up on the sparkly eye shadow ("If I wanted to look like New Year's Eve threw up on my face, I have a bag of confetti I could use," Kate had remarked. "Why do you have a bag of confetti?" Edie had asked, laughing), Edie and Kate sat on stools in the kitchen, tossing popcorn into their mouths. Then Edie thought to check her phone, which had been on silent since she got home from school that day.

There were three missed messages.

Arianna: Don't leave me in suspense!

Chris: ???

Evan: Up for a smoke tomorrow during lunch?

Edie stared at Chris's question marks, and her heart began to pound. "???" was right.

She didn't know why it was so hard to make this decision—

it was prom, after all, not life or death—but the thought of the way Evan's eyebrows would pinch in the middle, half disappointed and half critical, or the way Chris's eyes would avoid hers in the hallway again, as they had since the breakup, was just . . . too much. Right now, before she decided anything, all the different parts of her life were suspended in midair. And once she did, everything would come crashing down, she just knew it.

Kate must have seen the panic flash in her eyes, because she let the popcorn kernel fall on the floor and asked, "You okay, Vim?"

The casual use of the nickname—probably unintentional—made tears prick in Edie's eyes. And then she had an idea.

"Hey, you know that prototype your dad has in the basement?" she asked. "For the Elucidation Protocol? Do you think he would mind if we . . . used it?"

Kate raised her eyebrows.

"Let's see. Would my dad mind if I touched the thing he's always telling me not to touch under pain of death and the removal of my bedroom door?" She scratched her chin. "Yeah, Edie, pretty sure he would. Why?"

"I just . . ." Edie closed her eyes. "There's a decision I need to make, and it's kind of a big deal, and I just . . . I thought the EP could help."

"That is what it's designed for," Kate admitted. "Um . . ." She chewed her lip, the way she always did right before she suggested something stupid. This time was no exception. "Let's do it anyway."

Edie brightened. "Really?"

"Yeah, Dad's not going to be home until late," Kate said. She paused, tilting her head as she looked Edie over. "It really is important, right?"

Edie hesitated.

"Yeah," she said finally. "I wouldn't ask if it wasn't."

The prototype of the Elucidation Protocol was a little disappointing when you came face-to-face with it. The first time, Edie had narrowed her eyes and said to Dr. Rhodes, "This is it?" It looked like a headband with a bunch of wires attached to it, running along the floor to a little computer. The device wasn't the revolutionary part, Dr. Rhodes had explained. The substance that triggered the program was. He had made batches and batches of it, to the point that the other Dr. Rhodes, his wife, insisted he stop bringing it home, particularly when the protocol moved to its next stages and the original formula was no longer viable.

So she wasn't surprised when Kate plucked a vial of the stuff from a shelf in the—completely packed—closet of identical vials, without a second thought. She even *tossed* it to Edie, who caught it, thankfully. She sat in the padded chair—ripped across the seat from overuse—and buzzed with nerves as Kate arranged the wired crown atop her head like she was some kind of sci-fi prom queen.

"Wrap that heart monitor thing around your arm, will you?" Kate said. She was in scientist mode now. She had never been into science the way Edie was, but she was capable enough, growing up under her father's watchful eye. It was Edie, though, who knew how to attach the heart monitor to her arm so that it would pick up her pulse, who untangled the wires and made sure the leads were secured to her temples.

"You know the drill, but I'm going to give you the whole speech anyway, okay?" Kate said as she sat behind the computer to set up the program. "The protocol will run twice, once for each of the options you're considering. It doesn't see the future; it just helps you to see what *you* think would happen in each of two scenarios. The prototype is flawed in that it can't account for any other factors aside from the knowledge that you yourself possess, though it does assist in clarity of thought."

Edie nodded. She knew all this. Her hand was getting sweaty around the vial of substrate. She was worried it would tremble when she brought it up to her mouth to drink, and Kate would see it and know how terrified she was. About *prom dates*, of all things.

But it was more than that, wasn't it? Evan was intellectual, daring, opinionated. Chris was kind, openhearted, enthusiastic. And when she was with either of them, *she* was those things too; she was more than she could ever be alone, like Vim and Vigor and the Charge. It was a choice between dates, sure, but it was also a choice between Edies.

Wasn't it?

"I'll cue you verbally to start the second phase," Kate said. "So drink up, and it should set in after ten seconds. Don't be alarmed when your scenery shifts, it's perfectly normal."

Edie nodded and tipped the vial's bluish contents into her mouth.

♥ ♥ ♥

Edie twisted her arms behind her back to push up the zipper on her black dress. It was simple, hanging from off-the-shoulder straps and clinging just enough—not too much—to her belly and thighs. She tucked a stray curl into the twist at the back of her head; then, making sure that her little brother wasn't anywhere nearby, sniffed under each armpit to make sure she had remembered deodorant.

"Edie!" her mother sang from the first floor. "There's a boy here for you!"

"Coming!" she crowed back. She checked her winged eyeliner one last time in the mirror, stuffed a Band-Aid in her silver clutch in case her shoes gave her blisters, and made her way downstairs.

Evan waited by the door. He wasn't carrying a corsage, and she hadn't expected him to, but it was still vaguely disappointing, like he couldn't be bothered to do something silly even if it was just a nice gesture. But she pushed that thought aside as she went down the steps, particularly as his lips twitched into a smile.

He wore a black suit, white shirt, black tie. Classic. And at least he wasn't wearing flannel. His hair had just as much product in it as it usually did, and it looked so thick she wanted to bury her hands in it.

"Let me get a picture of you two!" Edie's mother said, and she rustled in her purse for her phone. Poking at it like it was a typewriter, she found her way to the camera app and held it up. Evan pulled Edie close to his side, grinning.

She smiled back, and with a click, the moment was captured.

After a hug that lingered a beat too long, Edie broke away from her mother and followed Evan to his old green Saab. She loved the way the car smelled, like old tobacco and men's deodorant. She wondered what she would find if she opened the center console, and made a list of guesses. A tin of mints, a lighter with half the fluid gone. Maybe, if she dug deep, the stub of a joint and a button from a winter coat. People's scraps said so much about them.

They didn't talk much on the way there, as Evan parked and they piled into one of the buses with everybody else. Edie loved seeing all the people in their formal wear stuffed between bus seats, some of the skirts so big they fluffed up by a girl's face. Evan chose a seat in the back, next to an open window, and he sat a little closer to her than was strictly necessary.

"You didn't want to sit near your friend? What's her name?" Evan asked. "Arianna, right?"

"She went on the early bus—yep, it's Arianna," she said, inordinately pleased that he remembered Arianna's name. "You corrected her grammar once, remember?" she added, on a whim, a little smile on her lips.

"Did I? God, she must hate me." Evan laughed. "It's a reflex. My mom used to make a horrible sound every time we made a grammar misstep. I think it was her attempt at classical conditioning."

"What was the sound?"

Evan's face contorted, and he let out a loud "EHH!" Like a warning buzzer mixed with an old car horn. There was a rustle of skirts as some of their classmates turned toward the sound.

Edie mimicked Evan's expression of horror. "She did that *every time?*"

"God forbid we used the word 'like' as a filler word," he replied sourly. "My parents split up when I was twelve, though, so her influence wasn't as strong after that. But you know what they say about the formative years."

"They form you," Edie supplied. "You lived with your dad then?"

"He's the responsible one," Evan replied, nodding. "So to speak. He hasn't noticed my unexcused absences yet, but I'm not complaining."

He *was* complaining, Edie knew. The same way she complained about her parents avoiding each other's eyes when they were in the same room together—by pretending it was better that way.

She wasn't sure where the question came from, but it was bubbling from her mouth. "Why did you want to be my friend, Evan?"

She had wondered more than once. And the answers she came up with ranged from "because I wanted to get in your pants" to "because your knowledge of cutting-edge neuroscience is downright alluring" and everywhere in between, but what he said surprised her anyway.

"You seemed as lonely as I was," he said, and he looked away, his hair tousled by the wind.

The bus rattled and rocked all the way to the Holiday Inn ballroom, which was decorated with different kinds of strings of lights, stars and roses and tiny lanterns. A folk-pop song with a twangy guitar was playing over the sound system, and there were a dozen round tables arranged next to the dance floor. A buffet table held deep trays of food, covered to keep them warm.

She spotted Arianna and her boyfriend, Jacob, already cuddled close at one of the tables, a plate of finger food between them. A hint of movement caught her eye on the side of the room, and she spotted Kate gesticulating wildly to Lynn. Edie blinked. Kate was wearing black pants and a glittery shirt that caught the light when she moved, and Lynn was in a red knee-length dress.

Kate's eyes found hers. Then looked away.

"Wow," Edie said. "This is a teen movie nightmare."

"You said it," Evan said. "I think I need a smoke. Want to?"

"A little early to bail, don't you think?" she said.

"I came, I saw, I prommed," he replied. "We can always come back. Come on, there's a place I want to show you."

They ended up a few blocks away, at the boardwalk. The smell of salt and seaweed was on the air, as well as the occasional whiff of cigarette smoke whenever the wind blew just so. The cigarette itself dangled from Evan's fingers like he was about to drop it, just like Edie's shoes dangled from hers by their little black straps.

He did put out the cigarette then, smashing it against the inside of a little tin he kept in his jacket pocket. A second later she thought she saw him pop a mint into his mouth, but she couldn't be sure. She ducked her head to hide a smile and followed him at his gesture. Then he was hopping off the boardwalk, drawing a gasp from her lips and a laugh from his own.

"Don't worry, there's a sandbar here at low tide," he said, and his pale hand stretched out around the boards beneath her. She set down her shoes, hiked up her skirts—all the while sparing a few choice words for boys who didn't understand how much harder it was to maneuver in a slinky dress than a pair of loose pants—and jumped down.

She splashed a little on the landing, but since her dress was black, it didn't really matter. She kept her skirt out of the sand, though, draping it over her elbow as she turned to face him. Yes, he had definitely eaten a mint—even from a foot away, his breath was fresh now, with a hint of tobacco.

"If we weren't in formal wear, I'd suggest we sit down and listen to the waves," he said. He ducked his head and, to her surprise, blushed a little. Or she thought he did—it was getting dark, so it was hard to tell. "Guess I didn't think this through very well."

"You know, it would probably be creepy if you had," she said, and he laughed, with less control than he usually had, so it came out like a bark.

And she realized, suddenly, that Evan—journal-carrying, smoking-behind-the-shed-on-school-grounds, pep-rally-ditching Evan—was nervous. That for all that he pretended to know himself and what he wanted, he was just as clueless about the whole thing as she was.

So she let her skirt drop to the sand, threw an arm around his neck, and tilted up on her bare toes to kiss him.

She felt his fingers digging into her waist, and the grains

of sand between her toes, and the firm pressure of his mouth. Then, at the nudge of a tongue, parting, giving way, the tension thrumming through him releasing. Salt and mint and cigarette. Waves caressing the shore, and the moon now emerging, and she was exactly the daring girl she wanted to be.

"Second phase in five . . . four . . . three . . . two . . . one . . ."

Edie twisted her arms behind her back to push up the zipper on her red dress.

"I got it, don't dislocate anything," Arianna said, coming up behind her. She was already wearing her dress, a yellow gown that almost glowed against her brown skin. She had gathered her thick hair into a knot just behind her right ear, and there was a flower pinned there, just as bright as the dress.

Edie's friend zipped up the dress, and she smiled at her reflection in Arianna's bedroom mirror. They had picked Arianna's house for its huge staircase—perfect for prom pictures.

Edie had *tried* to buy a normal, simple dress, but Arianna had forbidden it. "This is one of the only times in your entire life that it will be okay to wear a huge monstrosity," she had pointed out, and after a few repetitions, Edie agreed. Consequently, her red dress was a *gown*, with a full skirt.

And *pockets*.

She beamed when she moved in it and heard the layers swishing up against one another. Making sure her phone was secure in one of the pockets, Edie followed Arianna out of the master bathroom. A group had gathered at the bottom of the grand staircase, all the boys in their tuxes and the girls in bright dresses in almost every color of the rainbow. They were Arianna's cross-country teammates, and Edie liked them but didn't really know them. It didn't matter—she knew Arianna, and she knew Chris, who was laughing by the door with Arianna's date, Jacob.

When he spotted her, Chris's face—if possible—lit up even more, and he broke off his conversation to go to her side.

"Nicely done, Robbins," he said.

"You too, Williams," she replied, making a show of looking him over. He did look good. Unlike the penguinlike boys around him, he was in a navy blue tuxedo with black trim, his bow tie so straight it was like he had tied it with a level on hand. And he was holding a white wrist corsage. An orchid.

She grinned as he slipped it onto her, then caught his hand, and squeezed.

"I see you're committed to this occasion," she said. "Corsage, nice suit . . ."

"When I was a boy I used to dream about my prom night. . . ." He folded his hands under his chin and gave an exaggerated blink. "And about the gal who would sweep me off my feet, et cetera."

She mimed throwing up.

"Really, though, my granddad always says cynicism is unattractive in a young person," he said, a little more seriously. "Well, actually, he says, 'What do you have to be cynical about, boy? The whole world is at your feet.' And something about a war, I don't know."

"Meanwhile, there's my mother, who started to warn me against bad prom night decision-making and gave up halfway through," she replied. "Like, literally gave up. Sighed heavily and went into the living room."

Chris laughed. They took their place on the steps with the other couples. He stood close behind her, wrapping an arm around her waist. They smiled, stiffly, for the first few shots, and when commanded to be silly, Edie put on a comically deep frown as Chris pretended to collapse against the banister.

Before pulling away, he bent closer to brush a kiss against her cheek. She flushed with warmth.

They piled into a stretch white limousine that took them—in a cloud of vapor from the smoke machine—to the high school, where they got on one of the buses instead. They rode in the back, raucous enough to get scolded multiple times by the chaperone. Edie's stomach ached from laughing so hard, and they weren't even at the prom yet.

When they arrived, she and Chris paused in the doorway to marvel at the strings of light that crisscrossed the ceiling, and the luminous gauze that made up the centerpieces of the tables. There wasn't a soul on the dance floor yet, though the lights were already low and the music was playing. So she knew what Chris was going to do before he did it.

He grabbed her hand and pulled her toward the dance floor. "Someone's gotta get this started!" he said, by way of explanation, but she didn't need it. Her cheeks were hot as he pulled her into the empty space, and she felt the eyes of everyone in the room like fingers brushing over her, but then Chris was going through his repertoire of stupid dance moves, trying to get her to laugh with him: the cabbage patch, the shopping cart, the sprinkler. . . .

Edie sighed, bobbed her head to the music, and pretended to be holding a fishing pole. She cast her invisible line, and Chris became the fish, flapping wildly as she pulled him in. Then she fell against him, so embarrassed she couldn't help but bury her face in his shoulder. But it was all right, because in the middle of her spasm of humiliation, Arianna and all her friends had come to join them, and now she was camouflaged by a whole crowd of fools.

It took another song to get comfortable, and then Arianna was spinning in circles around her, and Jacob was dragging a handkerchief across his sweaty forehead, and Chris was trying to teach her how to do the electric slide, even though it didn't work with the music. She kept tripping over her skirt, and her legs were sticky with sweat, but it didn't matter, none of it mattered except how widely he smiled at her.

Sometime in the middle of one of those songs where they shouted commands at you—Edie's favorite, because she didn't have to think of her own moves—she spotted Kate at the edge of the dance floor, trying to coax Lynn to join her. Kate was in silver—no, not just silver, but a dress made of *duct tape* that wrapped around her from chest to knee. Lynn was in red, like Edie.

Edie caught Kate's eye, pointed at the duct-tape dress, and gave her a thumbs-up.

Kate gave her a confused look.

And Edie stepped to the left and turned, as commanded by the music.

The song slowed, and the lights went low, so only the starry strands glowed in a net above them. Chris's hands found her hips, and she put her arms around his neck. They swayed, leaning on each other to recover from the fever of the past few dances.

She touched her forehead to his, and he was sweaty, his skin radiating heat, but she didn't mind.

He had made her feel light, for once. So she tipped up her chin to kiss him. He cupped her cheeks, and they stopped swaying. She crushed the corsage against his chest, toying with the buttons of his shirt, with the perfectly straight bow tie.

This was it, she knew. The feeling people meant when they talked about love. And it was so easy to love him, so easy to love the person she was when he was around.

"You look happy," he said to her softly, over the hum of the music. "For a while, after the accident, it was like . . . like you didn't feel much of anything. And I didn't know what to do. But . . . it's nice to see you happy again."

It was nice to feel happy again.

But she couldn't get rid of the unsettling thought: *What happens when I stop being happy again?*

Kate did not count down her exit from the Elucidation Protocol. Edie jerked from the vision, startled to find herself sitting instead of standing and wearing jeans instead of a red gown. She ran her hands over her arms, feeling bereft. Lost.

Such a weird thing to have in your basement, she thought as she looked around for something to anchor her. Along the far wall were bookcases stuffed with books, sometimes two rows deep. This was a house of curious people. Kate's parents didn't even mind her comic obsession. Her mother had even called it a "feminist undertaking."

Kate stood in front of her and ripped one of the wires away from Edie's forehead. Her movements were sharp, her brow furrowed. Edie blinked up at her as Kate eased the crown off her head and set it aside. Then Kate took a phone out of her back pocket and thrust it at Edie.

"Here. Take it, it wouldn't stop buzzing," Kate said. She folded her arms.

"What is it?" Edie said, still feeling out of it. Had she mumbled something while she was under the influence of the EP? Something about Kate?

"Oh, no, this conversation can wait until you've checked your texts. Go ahead," Kate said.

Edie touched the screen, bringing up the last few text messages. They were all from Arianna.

> **Arianna: Well?**
> **Arianna: Did you choose a boy yet?**
> **Arianna: Tell me soon, because we need to go dress shopping together.**

She looked up at Kate, still not sure what was going on.

"Tell me," Kate said, her voice shaking. "Tell me we didn't just break my father's rules, risk me getting in serious trouble, and potentially damage highly expensive equipment so you could *pick a prom date*."

"It's not . . ." But what? How could she explain that it wasn't about a prom date, wasn't about Evan or Chris or dresses or dances? How could she possibly tell Kate about the whirl of panicked thoughts chasing themselves through her brain every second of every day, and the deep ache she felt every time she thought about the future, the past—hell, even the present?

"God." Kate closed her eyes. "When you agreed to come tonight, I thought it was because you actually gave a damn about me still. That maybe we could be friends again. And now I find out you would take advantage of me like this, for something so . . . so *vapid* and shallow and—"

"You're so *judgmental*, god," Edie snapped. "If you're not ragging on me for liking makeup, you're insulting me for caring about prom. Well, excuse me for not waging some kind of eternal war against The Man!"

"You don't listen, do you?" Kate's eyes filled with tears. "I thought we could be friends again! And it's like you don't even think of me, don't even see me anymore, not since . . ." She blinked the tears away. "Do you even *like* Vim and Vigor anymore? Or did you just come so you could ask me for this?"

"*You're* the one who doesn't even make eye contact in the hallway," Edie said. "And you must not know me very well if you think I'm just some airheaded idiot who's agonizing over a prom dress."

"Just go, okay?" Kate shook her head. "Just go, and choose a boy, and go back to pretending I don't exist."

She turned and walked across the basement. Edie listened to her footsteps on the stairs, and above her head, as they crossed the living room. She heard a door close upstairs and knew that Kate would be in her room by now, probably playing music louder than she should, and wouldn't answer the door even if Edie pounded on it.

So Edie got her bag, put on her shoes, and left.

They had been the last ones at the funeral, Lynn, Kate, and Edie. They helped Amy's aunts clean up, then sat on the couch in the living room, sucking down the last of what Edie mentally referred to as the funereal punch. All day she had been suppressing the horrible urge to laugh. Everything was funny—the priest's hobbling gait as he went up to the pulpit, the face Amy's grandmother made when she cried, the off-balance way the pallbearers carried the casket.

She felt like some of the wires in her brain were crossed to trigger the wrong reactions at the wrong times. As people stood around weeping, she got so angry she thought she might explode, and excused herself. By the time she made it to the couch with Kate and Lynn, she was so exhausted from the wild swells of the wrong emotions that she was numb.

Then Lynn's parents came to pick her up, so it was just Kate and Edie, waiting for their rides together, and Edie still couldn't look Kate in the eye.

Kate put down her mug, her hand trembling, and said, in a voice so small and so broken Edie almost didn't believe it belonged to her friend:

"Do you think it's my fault?"

She knew why Kate was asking. Because it had been Kate's

idea to drive to the 7-Eleven, and Kate who had been behind the wheel, and Kate who hadn't gotten out of the way of the drunk driver in time, and Kate whose whole body was shaking now.

Edie threw her arms around her best friend, held her tight, and forced herself to say, "No. Of course not."

But oh god, maybe she did, maybe she *did*.

That night Edie opened the Vim and Vigor folder on her tablet and scrolled through the images one by one. Kate had been writing this most recent Protectors story for almost a year. It was longer than most books, and she updated it weekly on FandomWorks. Every time Edie thought about giving it up, she found something that made her hold on—a phrase she recognized, a revelation about a character, something small.

Then a few months ago, she had discovered something bigger.

Kate had always teased Edie for being conventional in her "ships"—the couples she was most rooting for in fanfiction, even if they weren't together in canon. Kate was more interested in nontraditional interpretations of Vim and Vigor—Vim with other women (Transforma, mostly), and Vigor as asexual, or demisexual—and Edie liked to hear about those too, curious about all the possibilities. (Though it had been difficult to explain to her mother why she had so many sketches of two women kissing on her tablet.)

But Edie always went back to Vim and Antimatter, the son of their evil nemesis. The early comics showed them potent in their hatred for one another, almost killing each other every now and then. But then Antimatter's mother had died, and he started to shift, and the passionate hate turned to attraction. Enemies to lovers—one of Edie's favorite tropes.

And Kate had written it into her story.

Her Vigor was asexual, of course—that was Kate's favorite interpretation of all. But Vim and Antimatter were there, in her fic, the one she had been building for a year. It was almost like she was speaking directly to Edie.

That was when Edie started sketching again. Trying to talk back.

Edie paused on a drawing of Antimatter's gloved hand in Vim's slender one, their fingers twisting together as something exploded behind them. Maybe she didn't need to find the right words to say to Kate, or even any words at all.

Edie opened a blank email and attached the Vim and Vigor folder. When it uploaded, she typed in Kate's email address and wrote "I'm sorry" in the subject line.

Sent.

It was prom night.

Edie twisted her arms behind her back to push up the zipper of her black skirt. It was high-waisted, hitting her right below her ribs, and made of a stiff material that disguised the cell phone and lipstick she carried in the pockets.

She leaned close to the mirror to check the border of her lipstick, which was a vibrant orange-red.

"So you're really set on that getup, huh?" Arianna said from the doorway, her arms folded.

"Not much choice now, is there?" Edie smiled a little. "Come on. Let's go make precious memories."

There were strings of lights across the ceiling, just as she had imagined during the Elucidation Protocol, but none of them were shaped like stars. Instead, they were your standard Christmas light variety, little and twinkling and white. And the centerpieces on the round tables were just white flowers, lilies and carnations. Kind of hideous, actually.

Edie stood in the doorway and tucked her hands into her skirt pockets. She was scanning the hotel ballroom, at her leisure, watching Chris and his date—one of the cross-country girls, a short, sweet junior named Tonya—do the shopping cart, shoulder to shoulder. Evan was nowhere to be found, probably smoking under the boardwalk, if he had come at all.

Arianna turned back, her arm still looped around Jacob's elbow. "You coming?"

Edie waved her on.

Then she spotted them, standing at the edge of the dance floor, and she remembered the text she'd sent to Lynn and Kate a few days after the incident at Kate's house.

Edie: Protectors reunion at prom? <3 Vim

She unzipped her leather jacket and tossed it over the back of a chair. Underneath it she wore a garish purple T-shirt with an illustration of Vim on it. The superheroine was flying through the air, her cape rippling behind her and her fist outstretched, jagged energy lines radiating from her body.

Across the room, Lynn spotted her and waved. She was wearing her Transforma horns and an acid-green dress that clashed horribly with them. She looked like a bottle of radioactive waste, and her lips were dark purple.

Kate turned, and when Edie recognized the Vigor costume for what it was, she almost cried with relief, because it meant Kate had forgiven her. From the back, the costume just looked like a rippling black coatdress, but from the front, that bright red bustier was unmistakable. As was the sparkly red eye shadow on Kate's eyelids.

They looked insane. Ridiculous. And fantastic.

She crossed the room just as a fast song started playing. When she was close to Kate and Lynn, she struck the classic Vim pose, and all three of them laughed.

"Look, I brought something," she shouted, over the music. And she took a tiny picture of Amy out of her pocket. It was attached to a Popsicle stick and decorated with the neon-yellow Haze headdress. And glitter.

She knew it was weird. She hadn't really brought it for them. She'd brought it because she thought it might feel good to remember Amy. Also terrible—she knew it would feel terrible to remember, but sometimes good and terrible could coexist, right? They had to.

"That is . . . ," Lynn started, eyebrows raised. "Dark," she finished. "Very dark sense of humor you've got there, Edie."

But Kate was laughing. "Oh god, she would have loved it."

And Edie realized: Evan only liked her when she was lonely. Chris only liked her when she was happy. But Kate . . .

Kate just liked *Edie*.

Edie didn't blame her for the accident, then, not even a little.

"Let's go," she said. "I love this song."

And they *danced*.

Work In Progress
E. K. JOHNSTON

1.0

By the time the explosions stop, you feel like you have forgotten everything about your life before they began. There is only the dark, the muted breathing of your companions, and the desperate need to not be found. The mutineers have undoubtedly killed your parents—they were in the medical bay and would have tried to stop the captain from bleeding to death—and remembering anything would mean remembering them, so you don't.

Instead you pretend: it is a game. You only must stay quiet and stay together, stay clever and stay sharp, and you will win. This is what you whisper to the others. That there is a way out that doesn't involve a bullet or a one-way trip through an airlock. It's cold enough that you don't want to think about the black void that surrounds the ship. You never much liked it before, even though you liked to look at the stars. You had a lot of faith in the ship's hull, in its engine, in its crew, and all of that is gone now, bled out on the med-bay floor.

The other two are quiet, and you wonder if they regret having brought you. You are good at distraction, but you don't have a lot in the way of useful skills besides that. You do your best to keep them occupied anyway, telling stories the way you would if this was a sleepover. They never tell you to shut up, so you assume you are doing what they want. You certainly can't imagine picking anyone besides them if you'd been the one doing the picking. The adults were all shooting at one another and the other children were all crying, and much too young. Maybe that is why they took you with them: you were handy and you weren't screaming.

You eat the smallest ration and you don't complain, and when they ask you to keep watch while they risk trips out of the ducts for water or more food, you do it and you are grateful for what they bring back. And whenever you can, you remind them of what might be waiting when the ship lands, of the wide green fields and the wildflowers and enough room to run and spin and yell. You have only to make it that far, stay hidden that long, and then you might be safe. *Will* be safe.

You remember more, now. That it will be a long time until the ship lands. That the planet will be gray and only partially terraformed. That the mutineers who killed your parents will still be waiting with guns. You don't remind them of that when you speak, though. And they don't ask you questions they don't want to know the answers to. They only turn away, and say it's time to rest.

None of you has ever been really cold, even on the nights when CJ came to your bunk to avoid shouting parents, and Tab did the same to avoid crying siblings. There was always room for them in your bunk. There isn't room now. The ventilation duct where you hide to sleep is only wide enough for two of you to lie abreast in it. The third must be alone, and cold.

Space or company.

Choose.

You are in the schoolroom when it starts, of course, because it is the middle of the lighted shift, and you are still young enough that there are things you need to learn. The three of you sit in the hull-side corner of the room, passing the screen back and forth between you while you study. It makes Alex nervous, to be that close to space, but you ignore that, because your siblings sit near the door, and you have always done your best to avoid them. It saves your life that day, even though you don't like to think about it.

Alex is reading out loud about some city back on Earth-of-Old—because Alex is a storyteller's voice in the black—when the explosions start. The younger kids scream immediately, and you feel CJ tense. CJ knows the inner workings of the ship the best of the three of you, and that's how you know to worry. The void of space seems very, very close, and you put an arm around Alex to remind you both that the hull is strong.

You can hear the sound of gunfire, and the heavy tromp of grav boots. Whatever is happening, there is a worry that the ship's gravity will fail. That is when you know that it is not a drill.

CJ is moving, prying a panel off the back wall. Alex is frozen. The kids are still screaming, and you are standing somewhere in the middle. You feel like you've been in the middle a lot lately, drawing away from the other two even though you don't know what direction it is you're heading. There are things you want to do alone, but at the same time, there are things you want to share. You have to figure out who it is you want to share them with, and that turns out to be harder than you thought.

You don't want to share them with your own family, really, except that your older sibs are almost interesting now, and you wonder if you should stop ignoring them. This is probably why people build robots. It's much easier to talk to robots.

Alex is pulling you toward the gap that CJ has made in the paneling. Neither of them is yelling, but it isn't because they're calm. Quiet people don't attract attention, and attention right now will get all three of you killed. Behind the schoolroom, in the bones of the ship, you will be safe from gunfire. There is not enough time to take everyone. You don't hesitate for a moment, following them and then helping CJ to attach the panel and cover your tracks. It's only afterward that you realize the full weight of what you've done.

You want to be alone then, more than ever before. Alone with your grief and your guilt. But you are afraid that your loneliness would kill you, as surely as the bullets mowed down the kids you left behind, your brothers and sisters among them. Children are a drain of resources on a spaceship, and it's easy enough to make more of them if you decide later on that their numbers can be supported.

Privacy or security.

Choose.

You really, really would prefer it if Alex would shut up, but you can't bear the thought of what you'd all do in the silence. Alex's parents had been in the medical bay, and Tab's were goddamned bridge officers. They were dead for sure. Your parents, engine grease so far under their fingernails that their hands were never clean even after their allotted time in the sonic shower, might have held the guns that did it. You don't want the other two to figure that out.

They'd been shouting at each other for weeks, your parents had been, about the state of the engine and their prospects for promotion. They'd argued about the food and the water ration. They'd griped about their options during the dark shift, when they weren't working but weren't yet tired enough to sleep. You'd ignored them, slid out of your bed, and gone to sleep with Alex, where it was quieter.

You have always had Alex and Tab. Your parents have different jobs, but the children are all raised together, until aptitude splits them off. You three are the first batch of children born onboard, once the captain determined that there were enough resources to support you, and you have always loved her for it. Your parents didn't much care for the captain's favor—or for your friends—but there was nothing they could do. They had their jobs away from their quarters, and the alternative was endless loneliness.

You do what you can. You learn the ship inside and out, to make them know that you are proud of what they do. You study the star charts and you absorb everything about Earth-of-Old that Tab will tell you, and everything about the destination colony that Alex can make up. You are determined to be a child of the ship, and to make sure your friends are too, but that isn't enough to quiet the grumblings on the lower decks.

When the shouting is no longer something you can ignore, it is too late. There is gunfire, and the heavy step of those doing the shooting coming toward you. Alex is frozen and Tab is torn, but you are already moving. The panel shifts under your hands as you pry it free, just enough for three bodies to squeeze into the wall. You're not sure what will happen after that. Whoever wins the fight will know you're missing. It's not like there's anywhere that you can go. But for the moment, you and yours will be safe.

You drag them behind you, and refasten the panel. Somehow, you manage to stay quiet as the schoolroom fills with shooting and the screams are cut off. You are in the middle, holding Alex still and keeping Tab from crying out—or vomiting—as the sound of dying is replaced with the sounds of nothing, which is somehow worse.

The silence stretches on, broken only by Alex's whispers about the haven you might find when you reach the destination colony. You know the stories aren't real, but you can't bring yourself to voice corrections. You're afraid that if you do, they'll remember that you could leave the walls and ducts whenever you wanted to, and be safe there. You think. There had been other children of engineers in that schoolroom, and when the guns stopped, it had been very, very quiet. The three of you cling to one another and to Alex's stories, and you cannot make yourself let go.

Chance or reality.

Choose.

2.0

The thing you remember most clearly about summer is how quickly the heat of it can turn to cold when the sun goes down. There are hot summer nights, of course, when the three of you lie on the bed, covers thrown far away and none of you touching. But by the time the sun comes back, the cool breeze off the lake has mixed with the stuffiness held down by the trees, and Tab has reached for the sheet to keep the rest of CJ from shivering and waking you up too early.

Those nights aren't your favorite anyway. You like the ones where it gets cold enough that you all huddle together as soon as it gets dark. Sitting on the end of the dock after swimming, in spite of the mosquitoes, or lawn chairs pulled as close together as they can be around the bonfire. Those are nights for whispers and games that you have shared with no one else, for secrets and for plans.

You outgrew CJ's bed last summer, and Tab's bunkie is shared with too many siblings. This bed creaks whenever one of you rolls over, and whoever sleeps in the center has to climb out the foot to go to the bathroom, but it's in the attic, so no one complains when you talk and laugh too late. You all drift toward the middle when you sleep, and wake in a pile of arms and legs. Warm skin and soft breathing give way to giggles as you climb out and head down the rickety old stairs for breakfast, and whatever excitement waits you in the newness of the day.

The rare nights you sleep alone, you don't stretch out in the bed. You sleep where you always do: on the edge, facing inward. The whisper of the wind in the trees outside your window is a poor substitute for secrets, but if you close your eyes you can pretend. You have always been the best of the three at pretending: the dreamer who makes the games and keeps the tally of the worlds you have already conquered. It's harder to pretend when you are alone, but you do your best. When you wake up in the morning in the middle of the bed, you scramble back to the edge, and try to forget how comfortable it was to sprawl.

You can fit one person into places that three people can't ever go, but you don't like to do it unless you have to. *You can fit two people*, a traitorous part of your heart whispers. You can fit two people where three people can't go. You only ever do it when one of them is sick or stuck in traffic. You don't like it when they go somewhere without you, after all.

Two people in the front of the car. Two people to balance the canoe. Two people to split a Popsicle. You're not much of a driver yet, and if there's three in the canoe then someone's always resting, and freezies are better than Popsicles anyway and . . .

So many things are built for two.

Space or company.

Choose.

The best thing about summer is that you can spend it with your family without spending it with your family. There are a lot of them, and they are noisy, and you like that you can play with them sometimes and ignore them when it suits you. When you were very small, before the lake had internet access and before you had more than one younger kid to worry about, you only came up for weekends. But progress is kind, and now your parents can work away from the city, so you are here for all three glorious months of summer.

(It's really two and a half, CJ tells you, because CJ measures everything precisely. You are more given to rounding up. It makes you feel better.)

With five more kids after you, the bunkie shouldn't be a refuge, and yet it is. The sibs have bikes and pocket money for candy, and they're gone from sunrise to sundown, unless one of the twins scrapes off enough skin to merit a trip to find Alex for some first aid. You're not sure why you stay so clear of the pack, why you don't lead it. You had two years as an only child, but apparently it stuck.

You read a lot, inside because there aren't any horseflies there. When you go to the main house for snacks, your parents say things like, "Why do you read in the bunkie when you have all that nature?" and you look calmly at the ledgers and file folders spread out across the dining room table until they appreciate the irony and leave you alone. If they can understand the difference between working in the city and at the lake, they can understand the difference of reading too.

You disappear after dinner, and a lot of the time you don't come back. They know where you are, so they don't worry. They could shout for you and you'd hear them. They never do.

The mosquitoes are bad at dusk, but not if you're swimming or standing around a fire pit. CJ and Alex talk nonstop, but not in the way your siblings do. They talk about the future, things that could never happen and things that might, and if they notice that you don't say much, they don't make a big deal of it like your parents would. You keep your secrets, but you keep theirs too, and somehow that balances the scales. Sometimes you wish that you could just tell them something, anything, that would make the exchange more fair, but your tongue always sticks.

You can't even say something when you've all gone to bed and you hover on the edge of the mattress, too scared to get close and too scared to leave them. You imagine that they'd forget you immediately if you did. You're surprised, every summer, when you come back to the lake and they take you in like you've never left. You're not sure what you've done to deserve it, because it's certainly not that you've opened your heart up the way they do.

Privacy or security.

Choose.

Someday the world is going to come down very hard on Alex, and you kind of hope it's in the winter so that you don't have to see the ruination. In the summer, life at the lake is very different. There are a lot more people, for starters, but not in the obnoxious way. The people who come up from the city come for the quiet, so they are respectful. They buy their food at the local store (your uncle), if something goes wrong with the toilet they call a local plumber (your cousin), and they pay their taxes to the local council (headed by your mother), because property ownership is property ownership, regardless of how much time you spend in residence. Hipsters, it turns out, are good for something after all.

"We're not hipsters," Tab says, every time you mention it. "I don't think hipsters have six kids."

They probably don't, but it's one of your small pleasures to get a rise out of the city kids at every opportunity.

"I'm not from a city!" says Alex. Same deal.

They let you get away with it because you are a local, and because they miss you when they have to go back to their real houses, hours and hours away. Your real house is here: insulated walls against the cold and snow, a practical number of bathrooms, a television that doesn't rely on the weather for good reception, and all of your belongings in the same place, all the time.

It makes you want to scream a bit, how little Alex seems to understand about how the world works. It also makes you want to spend the rest of your life making sure the truth never comes out.

You don't sleep at your own house in the summer anymore. Theoretically, it's because you don't all fit in the bed, your arms and legs end up twined in ways that might be awkward to explain, even though you all know there is nothing to tell. Really it's because you want a vacation, and if you're somewhere else you can pretend. Alex is very, very good at pretending—and even better at ignoring innuendo—and you are rather shameless about using that as an escape. You make it up in other ways. You whisper when the three of you are roasting marshmallows, and you never roll your eyes, no matter what Alex says. You always let Tab sleep on the outside, even though you hate crawling out of bed to go to the bathroom.

You find that you have become the center, pulling them in the way the lake pulls their families back every summer. You are afraid that they are drifting, that one day they will get a job or go to a university that's far away, and you will be alone in a town that only has a population in three digits two and a half months of the year. They have come into your world for their entire lives, but you're not sure how you'll fare in theirs, if they would even want to see you when you try.

You don't want to see the world come down on Alex because you don't want to feel it come down on you.

Chance or reality.

Choose.

3.0

The longer you spend traveling on this, your first quest, the more you feel like your knight masters left far too much out of your apprenticeship. They never mentioned how terrible oatmeal tastes when you can't cook it without dropping in half a cup of cinders. They never mentioned how awkward it is to pitch a tent in the dark. They never mentioned that, away from the castle, all horses turn into beasts of the devil. They never mentioned that you would be lonely.

You're not alone, of course. Quests are not meant for one person, unless there is some decree from the queen or from one of the gods. Your companions are the ones you would have chosen anyway, with skills that complement your own—a mage and a . . . well, a thief, to be quite honest. Both of them are young, like you. The mage you know from the castle. The thief you had never seen before, but the familiarity with which you are treated makes you think the thief is also a spy. Both of them are terrible cooks.

The mage has a writing desk to use when you are in the saddle. You're not sure that you've done anything worth chronicling yet, but the scratch of the pen is constant, and sometimes in the evenings the mage has to make more ink to replace that which has been used up. You caught a glimpse of the pages once: flowers and trees drawn with fine lines, and lettering so tiny you couldn't read it in the seconds you had.

You have absolutely no idea what the thief's job is, and by the time you work up the nerve to ask, you've reached your destination and several things are on fire. Then it is your turn to act, with your bright sword and your strong shield and your noble courage. Mostly, you think, you are very lucky, but the skirmish ends with the dragon laid out at your feet and both of your companions still breathing, so you decide you can't have done too poorly.

The journey back is different. The mage sits closer to you, and asks you to check the pages over to make sure they are accurate. The thief makes fewer cutting remarks and no longer disappears for hours at a time. Most of your gear was lost to dragon fire, but you can all sleep in the same tent, and you do, though you leave your armor in saddlebags with the horses because the smell is pretty bad.

There were other apprentices when you were learning to be a knight, but they were competition. This is different. This is the sum of the parts, though you never really thought of people as parts before, and you're reasonably sure that between the three of you, there's very little you couldn't accomplish.

You miss the solitude of training, though. The hours on horseback, or firing arrows at the practice targets. The study of old battle tactics and military history. There's something to be said for teamwork, but there's something about blessed quiet that you long for, even as you plan for a future with these two by your side.

Space or company.

Choose.

When the mage-teachers pick you, of all your siblings, for further study, you are so proud of yourself you nearly burst. Pride, you know, is not an attractive feature, but your parents are too busy to be proud of all of their children, and gods know, someone should be proud of you, so you are. You do your best to keep it under control.

The classwork is easy, and you all but fly through it. Your

teachers commend your neatness and accuracy, and classmates are outright envious of your memory, and you do your best not to reveal how much effort it costs you to be so brilliant. For some reason, natural talent is considered more worthy than hard work.

In the end, you are chosen to chronicle the first quest of a new knight you've seen a few times around the castle. Like the others, the knight is tall and broad shouldered. You hope that somewhere under that thick skull there is a brain, or this quest is going to be very, very long indeed. The thief you're saddled with, for reasons passing understanding, has enough brain for all three of you. Pride should make this unattractive, but you can't stop looking.

You idle away time and ink with drawings of all the plants you see. Most of them are well recorded already in the archives, but you know that context is important, and it's always possible that you might find something new in the process. You are terrible at making camp, but your mage's fire is perfect, and so neither of your companions complain. You never wander far once the tents are pitched, even though you're always curious about what might be on the other side of the hills in the directions you're not going.

The dragon is beyond anything you might have imagined, and you can hardly watch the knight take it on. This, you realize, will be troublesome when you sit down to write your account of the battle. You decide that most of these must be made-up stories anyway, and resolve to ask both of your companions for their input when the time for writing comes. Now is the time for not being lit on fire, and you do your best to stay out of the way.

You're not used to asking for help, for different insights to use in your work. You suppose it's all right: these two are not your rivals for the teachers' approval. Your name will be the only one affixed to the scholarly work that you produce. All that will matter is that it's your hand that holds the pen.

You won't get famous drawing plants. You won't even get famous teaching other mages their craft. You'll get famous following a knight, this knight, and chronicling battles and victories for public record. It's a victory this time, with the dragon reduced to a smoking pile of scales and ichor at the knight's feet, but next time you might not be so lucky. If you stay home, you'll be nothing. If you venture out, well, it really could go either way.

Privacy or security.

Choose.

You agreed to come on this ridiculous adventure because they promised to feed you. You eat well enough in the city, most of the time, but you have to work for it. Now all you have to do is sit on a horse, follow the others, and there's three meals a day with better meat than you'd ever get from a month of picking pockets.

The horse is the biggest difficulty. The knight tries to teach you how to sit properly and reassures you that your seat is getting better, but the first few days are outright agony. Your feet burn and your thighs burn and your rear, well, suffice it to say that if you had to make a quick escape, you'd be unable to. That is the worst part of all. In the end, the horse becomes accustomed to you and you to it, and the knight smiles at you when you swing up into the saddle, and you wonder how in all hells this became your life.

The mage doesn't notice you very often, because there are so many flowers to draw and only so much daylight.

Your task, you were informed, is to keep the knight and the mage alive. Though both of them are very well trained and the best of their classes, they have not been out in the world before. If they need to buy food, you are to make sure they are not swindled. If their nobility appears to be blocking their ability to get the job done, you are to take care of it.

You are profoundly bored.

The knight assumes that you are companions in truth now, and treats you as an equal. If this bothers the mage, no sign is given. The knight, you realize, believes the stories, and since it is the mage's ilk that have written them down, you can't really be surprised that the mage believes them too. Companions on a quest, bound for life by their mutual triumph over danger, and friends and comrades for eternity. It's a pretty tale, and you wish you could buy into it as they have, but you can't.

You know better, and you know what waits for thieves. If you're lucky, you'll be knifed in the heart by someone you know who is trying to take your place in the gang. If you're unlucky, you'll be caught. Then it's torture for information, which you don't have, and a public hanging, which you would really rather do without. Thieves might get called to go on quests from time to time, but their endings don't change, not for real.

When the knight goes up against the dragon, you and the mage hang back and stay out of the way. The mage is clearly terrified, and you can't say you're not, so you say nothing at all. The knight puts up a good fight. Each swing of the bright sword is slower, though, and each stroke of the dragon's claws against the strong shield seems to put more pressure on what by now must surely be a broken arm. There's no opening for the killing blow, and you don't think the knight can last much longer.

You scream, loudly, and the mage cries out too, more startled than anything else. The dragon looks at both of you, as if aware for the first time that the knight is not alone, and in doing so reveals soft belly to steel. The knight does not miss, and then the dragon is dead at your feet.

They know what you did. The knight believes the stories more than ever now, and the mage is writing yours down as you ride. But still you cannot quiet that restless doubt and consider fleeing into the night before you reach the city walls. They would miss you, maybe, but then they would forget, and you wouldn't have to watch them do it.

Chance or reality.

Choose.

Hurdles
BRANDY COLBERT

"Feeling good about next week?"

My father asks me this before every track meet. The closer we get to an event, the more his questions about my preparedness replace normal inquiries, like asking about my day or how school is going.

"Yup," I say, watching the toaster. He didn't even say good morning.

"You know, some big scouts are going to be there." He opens the cabinet and reaches for his silver travel mug. "Carl from SC and Troy from Arkansas and—"

"I know. You told me. I'm ready."

My two pieces of toast pop up. Dad fills his mug while I slather on butter. He looks over when the knife clangs against the counter and frowns.

"Mavis, what'd I tell you about toast? If you insist on having that over something more rich in protein, you could at least eat it with peanut butter."

"I'll make up for it at lunch." I bite the inside of my cheek so I won't sigh as I walk my plate to the kitchen table.

Probably other people my age have way more exciting fantasies, but my dream come true would be only having to deal with my father at one place: school or home. Not both. Everyone at school loves him—his health and wellness students and my fellow teammates. I love him, but I think I'd like him a lot more if he were just my dad and not my coach too.

Jacob says I'm lucky. His parents don't understand what track means to him. But sometimes I wonder if my relationship with hurdles means more to my father than it ever will to me.

I get my period as I'm walking to my first class and make a detour to the English-wing bathroom. The bell sounds while I'm still standing at the sinks, digging through my bag for a tampon. Shit. I'll have to go up to the office for a late pass.

I take my time walking to the front of the school, thinking about the meet next week. I *am* ready—I'm always ready . . . the part of me that everyone's watching, that is. But something's missing. I used to feel a rush of excitement at least a week before I'd be competing. I used to go online to look at the members of the opposing teams to see who I'd be up against and then picture their faces as I practiced jumping.

This year is different. Dad is being even harder on me than normal because I'm a junior. He says now is when scouts are going to start looking at me, and that if I want to get to the

Olympics, I have to start treating hurdles like they're my job.

The older secretary is working the attendance office. She barely even looks up as she scrawls on the square of paper and rips it from the pad, sliding it across the counter.

"Thanks," I say, and when I turn around to walk back out, I run straight into a guy. I lose my grip on the late pass, and it flutters to the floor. "Sorry," I mumble automatically, bending down to grab it.

When I stand, I'm face-to-face with the love of my life.

"Hey," he says, appraising me with his sleepy brown eyes.

I haven't seen him in three months. I feel like someone has sewn my throat closed. I open my mouth, and all that comes out is air. I swallow and try again. "Hi. Bobby. I . . . Edwina didn't tell me you were coming back today."

He shrugs. "I think she liked it better when I was gone."

We both know he's right, but I don't acknowledge it.

"How are you?"

"Sober," he says with that wry smile that still makes my knees feel like pudding. "Been staying out of trouble?"

"My life is basically school, hurdles, and listening to my dad talk about school and hurdles, so . . ."

Bobby touches my elbow and I try not to melt into a liquid version of myself as he pulls me into the hallway, a few feet from the office door. "You want to get out of here?"

I stare at him. "Didn't you just get here?"

"Yeah, and two minutes back in this place is enough to remind me how much I fucking hate it." He cocks his head to the side. "Got my car back. We could go grab some breakfast.

Or head down to the beach? Your choice."

I can't think of anything I want more than to blow off the rest of the day and spend it with Bobby Neeley instead. I feel like another part of me comes alive when I'm with him. Even when he was just sitting in the same room as his sister and me, not paying attention to either of us, I've always felt better with Bobby around. We've never talked about it, but I think he feels the same way.

"I can't," I say, after the pause has become too long. "I'll have to miss practice if I get detention, and my dad would kill me. I have a meet next week."

There's also the matter of my boyfriend, Jacob. He knows I'm friends with Bobby, and how upset I was when he had to go to rehab. But Jacob is so easygoing and trusting, I don't believe it would even occur to him to think I could have feelings for someone else. And I *like* Jacob. It would feel dishonest to spend a whole day alone with Bobby, no matter how badly I want to.

"You sure?" Bobby raises his eyebrows, like it's possible I could be missing the best day of my life.

"Sorry." I bite my lip. "You should sit with us at lunch, though."

"If I make it that long." He salutes me and starts walking backward into the office. "Good to see your face, Mavis."

"Yeah. You too, Bobby."

The next day after practice, Dad says he has to wrap up a couple of things before we leave and tells me to meet him in his office. But when I get there, Jacob is sitting in the folding chair across from him. They're laughing, and like always, their ease with each other makes me uncomfortable.

I guess that's not fair. My father has been his coach since freshman year, since before Jacob and I started dating. Still, I feel like they should keep things strictly business. I don't like the idea of a guy who regularly sees me naked being all chummy with my dad.

I knock on the doorframe, and they both turn toward me. Both smile. Jacob pats the empty seat next to him, but I decide to stand. "Almost ready?"

Dad slides some papers into a folder. "Sure. I can finish the rest of this at home. Your boyfriend here distracted me."

Jacob grins, and I feel bad that I want to roll my eyes.

"Your mom's working late tonight," Dad says. Like he even needs to announce it at this point. Mom's an attorney at an environmental law firm, and she's working on a big case right now. I feel like I haven't seen her in weeks, and when I do, it's usually just a quick kiss good morning or good night. "So it's just us for dinner. Should we do salmon and brown rice?"

"Um, actually, I'm going to Edwina's for dinner." I pause. "If that's okay."

"You're going to leave your dear old dad to fend for himself?" he says in mock horror. "What if I end up eating ramen noodles?"

"You'll survive," I say. "Or, you know, you could live it up and swing by a Mickey D's drive-through."

Dad gives me a look, then turns to my boyfriend. "Well, what are you doing for dinner, Jacob? Do you like salmon?"

This time my eyes flick toward the ceiling before I can stop them. "I'm going to wait in the car."

I like being at Edwina's house—when no one is arguing. It's a nice house, clean and comfortable and decorated well. And her parents like me. They seem to find it fascinating that I'm good at something physical. None of the Neeleys have ever played a sport in their life. Edwina's father is an executive at a bank, her mother is a wedding planner, and Edwina is managing editor of our school's literary magazine.

Bobby's not particularly athletic or academic, and he always lists that as another reason he's the black sheep of his family.

"I'm mediocre at everything," he once told me at a party.

We were sitting on the back stoop of the house, and I knew I should be inside, looking for Jacob. Instead, I was drinking canned beer with my best friend's brother.

"You are not," I said, leaning back on my elbows.

"Tell me one thing I'm the best at." Bobby took a long swig from his beer. I watched his Adam's apple bob as he gulped down nearly half of the can in one drink.

I hesitated.

"See?" he said, nudging me. "You can't think of anything. Mediocre. At everything besides drinking."

He threw back the rest of his beer.

And I wasn't brave enough to tell him that I hadn't paused for the reason he'd thought. It's just that I wasn't sure how to tell him he was really good at being Bobby, and that was good enough for me.

Dinner at their house isn't so bad tonight. Maybe everyone is on their best behavior because he just got back a few days ago. The worst was when Bobby would come to dinner drunk and everyone could tell but no one would say anything. He picked a lot of fights, and his parents couldn't always keep their cool. Edwina straight up ignored him on those evenings, even the time he screamed across the table that she was a fucking bitch.

One thing I like about eating with Edwina's family is that it doesn't occur to them that I'm supposed to be avoiding certain foods. I put on muscle easily, but I'm still small, so nobody thinks I need to watch my weight. Dad is so obsessed with me staying in optimal shape that it's usually easier to just eat what he suggests. It's not like it's bad food; just boring. But my mouth waters at the smell of the lasagna that Mr. Neeley places in the center of the table, and I'm already thinking about having seconds before he's served the first helping.

After dinner, Edwina shows me a sneak preview of next month's lit mag. She pushes her red-framed glasses up her nose as she scrolls down the layout on her computer screen. Edwina generally dresses like an art teacher—all bright colors and big patterns and prints that don't necessarily go together but look amazing against her dark skin. It's the opposite of what has basically become my uniform: a plain T-shirt, long or short sleeved depending on the weather, but mostly short sleeved because we live in L.A.; dark jeans; and running shoes. Edwina always says I'm wasting my fashion potential, as if I am the sort of person who likes to call attention to herself.

"We still need submissions for our environmental issue," she says pointedly.

"E, stop trying to recruit me." I lie back on her bed and close my eyes. "Writing papers for school is bad enough."

"That's not *creative* writing," she says. "And you should kick ass at environmental topics. Hello, your mom?"

"Sure, I'll just whip up a haiku about her firm suing the shit out of an oil company."

Edwina sighs, but I know without looking that she's only doing so to cover up her smile. My eyes are still closed, and I'm so full from my plateful of pasta and cheese that I start to drift off. When Edwina speaks again, it takes me a moment to catch up.

"Wait, what?" I say.

She sighs again, but this one is heavier. Longer. She's quiet for a moment, then: "Does it make me a horrible person if I say I wish he hadn't come back?"

I keep my eyes closed. I don't answer her right away. Edwina knows how I feel about Bobby. She used to tease me about him when we were younger, but we haven't talked about it in a while. Not since Jacob and I got together. I think a part of her believes that it was a schoolgirl crush and I'm over him. She doesn't understand that my feelings are real.

"You're not a horrible person." I sit up and look at her. She's staring at her computer, but I know she's not seeing what's on the screen. "You're just being honest."

"Yeah, but people use that as an excuse to be a bitch." She meets my eye. "I don't want to be a bitch. But he was really mean to me before he left. For a long time. And now he's sober and we're just supposed to forget how he treated us?"

"He didn't mean it, E."

"Really?" She takes a shuddery breath. "Don't people say what they actually feel when they're drinking?"

"E . . ." I trail off because I don't know what to say. She's right. I cringed my way through more than one of Bobby's bad nights at the dinner table, but I guess a part of me hoped that once Edwina realized what was really going on with him, she'd forgive him for the awful things he said. That maybe his problem with alcohol would trump his vicious outbursts . . . even if he did mean what he was saying.

"He was never mean to you. Not around me," she says.

I sweep my box braids up in one hand and let them fall down around my shoulders. I don't know what to say to that, because she's right. Bobby has never said a mean word to me, not even at his drunkest.

I stay for another half hour, but it's not the same. I pretend to be overly interested in Edwina's short story, and she pretends not to notice how hard I'm trying. She once told me that I always seemed to take Bobby's side, even when he was at his worst. She didn't sound mad at me then, just sad.

Now she looks closed off. Like even though we're best friends, there's a part of her she can't share with me. Like if it came down to choosing between the two of them, she knows Bobby would come first.

I'm halfway down the walk before the front door of the Neeleys' house opens and I hear my name.

"Wait up," Bobby says. "I'll walk you home."

"You don't have to do that," I say, turning around. I only live three blocks away, and it's not too late.

But now he's standing next to me, and we fall into step together. When he was gone, sometimes I worried I would forget how he looked. Bobby hates being in pictures, so pretty much all I had was my yearbook. But I didn't like looking at his posed photograph, with the stiff, unsmiling face. It turned out I didn't need to. I'd never forget him. I memorized every line and curve of his face years ago, along with his strong jaw and the coppery brown of his skin.

The night is cool and crisp, and even though the moon is partly shielded by clouds, it feels like a perfect February night in Los Angeles.

"I know Edwina hates that I'm back," he says, digging his hands deep into the front pocket of his hoodie. "I'm honestly not sure my parents feel any different. And that just makes me want a drink. Or ten."

He doesn't look at me, so I don't look at him either.

"Have you called your sponsor?" Edwina told me he has one, but I immediately wish I hadn't said anything. That's not something she should be telling people. He should have told me first, or I shouldn't know at all.

"No. It's still weird. Calling myself an alcoholic. Feels like I'm talking about someone else."

This is a conversation for sitting down and looking straight into each other's faces, not one to be had on the go. But we keep trucking along down the street, so quickly it feels like we're seconds away from breaking into a run.

"Well, I won't let you have a drink."

Of course I felt guilty when I found out his parents were shipping him off to rehab. I thought about all the times I'd heard him slurring his words and seen him stumbling around and when I'd been drinking right next to him, knowing he'd had too much. But that wasn't just Bobby, that could be nearly anyone at a party on any given weekend. I hadn't known what was just a good time and when I should have been concerned, because Bobby's life didn't visibly fall apart. He still went to school and he still showed up to dinner each night; it only became an issue when people started smelling liquor on him during the day.

"I know I'm an alcoholic," he says, slowing down his pace just a bit. "But I hate the way that word makes people look at me. My parents don't say it. They won't even say AA."

Edwina told me when he was gone that she doesn't think it's a disease—just a weakness. Their parents feel the same way.

"My sponsor is cool, but he's this old white dude and . . . he's been where I was . . . where I am, but it feels like he doesn't know. What it's like to be me." Bobby stops in front of a house surrounded by clean-cut hedges with an arched wooden door in the middle that leads to the front yard. "Sometimes I think my parents are more worried about how it looks instead of how I'm doing. Like I've shamed our entire race."

This isn't news to me. I've spent more than one dinner at their house where the conversation turns, at length, to all the ways black people are failing black people. I'll never forget the deadly look their father shot Bobby when he brought up the fact that maybe he should examine how the systems set up in this country fail us instead.

"Well, you haven't," I say, wanting to touch him—hold his hand, hug him—but knowing I shouldn't. Even if he doesn't want me like I want him, it would be disrespectful to Jacob. "You got help, like they wanted. You haven't had a drink in three months."

"Three months, six days, and two hours." He sighs. "Do you ever just want to get the fuck out of here?"

"L.A.?" I look around at the manicured lawns and hear the song of the crickets and feel the cool breeze that rustles the tree leaves and floats over my face. "I don't know, it's not so bad. Maybe not as pretty as Santa Barbara—"

I stop. I shouldn't be so flippant about his rehab.

But Bobby shakes his head and pushes down his hood, running a hand over the top of his tightly packed curls. "Not like that, just, like . . . do you ever want to start a new life?"

I swallow hard, trying not to think about the fact that it sounds like he's leaving again. How he'll be eighteen in a couple of months and soon his parents will have no say in anything he does.

"I don't know." I haven't thought about that, not really. But I don't want him to feel more alone than he already does.

He doesn't say anything else about it. We spend the rest of our walk in silence. It's not uncomfortable, and I wonder what he's thinking, but I don't want to break the easy way we have of being around each other.

When we get to my house, the porch light is on. Dad's car is in the driveway, but the space behind it, where Mom parks hers, is still empty.

"I'd invite you in," I say, "but . . ."

"Yeah, it's getting late. I just wanted to make sure you got home okay." Bobby gives me a tight smile.

"Are you sure *you're* okay?"

"I'm fine. I'm gonna call Ray. My sponsor," he says in response to my confused look.

"Oh. Well . . . you know you can call me if you need anything, right? Anytime."

"Yeah." Bobby nods, and his smile loosens. Grows a little wider for me. "Night, Mavis."

He stands at the curb and watches me. While I walk to the porch and get out my key and turn it in the lock. He watches until I'm safely inside.

The next night, Jacob comes over to do homework. My dad is at some coaches' meeting and Mom has another late night at the office, so Jacob brings over dinner from the burger stand we like on Fairfax.

It surprised me how easily I slipped into the *we* with Jacob. He was my first everything: crush who liked me back and did something about it. Kiss. Sex. I noticed him the first week of track practice our freshman year, just like anyone else who's attracted to guys. He's objectively good-looking, with thick honey-blond hair and dark green eyes and a smile that lights up the entire school and is almost always meant for me.

I think what surprised me the most about Jacob is how comfortable I am around him. I never assumed I would feel so relaxed with any guy but Bobby. I don't like to think about it too much—I don't feel for him what I feel for Bobby, but I've given more of myself to Jacob. Physically, of course, but I'm honest with him in a way that I'm not with Bobby. Maybe because I know Jacob can handle it, because he has a family that loves and respects him and believes he's a good person.

I'm still eating by the time Jacob finishes his cheeseburger and fries. He steals one of my tater tots and swipes it through the dollop of ketchup on my plate.

"Your food okay?" He gestures to my mostly uneaten burger on the coffee table. We're sitting on the floor, in front of the couch.

"It's good, I'm just . . . I don't know." It seems like a waste, to not finish my burger when I know I'd get a huge lecture from Dad if he were here to see it. I should at least be able to enjoy my secret rebellion.

"Nervous about the meet? I watched you today at practice. You looked fucking awesome."

"Yeah? Tell that to my dad. He thinks . . ."

"What?" Jacob brushes his hands on his jeans, still looking at me.

"Nothing."

"Mavis, it's not nothing. Come on. It's me. What's up?"

I take a deep breath. "Sometimes . . . I just think maybe I'll never be good enough for him. I felt like I had a good practice too. One of my best in a while. Then he said my touchdown time had improved on the fourth hurdle, but I'm still slow off the block."

"Well . . ." Jacob sighs. "You know he pushes us because he cares."

"I live with him," I say. "I've heard that more than anyone."

"Fair enough." He hesitates. "Sometimes I'm jealous of you."

"Of *me*?"

"Yeah. You and your dad. He really does care about you."

I push my plate across the coffee table and bring my knees up to my chest. "Your dads care about you."

"Yeah, they're great. But I feel like I don't have anything in common with them." Jacob pushes his hair out of his eyes. "They think sports are a school thing. They'd probably get it if I wanted to run in college, but it'll never be a career to them. And your dad—"

"My dad will be severely disappointed if I don't make it to the Olympics," I say flatly.

Dad doesn't talk about it often, but he was close to getting there himself. He tore his ACL during the trials and that was it for him. It's so clichéd, him wanting me to succeed where he couldn't; coaching because he never went pro.

"You're gonna get there, Mavis." Jacob puts his hand on my knee and gently rubs. "It's not even a question."

Jacob believes in me the way I believe in Bobby. He always thinks the best of me, and sometimes I wonder if I deserve it. Then sometimes, when I start feeling too bad about how much more he likes me than I like him, I let myself wonder if he really likes me for me or if it's because I *am* good enough to get to the

Olympics. Or because I'm the coach's daughter.

So I kiss him. His lips are soft and sweet as ever. Familiar. And maybe, if I keep myself busy with him, my mind will stop going to places it shouldn't.

Maybe then I won't keep thinking about what Bobby said. About leaving.

I'm walking through the hall by myself, on my way to the cafeteria to meet Edwina and Jacob, when someone gently grabs my arm from behind. I stop, and before I even turn around, I know it's Bobby.

"I'm taking the afternoon off," he says. "Come with me."

"I seriously can't." I look down at my feet and then at him. His eyes are so deep, deep brown; so intense that I'm afraid to keep meeting his gaze. I feel like they're going to convince me to do something I shouldn't.

I thought I might feel differently about him when he was away. I wrote to him once, but he didn't reply. I didn't expect him to, and I took that as a sign. That I was meant to be with Jacob. That whatever I'd felt about Bobby before he was gone would simply fade into nothing in his absence. I didn't think it would come back like this. Stronger. Harder to ignore.

"We'll just drive around. I'll have you back by your next class. Promise."

I don't say yes, but I don't protest, either. And whatever he sees in my eyes makes him take my arm, lead me away. He knows the door we should use to avoid being seen on the way to the parking lot. I stare straight ahead, afraid that whatever spell I'm under will break if I look anywhere else. I'm terrified that I will look up and see Edwina. Or Jacob. Or, maybe even worse, my father.

But suddenly, I'm not terrified of getting in trouble. I'm with Bobby. His fearlessness makes me feel stronger, even if I know he's no stranger to the consequences of his actions.

His car is clean inside, but a bunch of empty soda cans litter the floor, and I've never seen him smoke, but it smells vaguely of cigarettes. Maybe a new habit he picked up in rehab? I don't ask.

"Where should we go?" He's pulling out of the space before I've buckled my seat belt. He may be brave enough to sneak out, but he's not stupid. We still need to get the hell out of here before someone sees us.

"I don't know."

I stare down at my lap. Would I do this with Jacob? Or would I tell him he's crazy, that there's no way we could pull it off, that we should just go to the cafeteria before all the good greens are gone from the salad bar?

"Burritos?"

I say yes immediately. Even though I know it will sit heavy in my stomach for the rest of the afternoon, maybe until dinnertime. Even though I've been eating like shit this week—lasagna and burgers and now this. I'm really going to have to step it up at practice. The meet is only a few days away.

Bobby doesn't say much, and that makes people nervous, to never know what he's thinking. But I've only ever felt comforted by that silence. It feels thoughtful. And so it's not weird to me at all that we don't really talk until we're halfway through our lunch.

"It's claustrophobic here." Bobby dumps more salsa over his chicken burrito.

"In this place?" I look around. We missed the big lunch rush. We're practically the only people in here.

"No, I mean . . . being back. Here. My life."

He takes an enormous bite and chews for what seems like forever. I wait. And when he's done, I blurt, "Are you leaving?"

He shrugs. "Thinking about it."

I exhale. "Where will you go?"

"Dunno. Maybe somewhere up north."

I stare down at the table. At the crumpled napkins between us, and the spilled salsa pooling on the table next to his arm. I don't know what to say. And he pauses so long, it feels like a good-bye.

Until he says, "You wanna come?"

Jacob is waiting for me by the girls' locker room before practice begins.

"Where were you at lunch?" His voice isn't possessive, just curious. He slides his arm around my shoulders as we walk.

Bobby and I didn't get caught, but I was too anxious to skip the rest of the afternoon with him. He dropped me off like he'd promised and told me to walk in like I owned the place. I did. Nobody stopped me.

"I had to do some research," I say. "For history. Sorry I forgot to tell you."

"It's cool," he says, squeezing me to him. I try to relax, but my whole body is tense, like a rubber band ready to snap in half.

"Edwina was freaking out about Bobby."

I turn my head to look at him as we walk. "About what?"

"He's been skipping classes. Their parents are pissed."

"Oh." His skipping classes is going to be the least of their problems soon if what he said is true. That he's probably leaving.

"Mavis!"

Shit. My father.

Jacob and I stop and turn and wait for him to catch up. The legs of his athletic pants swish together as he strides toward us.

"Hey, Jacob." He greets my boyfriend with a grin. "I need to talk to Mavis for a minute. See you out there?"

"Yeah, Coach." Jacob returns his smile and briefly turns it on me before he continues down the hall.

My heart thumps and thumps as I wait for my father to speak. Maybe he does know I skipped out for a while. I take a deep breath. Prepare myself for his lecture.

"Honey," he begins, and that's weird. Because he doesn't exactly call me honey when he's mad at me.

I blink at him.

"Is everything all right with you?"

My heartbeat instantly slows. "Sure, Dad. Why?"

"You haven't seemed like yourself this week, and I'm wondering . . . is it the meet?"

If only.

But I can't say it's something else, because then he'll want to have a big discussion about how I can't let myself get distracted. How I have to keep my eye on the prize. Keep excelling at what we've been working for all these years.

We.

I clear my throat. "I guess . . . I guess I'm a little nervous."

"I thought so," he says, practically smiling. Jesus. Since when should someone else's anxiety be a source of relief? "Look, I understand. It's getting down to crunch time, when you have to prove yourself. I've been there."

I chew on my bottom lip so I'm not tempted to say that we're not in the same position. I care about jumping hurdles. I love it. I feel my best when I'm sailing over them on the spongy clay-colored track. But I don't love it as much as he did. Or does now. And maybe I never will.

"But the scouts are coming to see you because they know you're one of the best," he says. "You know that too. And I know you don't want to let them down."

I nod, even though this is probably the worst pep talk I've ever heard.

"Stay focused, okay, honey? You've just gotta stay focused until next week. I don't want to see you getting preoccupied with other things during practice. We need to improve your start off the block. . . ."

I zone out. It's the only way I can handle this.

I wonder what would happen if I didn't show up to the meet. If I just disappeared. I wonder what would happen if no one could find me afterward, either.

When I tune back in, he's staring at me. Saying, "Okay, honey?"

I nod again. Smile so he'll think I not only heard him but

appreciate the feedback. "Okay, Dad. Thanks."

We walk together down the quiet hallway. Everyone has either gone home or split off into their after-school practices and meetings. Dad pauses by the door that leads to the athletic field, his fingers gripping the handle.

"And Mavis?"

I look up. "Hmm?"

"No more cheeseburgers until after the meet."

I told Bobby I didn't know.

I've been thinking about it nonstop, his question. All weekend, I could hear his voice no matter what I was doing. Brushing my teeth, reading for English lit, talking to my father about the upcoming meet.

"You wanna come?"

I figured he'd make the decision for me, leave when he wanted to leave and not tell me until it was too late or I had to choose at the last minute. He doesn't wait for anyone to get on board with what he wants.

So I'm surprised when he's standing by the fence after track practice on Monday afternoon. I let the girls on my team file past me on their way back to the locker room and take my time making my way up the hill to where he stands. It's warm out for late February, even in L.A., and he's wearing a black T-shirt with Eric B. and Rakim lyrics printed on the front. I'm sweating everywhere and stand back a bit in case I stink.

"Thought any more about it?"

He doesn't have to clarify what *it* is. Obviously it's the only thing on his mind, and he must know the same is true for me too.

"Yeah, I . . . I don't know."

We'd essentially be running away. And when people run away, they need to have something to run *from*, right? People don't just pick up and leave everything they know when they have a good life . . . do they?

Maybe they do for love.

Bobby nods. "All right. Well, I'm leaving tomorrow night."

The big meet is in two days.

I wipe perspiration from my forehead with the back of my arm. "You haven't told Edwina?"

"Fuck no. You kidding?" His eyes widen the most I've seen them in a long time. "You haven't said anything?"

"Of course not." Out of the corner of my eye, I see the boys are finishing up their practice. Jacob will be walking by soon. "I wouldn't do that."

"I know." Bobby's voice is even quieter than normal. "Look, I know it sounds crazy, Mavis. But I wouldn't ask just anyone. I think . . . you and I . . ."

I stare at him.

"I don't know if I could give you everything you have here. Maybe someday. But I promise I'd take care of you the best I could."

He can't even take care of himself.

That's what Edwina would say, and I hate that I'm hearing her voice right now, during one of the biggest moments of my life. Bobby isn't much for words, but what he just said . . . it's the equivalent of what I feel for him. I know it.

"What time tomorrow?"

"Late. After our parents go to bed." And the look on his face is so surprising, so un-Bobby, that it takes me a few seconds to place it: hope.

"I don't have a lot of money," I say, though I probably have more than him. His and Edwina's parents do well, but they cut him off even before he went to rehab. What little he has is saved up from the part-time job he used to have as an excuse to get out of the house.

"We can get jobs."

"What about school?"

What about the Olympics? What about my future?

I don't say that last part aloud, but the impatience more than flickers on his face. It lingers. I'm being too technical, asking too many questions about a future he's purposely trying not to plan.

The chatter from the guys makes its way over to us as they walk up to the school. Jacob looks over. I can't read the expression on his face, but he doesn't look as happy to see me as he always does. His eyes shift to Bobby. He doesn't look at all pleased to see him. Has Edwina been complaining more about her brother?

Or can he finally tell, after a year of being with me?

Jacob looks away first. Jogs to catch up with one of his teammates and claps him on the back to get his attention. But I watch him until he gets to the door. He glances back at me once more before he slips inside.

Bobby sighs. "Look, Mavis . . . I don't have all the answers. Except that I have to get out of here. And I want you with me."

He reaches out into the sliver of space between us and slides his hand along my hip. Under the fabric of my tank top and along the light brown skin just above the waistband of my gym shorts. I shiver all over.

He doesn't touch me anywhere else, and he doesn't try to kiss me. He doesn't have to.

I go about the next day like it's any other day of the week, of my life.

I eat lunch at our usual table and fawn over the new issue of the lit mag, hot off the presses. When Edwina pesters me about submitting, I say that maybe I'll send her something for the next issue. She beams so hard it makes my heart hurt.

I'm extra sweet to Jacob. He didn't say anything about see-ing me with Bobby, but I make sure to hold his hand between classes, and I change quickly before practice so we can walk outside together.

But every single moment of the day has a new significance. I wonder if it will be the last time I do all of those things, if this is the last chapter to the book of Mavis as I know it.

My mother's car pulls into the driveway a few minutes after Dad and I get home. I stare out the living room window as she walks up the path. She hasn't been home before ten o'clock in at least two weeks.

"Don't look so surprised," she says with a tired smile. "I'm not officially living at the office."

"Are you done with the big case?" I ask as she kisses my cheek.

She swipes at my face with her thumb, removing traces of her lipstick. "Almost. I'm going back after dinner, but I couldn't stomach another night of eating takeout across from Patrick and Lisa."

Dad can barely stop smiling through dinner. I watch him being cute with Mom at the table, and I wonder if he'd back off a little if she were around more. I know that's not fair. She's not always this busy, and she makes time for me when she's home. But it's nice to get a break, to have someone else at the table to distract him from going over stats for the millionth time or monitoring how much and what I'm eating.

"I'll get the dishes tonight, Mavis," Dad says when I start to clear our empty plates.

"Yes, you should go up and rest," Mom says after taking a sip of water. "Word on the street is you have a big meet tomorrow."

I shrug, even though I know my apparent apathy kills Dad. He doesn't have to tell me the meet is all he's thought about for the last forty-eight hours.

"I know I haven't been around much lately, but I'm going to try to make it tomorrow, okay, sweetie?" she continues. "I love watching you fly over those hurdles."

"Our girl's looking great," Dad says. "I can't wait for them to see her."

I kiss them and hug them and say good night, even though I know Dad will pop his head in before he goes to bed. I keep it together until I leave the room, but when I get to the stairs,

I feel that familiar ball of pressure behind my eyes and nose, like I'm going to cry. Only no tears come. And what kind of monster does that make me? What if that's the last time I ever see my mother?

I go up to my room and open my notebook and textbooks as if I'm going to start on my homework, same as any other weeknight. But I sit down at my desk only for a minute before I'm in my closet, rummaging through shoes and boxes for my largest duffel.

Bobby said to pack light, and I stare at my room helplessly as I wonder what I should leave behind. The clothing is easy—it's everything else I can't figure out. Do I take whole photo albums to remember every important thing that's ever happened, or just a few pictures with Mom and Dad and Edwina and Jacob in them? And what about my medals? There's a good chance I won't be running hurdles again for some time, if ever, but will bringing along reminders of my accomplishments weigh me down?

Mom leaves again for the office, and I slip my duffel back into the closet when Dad sticks his head in to say good night.

"You're going to do great tomorrow, honey," he says, leaning against the doorframe. "I'm proud of you."

"Thanks," I say. And then I wonder if I should say something bigger, something more substantial to tide him over until I see him again.

Like "I couldn't have done it without you" or "Sometimes it really sucks, but I know you're only so tough on me because you want the best for me." Or even just "I love you, Dad."

But the words get stuck in my throat. So I smile at him and he closes the door and I listen to him walk down the hall. Hear the water turn on in the shower, and then rustling around for the next twenty minutes until he flips on his sound machine and gets into bed.

Bobby texts a few minutes later and says he'll be by to get me in an hour. He'll park down the street and I'm to go out and meet him and tonight we will start our new life.

I didn't know I was going to say yes. Looking into his eyes yesterday afternoon, feeling his hand on my hip like I was already his, it was hard to say no. I didn't think about what happens if he starts drinking again, that no matter how much I try to help him, he's going to do what he wants. Will he go to AA meetings on the road? Find a new sponsor? We didn't talk about it.

And I'm old enough to get a job, but neither of us has any real skills. Will I have to serve up burgers I'm not supposed to eat or sell crappy clothes in a mall, because those are the only things I'm qualified for? College was never a choice—it was an expectation, but not just from my parents. I've always known I'll be on the track team wherever I go, but I like the idea of having a degree that says I put in the time, that I'm especially knowledgeable about a particular subject. I could get my GED, but it seems wrong when you grow up the way I did, full of support and love and encouragement.

Those tears finally spring to my eyes when I think again about my parents. My dad isn't always the easiest person to be around, and my mother is hardly around at all for many weeks at a time, but they're genuinely good people. And no matter what, if I leave like this, they're going to think it's their fault. They're going to worry. Even if I tell them I'm safe and with Bobby, they won't ever feel at ease. My father might never forgive me for wasting everything I've worked toward. I can't even think about how Edwina will take the news. Or what Jacob's face will look like when he realizes he didn't know me at all.

I could let Bobby go, alone, but the churning in my stomach lets me know that I'd worry even more if he ran away without me.

I want—I *need* to tell him all of this, but I just keep turning my phone over in my hands every time I start to call or text. I don't want to disappoint him. He'll tell me everything will be okay, that we'll figure out a way to make things work because we're us. We'll be together and that means everything will be all right.

I sit on my bed, my packed bag at my feet, and stare at the clock above my desk until it says he will be here in ten minutes.

My palms sweat as I pick up the phone. He answers on the second ring. "Hey there. What's going on?"

Jacob's voice is drowsy.

"Were you asleep?"

"Mmm, not totally. Always awake for you. Something wrong?"

I pause for too long, hoping he'll figure it out and force me to confess. But he *was* asleep. I can tell by the way he can't stop yawning and how his voice never picks up to its normal speed. He might not even remember I called in the morning.

"No," I finally say in a small voice. "Nothing's wrong. I just wanted to say good night. And I love you."

We've said it before. The first time was months ago, and I've always felt like a bit of a fraud, because while there is so much I love about Jacob, it's not the love I know I'm capable of.

It will never be the same as the love I have for Bobby. And there's no rule that says you have to love everyone equally, but I know the two should be reversed in my heart.

"Love you too, Mavis. Get some sleep. Big day tomorrow."

He hangs up with the softest click, will probably be asleep again within minutes.

I pace my room, drinking in every last detail with my eyes because taking a picture seems like it would be cheating. If I'm going to run away, it has to be all or nothing. Which is why I didn't pack any of the photo albums. Or photos. Except for the one of my parents on their wedding day that is my favorite, the one I took from their album and have had propped up on my desk for years. I've always liked it best because they look so in love, but it seems like a good one to have so I can remember they were happy before I came around. They can be happy without me.

I nearly jump across the room when Bobby's text comes through.

Outside.

I take a deep breath and I pick up my duffel and walk toward my door. Take one last look before I put my hand on the knob.

And then I stand still. I don't know for how long, but I don't move again until his next text comes through.

Hey, you ready? Need help with your bag?

The tears fall this time, drip all the way down my chin and into my collarbone. Which is more important? The love I have for someone who doesn't have enough, or the love that fills every other part of my life?

I thought I would know by now.

I thought I already knew.

You coming?

The Historian, the Garrison, and the Cantankerous Cat Woman
LAMAR GILES

THEN

We started this dark journey three years ago, me and Jermaine.

My mom, a librarian by trade, had been hired as the new Historian for this godforsaken town of Glen Creek, Virginia. She grew up here, told tough stories about lingering attitudes toward people with brown skin and the kind of hair you didn't see in the shampoo ads. Stories that concluded with her running away to New York when she was eighteen.

There she stayed through her waitstaff-financed college years. A good relationship that changed when two became three. And then single motherhood.

When Glen Creek's former Historian—the grandmother I never knew—got sick and broke the vow to never speak to my mother again, Mom became the prodigal daughter. She came home. And dragged me with her.

Enter freshman Tatiana. Shunned for my "weird" accent

and "city attitude."[1] Unable to bite my tongue when I proved myself a better mathematician than the subpar Pre-Calc teacher and he called me "uppity," I found myself in detention my very first day. Where I met the boy—there for defending some bullied kid, of course—who would change everything.

He wasn't normal. Glen Creek wasn't normal. These were facts everyone seemed privy to but me. Including my mom.

NOW

Jermaine's body, I wanted to touch it, to feel him again. I wanted that now more than ever. Isn't there some saying about that? We should show the ones we love how we feel while they're still here. Before it's too late.

I pressed the back of my hand to his forehead, the way my mother used to when I was feverish. He wasn't cold, exactly. Cooler than a person should be. The pool of blood slowly seeping from beneath him, soaking my papers, oozing to the edge of my desk, reminded me of thawed hamburger meat on brown butcher paper. I snatched my hand away. There's another saying: better late than never. That one's wrong, though.

Around me, the lair shook. Plaster dust rained from the aged ceiling. I considered running and letting Niya bring this place down on her head alone. But let's be honest, if I could leave here—*him*—I would've long ago.

"Stop it, dummy!" I said. "That's a support column."

Niya delivered another punch to the beam. A new set of

---

1.   How was I supposed to know Virginians were so sensitive about the quality of their pizza and their lack of boroughs?

cracks webbed out from beneath her bloody knuckles. It was Jermaine's blood, from where she had carried his corpse, not hers. Physically, Niya's kind[2] had strength and durability that were more than a match for mere concrete. Emotionally . . . she broke well before the pillar did. And that was *dangerous*.

What had she seen out there?

With maximum will, I kept my gaze fixed on her, not letting my eyes dart to the half-dozen puncture wounds along Jermaine's chest and abdomen. Or the shard of bone jutting from his right leg just below the knee. Or the agonized grimace etched on his still face.

Niya roared, whipping her black braids, flinging tears off her sloppy cheeks. When she punched the column that time, the vibrations opened a hole in the ceiling. A dusty display of DVDs fell through. It crashed onto the sparring mat, and low-budget horror/sci-fi movies spun in every direction. A faded yellow sheet of paper that I knew to be a 5 FOR $15 clearance flyer drifted down, arching back and forth like a leaf on the wind.

The punches stopped. Niya watched the flyer until it reunited with the broken display, then faced me. "I couldn't stop it, Tat. I couldn't save him."

"What happened?" I said, noting how detached I sounded. I couldn't help it, yet I wondered if I should make myself sound more emotional. More raw. Wasn't that what I should be feeling, with him lying dead behind me? Was there a protocol for losing your kind-of-a-superhero best friend who you loved

---

2.   Theri, or *therianthrope*: a shapeshifter of the feline aspect. A were-cat. Temperament and all.

with every fiber of your being?

If there was someone to ask, it was Niya.

"I don't know exactly," she said. "It was a routine patrol. Cemetery, hospital, high school. Checking for ghoulies[3] in all the usual spots. Not a damn thing popping all over town. We were planning to call it early, go back to his place, and . . ."

My shoulders slumped like a few of my bones had suddenly gone missing. I gazed into a dark corner, swallowing my hurt the same way I had the first time I saw him stare at her in a way I only dreamed about. Or like when I had a revelation on that Trickster God threat and ran to the lair, only to find them sweaty and kissing against the very column she now tried to destroy.

Niya, being as kind as she was capable of, rephrased. "We were done. Heading home. Then . . ."

She made spastic gestures with her hands; her mouth gaped. As if she was simultaneously trying to recall the unthinkable and describe the unspeakable. Maybe she was.

I still didn't know what the protocols were here, but I was a trial-and-error girl. So I crossed the room and embraced the rage-grieving girl who could easily snap me in two with her bare hands. After a moment of stiff surprise, she hugged me back, and dissolved into hiccups that were really sobs. She lurched against me like her legs might buckle. I spun her toward a nearby chair and made sure she wasn't facing the corpse she'd brought here in a fireman's carry.

---

3. A term of Niya's devising. An overly simplified catchall for the various threats in town.

"Tell me." I pushed my glasses higher on the bridge of my nose, insistent.

"It . . . it wasn't like anything we've seen before. It cut us off on the way to the car. This big Jabba the Hutt–looking blob. I could barely make out details because it was like . . . like . . . the shadows moved with it."

Normally, I'd be half listening, half indexing. Breaking down descriptions into categories and eliminating possibilities. Big—not a leprechaun, sprite, or dwarfish creature. A blob—so, not humanoid. Rule out vampires, zombies, werewolves, or our old nemesis Gentleman Gaunt. Cloaked in shad—

The top of Jermaine's skull. I could see it from here. Saving Niya from the sight meant I was the martyr. God, someone would have to tell his mom.

"It don't make sense, how it took him!" Niya said, drawing me back to her. "Jermaine's almost as strong as me. A little faster. I held its attacks off fine, but it tore through him like paper."

"I . . ." *Think, Tatiana. He's dead, but you have to focus on what's next.* "I never thought I'd say this, but you're correct."

She sneered, a good thing. Our old routine of barely there civility would help her focus.

I turned to a bookshelf, thankful to be looking at anything other than him. "Your power sets are similar. The strength and the speed. That you made it back, and he didn't—"

Something collided with the back of my head. It pistoned my face forward so my nose and mouth smashed into the spine of my Saharan histories tome. Niya's fingers palmed the back of my skull with uncomfortable firmness. "Are you blaming me? You think it's my fault?"

"Listen to my actual words, Niya. I didn't say anything like that." A trickle of blood salt-slimed from my nostril.

"Tat, Tat, the reasonable gnat. Why the fuck are you so calm right now?"

I ripped away from her then. Left chunks of hair behind. I screamed into the face of the girl who once tore the head off a gill-man with no effort at all. "Because one of us has to be! One of us has to think, and lead, and do something now that he's gone! You can't, so it has to be me. Always me with the solutions, always me with the plan. I don't want to plan, I want to mourn and scream and cry. I'm the rock! The one you both come to when you can't punch your way out. So that's why I'm calm. I'm not allowed to be anything else."

Shame masked her, and she flicked loose strands of my hair to the floor. "You are, you know."

"Are what?"

"Crying."

"I—?" Dabbing my fingers at my eyes, I felt the moisture.

Her crazy-ass tantrum seemed at its end, and she handed me two tissues plucked from a box near my computers. I mopped the blood from my lips first.

"I'm sorry," Niya said. "I know you loved him too."

That startled me. Because I could tell she didn't mean platonically.

She kept going. "I'm sorry if I harmed you, and I'm sorry for asking you to find the solution one more time."

"I need to know more about that creature, and we may need to call in help. Maybe the Dusk Thrashers, or the Salem Knight. If that thing's as powerful as you say—"

"I'm not talking about that thing. That thing can wait. I'm talking about Jermaine."

"You mean telling his people?" In my gut, I knew that wasn't on her mind.

"No, Tatiana. I mean resurrecting him."

THEN

It took four times of Jermaine saving me from some unexplained, fantastical threat before he gave up his lame deception and confessed what I already knew. Monsters were real, they ran rampant in our town, and he fought them.

I'd actually deduced it after the first time he swooped in wearing that ridiculous modified football helmet and motorcycle leather (a costume I eventually convinced him to retire), calling himself the Garrison (we benched the name too).

He started in on his origin story. Ancient bloodline, strength and speed, our town built on a broken ley line[4] that draws the Arcane, and so on. He seemed shocked when I cut him off.

"Got it," I said. "I've had it for a while. That costume doesn't change your height, your build, or the way you move. I'm sorry to tell you, but your Garrison voice sounds just like your read-aloud voice in English class. Only gruffer."

"The costume didn't fool you? Even a little bit?"

---

4.   Invisible mystical lines of energy crisscrossing the globe, connecting everything to everything else. Like the World Wide Web, just less pervy.

I patted his thigh, crusty with the green blood of the wood-skinned spriggans[5] he'd slaughtered saving me. "You read the comics; it worked for Batman. I know. It's okay."

"Now I wish I had told you sooner. Your mom made it seem like—"

"My mom? What's she got to do with any of this?"

Silence. No eye contact from a boy who'd just stared down a tree demon. I hadn't been as observant as I thought.

The three of us had a long conversation that night in my mother's study, a book-crammed room once reserved for my grandma. We talked about what the Historian of Glen Creek really did.

If Jermaine was Batman, Mom was Alfred. Dutiful assistant to the town's protector. Jermaine's bloodline wasn't the only one with obligations. When Mom ran away from home as a teen, it wasn't to escape an overbearing mother. She ran from destiny.

But Grandma barely formed sentences now and couldn't tell me and Mom apart most days. The Historian must be whole and present.

The way Mom explained it, she made it seem like a burden. I guess, for one person, it could be. That's when I said, "I can help."

It made sense. Many hands make light work, and all. Two heads better than one.

My offer hung between us. Her answer took too long, so I knew it wouldn't be the one I wanted.

"No," Mom said. "Out of the question."

---

5.   Tree monsters. They don't just live in a tree. They *are* tree.

"Why? It's, like, genetic, right? I'm going to have to do it eventually no matter what."

"We're talking about forces beyond comprehension. Dangers to the body and soul. Get something wrong, and the consequences echo into eternity."

"I'm not afraid." I looked to Jermaine for backup. "You've seen me out there. You know."

He sat silent. Forearms resting on his knees, hands clasped, counting cracks in the floor.

Mom said, "If you don't feel fear over the horrors in this town, then I know you're not ready."

Jermaine stood. "I should go."

"You don't have to," I said.

Mom immediately countered. "No. Get some rest. You've got school tomorrow, and I need to research what's brought the spriggans here. I'll be in touch."

"Yes, ma'am." He leaped nimbly to the windowsill. "Bye, Tat." Then he dropped into the night. It occurred to me that he must've come and gone that way many times as he and Mom kept each other's secrets.

"Mom—"

"You've got school too. Good night."

She turned her attention to some dusty volume.

The next day in school, Jermaine did a clumsy job of avoiding me. Going as far as changing desks in English. Toward the end of the day he saw me coming, dipped into the boys' bathroom. I followed him in.

"Oh, crap," he said.

"This would be the place for it." I sniffed, then decided mouth breathing was a slightly better option. "Why are you acting weird?"

"I was born weird."

"Weirder?"

He threw up his hands, a frustrated surrender. "I gotta stay away from you. All right?"

No. That wasn't all right. Pretty damn far from it. I didn't bother asking why. "My mother doesn't control you or me."

"Except she kind of does. The Garrison needs the Historian. That's time-tested. I don't understand half the shit I end up fighting. Without her, I might mistake a vetehinen for a merman[6] and get my arm ripped off. You know?"

My vision was pulsing; anger had me disregarding the nuances of monster anthropology. "Fuck her and her books. You're my friend. The only one I have here. She can't take you from me."

"I'm sorry for making things tense between you two. Everything's heated right now. It'll have to get better. Like you said, the job's coming to you eventually. Give it time."

I tried. There just wasn't much time left.

Spriggans murdered my mother in her study the very next week.

NOW

"Resurrection? No. Absolutely not!" I swept papers and a few flimsy notebooks into my satchel and retreated up the stairs.

---

6. The only difference between a vetehinen and a merman is who's naming them. They're both troublemakers with fish tails. He does need help.

Niya bounded behind me. We emerged in the surface level of our lair, an abandoned video store once known as Movie Meridian. From the moment I arrived in Glen Creek, I had wondered how such an outdated store survived in the age of streaming and digital downloads.

Easy. Magic.

Run by two warlocks for over a century—first as a general store, then a record shop, finally movies—the Meridian was a safe haven for supernatural beings who fought on the side of good. The couple sacrificed their lives buying Jermaine a few critical moments to close a dimensional breach during last year's Imp Siege. After, we found a will, gifting the store to us.

There we were, in a fully stocked time capsule of VHS tapes and DVDs (not even Blu-rays) that looked like an empty, abandoned storefront to unknowing observers. I circled the *Titanic* cardboard display and skirted the hole that Niya's earlier tantrum had produced. Not fast enough to escape her words.

"Fine. Don't help me, Gnat. I'll do it myself."

I faced her, as irritated by that nickname as her ludicrous proposition. "Really? You needed a flowchart and a coloring book to understand *Captain America: Civil War*. Now, you're going to do universe-altering magic on your own? Please."

She was across the room. I blinked, and she was an inch from my nose. "That movie had a lot of characters. And for Jermaine, I'll do whatever it takes. I'm surprised this is a hard sell for you."

"You and I are irrelevant in this. It shouldn't be done. By anyone."

"Shouldn't and can't are two different things. Is it possible?"

I could've lied. Instead, I hesitated.

"I knew it!" Niya said. "Thank you, Tatiana. I'll find out how myself. I'll comb the earth. You can go back to your life. I'll take care of this."

My head tilted. "You think it's that easy for me? I can feel his gravity pulling on me through the floor. Go back to my life. Him"—I motioned around us—"*This* has been my life longer than it's been yours."

Niya shrugged me off. As usual. "What then? Because I'm thirty seconds away from going on a quest. With or without—"

"I'll help."

She grinned, and her sharp canines seemed overly pronounced. "Dope! Brains and brawn, always a good combo. Now, we have to figure where to start."

"I know where." I made the first steps on our quest and pushed through the Meridian's entrance, triggering the tinkling chimes. "My grandma's house."

THEN

"I don't know how those things got to your mom, but they'll never hurt anyone else like that again. Not if you help me. Just always know I'm here," Jermaine said. "It's me and you."

We stood before my mother's tombstone, rain pouring, drenching us. He wouldn't leave until I was ready. He endured.

For the next two years it was as he said, me and him. Together we tracked the spriggans and eradicated them for what they did to my mother. Then it seemed like every week after, there was some new threat. Sorcerer, monster, god. Creatures from all of our world's myths, and worlds beyond. Some good, some vile. All drawn to the power seeping from the town's bedrock.

Most of the baddies we killed; some escaped, only to return with a new nefarious plan to take their revenge. As I got better at my inherited Historian role, nothing seemed a match for us. My knowledge, with his strength, was a no-lose combination.

Then, last year, the circus came to town.

The Ringmaster was an earth angel with designs on the Throne of Heaven.[7] He'd taken his show all over the country, into different realities, anywhere he could potentially snatch a creature of the Arcane who might serve in his treachery. While he gathered his forces, he subdued his recruits with magic, and used them as attractions.

COME SEE THE TUMULTUOUS THUNDER LAD!
DO YOU DARE STAND EYE TO EYE
WITH THE GREEK GORGON?
YOU WON'T WANT TO PET *THIS* KITTY!
SHE'S THE CANTANKEROUS CAT WOMAN!

The Ringmaster wanted Jermaine for his collection. He actually succeeded in capturing him, and he was ready to hop to another reality when I brought in an old ally, Father Reagan. A priest who caged exorcised demons in his own soul, drawing on their powers to fight darkness.

Father Reagan and Jermaine defeated the Ringmaster and freed the exhibits. Most of them scattered. One stayed.

---

7. That oldie but goodie.

The Cantankerous Cat woman.[8] Jermaine befriended her while he was the Ringmaster's captive. Her real name was Niya.

He welcomed her with open arms, saying we could use her help. It was no longer just me and him. That was the first promise he broke.

It wouldn't be the last.

NOW

My house was on the other side of town. Not a long drive, three or four miles through empty streets lined by old shops and older trees. While the scenery scrolled by quickly, tension in the car has a way of stretching time. I wrenched my hands on the steering wheel, willing our destination closer.

Niya couldn't sit still, shifting restlessly the whole time. Part of it may have been her feline nature. Part of it had to be second thoughts. She was an idiot on so many things. Even she couldn't feign ignorance when it came to the forces of life and death.

"What's at your house? Spell books? Potions?" she asked, a tiny plastic shaving curling from the door handle where she nervously dug one claw.

"No," I said, resisting the urge to bop her on the nose so she'd quit treating my car like a scratching post. "The Historian isn't a sorcerer. I have reference books there that mention the sort of magic you'll need. There are incantations in some of my books, but that's not enough."

"Why not?"

"Because you can't just read a spell and make magic. Maybe

---

8. Even a vicious monster like the Ringmaster got it right sometimes.

someone can recite some"—I made air quotes with one hand—
"'cursed Latin' or whatever in a movie and summon the dead,
but in real life just having a spell is like just having bullets. You
still need the actual weapon."

"What kind of weapon?"

"Willpower. You have to have intention, and an elevated
understanding of the forces you're dealing with. Most of the
time, that's still not enough. Your most powerful magic—the
kind that truly alters reality the way you want—needs a sponsor. Some being outside of our world."

"A demon," Niya said.

"More things live outside than we'll ever know. But yeah,
in some cases a demon. I know of some volumes that will point
you in the right direction."

"Me? Not us? I thought you were helping."

"I'm still contemplating what constitutes as 'help' in a situation like this."

"Let me clarify. Bringing back Earth's protector is help. Our
world needs the Garrison."

That stupid name. "Even if he comes back wrong?"

Nothing to say. She'd been thinking about it too.

"Shit!" I said as Trenton Street sailed by. "That was my
turn."

"Sorry I distracted you with saving the life of our friend."

More than a friend. For both of us. You know that, Mean Kitty.

The median on the street prevented me from popping a
spontaneous U-turn, so I'd need to drive a couple of blocks
before course correcting. Time I'd use to simplify this for the

kindergartner in my passenger seat. "I've thought about this way more than you, Niya."

"How? You didn't know anything was wrong until I brought Jermaine to Meridian."

"Because when I thought about it, it wasn't for Jermaine."

"So, who—?" She stopped short. Good. She got it.

"As you can probably tell, my mom's not around. There are reasons."

I waited for a reaction, prepared to deliver a stunning diatribe that I knew wouldn't change anything. Niya's attention was elsewhere.

"Stop the car," she said.

We were passing a park. I peered through the passenger window into the inky night beyond its low border wall. "For what?"

"Stop the car! Someone's in trouble!"

My brakes squealed when I mashed them. Niya ejected from her seat, hitting the sidewalk in a tight roll, then hopped the wall in a single bound before I came to a complete stop. She loped along on all fours for speed, and I lost her in the night.

Popping my trunk, I ran to the back of my car for the things I'd need. Armed, I sprinted into the park after her.

Screams and growls drew me toward the park's center. I'd been working out some, but there's not a ton of cardio in Historian work. I was huffing and puffing by the time I reached the melee.

Sprawled on the ground, pressing a hand to a sloppy gash on his leg and muttering incoherently, was a man I'd seen sleeping on various benches around town over the last couple of weeks. He scrambled away from the tornado of teeth and claws spinning in the center of a misshapen huddle. Niya was fully transformed, her dagger teeth protruding from her jaws, her fingers hooked, the tips rugged and sharp as serrated blades. She tore through a group of waxy-skinned beings with elongated limbs and stretched necks. When one whipped a tongue at Niya, slicing her at the shoulder, I recognized them as akanames. Filth lickers.[9]

Their nickname was a misnomer. They didn't lick filth. They licked flesh. Right off the bone.

The new wound amplified Niya's fury. She flipped over a charging akaname, ripping through the back of its neck while she was in the air. A few vertebrae skittered across the lawn like tossed dice as the akaname collapsed and melted into bubbling rot. She landed and rammed a hand through the stomach of another. When she flung it off her arm, it dissolved before it hit the ground.

One of the two remaining monsters went for another tongue wound. Niya slipped an escrima stick from a loop on her belt and put it between her and the deadly sinew. The creature's tongue coiled around the stick, snapped it in half. As it retracted, taking a chunk of the weapon with it, the akaname didn't account for the wooden shard it had left in Niya's hand. She raced the tongue back to the creature's snarling mouth and jammed the makeshift stake right through its eye.

I'd seen her in action before. Always knew how lethal she

---

9.   Think frog people with tongues you could use to shave your legs.

was in a fight. There was something more in her now. A rage and determination. There were five stages to grief, and one was anger. I knew where she was in the process.

While anger could fuel strength, it also dulls senses. Niya wasn't aware of the akaname behind her, about to strike a killing blow.

So I tackled it. Awkward.

It hissed and writhed. The bones beneath its loose skin seemed to realign as it attempted to twist off its belly into the position better suited to bite my face off. Best not to give it the chance.

Pulling the ceremonial dagger from my bag, I drove it into the beast three times. Lung, lung, head . . . assuming I'd remembered its anatomy correctly. It still writhed, but weaker. The hissing became moist. I kept driving that dagger into its skull. Over. And over. And over. And over. And . . .

"Tat." Niya snagged my wrist, stopping another downward swipe. She yanked me off the thing as it dissolved into a black puddle.

My head whipped about. The homeless man who had drawn us here hobbled off in terror. The hospital was nearby. They'd help him.

Niya's face shifted back to her human form; the claw looping my wrist transitioned from rough pad to soft palm again. She let me go, and I lowered my arm, still gripping the dagger's hilt hard enough to make my hand ache.

She panted, wide-eyed, excited. It's been said her kind gets aroused by battle. "Damn, Tat. You whaled on that frog creep.

Jermaine told me he'd been training you."

I stiffened. "You two talk about me a lot?"

"No."

That stung. I tried not to let it show, though her freaky cat ass could probably hear my heartbeat change or smell my disappointment.

From my bag I drew a bottle of water, passed it to her. "Here. Hydrate."

Snatching it, she just about tore off the top and lapped it greedily. When half the bottle was gone, she angled the open end toward me, but I waved her away. Never believed that "cat's mouth is cleaner than a human's" stuff. "That's all you."

More greedy gulping. Then, "What were those things?"

"Does it really matter?"

"I've never seen anything like them before. Where'd they come from?"

"This is Glen Creek. Where does anything come from?"

Her breathing returned to normal. Her shoulders slumped as the weight of the evening returned. "Guess you got a point."

"Let's get going."

Returning the bloodstained dagger to my satchel, I led her back to the car. To get this over with.

My house was off a main road, at the end of a rutted driveway. The path was bordered by unkempt cotton fields, where dingy white puffs blanketed acres and acres.

"Is this a plantation?" Niya asked.

"Used to be."

"Is there some spiritual significance to the Historian living here? Something to do with the blood of slaves? The darkness of centuries-long oppression?"

I shrugged. "I think my grandparents just got a good deal on it."

"Oh."

I parked before the massive wraparound porch, and we climbed the plankboard steps together, wood creaking beneath our weight. When I gripped the door handle, I hesitated. "My grandma's in here. She gets confused sometimes. Okay?"

Niya nodded and flicked her hand in a hurry-up gesture.

Inside, the foyer was so brightly lit that the pastel-blue walls seemed to glow. I went for the stairs, but Grandma rolled from the den, her motorized wheelchair humming.

I said, "Hi, Grams."

Her eyes fixed on me, bounced to Niya. Then, "Something's wrong."

"Everything's fine, Grams. We're just going to go upstairs and—"

She ignored me, maneuvered her chair closer to Niya, who said, "Ma'am."

Grandma said, "Janet is in so much pain. I can tell."

Niya's eyebrows furrowed. I waved her along. "We'll be in the study."

I climbed the stairs, and Niya seemed to have an internal debate about leaving my grandma. I said, "It's all right."

Niya joined me, whispered, "Who's Janet?"

"My mom. Told you, she gets confused."

From the second-floor landing, we entered the study, and Niya got her first glimpse of the organized confusion that was the Historian's library. Every shelf was crammed and bowed in the middle. Every horizontal surface was covered with dried-up pens, loose sheets, and legal pads. None of the visible paper was untouched by my careful, meticulous script.

The Cantankerous Cat Woman spun slowly in the center of the room, overwhelmed by it all. "You did all this? Why?"

"Elevated understanding. The Historian has to know this stuff better than anyone, and it's dense. I have to rewrite many things for my own interpretation. Notes and footnotes,[10] all the time."

Bouncing between a few specific shelves, I pulled select volumes and stacked them on a desk. Little pastel tabs protruded from marked pages, and when I opened the books some of my Sharpie-covered Post-it Notes unstuck and littered the floor.

"How can I help?" Niya asked.

"Do you read ancient Sanskrit?"

She blinked. "I'll sit quietly in this corner."

"Thanks."

That's how we were for the next hour. Me jotting down more notes, her awaiting my recommendations for doing the thing she shouldn't do. When the silence got to be too much, she said, "I'm sorry about how things happened, Tat."

"Things?" I stopped writing, though I kept my eyes on my work.

"I didn't come here to get between you and him."

---

10.   I love footnotes.

"I know. He explained. We don't have to talk about it."
Please, stop talking about it.

"We do, though. It's been weeks, and we're . . . I don't know.
Coworkers."

"What we do isn't the late shift at McDonald's. With all
that's at stake, I know how to manage my personal feelings."

"Except that's not true."

Slowly I rotated my chair to look into her stony amber eyes.

She kept going. "I think you want everyone to see this cool,
unflinching genius—and you are a genius. But no one's as cold
as you try to make us believe. I know he—*we*—hurt you."

Raising my palm, I said, "Stop." I snatched sheets from my
notebook. "Come to the attic. The rest of what you'll need is
there."

"Great talk."

I left my chair, making sure my satchel was still with me, and
the ceremonial dagger inside it. Crossed the threshold into the
hall. Grandma was there.

Her chair whined as she positioned it before the door.

Niya, quicker than I ever would've given her credit for, said,
"How'd she get that chair up here? Is there a ramp or something?"

No. There's no ramp.

Niya kept walking, surely thinking Grandma would move,
but stopped short when she collided with an invisible barrier
a foot shy of the study door. She rebounded off what seemed
like thin air. Pushing her hands forward, she pressed her palms
against the unseen wall.

"Tatiana!" She slammed a fist into the obstruction. "What is this?"

I said, "Me correcting a mistake."

Kneeling, with my satchel between my feet, I removed the dagger stained with akaname blood and held it out to Grandma with two hands. "I present the arcane blood of then, and the mortal blood of now." Gripping the hilt, I drew the blade across my left palm, raising a hot red line that quickly spilled onto the floor.

Grandma licked her lips, and her flesh began to meld with her chair, organics and mechanics blending into a shifting, bulbous mass.

"No," Niya said, clearly recognizing the creature my grandmother was becoming as she swelled, filling the hall. Shadows leaped from corners and eaves, drawn to her—it—like a cloak.

I said, "I request an audience with the Pall Merchant."

"Again?" The voice had the timbre of a rockslide and seemed to seep from the walls. It did not come from any human mouth.

My grandma, who hadn't really been my grandma for some years, completed the transformation into the thing Niya had struggled to describe back at the lair. The collector that had killed our lover.

"You did it," Niya said. She flicked her wrists in a manner I'd seen a hundred times, when she exposed her claws. Only her hands remained human. She flicked them again, with the same result. Then she stretched her mouth wide, searching for animal incisors with her tongue.

I retrieved the bottled water from my bag, the one she'd

drunk from in the park. Explained, "It's an old formula. Suppresses mystical abilities for up to a day. Added bonus for being odorless and tasteless."

"You bitch!"

"Name-calling won't do you any good now." I felt the Pall Merchant's presence all around me. The creature filling the hall was an emissary of sorts. A pack mule. The real power didn't bother to manifest fully here. That was okay. It was sort of like doing business over the phone.

The Pall Merchant said, "What is it, Tatiana of Earth Realm?"

"Another deal."

"I'm excited to hear what you offer now."

"I want one of the lives I offered you back."

Niya said, "I'm going to rip out your throat, Tatiana."

"Hmmm," said the Pall Merchant. "My kind isn't in the business of refunds."

"Not a refund. Even exchange. Take the theri instead."

The beast formerly known as Grandma shifted, its sides rustling against the walls. It had no discernible face, but it was definitely examining Niya in whatever manner it was able, somehow transmitting an assessment to its master.

"And which life is it you want returned?"

"Jermaine's."

"Not your mother?"

"No. I want him."

The Pall Merchant chuckled. The sound made my nose bleed. "You always have, haven't you?"

Niya threw her whole body against the barrier. Infuriated madness.

"Stop it!" I told her. "You're getting what you wanted. Jermaine's coming back." I directed my query to the Pall Merchant. "Right?"

"For a valued customer? Deal accepted."

The shadow mass spoke then, in my grandma's voice. "Janet is in such pain. Now Niya will be too."

It spilled into the study, through the invisible barrier, like water through a broken dam. Niya screamed for a long time.

THEN

We sat in the lair, and he kept putting things between us. A desk, chairs. He was nervous in a way that was new. When he told me Niya would be staying in Glen Creek indefinitely, his apprehension made sense.

"I thought her being here was a charity thing. Aren't we supposed to be finding her family or something?"

"We found them."

That "we" was not all-inclusive. "I don't understand. When?"

"You went to New York for that college visit. We got a lead."

The discussion had always been that Niya would find her family. Reunite with them. Leave. "And?"

"They'd been murdered by Gentleman Gaunt. Tat, did you hear me?"

I was supposed to respond. This was a situation where I

should empathize. Or sympathize. I always got them confused. "So, she should find him. Destroy him. We can put her on his trail."

He wouldn't look me in the eye. "I need to tell you something."

"What?"

"You should sit down."

"What is it?" I detected an echo. My shout bounced.

"I have feelings for her."

Laughs. From me. Wild cackling. He looked startled. I stopped abruptly. "Feelings? I go away for a weekend and you have feelings? I'm back now."

"That doesn't really have anything to do with it."

"I'm back now." I crossed the room, slid onto his lap, cupped the back of his neck with one hand, then felt a stirring near my thigh. "Do you feel that?"

Jermaine stood, cradling me in his arms. I expected him to do what he'd done many times when we were alone and there was no immediate threat. I expected him to come back to his senses. I expected too much.

He set me gently on my feet. "We shouldn't do that anymore. It wouldn't be fair."

"For who, Jermaine?"

"Any of us."

He tried to leave, but he let me block his path. "You said it would be you and me. You said nothing would come between us. You said you would love me forever."

"I know I did."

"So . . . ?"

"Things change."

That they do.

Weeks passed. We didn't talk in school. In the lair, all we discussed were current supernatural threats. Somehow he arranged it so the three of us were never together in the Movie Meridian basement at the same time. And like a typical stupid boy, he thought that would be enough to make things right. Then I walked in on them, and nothing could ever be right.

He suited up to go on patrol—with her, though he tried to be slick and not say it flat out. Like I'm stupid. Me? Stupid?—I offered him a bottle of water. "Here," I said. "Hydrate."

He drank it all and thanked me. Part of me wanted to be there when his powers failed. To see him blindsided. Ruined. And maybe, before he took his last gasp of air, when he looked to the sky for answers, I'd lean over him and say, "Things. Change."

But that would just be petty. Wouldn't it?

NOW

My mouth, pressed to his. Jermaine's lips were icy then. I didn't flinch away, and soon the warmth bled back into them. Our bond, with the help of the Pall Merchant's magic, pulled his essence back into his meat, knitting his wounds, refilling him. When he drew a ragged breath, taking some of the air from my lungs, I pulled away.

His eyes snapped open, and he sat bolt upright, as if waking from a nightmare. "What happened? That thing, where is it?"

He swung his legs to stand. Papers, tacky with his blood, plastered his back and knees. When his feet touched ground, his knees buckled. I caught him before he fell.

"You're moving too fast. Sit. Rest," I said.

He didn't fight, but I felt his neck crane. Heard the recently dead tendons creak. "Where's Niya? She was with me when I got attacked."

"Jermaine, I have bad news." I cradled his head to my chest. "But I want you to know, no matter what comes next, it's going to be me and you. I promise."

Waiting
SABAA TAHIR

Pineview is hot. It sounds like there'd be acres of shady redwoods around here, doesn't it, what with the "pine" and the "view"? Well, no pines around here. No view, either, unless you consider the California Aqueduct and the I-5 worth looking at. Even the spinach fields are dried up.

But the lucky yuppies driving from San Francisco to Los Angeles and back still need gas and food. So despite fallow fields and Valley fever and a nasty drought, Pineview endures—a pimple on the otherwise majestic map of California.

If I was driving by, I'd speed past, telling myself I'd get gas someplace less pathetic. Fortunately most drivers aren't me.

Since summer started, it's been busy, busy, busy. Which is good, because private school costs money, money, money, and I'll need that money in the fall. Though Dad doesn't seem worried. He threw me a party complete with Stanford colors when

I graduated last week. I swear, all forty residents of Pineview came. No, I'm kidding, it was more like fifty people.

Still kidding.

Anyway, my point is that Pineview is unremarkable. Which means that some people who live here just stand out. I'm not one of them. I'm brown, and *everyone* here is brown. I'm just a different kind of brown—South Asian, instead of Latina.

But Félix Sandoval—he stands out. He's got that look in his eyes, like he's doing something with his life. Like me, Félix is going to Stanford. Unlike me, he got a full scholarship because in addition to having annoyingly perfect grades, he is about ten feet tall and plays basketball. We're probably the only two kids in this entire stretch of the I-5 with a tree as their mascot in the fall. (Seriously, a *tree*? Come on, Stanford.)

"Poe!"

At first I pretend I don't hear Félix. I'm in the station's walk-in freezer, stacking drinks, and it is very plausible that his drill-sergeant bellow wouldn't make it back here.

"Pooooeeee!"

It's the stupidest nickname in the world, and I place full blame for it on my AP English teacher. A month ago, he made me read one of my poems out loud in class. It *happened* to be about death, so Félix started calling me Poe. Which is strange, because we don't exactly move in the same social circles. My friends play Assassin's Creed, read J. R. R. Tolkien, and worship Pink Floyd. His friends play basketball, limit their reading to the Taco Bell menu, and worship Floyd Mayweather.

You think I'm exaggerating. I am not.

"I'm in the freezer, Félix! Doing your job!"

I crack my back, cursing Sam—my best friend and the station's go-to stock boy—yet again for getting himself thrown in jail. (First offense, meth possession. He'd just turned eighteen. His public defender got a reduced jail term by persuading the judge that Sam was using with no intent to sell. In any case: Stupid. As. Hell.)

Félix was a desperation hire, the only person who applied for the job after Dad posted the help wanted sign. *Why* he applied is one of Pineview's greatest mysteries (along with why Señor Arena, who manages the Subway attached to our gas station, puts up with his crazy wife). Félix spends more money on one pair of jeans than I spend on iTunes in an entire year. Rumor is that his mom's a big-shot lawyer who sends him guilt money every month from DC.

When I shared my puzzlement with Sam before he left for prison, he cocked his head and lifted arched black brows I always wanted to trace with my fingertips. "I can tell you why he wants the job," he said. "But you'd get mad at me."

"Only because I'm mad at you all the time anyway." I punched him—a little too hard, maybe. But who cares? He didn't feel it because Sam's arms look like they got really hungry one day and swallowed rocks but never digested them.

I drop a case of Coke and head out of the stockroom to find Félix hunched at the counter, peering over my notebook.

"'Dear Sam,'" he reads out loud. "'Do they care about—' Hey!"

"That"—I grab the notebook from his hands and tuck it into

my backpack—"is none of your damn business."

"You're writing to the gringo, huh?" Félix says. "I thought you were mad at him."

"I can be mad at him and still write to him." I point at a tower of soda in the stockroom. "We have to move that entire thing into the freezer before the Coors guy comes at three. Hop to it."

"Yes, boss." Félix bows. "You finish your letter."

"Why, thank you, Félix, that's remarkably thoughtful of you."

"Don't get too excited." He grins. "I need a favor and I'm trying to get on your good side."

Félix's favor is cutting out early so he can take some girl from Joaquin High to the movies. She lives a half hour away, and the movie theater is another half hour away from that. So if he wants to be on time, he has to leave by four. Such is the dating scene in cultured and sophisticated Pineview, CA. I don't turn back to my letter until Félix is gone and the evening rush has died down.

> *June 5*
>
> *Dear Sam,*
>
> *Do they care about the drought in jail? Do you guys have to use less water? We're limited to two-minute showers. My dad loves it, says the water bill is lower than ever. Do I even want to know the shower situation in jail? Ha ha. Okay, sorry, bad joke.*
>
> *The store's been busy. I must say, I am shocked at the consumption of Subway sandwiches in this country, specifically the*

consumption of meatball subs, which we all know are the sloppy, gross younger brother of the Philly cheesesteak. How do people digest such foulness?

Anyway, at this rate, I might actually be able to afford half of a book for classes this fall! I wish I played a sport and got a scholarship. Or, you know, had a mysterious great-uncle who could be my educational patron.

You told me not to ask how you were, so I won't. I hope you're okay, that your cellmate isn't a horrible monster. I can't imagine you taking any crap, but still.

Love,

Ani

June 15

Dear Ani,

Thanks for the letter. My cellmate is all right. Talks in his sleep a lot about someone named Tomas. I think it's his kid.

Tell your dad I say hi. You think he'd want to hire a meth head once Félix leaves?

Sincerely,

Sam

My favorite time to work at the station is early in the morning, because no one ever wants to pick a fight. Pump's not giving a receipt? Too tired; they don't care. Out of Marlboro Menthol Lights 100's? Too tired; they don't care.

I'm opening this morning, picking out Pink Floyd's "Wish

You Were Here" on the guitar and reading *Harry Potter and the Prisoner of Azkaban* for the thirtieth time when Félix comes in. I look up in surprise.

"You don't get free drinks unless you're working, Sandoval."

"Chill out, Poe. I came to keep you company. It's Tuesday."

"You take a bath on Tuesdays?"

"You said last Tuesday that you hate the second Tuesday of the month because the gas tanker guy shows up and he's always a creep."

Félix waves his hands around a lot when he talks, and I shift back so he doesn't whack me in the face. It's been known to happen.

"I thought if there was a big, scary Mexican guy around," he's saying, "he might think twice about hitting on you."

"Félix, you are too pretty to be scary, and you are only three-quarters Mexican."

"You think I'm pretty?" He bats his dark eyelashes at me. I smack him with the Harry Potter book, and he grins. When he catches sight of my notebook, the grin fades.

"When does he get out?"

"Eight months," I say. "Six, if he doesn't screw anything up. Just in time to miss every opportunity to do something useful with his life because he'll be a convicted felon."

"Wow, Poe, bitter much?"

"We were supposed to get out of this place together," I say. "I always thought I'd be a doctor and he'd be a paramedic and we'd work in the same hospital, which is so stupid because paramedics take people to different hospitals, but still."

"And now . . . he can't do that."

"Not unless he waits ten years for his record to clear, and even then, he can't screw anything up in the meantime."

"That's why you're so mad at him. You guys had this whole boyfriend-girlfriend life plan. With marriage and kids and stuff?"

I squirm. "Sam and I aren't together. You've met my dad. If I even thought about dating a boy, he'd give me a horrible lecture about premarital sex and then I would have to kill myself from embarrassment."

"That's like my aunt Tina." Félix makes his voice shrill and speaks with a heavy accent. "'You want to keep your scholarship, mijo, you better not even look at a girl! You better not even *think* about a girl!'"

"Hope she didn't hear about your hot date the other day."

Félix laughs and picks at the lint on his jeans. "No danger of that."

I just give him a look, and he shrugs. "She was nice. Boring. I kept asking her, 'What do you like to do?' She didn't have anything to say."

"I thought guys liked girls who had nothing to say. Less talk means more . . . you know." I hit a wrong note on my guitar, and my face gets hot. Ugh, what am I, eleven? Also, Ani, way to play into harmful stereotypes of males.

Félix tilts his head. He's grinning, but his brown eyes are serious. "Not this guy."

June 20

Dear Sam,

That was quite an expansive letter you sent. You shouldn't waste so much paper.

You're not a meth head. If you'd been as smart as you normally are and refused to get into a car with your idiot brother, this wouldn't have happened. You'd be in the stockroom instead of too-tall Félix, complaining about how bad my guitar playing has gotten. And maybe we'd have a chance to talk about what happened the night before you got arrested.

Anyway. Don't mess with the guys who really do that stuff, okay? Stay away from the bad influences. Wait, is that even possible?

Enough about that. Do you read much in there? You want me to send you some books?

Love,

Ani

June 30

Dear Ani,

Books would be good. Nothing to do here but work out and it gets boring. Send me trashed books though. Nothing new. Don't want them stolen.

Sincerely,

Sam

July 7

Dear Sam,

I have enclosed five books, which you will probably get through in fifteen minutes. They are all on my reading list for English Lit 10A in the fall. Read carefully so I don't have to!

Dad says you of course can have your job back.

Okay, I tried to be subtle. I hoped you'd bring it up. But that didn't work. So here goes. What happened between us, Sam? I know you are in prison and you have big things to think about like your life and your future and surviving every day. And I would never say something unless I thought that it was more than just a kiss. Don't you dare tell me it didn't mean anything, because I can tell when you are lying, even over mail. We went from zero to sixty really fast, which makes me think that you'd been thinking about it for a while. And that makes me think there's a lot to say. Only you're not saying it. So I have to. Except . . . now I'm not really sure what to say.

Love,

Ani

Félix has been working here for almost two months, and I can finally go pee without worrying that he's going to burn the damn store down.

"Is it six yet?" He comes in from restocking the paper towels at the pumps, and even though it's about two thousand degrees outside, he's not sweating. My friends and I used to comment on it at basketball games. Every other guy would look like they'd been dunked in the aqueduct. Not Félix.

"Yeah, you can go."

Félix nods, hands in his pockets. He takes them out. Then puts them back in.

"Me and some buddies are going to a party in Fresno. You wanna come?" He doesn't quite look me in the eye. I get the distinct feeling that he's trying to be nice.

God, how embarrassing. A pity invite. He must think I'm such a loser.

Which I sort of am. Because instead of hanging out with friends, I mostly spend my time at the store, daydreaming about my best friend. About how his hands felt in my hair. And about how his chest felt against mine. And about—

"Uh . . . Poe? You home?"

Crap. "Party! Yes. I mean, no, I—I can't. I'm uh, I'm—"

"Never mind." Félix grabs his backpack and practically runs out of the store. He looks mad, which is damn strange because in two months, he hasn't gotten mad once, even when I've been grumpy with him. Before I can say anything, his truck is peeling out of the parking lot.

When he gets back the next morning, he's his usual cheerful self. And I feel so strange asking about his reaction yesterday that I play along.

> *July 30*
> *Sam,*
> *Are you okay? I haven't heard from you. I'm worried. Did something happen?*
> *Ani*

The three suits who come into the gas station are going to be trouble. I know it the second they step out of the slick black beamer. Bored, rich Silicon Valley jerk bags, propping themselves up by making other people feel worse.

"Hola." The white guy who walks in wears boat shoes and a suit jacket over a V-neck. The douche lord of the bunch. He tosses two bags of Funyuns and some beef jerky on the counter. "How's your day?"

It always starts out like this. Innocent. Polite, even. There's the lift of the eyebrows. The "look at me, I'm being nice to the locals" look.

"Fine, thank you," I say. "That will be eight thirty-three."

"Ooo." The douche lord's eyebrows go higher. "Expensive! How about I buy one, get one free, pretty girl?"

"The price is on the bag. If you can't afford it, maybe just buy one."

"Oh, I can *afford* it." He drops a hundred-dollar bill on the counter, and I'm forced to point to the sign that says I can't make change for large bills.

Now douche lord is irritated. And embarrassed. A bead of sweat rolls down his pink face. He pauses for a long time, considering me, before digging through his wallet—and handing me a ten. "You're not very friendly."

I make his change. He stares at me with watery eyes, his mouth puckering when I lay the change on the counter instead of dropping it in his hand. "Nice-looking girl like you," he says. "Stuck in a backwater like this. What a waste."

Ah. Here we go.

"Not even a night school around here to make something of yourself. Guess you'll be pumping gas forever."

"Guess so."

"Well, with an attitude like that, you're definitely going nowhere fast."

Usually when this happens, I ignore it. We get a lot of assholes in Pineview, and none of them are worth more than an eye roll. But unfortunately for both of us, I'm in a bad mood.

I grab the bags of chips out of his hands, throw his ten in his face, and point to the door. "I refuse you service," I say. "Get out of my store."

For a second, he looks like his head's going to explode. Then he opens his mouth. "You stupid b—"

The cooler door slams, and Félix's face is thunderous when he walks out. I take a step back. His shoulders are bunched up, his chin sticking out, and he is not pretty at all. He's scary as hell.

"You were saying?" He walks right up to the douche lord and keeps walking when the guy starts backing up, all the way to the door. "You heard her," Félix says at the door. "Get out."

The guy bolts, muttering something about illegal immigrants. A few minutes later, he and his friends are gone.

Félix mutters under his breath. "Maldito pendejo—"

"Félix, hey—"

"What's your problem?" Félix whirls on me, and he looks as grumpy as I feel. "You get a dozen guys a day in here like that. You can't pick fights with all of them."

I put up my hands. "I was just going to thank you. What's *your* problem?"

"I don't have a problem," he snaps, before going back into the freezer. I leave him alone for a while to cool off. (Har har. Because freezer.) When he emerges a half hour later, he doesn't look quite so mad.

"Sam hasn't written to me in more than a month," I say to him. "I'm worried. Why are you upset?"

"Because you care so much about whether Sam has written you that you don't notice anything or anyone else." He turns red as soon as he says it, and I'm so shocked that I barely register what he says next.

"All I mean is that you sit here, thinking about this guy who—él se fue, Ani. He's gone. And when he gets back, *you'll* be gone. You could be . . . living life. Having fun. But you can't stop thinking about him."

"What do you care?"

Félix looks at me so pityingly that I'm actually embarrassed. Because of course I'm not a complete idiot, I *know* why he cares, even if I haven't wanted to admit it.

"Why not just go see him?"

I mumble my answer, and Félix rolls his eyes.

"Inglés, Poe."

"I never learned to drive," I say a bit louder. "My dad can't take me because someone has to watch the store. And before you offer, I do *not* need—"

"Sábado," Félix says. "I'll pick you up at seven. Ask your dad if you can have the day off."

"How do you know visiting hours are Saturday?"

"My cousin Alonso is doing twenty for aggravated assault

and armed robbery. Sometimes I drive Aunt Tina out."

I almost say no. Almost. But I'm too worried about Sam. "All right," I say. "But you don't need to babysit me. I can go in alone."

The prison scares the crap out of me.

The barbed wire, the hard look in the eyes of the correctional officers. The soullessness of the place, like there are probably Dementors somewhere around here. It gives me the willies.

Félix insisted that he wanted to see his cousin Alonso, so he walked in with me. He didn't mention my bluster from earlier, about going in alone. I'm relieved.

I surreptitiously wipe my sweaty hands on my dress. I decided to wear one because Sam once told me I looked pretty in it, and I want him to know that I remember the things he said. But when I see the way the prison guards look at me, I wish I'd worn my oldest, grossest clothes.

It's just like in the movies. I sit behind a glass partition, waiting for Sam to show. The woman to my right is crying, pale skin blanched gray. The woman to my left is holding the phone for a little boy. "Papá, Tío Héctor me llevó a ver—" he babbles to his father—who is also crying.

And then I hear a grinding *beeeeep*, and Sam is led in by a guard. He's not bruised or limping. In fact, he's bigger than he was—he shouldn't have a problem stocking as much as Félix, that's for sure. But the mop of black hair I'm used to is gone— his head is shaved. And there's a sullen anger in his expression. It's the same anger Sam's brother used to have. But until now,

I'd never seen it on my friend's face.

He picks up the phone. I had a joke ready. I've forgotten it.

"I—I was worried about you." This is so strange and horrible. His eyes are so blank.

"Sorry."

"That's it? That's all you've got? *Sorry?* Don't tell me you didn't have time to write."

He drums his fingers on the table. Why won't he look at me?

"I shouldn't have come." To my surprise, my voice shakes.

His voice is soft. "Don't cry, Ani."

"It's something in the damn air! Look, it's not just me. Even that big dude three cubicles over is crying."

Sam cracks a smile, and my stomach drops. He's always had the best smile. One dimple pops out, and his big brown eyes, which make him look like a little boy no matter how tough the rest of him is, crinkle just a little bit. It was that smile that made girls come into the store to talk to him, starting three summers ago. Too bad it took me forever to notice it.

"Did you join a white power gang? Is that why you're not writing to me?"

"Christ, Ani, no." He looks around, uncomfortable. "I . . . how's Félix?"

"What the hell does Félix have to do with anything?"

"You mentioned him in one of your letters."

"Because I'm stuck working with him all day," I say. "I shouldn't have come. I'm stupid. I thought—" I wipe my face. "I thought something had happened, but you're fine. You have more important things to deal with than your stupid friend and a stupid kiss."

"It wasn't stupid." He glances up at me and away quickly. But I almost drop the phone at the look in his eyes. The same look as when he kissed me. Longing—like he needed more and didn't know how to get it.

"Then why aren't you—"

"Keep writing," he says. "If I don't write back . . . I'm sorry. But please, keep writing to me."

He hangs up the phone, nods to the guard. A moment later, he's gone.

My hands are shaking when I walk out. I feel so ridiculous in this dress. Ridiculous coming here and expecting anything more than a dismissal.

When Félix sees my face, he silently opens his truck door, then drives straight to an In-N-Out. He orders me a Coke and a shake and two cheeseburgers and fries, and I already know I'm going to eat it all. He parks on the edge of the lot, the AC blasting. As we're eating, I stop to listen.

"You like Pink Floyd?"

"After the four hundredth time you played *Delicate Sound of Thunder*, they started growing on me."

"You know the name of a Pink Floyd album?"

"Dios mío," he sighs under his breath. "I also read the first two Harry Potter books, Poe, not that you noticed."

I'm quiet for a long time. Sam was the one who introduced me to Harry Potter. Before that, I hardly ever read. "He and I have been friends for so long, you know. Such a cliché."

"When did you fall for him?"

"A few months ago. He was fixing the roof and my dad

was up there, laughing at something Sam said. I hadn't heard Dad laugh since my mom died. I tried to ignore it for a long time. Sam always had girlfriends, so there didn't seem to be any point."

"Pero like he had hookups," Félix says. "You were different. You're his girl. No one at school ever looked at you, because they didn't want to deal with him."

"The worst of both worlds. I'm not *his girl*, but people think I am. Thanks, Sam."

"So . . . what happened? Did he go Aryan Nation on you or what?"

"I think he has a lot to deal with. It's stupid of me not to understand that."

Félix sighs. I'm glad he doesn't tell me that I'm not stupid. Or that things will be all right. He just hands me my shake, and turns the music up.

August 15

Dear Sam,

I just had orientation and omg, the kids at Stanford are so rich. But my roommate isn't. She's from Palmdale, which is like this backwater of L.A., apparently. We bonded over living in overly hot places with weird people and no money.

I'm excited. Scared too. My English Lit 10A professor sent three more emails after that first one with the reading list. He's waaay too excited about the start of the year.

Love,

Ani

August 27

Dear Sam,

Did you read those books I sent? If so, please write a thousand-word report and summary on each. Due date is Friday. Kidding. But actually sort of not? Ha ha ha.

I'm so nervous about Stanford, Sam. Half of those kids have been tutored in five languages since before they could walk. I don't even know how I got in. You helped me with all of my essays. How am I supposed to analyze stupid poems about fish and the withering moors or whatever crap Emily Browning Brontë writes about without you around to explain?

I miss your letters, even though they were insultingly short. The store is lonely without you. Your brother sucks.

Ani

September 9

Dear Sam,

I know I've only written three letters. But I don't know why I'm even doing this. What, you want to hear about my life? I get up. I open the store. I deal with assholes all day. I dream about Stanford. I used to dream about you, but I try not to anymore. I go to parties with Félix every now and then. We danced together at the last one. But it was sort of a group dance . . . like there was a big crowd, so I don't know if we actually danced together or not. Whatever. I know you care so much about this stuff.

Maybe I'll go out with him. He smiled at me the other day, and my stomach got a little funny.

But then, when we were at orientation, I saw him talking to this volleyball player. And she was so pretty that even I wanted to make out with her. Also she was twice as tall as me. Like two of me stacked on top of each other would barely reach her forehead. She and Félix would be cute. Not that I care. Do I care? Why aren't you here, Sam? Why aren't we having this conversation in person? Is your release date still November 14? Don't screw it up. Please don't screw it up.

Ani

September 18
Dear Sam,
This is my last letter before I go to school. My new address is on the inside flap. Not that you'll write to me.
Ani

September 29
Dear Ani,
Thank you for writing to me. Your letters have made a huge difference. I reread them every day. Maybe a hundred times a day. I think of what your hand must look like as you write them. And your head and how you get really close to the paper and sort of hunch over it like an old granny when you write. My favorite is when you change pens in the middle and I can tell. You need to start throwing out old pens, Ani. Then you won't have to change them so much. I'm not making fun of you. I love that about you.

Also—I loved your dress, when you came to see me. I know how much you hate dresses. It meant a lot to me. You

*looked beautiful. I wanted to tell you, but I didn't. I have
been thinking about it, though. I can't stop thinking about
it, actually. Or about our kiss. And how it felt to finally
touch you, after wanting to for so long. Or about all the
other things I want to do with you. To you.*

*But that stuff doesn't matter, because this is the last letter
you are getting from me until I get out. My release date
is still November 14. And I'll see you at Thanksgiving,
maybe. But for now, try to focus on school. Don't write me
anymore. I don't want you to. I don't want you to think
about me. Go out with Félix—he was always a cool guy.
Forget about me. I'm not good for you anyway, and I don't
know how things will be when I get out. It sucks in here.
I've tried to keep to myself, and it's lucky I know how to
fight. But it's not always easy.*

Sincerely,

Sam

I wait in my room after class for Félix to stop by—a routine
that began because we didn't know anyone else at school, and
continued into the winter because it was so much fun.

Nayyana, my roommate, zips up her duffel bag on her way
out for the weekend and gives me a giant grin.

"He's going to make a move tonight."

"Félix and I are friends." I've said it so often that I should just
tattoo it on my forehead.

Nayyana rolls her eyes. "You're cold, Ani. I order you to
have fun tonight."

"Isn't the whole point of leaving high school to *not* have to go to stupid dances anymore?"

"It's his winter formal!" Nayyana blows me a kiss on her way out the door. "Reject him if you want, but as long as he's a gentleman, don't be too hard on him, okay? He's a good guy."

"What if he's not a gentleman?"

"Then punch him in the face, obviously."

The second she leaves, I kick off my heels—jeweled emerald slippers that match the strapless ankle-length dress that Nayyana insisted I borrow—and check my phone.

I haven't told Nayyana much about Sam. But after living with her for three months, I'm pretty sure she's in the "pick the basketball star over the convict" camp. She'd give me an hour-long lecture if she knew I was texting Sam right before going to Félix's winter formal.

I read over my message again.

Ani: Dad gave me your number yesterday. I'm glad you're out.

No response yet. Maybe I should have asked a question. He would have been more likely to answer.

At two loud knocks on the door, I jump, dropping the phone with a thud. I shove my heels back on and yell, "Come in!" As I stuff my phone into the ridiculously small clutch I saved from a wedding I went to four years ago, Félix walks in. I'm too embarrassed to look at him, worried that he'll act strange, or tell me I'm beautiful or something else that would make our friendship seem like less of a friendship and more like . . . something else.

But he just gives me his big Félix smile as he looks over

my dress. "Órale. Brings out your eyes. And thanks for doing this—I know it's not your scene. But Dominic is DJing, so we know the music won't suck."

I manage a quick nod, self-conscious as I walk down the hall, my heels bringing me to Félix's shoulder.

He chatters happily about his game tomorrow, and it's me who is awkward and quiet. Me eyeing him, noticing how incredible he smells, and how great his jaw is when he actually decides to shave it.

My phone buzzes in my clutch. *Don't answer. It's rude to answer.* Surreptitiously, I glance down and try to get a glimpse of the screen.

Sam.

All I catch is a flash of his name before I shove my clutch closed. This is Félix's night. I'm *not* going to ruin it by texting someone who thinks it's fine to ignore me for hours before finally responding.

Félix is right. The music doesn't suck. And despite the fact that all the guys here are fraternity boys, most of them are cool. Félix and I tear up the floor, and by the time we get into his truck and head back to Palo Alto from the city, I'm buzzing with happiness.

"I don't want to go home yet," Félix says when we reach the dorms. "But I don't want to go to Dom's after-party either."

So instead we park and walk through Stanford's dark campus. I clutch my shoes in one hand, my buzz fading with every second—because Félix is quiet. And he's never this quiet unless something is going on in that head of his.

We're passing through the shadow of Hoover Tower when he slows down.

"Ani." I can't see his eyes very well in the darkness. But maybe it's just as well. "You must know by now."

I'm almost tempted to make it difficult. But that's just mean.

"I know," I say. "But . . . Félix—"

This kiss has been coming for months, but it still surprises me. I feel the calluses on his hands as he reaches for mine, hours and hours of basketball practice compressed into a tough knot on each of his palms. His fingers shake a little, nervous with something he's tried to keep under wraps for ages.

It's not a bad kiss. It's not awkward, at least. It's fine. Nice. I even feel a little flutter—a little bolt of excitement.

If Sam hadn't kissed me months ago, and if I had never felt that wild electricity with him, then I would probably think that this is just how kisses are. That I'd feel even more the next time I kiss.

You're overthinking this.

But I'm not. I know I'm not. I pull away.

"I'm sorry, Félix."

"Qué desastre," he says. "You don't—okay, I get it. That's cool, Ani." He nods, pulls his hands away. His teeth flash in the dark. "I misread. I'm sorry."

He's so apologetic. Such a gentleman—and for a second, I hate Sam and the fact he kissed me. *Why, Sam? If you never had kissed me, then Félix and I might have had something.*

I *need* to end this awkward silence before I sink into the ground permanently, so I paste on a fake smile, hoping Félix buys it.

"I could really use a Double-Double and a chocolate shake right now."

Hearing Félix laugh is such a relief. Twenty minutes later, we're squeezed into our usual booth at the Rengstorff Avenue In-N-Out, arguing over Five Guys fries versus In-N-Out's. When he throws a fry at my head and calls me an idiot, I finally relax. We're friends again, like before. It's as if the kiss never happened.

"Félix is coming up." Nayyana peers out our window to the quad below, where my friend makes his way through the crowds of students heading out for Thanksgiving weekend. "You should probably pack."

I grab my backpack and start throwing clothes in. "I didn't think he was coming."

"Because you are an idiot who doesn't know what a lovestruck boy looks like."

"I rejected him. And he hasn't come by all week."

Nayyana rolls her eyes. "He's licking his wounds," she says. "How could he not? You picked a ghost over him."

"Sam's not a ghost," I say. But I'm worried. Maybe he is a ghost, by now. His texts to me have been painfully short. And he hasn't picked up his cell when I've called. I tried twice. Then I decided to stop being pathetic.

"I just hope your ghost is worth it," Nayyana says.

Me too.

"Poe! Vamanos." Félix does his customary two-tap knock on the open door. "You're not packed. Of course you're not."

He grabs the stuffed cheetah my mom gave me two years ago (which I may or may not take with me wherever I travel) and throws it into my bag. Then he surveys my desk and picks up Harry Potter 7, which I've been rereading, ignoring my organic chemistry book—which I *should* be reading.

And as he's packing, I notice his hands, long fingered and big. Beautiful really, strangely graceful. Why have I never noticed them before? Because he's always waving them around when he talks, maybe?

Or because I never wanted to notice them. Because noticing them would mean noticing other things about him. And that would mean forgetting about Sam.

Nayyana gives me a pointed look before turning back to her laptop and pulling on her headphones. "Look at how great Félix is," her look says.

A half hour later, Félix and I are on our way to Pineview. I keep expecting him to say something, but he stares straight ahead, occasionally tapping his fingers to the music.

He doesn't mention the game he won a few days ago, or how excited he is about Thanksgiving—even though I know it's his favorite holiday. Sam's return to Pineview—which Félix knew about, because I told him—hovers between us, making the air feel bitter and strange.

"Poe, I have to tell you something."

Please don't tell me you love me. Please. Please.

"Close your eyes."

Oh, shit. "What?"

"Just . . . I don't want you looking at me when I tell you

because it's too embarrassing, so close your eyes. Promise you'll keep them closed."

Our exit approaches, and he slows the truck. I squeeze my eyes shut.

"I'mreallysorrythatIkissedyouanditwillneverhappenagain butIvalueourfriendshipand—"

"Félix, it's okay." I open my eyes, and he's so red. It's actually quite adorable. I feel a sudden lurch in my stomach. Embarrassment? Attraction?

"I . . . I've felt something too."

"You have?" His head spins, Linda Blair fast. "What—what did you—"

"Things," I say quickly. "I felt things. Things that I need to think about."

"You mean . . . you need to see Sam first."

"I mean, I need to think."

He slows his truck to a stop in front of the station. It looks dumpier than it did when I left. But the smell of gas and concrete and dust make me smile. The lights are on in the apartment upstairs, and I see Dad's shadow move across the kitchen window. *Home.*

"Pick you up Sunday—sixish," Félix says. "Happy Thanksgiving, Poe."

I watch him drive off, my backpack at my feet. Shoes crunch the gravel behind me. *Sam.* Behind him, the store is shuttered, a sign posted up in his neat handwriting.

CLOSED UNTIL FIVE A.M.
FOR COPIOUS POULTRY CONSUMPTION.

Typical Sam. I mutter a "hey," which he returns, and then I just stare at him. Is he here? Is he real? Is he actually back? He wears his usual uniform—black jeans, a black T-shirt, and Chucks. His beanie is pulled low, and seeing him, so familiar— it's like he hasn't been gone and no time has passed at all.

But then I see the curl of a tattoo sticking out of the bottom of his T-shirt sleeve. New. He doesn't quite look me in the eye. And that makes me feel like a million years have passed.

"Let me get that."

He reaches for my backpack, because he's always been polite. He's *still* not really looking at me. But his eyebrows, those beautiful black arches I know so well, they furrow, like he's thinking up the answer to one of my crazy English 10A essay questions.

His finger brushes mine.

It's *barely* a brush. Like an eyelash kissing my finger—that's it. But it sends a shock like lightning through us both, and his whole body goes still. Everything but his eyes, which jerk up to meet mine, hot with everything he never said in his letters or texts or over the phone.

I step forward, hooking a finger into his belt buckle and yanking him close as he drops my pack with a thud and pulls me toward him at the same time. As Sam's eyelids drop closed, I realize distantly that Félix never had a chance. *Poor Félix*, I think.

Then Sam is kissing me the way he kissed me months ago, the way I hope he will kiss me again and again. And I don't think of Félix at all.

Vega
BRENNA YOVANOFF

Las Vegas

Pan in to show the flash and glitter of the Strip—eight lanes, twenty thousand people, a wide, unholy slice of magic. A miracle of color.

The boulevard runs the stretch of desert like a vein, pumping with the fast, fierce pulse of cars and crowds and money. Promising festivals, carnivals, a horde of newly minted millionaires, a sea of glossy beauties and slick, smiling criminals. Luck that always comes through.

Follow the camera as it moves, soaring down scorching avenues, finding its way through a sea of palm trees and swimming pools.

The air is dry and hot, the city an impossible oasis, jeweled with pirate ships and castles. Oceans of bodies, waves of cars, a crush of neon lights and flying paper.

The camera winds along narrower streets now, following cracked sidewalks, rows of stucco houses. It pans through low, sunbaked neighborhoods, sliding between chain-link fences and parked cars, and finally comes to rest on one small, knobby girl, so wild and electric she almost shines.

She's quick and fearless, hair a tangled nest. A slash of joyful noise and dirty jeans against the dull brown backdrop of the neighborhood, in the dusty yard under the acacia.

Inside, her house is perfect, a confection of pastel-painted walls, fairy lights, gingerbread. Ancient pink refrigerator, swirling red carpet. A row of Aerosmith posters in the hall.

In the summer, water beads on the air conditioner like sweat.

Her mother comes home after bedtime, smelling like flowers and smoke, and kisses her. The kiss is a tiny, cherished gift. A ritual. It lands on her cheek like it's landing on the girl in a story. One day, she thinks, she will be like the people on the billboards—lucky, gorgeous, dangerous.

The city is a promise. A fantastical landscape of winners, beauties, criminals.

She will belong here forever.

Elle

Most days, to most people, I was Elle, like the magazine, a smoky-eyed glam goddess, all smiles and wicked edges. Lizzie to teachers and kids at school. Libs, if Wendy was happy, and Elizabeth Marie when she wasn't—a name like the clock ticking on a pile of dynamite, a tangle of rainbow-colored wires. Those days, the explosion could be for anything. Breaking the good casserole dish, crossing the street without telling her. Calling her Wendy instead of Mom.

To Alex, though? To Alex, I was always Betsy.

From outside, the house on Vine Street was as ugly as a codfish. Ugly as a potato. But the inside was beautiful and bright, and every night, Wendy came home from the High Roller Club wearing her spangled uniform, bringing candy-red cherries and tiny paper parasols. Her hair smelled like cigarettes and Aqua Net.

She sat at the kitchen table, counting her tips into two piles. The big one for rent and gas and groceries, the smaller one for the mayonnaise jar on top of the refrigerator. The money in the jar wasn't for anything. It was a just-in-case, a backup plan for the chance that maybe something good would happen.

When I was little, I liked to sit and stare into the jar. It looked impossible. It looked like so much money you could own the world.

"Whenever you win a hand," Wendy always said, pressing the crumpled dollars flat, "you just take your chips and then walk away. People are so stupid about luck. They think when they're up, they'll always be up. Get all bent out of shape when their hot streak ends. Start thinking the world is against them when it's not. The world doesn't give a shit about you. Remember that, you'll do just fine."

But Wendy was hard and quick and practical. She didn't believe in luck or signs. She believed in staring down into that swiftly spinning wheel, and knowing your number when it came up. When she came home from work, the skin around her eyes was tired.

I sat at the table and watched her count. I opened and closed the tiny parasols until the paper tore. When I put the wooden sticks in my mouth, they tasted like pennies. I knew that if I wished hard enough, someday my number would come up and something good would happen. I would do just fine.

"And don't be spending all day next door with that weird little Reilly boy," Wendy said, but I always did it anyway.

Alex was the one who taught me about magic, believed in it when no one else did. He was just that soft, awkward way, though, always ready to believe in something brighter and bigger.

We played pretend and built fairy towns, sitting in his mother's garden, where flowers spilled over the beds and the broken-down fence like a party, a flood of confetti and bloodred crepe paper.

Your best friend is supposed to be the girl who sits next to you in math and has the same lunchbox as you, but a better haircut. Not two years younger, not a boy, not skinny and strange, with all kinds of ideas about magicians and G.I. Joes and God.

His brother, Milo, was loud and mean, but Alex never tried to be like him.

Sitting under the acacia tree, he'd reach his hands around to the back of my neck and press his forehead against mine, trying to make me see his thoughts, but I never could. When he leaned back, I would look into his eyes and see a pair of dark silhouettes, two tiny Betsys floating there, one at the center of each pupil.

♥ ♥ ♥

There's a certain kind of magic to being a kid with someone. They always have this little private piece of you. They own your heart, even if you don't remember giving it to them.

There's no point arguing, it's how things are. You're stuck together by all the things you've seen and shared—the day Max Holbrook said he saw John Cena at the gas station on Tropicana and everyone went down to look. The way the leaves flutter like pale green dollars in the spring, and how they turn all brown and crumpled in the fall. The time I cut my lip on the skate ramp and had to get four stitches.

The day that Alex and Milo's dad left, loading all his things into a U-Haul, and Alex climbed through my window and curled up in my bed and couldn't stop crying.

I was twelve, still too young to know how to act when things stopped being okay. And anyway, the difference was hard to recognize. It seemed like he'd already been leaving forever.

Next door, the house didn't explode or collapse. It just got quiet. I had nothing to say. At my house, we didn't whisper our sorrows.

After that first night, Alex stopped acting like it mattered. He didn't talk about it and I didn't ask, because what was there to say? My dad had been gone since I was born. I had never lost anything.

We grew like weeds in the heat, cooking like the dahlias that Donna Reilly planted in the gap between our yards and then let die when her husband left. We sat with the fence between us, trying to see our own blurry futures in the garden.

"I'm the sunflowers," I said, pointing to their stalks, how

tall and strong they grew.

Alex shook his head. "I'm morning glories."

The day was ungodly hot. The morning glories had all been dead for months.

Their dad had always been the beigest, heaviest thing about their house, with sandy eyes, like the saddest dog. He sent a postcard once from Malibu—just once. A picture of surfers, sunlight washing out their faces. In it, everything was pale, the sky and water and sand. Even the paper was soft, all frayed edges and bent corners.

I sat in the dirt, drawing fluffy clouds with a stick.

"I hate it here," Alex said, in a way that made me think he meant it.

I leaned against the fence and hugged my knees, ashamed because I loved it.

Wendy said that this was just the way things went. She put her cigarette out like the period at the end of a sentence. "Everybody leaves," she said. "It's good while it lasts, but everybody takes off eventually."

"If they just wait, though. If they wait for him, maybe he'll come back."

But I could tell she thought the idea was a stupid one. She didn't believe in people coming back.

In the middle of the night when I was honest, I didn't either.

All that was before, though—before I got tall and heavy eyed. Before I got a waist and hips and a job at the outlet mall. Before I got untouchable and sharp.

The days got short and the years got even shorter, like every part of me was speeding up.

Summers were bright and brutal. Too hot in the house or at the pool or in the shade. Too hot to move, too hot to breathe. I didn't mind. The sun felt like the stare of some giant, benevolent god, and anyway, the night would always roll in again, bringing a dry, flickering wind—not cool, never cool, but wicked and electric, making the city feel wide awake.

Sometimes in the afternoons, Alex and I would walk along the Strip, not quite holding hands. The sidewalk was crowded.

At Treasure Island, we stopped and leaned against the railing, looking out over the water.

The lagoon was lined with plastic, full of scummy water and fiberglass frigates. The sails were ragged from the breeze that blew all summer. It had leached the color out of the mast flags, turning the boats into ghost ships. The air smelled black and greasy like gasoline. After a minute, I lit one of Wendy's cigarettes.

"That's so bad for you," Alex said. It was the first thing he'd said in a while. "It's like sucking on a can of Raid."

"I wish I was a pirate," I said, not meaning it, but just to say something. "I'd be a pirate captain with a parrot and everything. You could be my guy."

"The first mate?"

"Yeah, that. We'd go all over the ocean and loot stuff."

"I don't want to loot stuff. I think it would scare people."

"That's kind of the point."

He didn't answer, just leaned his chin on his hand.

I'd started kissing boys. It didn't matter where. In the back-seats of cars, in the front seats. On the hoods at night, when the heat pressed down in waves. They never cared when our elbows made dents. They just pressed harder, and I pressed harder, waiting for summer to end.

Alex didn't know. Or maybe he did, but he never said anything.

It wasn't like the kissing meant something. They weren't anything I wanted to keep. They were mouths, hands, shoulders, hips, but not like people.

Some of them had bruises. Their eyes glittered like armor. Some of them shook like birds, electric, pulses racing.

Under the streetlights, I would look down into the hollows of their palms. In the lines of their hands, I saw all the things they did to keep themselves from crying. When they drove me home, I never let them come up to the front door.

Out in the lagoon, the frigates looked broken down and pathetic. All the mannequins were chipped and wore eye patches.

Alex slid his hand closer to mine, like he was reaching for me and didn't want to be reaching. His wrist was thin and freckled. His hand on the railing was palm down. I knew that if I took it, I'd be able to read the sadness there, so I didn't. But he told me anyway.

"I think Milo's going to join the navy," he said, all in one long breath. "He said if Mom doesn't kick her stupid, scuzzy boyfriend out, he's leaving."

That was pointless, though. We both knew Milo wouldn't

join anything. "Will she, do you think—kick him out?"

Alex shook his head. "I think they're going to get married."

I touched the base of my throat. "Oh."

"It'll be okay."

"Except that Milo will leave, right?"

"Probably."

I looked out at the water and imagined seagulls picking over the wreckage. "I didn't know he was thinking about it."

"Yeah. Neither did I."

"Maybe he should be a pirate too. He'd make a good one."

"But you wouldn't." Alex turned to look at me. I'd always thought he'd wind up taller than me eventually, but he was fifteen now, and still kind of like a kid. "You should be a mermaid."

"And sit out in the middle of that pond, with everyone's Coke cans and candy-bar wrappers floating around me?"

"Mermaids don't live here," he said. "I mean real mermaids, wild and rare."

"Real mermaids." I laughed, blowing smoke out toward the water.

"If I could do anything," he said in a strange, husky voice, like he was trying hard to make me see, "anything in the world, I'd make you a mermaid. You could live in the middle of the ocean with the dolphins and the whales."

"That might be nice," I told him, grinding out my cigarette on the railing.

He nodded and moved closer, but we didn't touch each other.

After a while, we walked home.

♥ ♥ ♥

We went to parties, drank rum and Coke in crowded rooms.
Not together, but not exactly apart.

A small but certain distance had opened between us, the
way planets orbit but never touch. The rum tasted sweet and
poisonous.

I never imagined I was in love with the boys I held down
in cars, the ones who held me down in parks at night, the trees
throwing heavy shadows. Cigarettes, cuts on their knuckles, a
smell like tar, aftershave, exhaust. Breathing against their necks,
I breathed asphalt, basketball courts, laundromat detergent, the
wet ground, pressing up against my back. It was like the end
of the world or something just as comforting. I breathed it in
huge, rocking gasps.

Alex was different, though, addicted to the girls who ran
their fingers through his hair, sprawled in his lap. Their eyelashes were long and brittle, black spiders on their cheeks. To
kiss them, he had to imagine he was in love.

The party was at some rickety loft near downtown, all
exposed concrete and empty, echoing ceilings.

I was dancing right up next to the DJ, eating Skittles, wearing a sequined halter, cutoffs, and not much else.

Alex was on the couch with a girl in a vinyl dress. I'd seen
her at Crave and in the mosh pit at Hurricane. She was cute, in
a squirmy puppy kind of way, with sweet, shiny lip gloss and
high black boots. Skinny legs, okay face. They laughed, Alex
stroking her hair, the outside of her arm. There was a greasy
smear from the corner of his mouth to halfway up the side of

his face. It was clear and colorless, but I knew that up close it would smell like candy.

I watched them. Her cheeks were round and berry pink, but her eyes had a hard, hungry look.

When Milo came slouching over with his collar up and his hair gelled all the way to heaven, I wasn't happy, but I wasn't sad. He hadn't left town when he said he would. He was never going to leave. He was taller than Alex, with a mouth like a dangerous magic trick.

He slid his arms around my waist and whispered, "You look hot."

The room was a hundred and ten degrees. "I always look hot."

He laughed, and his breath felt like static on my cheek. He was a game I liked to play sometimes.

There was a little coatroom in the back. He bit my neck and then it was all dark room and hands and teeth and the high, white voltage of my skin.

In the morning, I woke up on a dusty couch with stuffing spilling out. Milo was already gone.

Alex and I drove home in the pink-gray dawn.

He looked strange, hollow around the eyes. I wondered if that was how I looked when I came home in the dark with teeth marks on my neck, my mouth bitten, my arms bruised. I didn't think so, somehow. I think I just looked normal. I think I felt okay.

"Have fun last night?" I asked in a scratchy voice, full of gravel and rust. I sounded like I'd been screaming.

He made a noise from the passenger seat, but it wasn't a word.

"Are you okay?" My voice was clearer, and I glanced over.

He was staring out the window, watching the palm trees wash by in waves. He sat with his arms crossed and his elbows cupped in his hands. "That girl," he said.

"She didn't look so bad." The light glowed red, and I braked. On the radio, someone was singing a song about a girl who gets kidnapped by pirates.

Alex cleared his throat, staring out the window. "I guess she used to . . . be with Milo."

I didn't tell him that sometimes you just wanted to kiss someone who didn't matter to you. How it was just a rule that where there were parties and drugs, you ran into all this other stuff too—lonely, hateful people standing on the edge of whatever thrilled or hurt them. "Everyone's been with Milo."

When he turned to look at me, I could see something dark floating in his eyes, and I looked away. "That's kind of the problem."

I sat with my hands on the wheel, waiting for him to tell me how Milo and I were a problem.

"She wants to be his girlfriend," Alex said. "She only picked me because she wanted to, like, *punish* him."

The idea was weird and sad. It seemed probably true, but I couldn't see the appeal of being Milo's anything. I didn't say that maybe she'd picked Alex because he never called anyone a slut, or because his jokes weren't at the expense of someone else, or even just that he always had clean fingernails and smelled like gum.

"It's so stupid, though," I said, trying not to sound impatient. "Why does it matter?"

"It doesn't," he said. I could tell he meant it shouldn't but it does. "She just seemed nice. How can she be nice and still be trying so hard to hurt someone else?"

"I don't know," I said, because the alternative was to tell him all the ways people were nice and the ways they were still just horrible.

We were quiet the rest of the way home.

On our street, I killed the engine. "Do you want to get some pancakes?"

He shook his head. "I need a shower."

"Hey," I said, reaching for his arm. "Hey, it's going to be—"

"Don't say okay," he said. His voice was hard and hoarse. "Because it's not."

My fingers touched his T-shirt and he pulled away. I stopped talking.

"I don't feel good at all," he said in a voice I could barely hear. "I need to go in and shower."

I sat behind the wheel and watched him walk, faster and faster, until by the time he reached the door, he seemed to be floating. Every time I blinked, he would be farther away.

I didn't notice when he stopped calling. When he stopped coming over. Let my texts go unanswered for way too long. I told myself I didn't notice. After a while, he didn't answer at all.

I wasn't hurt, though. I wasn't lonely.

There were parties to rage at and people to see. I had the

constant, jittering hum of the city. The colored lights, red and green and blue.

Alex

For a second, there was nothing.

Only tires hissing, lights that passed in flashes. A noise like the end of the world.

Then the window splashed into my lap in a shiny, crunchy wave and a billowing white wall exploded in my face.

No.

Back up.

Before that, there was everything. The house. The garden. My mom, digging holes to plant butterfly bushes. My dad, painting sad, twisted faces. I was dumb and little, the kind of kid who believed in world peace and the Easter Bunny and all that other stupid shit.

Talking to Elle—Betsy—through the backyard fence, with her tangled hair and her fierce heartbroken face, I was so in love with her, but not the love that TV and movies talk about. That came later.

The way I left home was almost an accident. It wasn't because of her—not the parties or the guys or the way I felt when all her recklessness and noise started to look dangerous. And it was all because of that.

Vegas was a murky ocean of porn and dirt and greed, and every time the bad parts showed, I hated it more. The movies and commercials make it seem like some ecstatic celebration, but the secret is, winning never feels as good as the moment right before. No one wants to admit it, that they come here for that moment, crave the ugly free fall of not knowing. That they come here to lose.

Betsy loved it too much to ever really look at the bad parts.

But I was starting to think they were all bad parts.

The day I moved in with Milo was the day I stopped being soft.

Betsy was sitting on the floor of my new bedroom, helping unpack my clothes. She'd been seeing some guy from downtown with bloodshot eyes. Some guy who liked to party, which could be taken however you want to take it. Mostly, it meant he could get drugs. Milo could get drugs too. By then, everyone we knew liked to party.

"Do you love him?" I said.

She was smoking something without a filter. Her nails were a bright glittery green, the color of poison. The look on her face was tired, like the idea made her so bored she could taste it. "Who's going to love a train wreck like that?"

"What about Milo, then?" It wasn't like I thought she'd say yes, or that I had to compete with him. *I* loved Milo, but still. Milo wasn't good for anyone.

She laughed, and it was like something breaking.

I didn't trust myself to say the real thing, the one you can never actually say. *Do you love* me? I said something else instead, raw and tight and almost the same. "Do you love it here?"

And she didn't have to say anything, because I knew.

After that, I didn't know how to be around her. I couldn't blame her exactly, but I couldn't be a good friend, either.

♥ ♥ ♥

Moving was the only way to leave behind the quiet that had filled my mom's house and gotten inside the walls. The whole place had turned jagged, like a piece of glass stuck in my throat.

And anyway, it's what you do when you turn eighteen. You move out.

There was a small voice in me that said the place with Milo on North Jones wasn't enough—go farther, drive west until I hit ocean. I wasn't brave enough.

Instead, I followed Milo. It seemed my whole life, I'd always been following someone.

I didn't say a word when he did shots before work. When he drove too fast or got in fights, when he made every bad decision the city was offering. I just sat and waited till it was over, like I was watching the movie through my fingers.

Nights were long and sprawling. Every place we went felt sticky. When we stood in the mosh pit at Seashore, I saw girls with plastic smiles. Milo at the bar. Lights so dark and bright it made my eyes hurt.

I leaned against the wall and tried to picture what Betsy would do. It wasn't like I thought I should be someone different or needed to love all the things she loved. It was more like if I could find some way to live how she lived, I'd be stronger. If I could just give up, things would stop feeling so bad all the time.

The night was dry and slow and heavy. We went out, because we were always going out.

In the crowd around the back bar at the Vault, Milo was doing flip tricks with his lighter. "Want to hit Crave?" he said.

He smelled like smoke and tequila and bad decisions begging to be made.

"Sure," I said, and even saying it felt like a widening crack inside me. "What the hell, right? I'm here to lose."

"What?" he said, but he didn't wait for me to answer.

I got in the car because why not and because he was my brother. We never planned for anything or talked about the future anymore. I'd stopped imagining one. And anyway, it wasn't like it mattered. Or else, it mattered so much I thought my heart would break.

It didn't break though.

We were on Casa Buena Drive, with the radio off. The wind was hot and frantic. It sounded like the ocean.

"Watch this," Milo yelled, and I thought of Betsy like I could almost see her next to me—like the dry, tarry air was blowing in her face instead of mine.

I saw it suddenly, the ways she thrashed and raged—all those times, I'd tried so hard not to dive in after her, and now here I was in Milo's front seat with the needle climbing, looking for the rush, the jolt, the thing that made my heart beat faster.

The city swept by in flashes and when we blew the stop sign at Clemont Street, my pulse felt like a bird trapped inside a bottle.

I told it to slow down.

Buildings whipped past. Milo was driving stupid and loose, the way he did when he'd been drinking—this easy daredevil indifference, where you couldn't tell if he was just that good, or just that lucky.

I didn't tell him to slow down.

The anxious clanking of my heart only made it clearer, how lost I was, how small and uncertain, and I made fists, thinking of Betsy. Thinking of the brave, unbreakable person I didn't know how to be without her. The city was a glittery nightmare, and this whole time, maybe I'd only ever been brave because of her.

Milo threw his head back and howled into the dark, his grin like a white slice of victory. A hazard sign. Lights and cars flashed by in neon smears, like this was all some kind of fast, blinking game, and I closed my eyes.

For a second, there was nothing, just me inside my head. Then it all crashed in again—Milo howling next to me, pounding on the steering wheel, the tires whispering against the road. The city around us roaring like the sea.

"Go faster," I said.

When the truck hit the passenger side, I don't remember anything but the sound of breaking. A noise like the end of the world.

A white wall billowed up in my face and then broke over me. The window splashed into my lap and then so did a whole lot of blood.

The ambulance came after that. There was blood on my shirt and in my mouth. My shoulder felt like a bomb had gone off.

These are the parts I remember most: the sirens. The way the paramedics stood over me, businesslike and blank, then the hospital, the lights, the clean, stinging smell. It was numb, painful, over, and anyway, the ending didn't matter.

I came here to lose.

At the place on North Jones, no one was home. Our roommate, Darryl, was in Tahoe. Milo had flunked the Breathalyzer.

I had a sling for my shoulder and a bottle of pills, but I couldn't figure out the dosage. I couldn't get the cap off the bottle. I couldn't take a breath without sounding like I was crying.

I called her.

Elle

His voice on my phone was muffled, low and lost and half underwater. A message in a bottle, the call of someone out to sea.

"Betsy," he said, careful and flat. "Please, when you get this, please come over."

His apartment complex was the cheap, dingy kind. All the buildings were stucco, and even in the dark, they all had the same burned feeling, like they'd shriveled in the sun.

It was after midnight. The air felt used up. There was a streetlight shining down onto the stairwell and the patio, but the corners were dark spaces. A coffee can sat next to the railing, full of ashes.

I let myself in. When Alex was home, he never locked the door.

For a minute, I stood in the hall, feeling like a criminal. All the lights were out.

The air smelled like old cigarettes, and I could hear music, playing low in the living room. I followed it.

I came into the room Gunslinger Elle—bandit jeans and Marlboro Man bravado—and all that disappeared so fast. Instead, just picture Betsy, standing with her hands shoved down in the pockets and her eyes wide and dry and burning.

When Alex looked up from his phone, the sight of him made me flinch.

One side of his face was a purple wreck. The skin looked dark and tight and swollen. There was blood crusted under his nose and cracking on a cut beneath his eye.

He was wearing a white shirt, but it was dark in places, and I stood in the doorway thinking, *Say something, say something.*

The only thing I could think was, "You shouldn't still be wearing that."

He made a face and shook his head. "I can't take it off. It hurts to move my arm."

There was a bottle of something prescription on the coffee table like he'd been staring at it.

"Can you open that?" he said.

I sat down and popped the lid, letting pills spill into my hand.

"Water?" he said, sounding slow and tired. "Cold?"

In the kitchen, I took all the ice cubes out of the tray and put them in a glass. Then I stood looking at them while they melted slowly and sweat ran down between my shoulder blades.

My reflection in the window was shock eyed, tangle haired. I went back out to the living room, carrying the glass like a prayer.

Alex drank and swallowed pills. He laughed the nervous,

eyes-down laugh that used to make him seem so old when he was twelve. Now, with his face turned away from me, and his eyelashes making shadows on his cheeks, it sounded young.

"How come no one's here?" I wiped at the blood underneath his eye, and he winced.

"You're here."

"You know what I mean. Where's Milo?"

"Police station. I don't want to talk about it."

. "How'd you get home?"

"My mom. She got me from emergency, but she . . . uh, she had to work."

"At one in the morning?"

"Tomorrow. I said I don't want to talk about it." He leaned back until his head rested against the couch.

"Did a person do this to you?"

"A car."

I didn't look anymore, like maybe if I didn't, he'd change back to normal, but his voice kept sounding wrong, even when I watched the carpet. My skin felt brittle and weightless like ashes. "How does it feel?"

The question was a broken rule. A thing we never asked each other. Too dangerous, too private. Never say it out loud, because then the other one might answer.

"Like nothing," he said. "Like I'm not really bleeding. Like it isn't really my blood."

The flatness in his voice was awful, and so I nodded. The blood had never been my blood. Sometimes, in crowded clubs at night when I was lit up with the wild manic rush of it, moving fast, fast, fast, I wasn't sure I had any.

He bowed his head. "Will you stay here with me tonight?"

We leaned against each other. "I'll stay with you forever."

"For real?"

"No," I said, because I couldn't stand to lie to him. "But I wish I could."

He breathed out, let himself sink deep into the couch. "Because you love it here."

We sat with our whole bodies touching. "Yeah, I do."

"Maybe Vega is a girl," he said.

His voice had gotten slow and thick. I nodded. He'd called the city something mumbling and wrong, named it like a person, but I didn't even know if he was doing it on purpose. Maybe all it meant was that the drugs were kicking in. I'd always been so sure he'd never actually see—not the way that I did—Vegas in all her shiny, messy glory. But now, in the dark, in the terrible quiet, I thought maybe he got it.

"I can't survive," he whispered. "She's too hungry. Bright and glittery, but sick."

And then I knew the magic still escaped him. We would never see the same thing.

"I'm poisoned," he said. His voice was raspy and his face was pale. He looked poisoned. "It isn't good for you here."

I watched the side of his face, blood still crusted around his mouth like someone at the hospital had started to clean him up and then gotten bored. "You mean it's not good for *you*."

"Anyone," he said. His voice was low, and he still wouldn't look at me.

I had a sinking feeling that he was wrong. That certain people could survive it. That this place was a dirty, thrilling home for some of us. The hard-edged. The ragged, jagged losers and the criminals.

Everything seemed huge and powerful in the dark, the sweat soaking into his collar, his gently curling hair. I put my face against his neck and his skin smelled like salt. There, in the hot, dark room, I imagined that my tears turned to ice as soon as they touched his shirt.

"You can go," I said, holding his good hand so tight it hurt my throat. "If you want to."

He nodded and I closed my eyes, thinking that this was an unhappy ending. A moment. That maybe I finally got it.

The day I came home to Vine Street to see Wendy, there was a cigar box on the floor of my old bedroom. It was one of those vintage painted ones, with little hinges and a picture of a fifties-style mermaid on the lid. When I picked it up, it rattled like a tray of bones.

I dumped everything on the carpet. With my hands in my lap, I sat looking at all the things he'd left me with. A dollar chip from Treasure Island, a handful of Skittles, a dead morning glory. The postcard from California—that pale picture of the ocean, soft and faded as old silk.

On the back, in smudgy pen, his dad had written:

> *Went out to see the waves before heading to Seattle. Saw these*
> *dudes and thought of you.*

*Venice ain't my bag—still too much sun—but I think you'd
like it here.*

For a long time, I sat holding the postcard. Imagining the
shape of Alex. The empty space where he belonged seemed to
sit like a rock inside me.

The hinges of the cigar box were rusty and the label was
rubbed off around the edges. I was almost ruined by the way you
could fit everything you needed to say into a box the size of three
stacks of twenties. And all those times we talked about this place,
how much he hated it, I didn't ever think he'd actually be gone.

"Everybody leaves," said Wendy, standing in the doorway,
and she sounded so sad. She sounded sorry, like she was giving
me this one tiny apology for every day of my life.

I nodded, thinking about the bottomless uncertainty of dis-
appearing. About staying. How hard I'd always tried to make
myself believe that being dangerous is not its own kind of
gamble.

Wendy leaned in the doorway, watching me gather up the
bits and pieces of Alex's good-bye—all the things he'd left me.
Her expression was strange. Suddenly, she stepped fast and light
into the room and did something she hadn't done in years. She
kissed me.

Later, I sat in my car in the hot, relentless dusk, holding my
elbows in my cupped hands like I was holding myself together.
The box sat next to me in the shotgun seat, a silent passenger,
waiting for a sign.

I thought about mermaids, wild and rare, girls with muddy-colored scales and murky water plants tangled in their hair, their eyes reflecting pounding waves and schools of whales. Maybe I was never that girl at all, or else I was only that girl when I was with Alex.

In the dark, I felt small and angry suddenly, nine years old again, looking at Alex through the fence. A little girl with no friends or father or future, just hoping for some magic.

My reflection in the window told a different story. Fierce, fearless girl, dust sticking to her skin, smoky eyes and too-sharp teeth.

But that's not right.

A black-haired girl who sat in the dark once, with a very hurt, very sad, used-to-be-small boy, and cried hard mermaid tears into his T-shirt, which was crunchy with dried blood.

Vega

The wind comes sweeping over the asphalt, hot as burning houses. It gusts between casino signs, between the blank-eyed gamblers who roll and roll for a lucky break that never comes.

The girl is alone, counting her chips in a city that never wants you to stop moving long enough to count. Here in the dark, the silence feels like an empty church, an echoing. No one has to be alone, and everyone is.

In her car, she cranes her neck to look at her reflection. Ravenous eyes, a raw red mouth, cherry chapped from biting her lips. There is a girl in the rearview mirror who would burn down everything if she got the chance.

Luck is a kind of magic all its own, a full and blooming promise. But here is a secret: it always runs out.

She leans her cheek against the glass and remembers how she used to dance and play her mother's CDs.

If she were living someone else's life, her mother's maybe, the ending would be different. It would be easy to let go. She'd never feel sad for no reason. She'd make a playlist of all the superhero songs she can think of.

But even in the bright, dishonest history of her mind, the ending is the same. She could be her mother, her alter ego, her own skillfully invented self, someone else. The sadness doesn't leave. When she turns the knobs in the bathroom, a rattling noise leaks out of the faucet like crying.

She presses her forehead to the steering wheel and tries to see her thoughts. In the darkness behind her eyelids, she can almost picture it. Vega is a sleek and sooty mirage, a gorgeous beast. Vega is her, and those, and them. She wonders if she's scared to leave because Vega might come with her.

It's forgivable to love something so much that it becomes you. The transformation happened years ago, and now she and Vega are like a glossy, monstrous pair of sisters, dripping black. She is just another fierce, mythical creature in this land of winners, beauties, criminals.

The part of the story she has never doubted is the house and the garden. Alex. The way they always found each other's eyes. The way they loved each other more than family. And when she's waited long enough, she turns the key. In the end, it's not that hard. For the first time in her life, she knows what happens next, knows what she's going to do.

Drive west like someone flying away from the devil.

Drive to the edge of the world, all the way to someplace softer, and not look back.

A Hundred Thousand Threads
ALAYA DAWN JOHNSON

December 15, 2078. The first of the V-mails never sent. The mask cracked.

Hello, Jaime.

I just thought you should know, that scarf I gave you isn't a double brocade. It's technically a brocatelle. It's a weave type that tends to stiffness, which is why I used the heirloom cotton that Rosa brought me back from Oaxaca. So it would be soft, but you could still read every stitch with your fingertips. I'm glad you refused to give it to the Colibrí. Even facing a masked vigilante pointing a gun to your head, you wouldn't let her take what I had freely given. I could have kissed you, cabrón, if you weren't so busy betraying me.

Right. Deep breath. See—I'm telling you something, Jaime. I don't always hide myself from you. But you—who you are—who I am—sometimes makes it necessary. Whenever we're together these days all I can feel is this barrier, like some overgrown cactus with spines that tear apart your hands and chip the machete and grow back thicker than before the next day. Did we ever talk, Jaime? I think we did. I could swear that we did, and yet now all I can do is weave and weave and pray that you'll understand what I mean when you feel the stitches. I loved your hands from the moment we met—you wouldn't remember . . . I—

They say that you're falling for the Colibrí. Berenice told me you spent all of Paco's party talking about how sexy you find her, how much you admire her. Berenice was surprised because you'd never been particularly interested in politics, let alone the class struggle, and now she was worried that you might leave me for some bandana-masked Zapatista vigilante who's stealing from our rich parents and giving it away to the poor. Some down-city lady Chucho el Roto. I laughed and told her that you were still firmly in my clutches.

But you're not, are you? After tonight . . . you met her. Pure dumb luck, when the Colibrí is busy robbing five hundred thousand pesos of rocks from your own aunt's neck—

Jaime, I've been thinking about making something with our story. You and me. Ha, you and me and the Colibrí. A video, a documentary, a collage of lost and hidden histories. If you saw it, you'd know me. And you might just hate me. Here, this is how it would start. Imagine the smoky voice of the narrator, suspiciously similar to the Colibrí's—but then, according to Berenice, everyone wants to be her these days:

December 2078. An eighteen-year-old girl sits on the balcony of a west-facing tower of the Estratósfera, the elite citadel that rises above the flooded streets of Mexico City. The lights of the towers and the monorails stretch out behind her, reflecting the black water of the canals, and disappear into the cream of the December smog. We pan across the famous towers of the city's political elite, from here smudgy silhouettes: Cuauhtémoc, Anáhuac, Balderas. The girl is dressed in only a thin white huipil blouse, decorated at the collar with fractals of red and orange diamonds in thick embroidery thread. They are neatly done but faded with age. The girl stitched them herself in another world, with another name, with another mother. Before she was adopted into this strange, glittering mirage.

How is this, Jaime? Mi Jaimecito? Is this honest enough—

Her arms are bare, and even in the ambient light of the Estrato, the bruises are starting to show, purple against brown. A laceration stretches from her collarbone to her chin, shiny with medical sealant. Self-applied. Her hands tremble slightly. Her eyes are red and glassy—a surprise. Aurora never cries.

And cut. You complain about not knowing me, Jaime, but when have you really tried? Aren't you just afraid, deep down, of who I might be? Not that fresa girl you met at thirteen, a mildly shocking dresser, a better kisser. But someone whose very existence threatens you?

No. No, chinga tu madre, Jaime, how could you—I know you're blind, but how could you have looked at her like that, how could you have flirted with her like that, how could you even now be trying to get in touch with her again?

December 17, 2078. I found this early, within a few hours of you posting. Even so, your uncle's spy team managed to scrub it from the net the next day.

My name is Jaime Torres de la Garza, and I'm recording this poem for—for who? It used to be easy, they were all for her, I inhaled free verse and exhaled pentatonic scales and they all traced the contours of her cloth beneath my fingers, and kept the shuttling rhythm of her loom. And now—someone new. A different sort of beat. I don't know how to reach you, Coli, so I'm posting this publicly. The gossip feeds will fucking eat it up.

> *Above the Highline direction Borealis,*
> *Which I hate to ride because I still remember the last time I had*
>   *my eyes,*
> *I felt you a moment before you spoke*
> *Manifested like the spirit they claim you are*
> *In my uncle's private car*
> *To tell his wife just how much you admired the look*
> *Of the rocks around her neck.*
> I'll give you some flowers in exchange, *you said,* or would
>   you prefer feathers?
> *And touched your crown, which I imagined buckling and glinting*
> *Like a morning oil slick on lake Xaltocan.*
> I hear Moctezuma loved them, *you said.*
> *And I laughed.*
> *I gave you my jacket and my obsidian ear plugs*
> *Because I wanted more of the deep dry of your voice*

When you stole from us.

The outlaw gave a speech, but unlike in the old telenovelas

It was a woman who had come down from the hills

To accuse me of crimes I'd been born to commit.

This will go to the families of the women you disappear,
the farmers whose land you've stolen or drowned or
poisoned past use. Think of it like a tax, Doctora Torres.

You asked me for my scarf, but that, I told you, I would fight for.

Fight for what?

*An angry jab of that rough smoke voice, an angry press of one finger
against my chest.*

I thought:

For that silk sheath of hair always scented with plumeria.

For that laugh like cane liquor, a burning draft.

*For that last unmelted iceberg, and all I've never seen beneath the
surface.*

I said:

For double-brocade weaving of blue and gold and jade in
heirloom Oaxacan cotton, with a greco motif reminiscent of the crenellations at Monte Albán.

You removed your finger, you left as silently as you came.

I would tattoo my chest there: a teardrop with a fingerprint.

But they say that it hurts

My love

And I'm already burning.

January 3, 2079. Spilling your secrets to the outlaw in the mask.

Tell me how you first met the Colibrí.

Well, I was taking a private rail car with my aunt, the mayor's wife. And you—she got it to stop on the tracks somehow and held us up. . . . I wrote a poem about it.

How did you feel, that first time?

Like I never wanted her to stop talking. This is weird. Do I have to talk about you in the third person? Who makes a documentary about themselves, anyway?

I want a record.

For what?

In case anything happens. Will you help me or not, Jaime?

I'd do anything for you, Coli. I'm . . . I'm going to leave Aurora for you.

You're—I thought you loved her.

You and I talk more than Aurora and I ever did, and we only met in person that one time when you were robbing me! I can't stand it anymore, no matter how much I try, she won't let me in. Maybe that's all she is, in the end. A fashion-obsessed Estrato girl.

And you're really that different? I don't remember you doing anything when your uncle gassed and shot at those protestors who came to Los Pinos.

That was the president's call, and anyway what do I have to do with—

And you know the femicides and disappearances they're protesting are very much a family business—

Oh, not you too! There's nothing I can do about Beto; he might be my cousin, but he's unhinged, we all know that. Like I told Aurora, there's no point in getting disowned by my own family for something I have no control over.

So maybe she's not only fashion-obsessed after all.

You're different. You . . . try, at least, to understand me.

Me? A criminal revolutionary with a billion-peso bounty on her head? That your uncle put there? I've never taken off my bandana in front of you.

I don't care. These eyes don't really *see* anything, you know, they just recognize patterns. A new face is just noise to me. Your voice, that matters. Your touch . . . would matter.

And yet I recognize that scarf, Jaime.

January 4, 2079. Imagining conversations we could never have.

You said the other week that you loved me but you didn't know me. That I never let you in. And I—this is hilarious, right?—couldn't even respond. I was angry. Open up? You have no idea how much you're asking of me. You couldn't. Your life hasn't been easy, I know that, but it has fewer layers. Your uncle is the goddamn mayor. You've lived your whole life in the Estrato. You navigate this fresa life without anyone questioning your right to it—your pale güero skin, your perfect accent, your grammar that can slide from high castellano to fresa slang without ever passing through that muddy, indeterminate zone of a poor india who barely speaks Spanish. I spent years in dread of a careless *s* slipping out in my second-person past tenses, of being too vulgar, of not being vulgar enough. I trained my voice out of rising and dipping with its double entendres, and into that flat nasal twang I needed to survive up here.

That's why I started weaving again. That's why I make all my own clothes. I discovered my superpower at thirteen: reinvention. I could be whoever I wanted to be, so long as I dressed the part.

Your friends never understood why you bothered to date me, when you could have whatever lily-skinned supermodel you wanted. But they don't understand, you wanted me *exactly* because of how good I am at playing fresa, how good I look on your arm, how neatly I have folded myself to fit into your life. When did you decide to fall in love with me instead of use me?

When did I?

I got messy. I tried to tell you about what mattered to me. I tried to get you to see all the injustice that makes even sweetness taste like poison up here, but you never wanted to hear me. Oh, if the Colibrí talks about redressing systemic wrongs you pause and consider what she's saying. But when it's just Aurora, your fresa girlfriend, somehow it doesn't seem to register—I'm always exaggerating, or getting emotional, or not telling you enough. Do you remember when I finally forced you to talk about Beto? I sat there in the hallway even though I knew that Rosa could hear us and my voice got low, the way it does when I get angry.

You backed against the wall, I remember. And I growled that you *knew* that your own family was associated with the kidnapping of those girls. You flattened your palms against the marble, one finger at a time. Your voice had as much color as one of those rags Rosa uses to mop the floor.

And you said, because you are a coward: "And what can I do about it?"

But you knew about those parties, the unpaid domestic labor, the sexual slavery, and, yes, the murders. You knew about your cousin—and so did your father and uncle. You were finally hearing me, though. I felt this sick, lurching thrill, because for a few dizzying seconds I wasn't lying to you at all. You heard me and you didn't even want to. You saw me and you flinched away. I felt taller than you. I admit it—I felt better than you.

I told you, "Aren't you an artist? Aren't you a musician, a poet? Do you know what great poets in this benighted city used to do? They'd die in prison protesting their government's evil."

And you froze. You jerked and reached for my hands and brushed my calluses from the loom with your calluses from the guitar. You bent your head and rested your forehead against my collarbone. I breathed the eucalyptus and grapefruit of your shampoo, and I remembered why I was here, and I remembered how you lost your eyes, and I remembered why I could never hate you, even if I didn't always respect you, and your breath hitched and you said—

"I'm sorry, Aurita. I'm sorry I'm not stronger. But I can't face down my father. Even the Colibrí can't."

"Maybe she can," I said.

But that was it, you were gone already. "She has better things to do, I hope. Beto isn't the *government*, he's just a fucked-up man-child with too much money—"

And I asked you about your uncle, your brothers, and your father.

Now you pushed me away. You were angry, finally. "My father doesn't have anything to do with that!"

I laughed. I'm not proud of what I said to that, Jaime. We don't know what relationship your father has with those women, if he engages in the trade or just tolerates it.

But tolerating it is evil enough. You would understand that if you really believed that those of us struggling down below were every bit as human as you are, as you imagine me to be.

January 5, 2079. Rosa Trujillo Ramirez interviews with a disguised associate of the Colibrí's. Amazing what she saw when I wasn't looking.

You mentioned that Aurora has been arguing with Jaime? About what?

I hear a lot, you know, as the housekeeper. Those Estrato types tend to forget when I'm around. This was back in November, just after Mayor Torres put that billion-peso bounty on the Colibrí's head. Aurora was telling Jaime that she'd heard rumors that his cousin Beto was planning another of his famous clandestine parties. The kind that go on for three days at a time, attended by senators and bankers and businessmen and narcos. Jaime's cousin Beto is much older than him, Mayor Torres's son from his first marriage. He had been in charge of city security until the Highline terrorist attack. I remember because it had been in the news, how it had been his own cousin's fault that Jaime went blind.

Jaime didn't want to listen to her, of course. He couldn't do anything about it, he said.

Aurora laughed. Oh, the way Aurora would laugh when she thought that no one but Jaime could hear her. "A laugh like cane liquor, a burning draft"—I remember that from one of those poems he published yesterday. The ones they say are for the Colibrí. But I know. He wrote that for her.

She said, around that laugh, "You don't have the first idea where your daddy goes, junior."

He used the Lord's name in vain and then said "Aurora" with the exact same tone. And he told her, it was so strange, he told her she was *hidden*, like a switchblade in wrapping paper.

His face looked at her, so bleak with those special eyes, and I remembered—did you know?—that he couldn't cry. They had to remove his tear ducts along with what was left of his first pair of eyes.

He can't really see, you know. Those eyes allow him to sense things, but it isn't processed visually.

You don't say? Maybe that explains the scarves. Aurora would spend afternoons on the balcony, reading while she worked on her loom. He would find her after he had finished his music lessons, and they would just sit together. Sometimes he would touch the fabric and admire the pattern, since she tended to weave in brocade. And then she would tell him if it was red or blue or had eagles or jaguars and the sort of skirt or jacket or thigh-high boots she planned to use it in. They were so quiet, and yet every time they spoke it seemed as though there was something else beneath it.

And what do you think of Aurora?

You say you're with the Colibrí, you're one of her band? No, it's all right, I can guess why she wants to know. May God always bless the Colibrí; up here in the Estratósfera they think she's a criminal, but they don't know what it's like down on the lakes. The narcos and the government, they'll take all the money you have and kill you for more. But the Colibrí, she gives it back. Some say the narcos kidnapped her daughter, others say she was just born a man-hater—as if you have to hate men to see the evil in those bastards. She's a saint, stealing back what's rightfully ours.

So Aurora, she wants everyone to forget where she came

from. Most everyone goes along with it, but I don't believe her act. She was thirteen when she lost her parents in the Highline attack. That's old enough to know where you come from. So I don't know how she managed to turn into that girl who's always on the gossip feeds. She's more fresa than a born fresa.

So she never talks about it.

Not even to Jaime—though, I admit, I always thought there was something different between them. He was in that blast, the same as her, and he lost his eyes in it. So it seems to me that neither of them can really forget how they got to where they are, but they don't talk about it. Not to me, not to their friends. Not even to each other. And yet he spent nearly every day here before the troubles between them—ah, may God always bless the Colibrí, but those are two I wish she could have left in peace. After all they've seen.

Did they ever mention his cousin Beto again?

Not where I could hear. I think Jaime didn't like to think of his family that way. But Aurora was right. All those juniors, even the ones who would never go, know what happens at those parties. They know about the disappeared girls, the ones forced to prostitute themselves until one day someone killed them for nothing at all. My little niece, the daughter of my oldest sister, is one of those missing girls. My God, I hate these people sometimes. My God, may the Colibrí give them what they deserve.

January 10, 2079. I could barely stand to say your name.

You did it, then. You broke up with her.

You almost sound as though you want me to apologize.

How do you even know that I'm attracted to you?

Don't you keep calling?

It's not safe for us to meet. I'm not your girlfriend.

I know. It's okay. I admire you. I love you.

You can't love someone you don't even know.

Aurora was . . . is . . . I've never seen your face, I don't know your name and I know you better than I ever knew her.

You were with her for over a year.

The only language Aurora really spoke was her loom and her clothes. Too bad for her I can't fucking see them.

Communication isn't only about talking. What do you and I even have in common? Have you even wondered about everything I'm hiding?

You'll never know all of anybody. But you can love what you know about them.

But what you know might be the wrong part, Jaime.

February 7, 2079. A disguised associate of the Colibrí's interviews Daniela Q, when she was still at that gossip rag.

How have your readers reacted to the latest activities of the Colibrí?

Our fan base at *Mejor Que Tú* magazine is teenage juniors and their elevator-riding tween groupies. Most of our attention has to be focused on the tabloid angle, the Jaime/Colibrí speculation. These days, that includes Aurora, though before she wasn't particularly important in the feeds—I mean, it's not every day a Zapatista lady thief who runs around in a hummingbird feather headdress and a bandana mask steals some mireina's tabloid-star boyfriend, you know?

The Colibrí has been making her way through the whole city senate—she's robbed five in the last month! It's uncanny, the way she gets past their security. Chucho el Roto for the twenty-first century. She claims in her videos that she acts alone, not for the Zapatistas or any organized group. This didn't stop the city legislative assembly from raising the bounty on her head on the grounds that the Colibrí is an operative for the New Zapatista Liberation Army. It's still political poison to associate with them, though that international tribunal cleared them a few years ago. Now the theory is it was really some narco hit. Anyway, no one in the office pays much attention to the political side. Mostly all the juniors and wannabes have been swooning over the message that the Colibrí sent to Jaime in her last video. Did you see it? She's in the woods somewhere, face hidden by the bandana and the headdress. The girls are all trying to imitate that voice, that sort of take-no-prisoners gravel swagger has gotten very a la moda. But we have an expert in-house who swears she uses a sublingual vocal mask—which makes sense. If anyone could find the Colibrí, the mayor would stick her head on a wall in the zócalo, like the Aztecs. Here's the video.

> *There's something my grandmother used to tell me, Jaime: Never trust a man with power over you. And sure as hell don't kiss him. Well, I haven't yet, but I need to know—what am I to you? A poor indígena who should be grateful you bothered to notice her? Or just a challenge, a new flavor now that you've gotten bored of the old one? You seem to think I should notice you—so tell me why. How are you worth it? If we're both symbols, between the bloodred fruit and the spiny cactus and the eagle and serpent in its claws—which is you and which is me? The sour cactus pear? The eagle alighting with the will of a god? The serpent struggling in its claws? The cactus is poisoned, Jaime, poisoned from the roots. What good are your spines if you won't use them? Go back to your good fresa girl if that's all you want out of me. I ain't waiting.*

Well, I can only imagine how Aurora felt watching that one!

Has she done anything in response?

Did she ever! She revealed herself in public for the first time in a month last night, at the gala fundraiser of Todas Juntas, that woman's crisis charity that her mother runs. If she was hurting, she didn't show it last night. She stepped out of the Hill family car in her most incredible outfit to date: a floor-length ball gown trimmed in eagle feathers. The fabric was some kind of hand weave in blue and gold and white—no one knows

where she sources her fabrics, she must special order them—
and it swept upward over a fitted bodice studded with jade. The
most astonishing thing, though, was her hat. It was all fabric,
stiffened and folded in a way that looked distinctly eaglelike,
with these long feathers woven in to brush her shoulders. She
looked more dangerous than beautiful in that outfit, a genuine
predator. And, given who stole her boyfriend, it was a response
more perfect than words. Eagle eats hummingbird. Sorry, no
disrespect intended to your boss. I know relationships end all
the time.

None taken. She saw the outfit. It was well done.

Aurora's always spoken more eloquently with her clothing.
She gave me a brief interview, though she refused to so much
as mention Jaime. All she would say about his new maybe-
girlfriend was, "I sympathize with many of the injustices that she
decries in her videos. I, of course, take issue with her *methods.*"
The look on her face when she said "methods" will probably pay
my rent for a month. Subtexual gold, the commenters love it.

I did an interview with them before the breakup. It didn't
go anywhere at the time, but now I'm remembering this odd
exchange between them.

We were adjusting the cameras, so Jaime started flicking
through his feed, which he can do just by accessing something
with his eyes, I'm unclear on the details. He was ignoring
everyone, and Aurora turned to him and said:

"Who *would* you be if you had to face just a little of your
discomfort?"

It sounded harsh to me, but he barely raised his eyebrows. He didn't look at her, he just said, "Less fucked up. The same as you would be if they hadn't killed your parents."

She bent over as though he had punched her. He didn't seem to notice for nearly a minute. But just when we had finished with the cameras, he reached over, squeezed her hand and kissed it, and I thought—I swear to God, shows you what I know, no wonder I'm still single—that theirs was a true love.

April 19, 2079. The poisoned roots.

How do you feel knowing that your family is intimately involved in a corrupt drug-funded slavery and prostitution ring?

You actually want me to answer you on camera? Beto could go down tomorrow and all I'd feel is relief.

And what about Mayor Torres? Or your father?

Coli . . . they're not perfect. They're corrupt machista assholes, fine, I'll give you that, but I can't believe that they know about this. I just can't.

If you do, how could they not?

Don't make me answer that. I'm worried about you. I've heard things.

What things?

That you're threatening city assembly members. That you're

connecting them with high-ranking members of the Conquis-
tador cartel and sending the information to pirate net broadcasts.
That you managed to hack the mayor's personal video channel
for an hour. And that—

What? Tell me.
You're breaking into our homes. Stealing things . . .

Oh, say it ain't so, Jaimecito. Things?
They won't tell me specifics, Coli!

But you know.
How can I know?

*Say it, baby. Say it. Don't play innocent fresa boy with me. You
know what I've been doing because it's in the center of the frame you've
been trying to pretend isn't actually on the wall all this time.*
Wait—the girls? You've been stealing Beto's girls?

*They're human beings that someone else bought. Or do you think
there are different rules for lake-dwellers and indígenas like me?*
No, of course not! Of course you can't—you're freeing
them. Of course.

You sound surprised.
I just don't understand why my father—he said you were
stealing things and that I had to stop betraying my own blood
and help them catch you. He said that you're just using me to
get to them. I know it's not true—

Oh, but it is, Jaimecito.

You're not—it is?

I'm only talking to you like this because I want you to hear me, at long goddamn last. I want you to see, er, metaphorically speaking—

Oh, for God's sake, Coli.

Sorry. I mean that you have spent your whole life shying from real responsibility. And you do it by denying your awareness of the evil around you. Well, now you're talking to me, Jaime. Now you know. So yes, I'm using you. I'm using you because I want you to help me.

You want me to help you. Help you how?

I can tell you the names of girls my people have confirmed are missing and almost certainly have passed through Beto's orbit. I can even give you vocal clips for a few of them. You visit your cousins and talk to the domestics of your aunts and you get yourself an invite to one of those terrible parties and then let me in the back door. I get those girls out one at a time.

You can't be serious!

Why not?

I could get killed!

You know that your own family is capable of killing you and you still defend them?

Defend them? Look at me, I can't stop laughing and I'm so scared I could puke. My father told me to denounce you and I told him to go to hell.

So pick a side, Jaime.

Don't ask me this, Coli. I want you to survive. I want us to meet in person again. My uncle and my father are planning something. They want to find a way to bring you down.

Tell me something I don't know, mi vida. So will you?

I don't want to die.

Neither do I.

Send me the names. And the voices. God help us, Coli, but I won't let you do this alone.

May 8, 2079. I nearly sent this. I very nearly did.

When I knew you were going to leave me, Jaime, but you hadn't done it yet, I would lie in my bed and imagine all of the ways I could convince you to stay. And the wildest thing was, I knew that I could! All I had to do was betray my family and everything that I'd dedicated my life to. And now you're gone, months gone, and I've had my cry, as Mamá would say. Now it's time to get back out into the world!

The trouble is, I see the world through your . . . well, not eyes, obviously, but your voice, your poetry, your laughter, those silly songs you would improvise for me on our walks. But you don't want me. Not the parts of me that I could give you, anyway.

I was making you a scarf. I'd had an inspiration the night of the first V-mail I never sent, and I sat in my backstrap loom though it hurt like hell from the bruises, and I worked out the basic pattern. I'm finishing it now, Jaime, and oh, it's so beautiful. You would have loved it. The colors of the ocean mixed with a thread that shimmers like a quetzal feather. The embroidery is thick, nearly a quarter of a centimeter high, a pattern of feathers. I finished it and hid it under my bed. I think Rosa found it, though.

I've started to regret not telling you back then, so I've decided to say it out loud now and see how I feel about it. It seems to me that I've spent so long unable to trust anyone, that my secrecy has grown inside me like a tumor. Maybe you would have understood; maybe you wouldn't have blamed me.

But now you would, I think.

Here, a truth.

My parents didn't die in the Highline attack; my mother is still alive. I was with the New Zapatista Liberation Army, protesting the new station, and I saw the bomb just before it went off. It wasn't our bomb, Jaime. You have to believe me. The government blamed us, that's all. There was a boy my age nearby, in the path of the blast. And I grabbed him and pushed him onto the tracks. He and I woke up in the hospital, forever changed. The Señora Hill—Mamá—adopted me. I've been able to use her access—and yes, yours, Jaime—to pass government information onto my mother and the others in the movement.

I never meant to use you when we met. I was surprised that you even wanted to talk to me. I thought we had so much time, I thought that I could control how much my mother demanded of me. I couldn't. And I couldn't tell you. For years I had a nightmare where I would tell you who I was, and then I would wake up to a different nightmare, where I couldn't.

So I tell you now, when you can't hear me. Maybe this will go in my documentary, my collage, my forbidden portrait of a distorted heart.

June 3, 2079. I cried the first time I watched this. You found poetry even in betrayal.

You had the most beautiful voice. I read the rumors about the sublingual mask, but I didn't believe them. That voice went through me like a dart, mezcal and woodsmoke, something cold and something still burning.

I had given you information about four girls I was able to find. Two in Beto's apartment and the other two with a lowlife friend of his who lived a few floors down in Cuauhtemoc Tower. I told you that I had tried to look discreetly among my uncle's staff and my own family's, but I hadn't. I realized, and then couldn't stop remembering, the way the girls would always change in my uncle's house. Their soft voices folding into one another, the texture occasionally brightened by sobs in a bathroom, my aunt's quiet disapproval of the sentimentality of her waitstaff. Once, stumbling home late and drunk from a party, I smelled blood on the pool house bathroom towels. My brother told me one of his girlfriends had gotten her period. And I remember thinking, but not saying, *Period blood doesn't smell like that, Jorge.* So I told you about Beto. I figured it would be enough.

"And your parents?" you asked, so cool and so sharp. My heart rocked against my breastbone.

"I don't know," I said.

"Yes you do, Jaimecito," you said, and disconnected the call.

A week later you got in touch again. "I've got the four out," you said, warm this time. "I've been thinking, would you like to visit me?"

I came to Star Hill three days later. Though you kept the bandana up, you didn't blindfold me, because outside of Estrato tech my implants struggled to make sense of the world. The lake and its reflections made me feel as though I had fallen through a looking glass. You brought me there on a flat-bottomed boat and I held myself rigid, the stink of that black water filling my nostrils. I couldn't even catch a whiff of that foreign-familiar smell that I remembered from the time you robbed us in the railcar. You poled the boat well, I'm sure, but every time we rocked I was convinced we were about to fall in. You must have been laughing at me the whole time. And all I wanted to do was touch you, at last, to make sure that you were real.

We stopped, I couldn't tell where. I could get a read on a small structure with just one other person inside. My network connection was laggy. It couldn't register locations, let alone faces. I stayed inside the boat. I didn't trust myself to get out on my own. You climbed back in and handed me a glass.

"Pulque," you said, when I sniffed at it.

I'd never had pulque before, but I took a sip. It was sour, viscous, bubbly. Nothing like a good beer. Berenice once told me they fermented it with dog shit, but I thought better of asking.

"It's good stuff," you said, laughing a little. "But give it to Juanita if you don't want it."

Juanita, the person whose face I couldn't read, introduced herself. Her hand dwarfed mine when she shook it. She was at least a head taller than both of us. She took over the pole in back and you sat across from me at the front of the boat. You told Juanita to take us through the chinampas garden plots, which I'm sure would have offered a beautiful view for someone else. I wondered what you wanted. Why had you agreed to see me after keeping me dancing for so long?

"I'll take you back anytime you want," you said. "If it's too hard just tell me."

I took another determined swig of the pulque. "It's not too hard. I'll adjust. I'm just used to . . . having more information."

"You're not used to being blind."

I tilted my head, though even as I did it, I recognized the gesture as something Aurora would do when I said something she didn't approve of. I missed her. When had that happened? "I'm always blind, Coli," I said. "What I do now isn't seeing." I could only rely on my unaugmented senses to orient myself. The rain started. It washed over our little corner of the world, a soft rush that nearly drowned our voices, drumming on the tiny pavilion roof.

The air smelled clean, and green, and silent.

"We're entering the chinampas plots," you said. "The corn is half again as tall as you are."

I could have laughed. My implants had made the figures look like swaying giants. They had never seen corn before. And, I thought, didn't that make me precisely the sheltered, privileged Estrato boy she said I was?

"Isn't it dangerous to grow food with the polluted water?"

You had leaned toward me in our silence, but pulled back now. There had been something—a scent, a memory, a familiarity in that gesture. But I couldn't hold it. You turned very Colibrí, as if there were cameras ready to broadcast one of your "messages to the people."

"The chinampas traditionally are nonpolluting. And we have ecologists working with local farmers to introduce algae and plants that are cleaning up Estrato waste."

"It's not only Estrato waste," I said.

"Sure," you said, "you assholes outsource plenty of it to multinationals too."

I sighed. "Didn't I help you?"

"You did," you said, with something odd in your voice. "But I'm still not sure if it's because you want to get in my pants or because you care."

"I care," I said, softly, but you didn't respond. We were silent for a while.

"Look," you said, "it's a double rainbow."

I looked up and tried to get a read, but outside of the boat everything was noise. I shook my head. "It wouldn't be much use, anyhow. Aurora . . . she used to describe colors to me."

"Tell me, how would she have described a rainbow?"

I was surprised that you asked, but even more surprised when I started to answer. I had tried so hard not to think about Aurora in those months of pursuing you, as though to admit what I had loved about her would mean admitting that I had made a mistake. But you asked, and there she was, smiling against my ear.

"It's really a circle, she told me that first. But the earth cuts through it, so we only see one half. There's never an end to a rainbow. And the bottom band is purple, as faint as chiffon. Quinceañera chiffon, Aurora called it. Though she made her own quinceañera gown, and didn't use any chiffon at all. Then a blue of a sky in a sun shower, the blue of lapis lazuli dusted with chalk. Green so green it seems fake and flat, just to prepare you for the purity of the yellow. Somewhere in between gold foil and parrot feathers, she told me, the ones that puff out close to the neck. And then, last, the crimson that bleeds into the gray of the clouds behind it. And just where they mix, the red of freshly spilled blood."

"Oh," you said, and I caught it again, that sweet breath of something familiar. But the rain was dissipating, and the breeze blew it away. She twisted in her seat. "Juanita, let's get back. Bartolomé should be here soon and I need to talk to him about the next raid."

We went back to the first structure, which turned out to be a cantina. I had finished my pulque, somehow, so they gave me another. It tasted better this time. I sat with Juanita while you went off to talk to the priest with the booming voice. He was talking about going into the Lomas, because the girls who weren't killed immediately always seemed to pass through there.

You said something I couldn't make out and then both of

you moved out of hearing. I took a long gulp of my second glass of pulque.

"So, whereabouts do you live?" Juanita asked. "Far from here, I'm sure."

I felt my throat jumping, the way it does when I'm scared or sad. "Lomas," I said.

"Ah," she said. "I hear it's nice up there. Not even flooded."

I could only nod. I hadn't told you anything about my family. Nothing about the slow parade of desperate girls. Had I doomed myself when I agreed to help you? Had implicating Beto led you to my own home? I started shaking and told Juanita I was cold.

"Take the boy home, Coli," she called. "Our pulque's too strong for him; you don't want his junior friends to think we've poisoned him!"

There were six others in the cantina now, and they laughed. You came back and put your hand on my shoulder.

"Is everything okay?" you said.

That was your mistake, you know. Even though the voice was still lower and rougher, the *tone* was like a dream I had been dreaming for a year and forgotten upon waking every morning. It was everything I had missed and tried to forget and resented and never, ever understood.

I stood up and gripped your hand. You knew.

You let Juanita take me back. By the dock, as you handed me down into the boat, you gave me a scarf. The raised pattern was of feathers, you said, quetzal blue. The weave was so tight that the cotton felt as smooth as your hair, falling over your shoulders. It was a work of art, Aurora, and you gave it to someone who could only appreciate half of it.

I pulled down your bandana and leaned in as though to kiss you.

"How is this possible?" I asked. My voice cracked twice on the last word. I could not believe how much I believed it.

"I never could tell you," you said, in both of their voices. "But I still need your help, Jaime, Jaimecito. We still—"

"I'll let you know," I told you. That voice I loved, I couldn't stand to hear it any longer. I couldn't stand to smell you and touch your fabric and the feathers of the headdress that you still hadn't taken off. You nodded and let me go.

So this is my answer:

No. I can't betray my own blood for someone who has never, behind either mask, never once shown me her true self.

August 5, 2079. The sleeper agent.

It turns out that Aurora has a very interesting history. You're her real mother.

Dios mío, Aurita, do you think this is a good idea? Are you really recording this?

I'll keep it secret until it's safe to use. So you're a councilmember for which organization?

The New Zapatista Liberation Army. Why are you asking me things you already know?

Because I might not always be around to know them, Mamá. Just speak, you owe me that much.

We intended for Aurora to be an agent on the inside, and she reported back to us for years, it's true. But about a year ago, the assembly had agreed that we needed more leverage in the fight against the redistricting for the new Highline stations—yes, they're planning to destroy the entire neighborhood to extend that so-called Estratósfera. They won't even allow us to use their goddamn monorail or set foot in those towers, and their proposed payment is more of an insult than honest robbery would be. They are going to destroy our sixteenth-century church, which we only managed to save from the flooding with the savings and work of generations. They're going to destroy our homes, our public spaces, an entire Nahua community, for a shopping mall and luxury apartments. How could we not fight back? But I supposed that Aurora had spent too long up there among those criminals. I supposed that she had forgotten where she came from. Perhaps it was too hard on her, to have to pretend to be an orphan in the blast. We rarely got to see her. And then her father died last December, and she couldn't even attend the funeral.

You don't seem very sad about it.

Of course it hurt me to lose her! I pray for her every night. That first year I cried so much I lost my salt. But there was no one else, and we had to take advantage of the opportunity. She and her aunt were our only activists to survive the blast. But then we realized, no one in the hospital had any idea who she was, and that rich woman was begging for an orphan. We had to let her go! She had a special role to play in the Hill family.

But this year we told her . . .

You told me to kidnap Jaime.

I wish I had fought harder against the idea. It goes completely against our principles. Just because they accuse us of unspeakable acts doesn't mean we should lower ourselves to their level. You refused, and that was the last I heard from you for months. Not until I saw the Colibrí . . . Aurora, does anyone else know what you're doing?

Just Bartolomé and a few from the band, Mamá.

At least your cousin is there. He's always looked out for you. Oh, what will become of you? You can't come back here. And if your Estratósfera family ever discovers what you've done? If your precious boyfriend ever finds out? Oh, then I won't even have your body to bury, and they'll still build a tower where our home used to be.

August 10, 2079. You knew that I knew, and I loved you for it.

You finally call, Jaime? I thought you hated—

There's a body in the bathroom, Coli. My father told me to wait in the greenhouse. But I'm in the laundry room instead. I can still hear them talking upstairs. They want to clean it up quietly. But it's a woman, Coli. A young woman dressed like a maid, but her face doesn't register.

They . . . where are you?

At my uncle's house in Lomas. I don't know how you get into our houses or do what you do, but I think you should come here.

You do.

I know your people have stayed away from Lomas since—but I think you have to come here now. I can't stand this anymore.

Jaime, Jaimecito, what can't you stand?

I can't stand that you might have been right.

August 11, 2079. And there comes a time when all that's left is your own blood.

Juanita was sure it was a setup. You had refused my calls for a month. Our spies said you seemed to be working for your father. You had rejected me, so why call for help? I agreed with her, but I argued that we should go anyway. Your voice was so strained and quiet. You didn't want to say it, not a word, and yet you were trying to tell me something anyway. You only called me Coli, which meant you hadn't exposed me to your family.

Juanita shrugged and said, "Let's get those bastards, then. If we're lucky we'll get enough to bring down the mayor. And if we're not, God will still take care of it when we're worm food."

I reached up to hug her, which is a joke between us because she's so big I can only reach her shoulders. "This is why I love you," I said.

And she smiled and said we should make sure Bartolomé was willing to risk his neck for my junior boyfriend.

He was, Jaime. Which you know. Or will know, if you survive.

It was one in the morning by the time we arrived, dark from the thick smog blocking out the moon and even the lights of the Estratósfera towers to the east. We decided that I would go in first. Bartolomé would wait for my signal dressed in full Colibrí gear. We're almost exactly the same height and build; with the sublingual vocal mask it would be hard to tell. I got in—no, I won't tell you how. I still don't know if you'll betray me, Jaime.

The greenhouse was dark and empty. I had to break open the padlock. The flagstone paths inside were covered with dead leaves and flowers and dirt. I flashed the ultraviolet light that I couldn't see and waited.

You snuck up behind me—you didn't need light to find your way, after all.

"No headdress," you said.

I jumped and swung around. You were alone. "The Colibrí is waiting to see what's really happening."

"They already got rid of the body," you said. "A truck came."

"Convenient."

You smiled. "But I got the license plate. My uncle's press secretary is driving."

It was a very good offer, Jaime. Not your father, not your property, but damning political leverage all the same. I sent the photo to Juanita and told her to follow with Ulises.

"What happened?"

"I don't know."

It hurt to see you. I had thought of you so much in the last month that I hadn't expected it to. But you had chosen to be the rotten fruit of your family's rotten tree. You hadn't chosen the hummingbird.

"Why am I here, Jaime?"

Your throat jumped. "So you can tell me to my face," you said, "why you lied to me. I *loved* you, or I loved both of the creations I thought were you—did you ever feel anything for me? Did you ever regret using me? Did you think, oh, poor blind Jaime, he can't tell the difference?"

"You came after *me*! I never asked for your love affair with the Colibrí."

"You sure didn't reject it! You seduced me with my ideal woman, and none of it was real."

That made me freeze. Because my heart was breaking, I suppose, though I had thought it was already in pieces. "Was she really? Did you really love nothing about Aurora? I wove you a thousand stories in a thousand threads, everything I could never tell you . . ."

You took a deep breath and put your hand to my cheek. "No," you said, and shoved me to the floor. Glass shattered and floodlights blinded me. I fell at your feet and found my com by touch, to yell at Bartolomé to get the hell away from here. It was too late, of course. He'd already come inside when he hadn't heard from me.

Someone yelled, "Hands up, Colibrí." And you left me there on the floor, ran to stop your father's soldiers from killing us.

And instead they shot you. Bartolomé they left to drown in his own blood among the poinsettia.

No one suspected me. They cleaned me up and took me back to Mamá's and said they would tell me when your condition changed. They were all laughing, what a good joke, they said. Of course it could only have been a man who robbed them like that. But what a good joke to play at being a woman. Poor blind Jaime probably didn't even know. Don't worry, they told me, we won't let his identity go public. Poor Bartolomé. Even in death he's stuck with my secrets.

We caught your uncle, by the way. Definitively connected him and your cousin to various femicides and disappearances. Impeachment hearings start tomorrow. I'm praying to the virgin you'll be awake to see them. Hate me all you want, hate me for the rest of your life. But you always knew me, mi vida, you knew more than I could ever tell you.

October 3, 2080. Some wars end because the soldiers refuse to fight.

Daniela Q: Let's move to something more personal. Just this past week you've been taking your first public steps since your near-fatal shooting last summer. Five days ago, you testified in the legislative assembly about the need to unilaterally restrict further Estrato development. So I have to ask, why now? Why has the junior golden boy at last turned political?

Jaime: I spent a lot of time on my back, to be honest. The Colibrí gave me—gave us all—a lot to think about. She gave us a promise that I think we all have to try to make real. She told me once that I never faced my own discomfort. Her death made me face it. She showed me a . . . truth, about myself, about herself, that it took me a long time to understand.

Daniela Q: Your family has been through a number of changes. Your uncle was forced to resign as mayor before the impeachment hearings began. Your cousin Alberto was assassinated by a presumed cartel member. And unlike every other Torres of the last five generations, you're studying law at the public autonomous university.

Jaime: I never wished misfortune on my family, but I do want justice. I'm lucky to have finally understood how I can use my influence and position in society to help redress the wrongs of systemic inequality.

Daniela Q: Are you writing poetry again?

Jaime: Yes. I've even written a couple of songs lately.

Daniela Q: Is there a special someone?

Jaime: I'm not sure, to be honest. There's just someone—I'd like to get to know better without all the pyrotechnics. I have this feeling we might just get along.

October 4, 2080. The thread and the loom.

Hello again, Jaime. I admit, that poem caught me off guard. A year without a word, and now hearings in the assembly! But I believe you. It's been a hard year for both of us.

I put this together for you and I thought I wouldn't send it, that it would just stir up bad memories. But then I reread that poem, and I realized that you knew me—that you knew us—both of them who were always, always me.

I'll read it and then I'll press send. It's time you learned the whole story.

> *I met an iceberg who wouldn't tell me her name*
> *But wove it in a hundred thousand strands of blue-black thread.*
> *The color of the lake, polluted, she once told me,*
> *Is the color of a hummingbird's crest.*

Before She Was Bloody
TESSA GRATTON

. . . and I made the Sahenate strong because I had three hearts.
—*from* Seven Hundred Declarations of Safiya the Bloody

White petals fluttered in the air that day, hovering over the marble garden that surrounded my grandfather's palace for a quarter mile in every direction so that no one might approach without being seen. Dedicated currents of magic held the petals suspended in swirls and starbursts to celebrate the return of the Sahe Sahenam, king of kings, from a border war in the northern foothills of Syr Saria. An extravagance, I knew, but that the Architects under my command could so easily ensnare the wind made me heady with power.

No one could see my smile through the sheer red silk of my veil, and so I unleashed it, full of joy at seeing my brother Dalir in his lacquered armor and vibrant blue headscarf, marching across the fused-sand pathway through the garden. It had been months since I'd seen him! And my success here at home in quashing a thread of rebellion was news both he and Idris the Great, our grandfather and the Sahe Sahenam, would relish.

But there, beside Dalir in a place of honor, was a dark young stranger wearing the plated leather armor of the Sarians. My dearest friend and body twin, Farah za Sarenpet, touched my elbow in a quick, familiar caress; she too had noticed the handsome stranger at Dalir's side.

Grandfather paused at the crescent ablution pool to dip his hands and touch his eyelids in deference to She Who Loves Silence. Dalir followed suit, as did the first and second generals and all five glorified captains in the royal party. But the stranger merely knelt respectfully and never touched the water.

He was no devotee of our goddess! How intriguing! I skimmed my elbow against Farah's bare arm, and she leaned ever so slightly nearer, to tap our silent language onto my wrist: she agreed with me that he was beautiful, but in the way of heathen horses, strong and stocky and proud as he strode up the shallow marble steps, and not so graceful as Dalir. I let my smile curve wickedly as I reached out to welcome my brother, whose narrow face broke into a grin that matched. He surged faster, skipping every other step to dart around Grandfather. It did the gathered mirza—the small princes of our empire—and all those who'd been away at war very well to see the affection between us, reminding them we were incorruptibly loyal to our family.

"Sahizada," I said over our clasped hands. Dalir kissed my

knuckles, drawing me closer, and with catlike speed tugged free the diaphanous red veil from across my eyes. Always a trouble-maker, my brother.

"Sahiza," he said, equally formal. "You must meet my new friend, the third son of the Sarian malka, who saved my life not once, but twice, and you must meet him with your eyes uncov-ered, for he has earned as much. Oh, and you too, Farah," he added fondly, and my body twin obeyed by uncovering her eyes.

Dalir turned, sweeping his arm out toward the stranger, and announced for all those gathered, "Here is Enver Kirazade, my newest, dearest friend!"

Enver bowed but did not cover his eyes with his large hands as would have been polite, especially before me, Safiya za Idris Sahiza, the granddaughter of Idris the Great and the Moon Eater's Mistress. I let him see my importance, and he proudly met my black eyes with his own. His were a crystalline brown, direct; his lips parted to speak, but he said nothing for a moment too long.

I made him pay for the hesitation. "I think your friend is unused to the beauty of our city," I said to Dalir.

"How could anyone be used to beauty like Your Glory's?" Farah asked sweetly. Her fingers pressed my wrist in wordless admiration.

Enver still did not speak. Despite his youth, he wore a short beard framing his jaw and chin, highlighting the rough planes of his face. His brown skin reminded me of fire, not the desert of my people or the obsidian of the Bow.

Our staring moment was interrupted by Grandfather: "Only

the Moon Eater himself," he said affectionately, in reply to Farah's question. Then he kissed my cheek and bade me replace
my veil before facing the gathered princes for his homecoming
speech.

*Our glorious city has belonged to many in the past. Its foundations
were built by prisoners and slaves for the first dynasty of Bes and
Sarenpet, before the Rise of the Holy Syr, when the desert kings of
Farz united under Isra the Great. Isra and the Holy Syr conquered
the lands around the White Sea from the northern Syr Saria, west
across the dunes to the Land of God, and as far east as Samar
and the Singing Desert. Under the Isran Dynasties, the city grew
tall and elegant with the sweeping architectural magic of She Who
Loves Silence and her shadow god, the Moon Eater.*

*Idris zada Ziya, my grandfather, brought his Silent Rebellion
to the city and claimed the throne of the king of kings. So the true
Sahenate was born, and Ashesan became the Sky Blue City. But
it is mine now, and in my heart it is the red of blood.*

—*from* Seven Hundred Declarations of Safiya the Bloody

That night, after prolonged feasting and revelry in celebration
of the return of the Sahe Sahenam, Farah and I dashed into our
shared bedroom, giggling and throwing off scarves. The heavy
door closed behind us, iron bar slamming down. It reverber-
ated through the tiles beneath our bare toes, and we danced in
drunken pleasure. We were finally alone again!

I wound our fingers together, spinning us in circles, and
Farah asked, "Did you see him eat with only forefinger and

thumb?" I fluttered my lashes and replied, "I paid more heed to his eyes than his mouth."

"Silly choices you make sometimes." Farah kissed me. "Mouths tell more."

"Blood tells most," I murmured, turning my cheek imperiously to offer her my pulse.

Little kisses bit their way down my neck, like spice in sweet cream. Farah slid her hands around my hips and asked, "Will you slice open his neck then?"

I lifted one of her hands. "The palm is more intimate," I said against her soft skin.

"Oh, Safi." Farah laughed breathlessly, kneeling. She touched her forehead to my belly and sighed longingly.

"Pretty love," I whispered, longing too. For I was the Moon Eater's Mistress, and could have no other. We posed together, silent, wishing, imagining ourselves players on a stage, and somehow that made our heartaches easier to bare.

You have heard the saying, certainly: first for her, second for him? The oldest serves She Who Loves Silence with a crown and steel will; the second gives all to the Moon Eater, the shadow god who hungers so for the spirit of our goddess he must be satiated with the bodies of her devoted. For such was I born, and became the Moon Eater's Mistress when I was of age to satisfy him.

—*from* Seven Hundred Declarations of Safiya the Bloody

Late the next morning, the Royal Mask Architect woke us from our nest of pillows and heart-soft sheets. Sunlight streamed through the goddess-eye windows cut like constellations into the white walls of my private chamber. With him came my girls carrying warm cheese-stuffed lamb, coffee, and hot water for washing.

He was a bony man in the simple blue robi of the Architects, laconic and polite, with the white dots of his station arcing across both cheeks. While we dressed, he turned his back and delivered overnight news of which mirza had drunkenly stumbled down the stairs, which had been caught kissing his cousin's husband, which had declared a poem to my glorious justice. That had been one of the mirza opposed to my sanctions against rebel families, and his poem was no doubt meant to return him to my good graces.

I said as much as Farah and I wrapped each other in matching robi, loose and sky blue, tied jackets tight to our ribs and decorated each other's fingers with rings, wound up our hair under identical white scarves.

The Architect took his turn to paint blue and black stripes and dots onto our faces to obscure the underlying design of our skulls and make us into mirror twins as defense against assassination. When we left the chamber holding hands, the Satriya guards took us in, not knowing which of us was the Sahiza, so even they could not give it away by body language. Farah had been chosen for this when I came into my blood and body, for her similar stature and shape. We practiced walking alike, skipping in complicated patterns, and playing imitation games to further confound all but those most intimate with us. Though, since Grandfather had been gone and I had become the sole representative of the Sahenate blood in the city, we'd ended our more silly endeavors.

It was a short walk to the House of the Moon, a dome of midnight-blue tiles centered in the Holy Year Courtyard, where it was my daily duty to wake the Moon Eater with my joy and body. We strode through the thirteen rows of twenty-eight pillars rising toward the bare blue sky, ecstatic flow tingling in the soles of our feet; we were thinking of Dalir's friend Enver Kirazade, and for me at least, that desire would transfer well to the Moon Eater.

But waiting for us at the ablution pool at the House's eastern entrance was the second general of the Sahe Sahenam's army, Eskandar zada Shahin, younger brother of my grandfather, and the Moon Eater's Lover before me. It had been he who had instructed me in all the ways he found most successful for waking our shadow god.

"Uncle." I greeted him eagerly, clasping his hands across the narrow crescent of the pool. My great-uncle, despite being a military man now, kept his beard unshaven in honor of his former position. He smiled and kissed my knuckles.

"Your Glory," he said in his gruff way. "I have missed the Moon Eater these six months and request your blessing to awaken him in your place today."

"Of course, Uncle. I feel certain our Moon Eater has missed you, as well. Come." Though disappointed I'd not have my own time with our lover, I dipped our hands together into the clear water and we touched our eyelids for She Who Loves Silence before entering the House.

Beneath a low, wide dome, tiled in patterns of the deepest

blue ceramics a fire can create, lies a slab of dark granite. The altar holds seventeen massive teeth, fangs as long as my hand and molars ribbed like stone. The teeth are as old as the moon itself, fallen from the Moon Eater's jaw thousands of years ago. I stopped halfway between the door and the altar, kissed my fingertips, and turned my back as my great-uncle continued on alone.

I pressed my hands between my breasts as I listened to the quiet sounds of pleasure the former Lover gave to himself and to the Moon Eater. It warmed my skin, and I thought of the moon-wide mouth of the Moon Eater, his teeth as bright as stars. I thought of Farah's gentle hands and, unexpectedly, of Enver Kirazade's solemn eyes. I welcomed the shiver of pleasure in the small of my back, the tingle in my breasts and belly, but the gift of awakening was not for me that morning.

So I breathed deeply to hold it all in until my uncle finished, welcomed the Moon Eater by his secret name, and joined me. He put a hand on my shoulder. "My thanks, Your Glory," my great-uncle said.

The forces of this world are harnessed in four forms: rising, falling, flow, ecstatic. Our Architects perfect their science by the study of these forms, experimenting with their interactions to build all the great structures of our civilization. Patience and passion are required for mastery. I have always struggled to apply these forces to my own life: falling into necessary compromise, rising to meet my own best expectations, flow that cannot be contained, and ecstasy always the intention.

—*from* Seven Hundred Declarations of Safiya the Bloody

In the past six months, while the Sahe Sahenam and his heir were at war, it was I who held the seat of the king of kings, spoke for my family, and cast deciding votes or vetoes. I had little authority to act on my own, but had learned to pull threads quickly, or was perhaps born with the skill.

I have always loved the grandeur of the Hall of Princes, the dizzying white-and-black striped domes stacked upon one another, up to the pinnacle dome so high it can be seen from all corners of the city. The cross-shaped council table rested low in the center, messily covered in inkwells and parchment, cups of wine or tea or spiced water, surrounded by pillows and rugs in every bold color of the desert. At the western head was the gilded chair of the Sahe Sahenam, where I had knelt every three days for the past six months. That day I returned to my position at the east, across from him, for now I held only my own rank again: Her Glory the Moon Eater's Mistress.

As the mirza gathered, Designers from the schools of Architecture used crystal styli to draw lines of falling and ecstatic force to keep sound from traveling in or out of the Hall, and I chatted with my uncle, who sat himself beside me. Farah knelt at my back, collecting notes for me and making certain we had a carafe of hot spice water for ourselves.

The Sahe Sahenam arrived with the last of the mirza, Dalir beside him, and the stranger Enver Kirazade, too. My grandfather wore an elaborate headscarf with a thin veil to cross his eyes; he cared not for the masking paints my generation favored over veils. Dalir's head was covered but his face striped with thin lines of gold and black to distort the planes of expression.

Enver was bareheaded and ferocious in padded robi that added to his girth as he shadowed Dalir like a bodyguard. My heartbeat picked up at the sight of him, but I gathered myself to stand and greet Grandfather, welcoming him home to his Hall of Princes.

My speech was cut short by one of those princes raising his voice to complain of my meddling ways to the Sahe Sahenam. Little did he know I'd hoped for the very thing, so I did not seem too arrogant and prideful in bragging to my grandfather of my deeds. Let it seem like humble defense of practical, necessary moves. One can achieve much more when others do not even realize they do your work for you.

I folded my hands and stood, listening as they described the order I'd given to hunt out the extended families of the three rebels caught sneaking into the palace. They'd used masks of Human Architecture to transform their faces into the three youngest cousins of the Ario family. Though the mirza had wished only to gut and hang the perpetrators and their confederates, I'd had their nephews and nieces, husbands and wives, and parents imprisoned too, and every third one executed by lottery before the mirza knew it had happened.

They accused me of barbarity; I reminded them of the Silent Rebellion that had gained my own family this very throne.

They claimed I was too young to be so cold; they insisted the Moon Eater's Mistress must be passionate and welcoming, not blood-hungry and hard. Their words cut at me, fueling my certainty that I'd been right. They had no idea what the Moon Eater longed for in a lover! None could but for myself and my uncle, the general at my side.

Even as I held my own against the princes, though younger than all of them, never biting insults back at them or letting my defense turn strident, I loved every livid, bracing moment. My grandfather finally ordered me down, and all the princes too. He agreed with them that I had overstepped my authority, but agreed with me that the mirza should have had this idea on their own, not been taught such efficient methods by a sixteen-year-old girl. Though I could not see his face clearly through his veil, the wizened irritability in his voice turned gentle toward me, and I felt his approval like a fire in my veins.

The meeting moved on to the needs of the northern army and rumblings from the heathen steppe in the far northeast, as well as integration of a new system of irrigation the Flow Architects had finalized. When the council ended, Dalir caught my eye, and I nodded, silently agreeing to meet in our favorite garden.

Near skipping with triumph, I led Farah and our contingent of guards through the Little River corridors of the rear palace and into a small flower garden tucked awkwardly between the kitchen domes and high walls of the royal barracks. A pool shaped like an eight-point star held the center, and eight narrow paths of crushed pink salt ran out from it. Between the spokes, pink desert roses and thorny violet sata vines tangled, messy and violent. We'd loved it as children, for the thorns could not hide assassins, and if our Satriya guards stationed themselves right, we felt free of their oppressive presence and could run and dance and play rather loudly without being overheard. I spent many hot afternoons immersed in that star pool.

I sat on the edge with Farah and played my fingers along the intricate pattern of tiny blue-white-orange tiles. Elaborate golden writing declaimed a prayer to She Who Loves Silence at the bottom of the pool, words glinting through still water. As always, I tapped the surface to disrupt it all. I smiled. Farah sat with her shoulder against my spine, and we waited for Dalir.

He came quickly, Enver a heavy shadow at his heels, and ordered his men to join mine at the edges of the garden and in strategic places above and around us on the arches and steps. "Safiya!" Dalir exclaimed, seating himself on the droplets of water I'd splashed onto the tiles. "You are a demon."

It was difficult to say if he was more impressed or horrified. I shrugged, slipping off my entire headscarf and tossing it across Farah's lap. Pieces of my hair fell out of their braids and loops. "It was the right move, Dalir."

"But some of those killed were children."

I lifted my eyes to his, dark like mine, but softer. "You will be Sahe Sahenam when Grandfather dies and must accustom yourself to brutality."

His mouth pinched. "I have seen brutality, at war. You cannot imagine the filth and horrors I have seen, and—and done."

"I think she can," said Enver Kirazade, the first words he ever spoke to me.

He crouched between two bobbing roses. His elbows rested on his knees, hands loose between them, but I was not fooled; he was at the ready, some hidden knives mere inches from those hands, to spring between my brother and danger, perhaps between me and danger as well. He stared at me, and my tongue dried out, my fingers quieted against the pool water.

Farah laughed suddenly, soft and amazed. "Speechless," she whispered.

I scowled, but not at her. At Enver Kirazade, who had made me stare.

He said, "What gave you your vivid imagination, Your Glory?"

At that moment my imagination was at work only stripping him of armor, pulling his hair, finding his tongue with my teeth.

Dalir answered, "Our grandmother's stories of the Silent Rebellion."

"I would like to hear those stories," Enver said softly, as if he and I were alone together, his words meant for silky pillows. I pressed my hips down against the edge of the pool, which arched the small of my back, making me sit taller, but also more aggressively, and Farah touched the back of my neck, offering me my veil. But I did not want to hide myself from them.

I said, "Dalir heard the stories too, exactly as I did, but he did not *listen*."

My brother scoffed, and I whipped toward him. "You forget the way Grandfather infiltrated the palace, you forget the devious methods our family used, the fast, efficient destruction of our enemies, the culling of the opposition in order to take the firmest possible hold, Sahizada. Such methods can be used against us, now that we have taught them. Our grandfather stole a throne, and it is your job to keep it secure."

"We won because She was with us." Dalir touched his eyelids respectfully. "She gave Grandfather Her blessing. So long as
She is with us, we are safe from those kinds of rebels."

"We are never safe," I snarled, leaping to my feet. I glanced
between my beautiful, peaceful brother, who seemed to have
learned hesitation while at war, and his new friend, hulking like
a griffin, dangerous and keen. No wonder Dalir's life had had
to be saved not once, but twice!

I left them there, all three, and instead of going to the barracks to wrestle or run, instead of stomping through the halls
in search of relief—displaying my sudden wild mood for all the
palace to see—I shut myself into my chambers to pace and plan
and wait until it was a new day and I could take my frustrations
to my Moon Eater alone.

> *She Who Loves Silence is a huntress. Her silence is that of patience
> and cunning. But too many of our people forget that. My brother
> did.*
> —*from* Seven Hundred Declarations of Safiya the Bloody

There are so many moments I remember from those last days
when I had only one heart: leaning close to Grandfather as I
helped him design the Moon Eater mosaic for the small dome
of his mausoleum; one of the princes, Rabiah za Ziya, coming
to me for help convincing the mirza to accept her proposal to
rearrange the tax plan for the small kings—we drank rose tea
and she flattered me again and again; dancing with Farah and
our instructor, stealing kisses between sets; Dalir bringing me

sweet cheese and his apology, then the two of us climbing to the top of the Bright Star Minaret to argue ancient philosophy until the morning song rang out across the city; Dalir again, laughing at some silly thing Farah said, his beard shaved to match Enver's and thin white lines painted in repeating patterns along his cheeks; Dalir and his shadow sparring with het sticks in the Heaven's Clock Courtyard, while a crowd of Satriya guards looked on and Farah and I held hands so tightly we bruised each other's knuckles; Farah touching Enver Kirazade's wrist as soft as a songbird to get his attention, and both of them going still; steam rising from the waters of the women's bathhouse, turning Enver's hair into ecstatic waves, and he did not cover himself despite my arrival and Farah's and three of our girls and two women Satriya. Enver looked at me and then Farah, as the steam stuck our thin robi to hips and breasts and melted the perfect dots painted to our foreheads, turning our faces into streaks of rain. I said, "Did no one tell you, griffin, this is the women's bath?" and he stepped so close to me the guards unsheathed their curved swords. He said, "You make me forget there is any difference in our bodies, for surely there is not in our spirits." I smiled. I bit my bottom lip so he could see it. And Farah said, "I rather like the differences between your two bodies." She touched my wrist, and his wrist, and the moment lasted forever.

She Who Loves Silence wishes for us to treat our bodies with the respect we give to the finest Designs, for that is what we are.
—from Seven Hundred Declarations of Safiya the Bloody

Dalir whispered to me as soon as he returned from war that I should know how to use a weapon, even if I would never carry one as the Moon Eater's Mistress. "She Who Loves Silence wishes for us to treat our bodies like the finest Designs," he reminded me. I teased him, disagreed for fun more than principle, until he suggested Enver Kirazade could show me.

We began one morning nearly three weeks after his arrival. I was fresh and exhilarated from visiting the House of the Moon, eager to show off, but more eager to learn with his hands on me. Farah knelt on the marble floor with ink and parchment, practicing her calligraphy, and our Satriya slouched beside the doors and open archways of this small weapons room. Enver waited in the center of a hexagon of padded carpets, and I leaped onto him immediately, twisting my arms around his neck and sliding a leg between his, in a quick grappling move I'd learned to use my weight against a heavier enemy. He hardly reacted, grunting as he shifted his stance to accommodate me hanging from him. "You should go for my eyes instead of my throat, for you are not strong enough to cut off my breathing."

"You were ready for me!" I complained.

He turned his face slightly; his left eye was beside mine. "I was not ready for you," he whispered, meaning something far more important than wrestling.

I forgot who I was, where I was, I forgot everything with that single desert-fire eye on mine, his arm around my ribs. I was nobody except for the thing we were together, for an instant, for a perfect soft breath.

And then it all came rushing back. I was Safiya za Idris

Sahiza, the Moon Eater's Mistress, and I could never have him.

He pulled me around his body and kissed me. It was wild and hot, and his large warrior's hands gripped my hips, holding me against him so I could dangle or cling. I wrapped around him, kissing him back. Never before had I been kissed by a man or boy, or with such roughness and open passion. He wanted me, and he thought he could have me. It was a kiss of offering as much as taking, without the yearning I was used to, without the terrible teasing knowledge that a kiss was all it could be.

Because he did not know.

I realized it even as my body burned and melted and I clung to him, as his teeth chewed at my mouth and jaw, devouring me. I slid my hands down his arms, thighs tight around his waist, holding on as he tasted my neck. There at his elbow I found the hilt of a flat knife sheathed in the leather gauntlet. I slid it free and ended our kiss with the tip of the blade in the hollow behind his ear.

Enver gasped, startled as he'd not been by my grappling. His eyes slowly focused on me, my mouth, then dragged up to my eyes. "I love your ruthlessness," he said thickly, beginning to smile. "I love *you*."

"No," I said, cutting his neck.

He released me as blood streamed in a solid line down to his shoulder, soaking into his robi. I tossed his knife to the rug and backed away an arm's length. "I am the Moon Eater's Mistress. You cannot have what you want."

Farah appeared at my side, and took my hand. Hers was hot,

her breath as fast as mine. Enver looked between us, confused. He said, "It is a religious title, is it not?" Finally he touched his hand to the wound on his neck, fingers finding sticky, flowing blood.

"Yes," Farah answered in a whisper. "But so much more. She belongs to the Moon Eater. She is the embodiment of His longing for She Who Loves Silence, when the goddess will not have Him, so that His hunger does not tear even the stars from the sky. We must sacrifice our need for Safi in reverence to His."

It made me want Enver all the more for how gutted he looked, how sad. "Both of you?" he asked, touching Farah's wrist.

"She belongs to the Moon Eater, and I belong to her," Farah said, like an apology, and she wove our fingers together, and we left.

Never think the sacrifices one makes for the Moon Eater are not repaid with gifts such as self-awareness and confidence. Had I not been taught to give, how might I have ever understood the nature of taking?
—*from* Seven Hundred Declarations of Safiya the Bloody

We cried, Farah and I, angry and mournful and even laughing at how we both wanted him and both wanted each other, and mostly just that we were so full of wanting we might die.

I said, in the last dark hour before the morning song, "Farah, you should have him. You can, both of you, and it would be like I was there too. For you are my body twin, and the twin of my heart. That will keep him here, with us, if you take him and make him your husband."

"He wants me differently than he wants you," she whispered.

We lay wrapped around each other in the silken pillows and heart-soft sheets, staring up at the constellation of tiny windows cut into the ceiling of our chamber. Gentle moonlight ghosted through, making only our eyes shine in the darkness.

"Kiss him the way he kissed me, and that will change," I replied.

She paused, then touched her cheek to my shoulder.

I shoved her over and rolled on top of her. I grasped her face in both hands and kissed her hungrily, as I had never allowed myself before. I imagined my hands large and hard from war, my shoulders heavy and strong, my mouth and jaw rough. I became him in my mind's eye, kissing Farah as if I could have her, knowing we belonged together. I kissed her messily, madly, with my tongue and teeth, toying too closely with giving too much. But I was not Safiya the Moon Eater's Mistress in the center of that kiss; I was Enver Kirazade.

Opening up to me, she returned it, soft beneath me, and her hands found my ribs, gripping through my thin robi. She danced her fingers at the collar, eager and sweet. She said, "I love you, Safi, I want you," and I kissed her eyelids.

It was not morning, but I got up, groping for her jacket and headscarf. "Go," I said. "Take this all to Enver, for me, and for you, and for him."

"And you?"

"I love you too," I said in a dark voice, a longing voice. I had to get to the House of the Moon before I spilled my desire where the Moon Eater could not relish it.

Shoving Farah out the door before me, I ran for the House with two Satriya guards scrambling after me. I splashed water from the ablution pool onto my face. A near-full moon still hung high enough to pierce the smoky glass eye at the pinnacle of the dome. I threw myself at the altar, shoving aside the fossilized teeth. Then I disrobed to stand naked for the Moon Eater. "It is early, but I need you now," I whispered. "Is that all right? I was never taught to need you, only be ready when you needed me."

Though sometimes I woke him slowly, teasing myself and him, sometimes I sat or lay myself back on the altar to show off my loveliness to the dome's eye, sometimes I stretched out my time alone in the House of the Moon, that morning I pressed my bottom to the edge of the altar and dug into myself immediately. I was desperate and not understanding everything I felt in my heart, the conflict, the sharp line between furious love and wild denial.

I whispered the Moon Eater's secret name again and again, beckoning him, begging him, with my voice and my wracked body, until he was there.

My brother always knew I would make a better king than he.
—from Seven Hundred Declarations of Safiya the Bloody

Loose and languid, I made my way back to my chamber, where at least twice as many Satriya waited. The Royal Mask Architect was just ducking out, no doubt surprised to have found me already gone. "Your Glory," he said, searching the hall behind me for Farah. "His Glory the Sahizada is inside. I have left a pot of paint for you. Shall I return inside to design your lines?"

"No." I brushed past him, closing my chamber door. Dalir sat on a pile of cushions beside my low calligraphy table, his legs curled beneath him and cradling a pot of paint divided into three sections: black, white, gold.

"You've been busy, and the sun is hardly up," Dalir said, a smile brightening his eyes. He dipped the narrow brush into the gold paint and skillfully drew a perfect line along his jaw, mirroring the edge of his carefully trimmed beard.

I sank to my knees before him and took the brush to finish his gold lines. "Whatever do you mean?" My words were as light as the touch of the brush on his skin.

He laughed. "Marriage alliance, and a good one."

Pleasure infused my answering smile. "You think so?"

"I do. I also know it is hard for you. I admire your dedication."

"It is no more than you would do, were I to be the king of kings and you the Moon Eater's Mistress."

"Maybe." Dalir shook his head, and I tsked at him for disrupting my design. I chose a different brush for the black paint. He closed his eyes and continued softly, "I am grateful for you, for what you can do. I know our Sahenate will be stronger for it, even though it sometimes curdles my stomach like bad milk."

I paused with the tip of the brush just off his cheek, and, full of warmth and the certainty that our futures would be great, I gently kissed his lips.

"I'll make you proud too, sister," he said, and then he bared his teeth.

"Dalir?" I dropped the brush.

My brother shook his head, mouth in a rictus twist. His skin suddenly gleamed with sweat. "I can't—I can't," he gasped.

The lines of gold I'd painted parallel to his beard line sank into his skin as if acidic. Dalir fell sideways, face drained of color, greenish even, as the paint ate into his flesh and his bones caved in.

It was over that fast.

My brother, Dalir zada Idris Sahizada, was dead.

I hovered over him for a shocked moment, unwilling to touch his face, or the remnants of paint there. His beauty had crumbled, wilted, and he was only a body in dark orange robi.

The pot of paints rested as if innocent beside my knee. Standing with it carefully clutched in my hands, I went to my door. A pounding filled my ears, my heart, *my heart*, so I could not hear myself as I called for the door to be opened and went out. I told my guards to take me to the Royal Mask Architect and told my brother's Satriya to wait and allow none but myself inside.

Every step jarred my skeleton. I thought I would break apart, tendons gone soft, disintegrating, nothing to hold my bones together.

Through the winding halls of the palace I went, holding the paint pot aloft like an offering, barefoot still and my head-scarf untied, loose about my neck. Were it not for the Satriya surrounding me, none would know I was—

I was the heir.

Safiya za Idris Sahiza, the Moon Eater's Mistress, was dead, too.

The warren of workrooms in the palace's wing of Design surrounded a central glass-domed library, and it was there I found the Royal Mask Architect, sketching invisible lines of force upon a vellum sheet with a crystal stylus. He looked up, startled, and covered his eyes immediately. "Your Glory!" he said.

I slammed the pot onto his worktable, drawing all the attention of the Designers and apprentices in the library. "Let no one leave," I ordered my guard.

Sun streamed down through the elaborately honeycombed glass dome overhead. All attention was upon me. I pointed to the pot and said to the Royal Mask Architect, "Put that on your face, now. The gold."

Without hesitation, he reached to dip a finger directly into the paint. The moment he touched it, I said, "Get it off, quickly, it is poison. And tell me who mixed it, for they intended to murder me."

His plain dark eyes widened, and he wiped it immediately onto his vellum, then with the stylus drew strong enough ecstatic force into a protective cage over the pot that even I could see the spark of it for one brief moment.

"Alis zada Beyar delivered this to me," he said sadly.

"Bring him," I said to my guard. "And find his family and friends." As they interrogated those present and left to track this boy down, I stood before the Royal Mask Architect and told him to paint a holy design onto my face.

I closed my eyes as he obeyed, first mixing his own paint. He streaked black in a wide swathe across my eyes, then silver in crescents over it, for he believed me still to be the Moon Eater's Mistress. My stomach churned, burning up my throat. I swallowed back the fire. He painted dots beneath my lip, traced silver shadow lines beneath my cheekbones, shading my face into an unfamiliar shape.

> *Few have known until this confession, oh my children, that I gut-ted a man with my own hands when I was sixteen. That is the moment I gave up the Moon Eater and became Hers instead.*
> —*from* Seven Hundred Declarations of Safiya the Bloody

Alis zada Beyar was forced to his knees before me, shaking and tearful. He was hardly older than me: he spat and said I had murdered his niece in my execution lottery. She'd been the youngest blood relation to the rebels, a girl of seven years old. So I understood, even as I took a curved dagger from one of my Satriya. I understood, even as I stabbed it into his side and dragged it around in a smile across his guts. I understood, even as I ordered the Architects to use whatever forces of flow or falling, rising or ecstatic or taboo Human Architecture they needed to keep him alive to face the Sahe Sahenam, to face justice for the murder of Dalir zada Idris.

The Satriya guard, the Royal Mask Architect, and all the Designers present gasped and bowed when they heard it, covered their eyes, and whispered my name.

My hands were covered with his blood; scarlet gloves, the

brightest kind of paint, and mixed by She Who Loves Silence
Herself.

> *My husband insists there is no shade to brutality; it is only itself,*
> *never too much or too little. My heart twin tells me he is wrong,*
> *that I have spent forty years discovering every shallow shadow and*
> *deep ravine of my brutal heart. She would know, she insists, but*
> *my husband argues he does not need to soften or complicate my*
> *legacy; he loves it completely.*
>
> *It does not matter anyway, because my bones are eating them-*
> *selves, and I will be dead soon, before both of them. I am glad.*
> *They should have had each other without me, and now they shall.*
> —*from* Seven Hundred Declarations of Safiya the Bloody

I was safe, surrounded by trusted Satriya, when I returned to
my chambers with Grandfather so that Dalir's body could be
prepared for She Who Loves Silence. There was a roar inside
me, a storm of purpose, building toward something I could not
yet see. A future, an ambition. I would be both myself and my
brother, I would make our Sahenate even greater than Grandfather had done, and no sympathy or hesitation would stop me.
I would devour the world.

As Grandfather bowed over Dalir, eyes shut, his moan like
a song sinking below the waves, I whispered to my great-uncle
Eskandar that I must find Farah, my body twin, for the assassin
had come after me, and her function was to make such attempts
doubly impossible.

And so I went, with blood staining the soft, intimate lines of my palms, blood streaking my robi, hair loose, and face a holy mask of silver.

Enver Kirazade had been allotted a room near Dalir's system of chambers, off a looping, elegant corridor tiled with gentle pink-and-gold ceramics. Satriya guard blocked the entrance, but they moved immediately for me, and I shoved through the door.

They were sprawled across massive red pillows, tangled in scarves and sheets and robi.

Farah gasped. One hand clutched a scarf over her golden belly, the other clawed at Enver's fire-dark chest. He lifted onto one knee, hand out. I could not help but focus on the puckered scars constellated on his shoulder and collarbone like an Architect's dots.

I stood, disheveled and bloody, and said the first, most salient thing: "I am no longer the Moon Eater's Mistress."

Farah shook her head, confusion and the first spark of anger brightening her luscious brown eyes. Enver's hand tightened to a fist and he said, "Dalir," with dry despair, for he understood he had not been present to save my brother's life a third time.

"Here is the blood of his murderer." I held out my hands, hardly recognizing the harshness of the desert wind in my voice.

Both stood. Farah took Enver's hand and, naked, they approached me. I touched their hearts, and then touched their faces, smearing blood onto their skin. I had nothing else to say. Tears dripped down Enver's cheek, onto my fingers. Farah too cried, putting her arms around my neck and head, cradling me, and Enver held us both, trembling with his own grief.

O my children, the children of my children, O my people from the center of this city to the farthest reaches of my Sahenate: if you are to thrive, you need more than one heart.

—*from* Seven Hundred Declarations of Safiya the Bloody

Unus, Duo, Tres
BETHANY HAGEN

At St. Marcellus Boarding School and Elaborate Prison for Misbehaving Rich Kids, Wednesdays mean Mass, composition, and rugby later out on the field.

Mass is mandatory, rugby is not.

The chapel attached to St. Marcellus is even older than the century-old school building, having been part of the monastery that once stood on the grounds. And, like silent ghosts from the monastery's past, statues of saints watch from the shadows, their faces pinched and narrow and sad—save for St. Martin de Porres in the far front corner. He's the one black saint in the chapel for a mostly black school in the heart of Savannah, Georgia, and there's something in his face, a weight of watchfulness and concern, like he's carrying the brunt of the prayers from the students here.

Of course, I imagine he'd be rather reluctant to ferry my

prayers up to heaven if he knew the solemn black boy in front of him was actually a member of the undead.

Mass is far from fatal for me as a vampire, if you were wondering. In fact, I rather enjoy it. Not the religious aspect necessarily, but the quiet dignity of ritual space, the soothing repetition of chants and hymns, the pantomime of drinking blood.

Mostly I enjoy it because Casimir enjoys it.

He kneels in the row before me, and I can see a spot of blood seeping through the snowy white of his collar. A human might heal from a vampire bite within a few hours, but for another vampire, it takes longer. And I'll bite him again before it's healed anyway.

Above the haze of incense, I smell the blood. Other blood smells of salt and silver, but Cas's blood smells deep and sweet. Three years ago, when I was fifteen and human, I stole a bottle of my grandfather's wine and drank it walking along a crowded Miami beach while Grandfather and his young wife partied the night away. I'd never had anything stronger than beer before that, and I'd been fascinated with the spicy, sweet headiness.

Cas tastes like that. Like that first sip of spiced wine along the shore, and when I taste him, I taste Caribbean wind and billions of far-flung stars sparkling in a net over the sea. I taste the saltwater roaring against the sand, the vibrant city glowing in defiance of the night.

I taste eternity.

I look down at the rosary twined between my fingers, the white beads moving against my dark brown skin. I don't pray, but I count the beads in every language I can think of, moving my mind along them so that it's not tempted to move along Cas's body instead.

Unus, duo, tres . . .

Ena, dio, tria . . .

Eins, zwei, drei . . .

It doesn't work. Cas is my only prayer, my only meditation, and he has been since we met this year, both orphaned boys cast adrift on a sea of trust funds. I shouldn't have done what I did to him, I should have protected him, spared him, but I am not a good person. I am a selfish person.

And I wanted him. I wanted to bite him, wanted him to drink my blood, wanted him to change into someone like me.

Chanting from the altar dissolves my thoughts, and then I'm walking down to take communion, which doesn't burn my skin any more than the crucifix attached to the rosary I hold. After more prayers and chanting, we are set free to class. Casimir flashes me a grin as we gather up our things from the pews and move toward the door. We usually keep a careful distance between us in public. Partly it's St. Marcellus—even the historically progressive Jesuits might not be ready to see two boys holding hands in church or kissing against the lockers—but there are even deeper reasons.

Three years ago, I would have loved St. Marcellus, especially after being sent to school in Europe for so many years. Walking into this school where most of the other students were black felt like I could finally breathe the air in as deeply as I wanted, like I'd been holding my breath without knowing it. But that feeling, that easy breathing, only lasted a few seconds; I was finally in a place where I shared so much with the other students, and yet the one thing we didn't share cut any chance of belonging into tatters. I was finally a part of a community that shared so much with me, a part *of* and yet necessarily apart *from*. The students at St. Marcellus should be my friends, my peers, my home . . . but I didn't come to St. Marcellus as just another young black man. I came as Enoch, the vampire.

This apartness, the insatiable hunger for blood, is why Cas and I keep our distance not only from each other, but from the other students. It's best to hunt far from home and appear solitary at all costs.

But we allow ourselves these few daylight moments in the jostle of the crowd, where the murmur and hum of two hundred other voices can hide our own.

"Did you see that new girl crying during Mass?" Cas asks me, his head turning this way and that as we push through the narthex to get to the front doors of the church. He's looking for someone.

"I was only looking at you," I say honestly.

Cas flushes, pleased. Unlike me, Cas looks like the pale vampires from children's storybooks. Bisque-colored skin and large eyes rimmed with thick eyelashes. His hair is black and wants to curl at the ends, his cheekbones are high and delicate, and his lips . . . well.

I like his lips.

"What did she look like?" I ask, deciding not to pursue that line of thought until we're alone.

Cas thinks for a moment. We walk through the wooden doors of the church toward the imposing stone edifice of St. Marcellus's main building. The early April wind is warm and humid as it blows past us, and there's a faint whiff of the decay that always seems to linger in Savannah, like the smell of a cemetery after a long rain.

"She looked gorgeous," Cas says finally. "And sad."

The way he says it bothers me, although it takes me the rest of the day to puzzle out why. But it comes to me that night, as I lie in bed and watch the moon swell and shrink and drift her way across the sky. It bothered me because the tone of voice he used to talk about the girl, filled with fascination and desire—it's the same tone I imagine I use when I talk about him.

I hunt at night, and right now I'm hunting for the only thing I want.

I find him in the library, near the fireplace, sprawled in a leather armchair with a book on his lap. He's wearing a T-shirt, too tight for his leanly muscled frame, and pajama pants with ducks on them. Ducks with little red deerstalker caps.

"Your pants are ridiculous," I say as I approach him.

He tosses the book aside. "So take them off me."

"I didn't say ridiculous was a bad thing."

Cas stretches in the chair, the hem of his shirt riding up over his flat stomach. There is a line of dark hair beneath his navel, which disappears under the waistband of his pants, under the ducks and their stupid little hats.

"I'm going to kiss you," I warn him.

"Good."

"It's going to hurt."

"I wouldn't have it any other way."

And that is one of the many numberless reasons I am soul deep in love with Casimir Nowak.

Within moments, we are in the darkest corner of the library, pressed against the cold stone of the old library walls. In the dark, his eyes glitter like onyx, like some sort of strange cat's, and I know mine glitter back at him. It's one of the few true signs of the monsters we are.

A crescent moon glows through one of the old windows, as pale and weak as a sliver of old bone, but we pay it no mind. There's only our lips and hands and breath, my fingers gripping the back of Cas's neck so hard I know it will bruise, and then that sweet surrender when he bares his neck to me and I sink my teeth into his skin.

It's different than feeding from a human, biting Cas. A vampire's blood is much more potent than a human's, much more intoxicating. I don't bite Cas to sate my hunger; I bite him because I love him. And he lets me bite him because he loves me.

The difference between a human's blood and my boyfriend's blood is like the difference between water and wine. One you drink to survive, and the other you drink to *live*.

I can feel Cas's heart pounding in his chest as it's pressed to mine, even through the wool of my uniform sweater and the cotton of his T-shirt, and he makes the smallest whimper of pain as his blood wells up to touch my tongue.

I hate myself for loving that whimper. It's my greatest sin, and it's been with me since I was turned into the predator I am today. But in these moments of pain, Cas becomes more beautiful and dear to me than ever.

My fingers grip his neck harder, and I want to squeeze him, shake him, scratch him, but I settle for feeding at his neck, for now, and then he gasps—not pain or pleasure, but alarm.

My head snaps up, and I spin around to see a girl standing between the rows of wooden stacks, lips parted, staring at us.

Cas transforms next to me, his body rippling with the same fascination and longing I witnessed in him earlier today, and then I know. It's the girl from Mass, the crying one.

Cas didn't lie: she *is* gorgeous. Heart-shaped face, delicate pointed chin, straight nose. Warm light brown skin, dark eyes, and long hair. She has curving, Cupid's-bow lips that could rival Cas's for my attention. A Virgin Mary medal glints at her long neck.

I wipe at my mouth, and the white sleeve of my uniform shirt comes away bright crimson with Cas's blood.

"I'm sorry," she says, and I don't think I'm imagining the breathlessness in her voice or the way her eyes keep sliding over to Cas. Against his white skin, the smear of blood on his neck is obvious, even in the dark, and I know that she can see that inhuman glitter in our eyes.

"I'm new here and I couldn't sleep and I just . . ." She holds up a book; through the dark, I can see how tightly she holds the leather spine. But she's not afraid—no fear spikes her blood. There's intense curiosity in her eyes, and a taste to the air around her that I can't identify.

Interesting.

"I should go," she whispers. "Good night."

And then Cas and I are truly alone.

Esther Gonzalez, unlike Cas and me and most of the other students here, is not a spoiled troublemaker sent away for penance. She has no record, no distressed notes from former deans outlining misbehavior, and she has perfect grades. The only spot of interest in her file, which I'm currently perusing in the dean's office in the middle of the following night, is an eighteen-month gap in her studies prior to this month. There's no explanation, although she tested into all the highest-level senior classes, so clearly she kept up on her schoolwork somehow. Her parents live here in Savannah, only a couple miles away, so perhaps that's the reason she chose to come here.

But still. It's strange, and her being here is strange, and her crying in Mass is strange, and I resolve to watch her and learn more.

It's not a terrible task, actually.

That week, Cas befriends her, and since he and I try to avoid each other during the day, I get the added bonus of watching him too. I watch them laugh together in the halls, study their calculus textbooks out on the lawn, sit together at lunch. They look good together—Cas graceful and tall, and Esther sunny and smiling—and my heart squeezes with jealousy.

It was never a question that we could also love girls. No, it was simply that it was also never a question that we only wanted each other. That we would give each other forever.

And during our nights together this week, I wonder if he thinks of her when we kiss, if he wishes she were here with us.

Or worse, here *instead* of me.

The truth is, I know what Cas looks like when he's falling in love. I saw it when he fell in love with me. And now I have to watch as he falls in love with someone else.

Esther finds me in the garden a week later. I know she's seen me watching her, and I can tell she's drawn to me, mesmerized maybe. I'm not sure how I feel about that.

I don't lift my head from the book I'm reading. I don't acknowledge her at all, even as she sits on the bench next to me. She sits on the very edge and she holds herself completely still, as if she's sitting next to a cliff's edge, a posture not of fear but of respect. Respect for the danger next to her.

I finally raise my eyes to hers, but I don't speak.

"You're different," she starts. From somewhere deep in the nearby chapel, organ music plays. Practice for Mass later. "You and Cas."

I can lie. I can invent a thousand stories, weave a thousand tales, to explain that night in the library. The glittering eyes, the blood dripping from my mouth.

But I find I don't want to. I want her to know. To scare her? Humiliate her? Seduce her?

I don't know.

"Yes," I say, as neutrally and coolly as I would say anything. I sound like I'm answering a declension question in Latin class. "We're different."

She nods. Like in the library, she's not scared. Deep intelligence and curiosity sparkle in her eyes, and a smile tugs at the corners of her mouth. She reminds me of Cas, suddenly, that constant smile, that joy for living pressing so close to the surface. What's it like to smile like that? To live like that? Even love is serious work to me.

"The blood and your eyes . . . ," she says. Pauses, then speaks again. "You're a senior, but you don't act or talk like anyone else here. What kind of different are you?"

"Why don't you ask Cas these things?" I ask. "I notice you two are spending lots of time together."

Her cheeks darken in a blush, and I feel that jealousy like a vise around my chest again. But then she says, "Because I wanted to talk to you. I want to know *you*."

And the way she says it.

And the way she says it.

I take a deep breath. "What do you want to know?"

"Everything."

And then I find that I want to tell her everything.

So I do.

I tell her that my parents died when I was in junior high. That my grandfather and I never got along, even after he became my guardian. He believed in his money like people believed in their gods, maybe even more than that because he created his business empire ex nihilo, built his money and legacy from scratch, and so his idol was actually a depiction of himself. And who loves anyone more than themselves?

Money's never held any sway for me, but power—now *that*

was something I could crave, and crave it I did, even from a young age.

I tell her that after years of battles with teachers and fights with other students, I landed at a boarding school in Rome— much like this one, actually—filled with more rich, disaffected people at various states of rebellion.

And Rome is where I met them.

They were beautiful, like Cas and Esther are beautiful. And they were different colors, different sizes, different ages, boys and girls, some young enough they looked like children, some old enough that they easily passed for adults. They found me outside a club after someone had tried to rob me. I'd stopped him, of course, had beaten the would-be thief until he fell half unconscious to his knees, and then I looked up to see them watching me in my fit of righteous violence.

They smiled, and then I knew I'd either finally found the nameless power I was looking for . . . or I was about to die.

How could I have guessed that it would be both?

Esther's face is rapt as she listens, and seemingly without thinking, she's slid off the bench and now sits on the ground in front of me, her legs crossed like a child listening to a teacher tell a story.

"And that's how you changed?" she asks.

"Yes. The power I wanted wasn't over money or politics. This was the power I'd been seeking all my life, without know-ing it."

She realizes that I'm not talking about the past right now, that I'm talking about something present. "This?" she asks, confused.

I gesture to her sitting at my feet, and then, to highlight my point, I reach down and take her chin in my hands, tilting it upward. Her breath catches as I run my thumb along her lower lip. *"This,"* I say.

"Oh," and all at once as her pupils dilate into huge black pools, her breath shudders out.

And it's then, with my thumb against her lips, that I smell it. Taste it in the air. Feel it pulse against my thumb.

Esther is sick.

Very sick.

It's early, I think, at least early enough that it took me this long to detect it, but there's no doubt now as I fill my lungs with the air between us. The sickness is deep in her blood, and it will be fatal.

I search her eyes. Does she know?

She stares back at me, evenly, bravely, and I see that of course she knows. Pain is creased in tiny lines around her eyes, there's a slightly ashen cast to her skin that wasn't there even as recently as last week. I start to say something—what, I don't know—but then I think better of it and decide to continue with my story until I've processed this.

I let go of her chin, even though I find I don't want to. "Anyway, within a few months after my sixteenth birthday, I was changed. And then a few months later, I deliberately provoked a fight with a teacher so my grandfather would have no choice but to find a new school for me. The Roman vampires were . . . they lived how they wanted, as bloody and wild as they wanted. And I couldn't live that life with them any longer without losing myself."

"Because you hated it?" she asks.

"No," I say, and I hear the self-loathing in my own voice. "Because I loved it too much."

A cloud passes over the sun.

"So it's true," she says after a minute. "*Vampires.* At my school."

I search her face again. I want to bring up her sickness, I want to know everything. Is it why she missed school for those eighteen months? Did she go temporarily into remission? Is it why she's going to St. Marcellus—to be close to her parents in case her illness takes a turn for the worse?

But no, those aren't even the questions I want to ask. I want to ask real questions.

Are you scared?

Will you die without ever having been in love?

How much does it hurt?

Will you let me kiss you?

I bite back the words, wrestle down the urge to pull her close to me and press my lips to hers. *Cas* is fascinated with her, *Cas* should be the one to kiss her. Except that she didn't seek Cas out, she sought *me* out, and now that I can feel the aura of pain and vulnerability around her like a scarlet glow, I can't think of anything other than kissing her.

She breaks the moment by speaking again, her thoughts on something else entirely.

"But how can you . . ." She bites her lip, that full lower lip, and it takes so much effort to drag my gaze back to her eyes.

"The sun," she finally says. "The crosses in church. Communion wafers."

"Stories," I say simply. "Or maybe they weren't, a long time ago. Maybe we've evolved."

She breathes out, nervously. "*Can* you die, then? Are you immortal?"

Immortal.

Once again I smell the sickness in her blood, slowly choking the life from her body. Never once has the word "immortal" given me pause. Never once have I thought about what immortality might really mean.

Not once until now.

"We can be killed," I say quickly, and my earlier coolness is gone. Replaced by something I don't understand. A need to feel close to her, similar to her. A need to feel mortal. "We can starve. And a stake through the heart will end us."

She smiles. "I learned that from Bram Stoker."

I almost speak again, almost finish my thought, but the distant organ music swells and the clouds close up even more over the sun; in the now-dim light, her eyes are almost black. Pain sings through her skin.

She's beautiful.

And I hate myself for noticing how beautiful she is when she hurts.

So I put the long-forgotten book in my bag, and I stand. "I suppose I just have to trust that you won't stake me in my sleep now."

She raises an eyebrow, her lips twitching. "So you do sleep? In a bed?"

"In a bed," I confirm, shouldering my messenger bag. "A real bed with blankets."

"No coffin? No soil from your homeland?"

"Coffins only fit one body," I say. "And I think soil in my bed would kill the mood."

Her mouth parts in surprise, and I brush past her with a small smile.

But my smile fades as I exit the garden and walk toward my room.

I lied by omission back there. Because there is a third thing that can kill a vampire, and kill them more painfully than any stake ever could.

Bad blood.

Poisoned blood.

Sick blood.

I can extrapolate infinite life from just a few swallows of human blood, and so, conversely, I can extrapolate infinite death. If I drink from a tainted source, I will die within minutes. Maybe hours, if I'm unlucky enough to suffer that long.

One taste of Esther's blood and I'd die within a day. She'd be the literal death of me, dark eyes, full lips, and all.

At first, Cas and I don't talk about Esther. We don't need to; the confusion and hungry pain is already in every kiss, in every bruise we leave on each other. But another week passes, and as we sit in the dark, empty chapel one night, our clothes rumpled and my mouth still wet with his blood, Casimir finally brings her up.

"Esther's sick, isn't she?"

It takes me a moment to answer. When I do, my voice is flat. Hollow.

"Yes."

"You knew. Didn't you?"

"I've been a vampire longer than you, Cas. My senses are stronger."

He runs his uniform tie through his fingers. It's off his neck because I yanked it off an hour ago in my desperation to get under his collar. "You should have told me."

"Why? Because you're in love with her?" I meant it to come out in a dispassionate voice. Matter of fact. Kind, even.

That's not at all how it comes out though, and my bitter words echo against the stone walls and glass of the church, and I hate myself for that. Who am I to lob accusations against Cas when I myself have been thinking about Esther constantly?

Casimir's voice is pained. "I'm in love with *you*."

"Why?"

It's the first time I've ever asked him this, but suddenly I need to hear the answer. I've killed people. I will probably kill more. Once a week, I go down to the river and I hunt innocent humans, take from them without their consent, and leave them slumped against alley walls, to wake up with no memory of what happened.

I like it more than I should, the blood and the teeth, but more than that, I like the way the humid river air kisses my skin as I prowl. Boys like me are supposed to be afraid even when we're innocent, but I'm not innocent or afraid. Instead, I get to move with power, with freedom, with the bone-deep knowledge that I cannot be hurt or killed in the ways that they might try to hurt or kill me. I am all the things this city doesn't want me to be when I hunt—black and male and unafraid. That I crave this might have been inevitable, but the change is chemical, absolute. I drink life now, and I drink it without shame and with the kind of satisfaction that sparks along my skin.

I took Cas's mortal life from him for no better reason than I was in love with him. Even now, my love for him is indissolubly united with my hunger for his blood and his surrender to me.

I gave him forever, but who would want that kind of forever?

Cas climbs over my lap, fists my shirt in his hands, and kisses me fiercely. "I love you because you're Enoch. And that's enough for me."

I look up at him in the dark. "But will it keep being enough?" I know my voice and face betray every doubt, every fear, every corner of my loneliness.

"Of course," Cas promises in that impetuous, passionate way of his. "Forever and ever."

And for the first time in the six months since I turned Cas into a vampire, I bare my neck and allow him to bite me. And as the pain and ecstasy flow through my veins, I let myself feel every ounce of it, closing my eyes and wondering if this is how death would feel. Sweet and welcoming, sharp and dizzying.

And then Cas turns and kisses me, his mouth warm with blood, and I stop wondering anything at all.

The next evening, I stand outside Esther's window on the lawn, lost in thought. Last night, with Cas's teeth buried in my flesh, I decided that I needed to bring Esther closer to us, even though I also know that there'll be no coming back from it if I do.

But I know Cas is falling in love with her, and if I'm not mistaken from my days of watching the two of them, she might be falling in love with him.

They've both been waiting for me. To give a signal or permission or consent, I'm not sure. But somehow, they both sense that I have to be part of it, and for that I'm both grateful and mortally wounded.

It's easier to be stabbed in the back than fall on the dagger yourself, you see.

But my jealous martyrdom is complicated by two things.

First, that Esther is dying, and even I'm not cruel enough to deny Cas and Esther each other when she'll be dead within months.

Secondly, that I also want Esther. Even without her blood, I want her—her mouth, her slender fingers, her curious mind. That mind is so present, so alive, so compassionate. So much like Cas.

I rap on the window, and she's at the glass a moment later, wearing a white nightgown with spaghetti straps and lace trimming, her gold Virgin medal gleaming at her neck. I almost laugh—she couldn't look more like a vampire's victim if she tried.

"Cas and I want you to come with us," I say.

Her face—*it's growing thinner*, I notice, *it won't be long before she has to leave school*—lights up with a smile. "Okay."

I extend a hand and help her climb out the window. "You're not going to ask where? Or for what? Do you crawl out of your window for every vampire who knocks?"

She quietly slides the window closed, and then she turns and looks up at me with shining eyes. "Only the vampires I want to be with."

Behind her, I see our reflection in the shadowed window glass. We are a study of contrasts in that reflection—black skin and bronze. Tall and short. Muscular and slender.

Dead and alive.

For a moment I imagine us together in the daylight, together like a normal couple. Holding hands, walking down the hallways, kissing in the corners where the teachers can't see. But the reflection is missing something, and that's Cas, and I can't fight the sear of guilt for even fantasizing about a future that doesn't include him. A future I don't deserve, and that Esther may not even have.

We walk in the moonlight across the lawn, a short walk, but a lovely one. I adore the sound of her bare feet on the soft new grass of spring.

"Where are we going?" Esther asks.

"The chapel," I say. "They leave it unlocked at night, and unlike the dorms, there are no prefects to catch you and report you to the dean."

"But you also use the library to meet," she points out.

"Yeah, and we got walked in on by a nosy new girl, remember?" I say with a smile. "Trust me, the chapel is much better for late-night troublemaking."

We reach the flagstone path to the chapel, and Esther seems lost in thought. "I've been wondering something about that night I caught you in the library . . . why were you biting Cas?" she asks. "It's not the same as feeding on humans, right?"

"Right. It's for fun, for—" I hesitate to use the word because it sounds old-fashioned, even for me. "For pleasure."

She looks at me. "But doesn't it hurt him?"

We reach the unlocked back door of the chapel and stop, and I lean closer, and run a finger along the smooth column of her throat. She sucks in a breath, her eyes fluttering closed.

"It hurts, doesn't it?" I whisper. "You're hurting right now."

She nods, barely, but her eyes squeeze tighter and I wonder if it's the first time she's been able to be honest about her pain. The first time she hasn't tried to be brave, the first time she's admitted . . . it hurts. It's the first time I've admitted that I know she's sick, and she seems almost relieved by it.

"When I bite Cas, I hurt him. And then I get to make the hurt go away. I stop the pain. And he kisses me after, like I've given him a gift. Giving pain is only one half of the scale, Esther. Taking it away is the other. That's why I bite him."

"Because he's grateful?"

"Because I love him."

She doesn't accuse me of perversity, but instead she opens her eyes. I move my hand to her throat, pressing my palm against the side. Her pulse thrums wildly, for once not with pain, but with fierce feeling and lust.

"Love is pain," I tell her seriously. "We feel it here . . ." I drop my hand to her chest, where I tap gently once, above her heart. Goose bumps blossom on her skin around the place my finger touched. "I just make the feeling real. A physical thing.

Something we can hold on to."

"What can you hold on to?" Cas asks, coming up from behind us.

"He's telling me why he bites you when you kiss," Esther says.

"Oh, he could talk about that for *ages*. We better cut him off now before he really gets going."

I roll my eyes, and we go inside the chapel.

Esther walks inside ahead of us, her head swiveling to take in the empty space, lit as it is with the faded jewel tones of moonlight through stained glass, with shadows draping the saints' statues like shrouds and the distant smell of incense still hanging in the air.

Cas and I have seen it a hundred times, and so he hangs back next to me. He finds my hand in the dark. "Thank you," he whispers. "For bringing her here. For letting me—us—be together."

I nod wordlessly. I don't trust myself to speak.

He lets out a long breath as we watch her white-clad frame move through the shadows. "It will be hard—not to bite, I mean. But we can't."

I nod again. Cas knows the rules; I was sure to drill them into his mind after I changed him. No bad blood. Never ever *ever*.

I find my voice. "You can kiss her, of course. Touch her. But if you feed from her, you'll die."

He closes his eyes, briefly. Even for a soul as gentle as his it's a hard thing to ask a vampire. To separate one kind of lust from the other.

But it's the most necessary thing to ask.

I plunder the sacristy for some cheap wine, as yet unblessed, and we find a comfortable alcove underneath St. Martin de Porres to drink it. Esther sits between us, leaning against Cas's chest and her legs slung over my lap. Cas plays with her hair, and I feel the turning of my jealousy, softening into something else.

"I saw the doctor yesterday," she says after we've been there a while. "I already knew it, could already feel it, but he confirmed it. The leukemia isn't in remission any longer. We did chemotherapy before, but this time it's too advanced. Blood transfusions might work, for a little while at least. Mom and Dad want me to come home right away, but I begged them for another week."

"Why?" Cas asks. "Don't you want to be with them when you're . . ." He can't finish his thought. Sweet Cas with his sweet immortal heart. He's known Esther barely a month, and already the knowledge of her death tears a hole through him.

Esther meets my eyes as she answers. "I wanted to have more time with you."

Cas can't speak after that. He closes his eyes and swallows hard, like he's swallowing back a scream. The only response he can give her is to rub her hair in between his fingers, the same way you might rub a rose petal between your fingers on a summer's day. She responds by wrapping her arms around him in a hug and holding him tight, and they're both so beautiful that I could watch them forever.

Of course, we don't have forever. Not with Esther.

The night becomes hazy, heady with wine and murmured conversations in the dark, and I begin to lose track of time, all time except for the moment where one thing becomes very clear to me.

I was right, and over the past three weeks, Cas and Esther have fallen in love.

Clarity and grief and—yes, still jealousy—cut through my heart like an icy sword, leaving only bloody intention in its place. I look up at the silent statues flanking the chapel walls, and instead of seeing the saints, I see the face of every human I've ever attacked. The three I killed when I couldn't stop myself in time. The countless others I've bitten and left weak and vulnerable in the night. I see the uncountable, unknowable others to follow in the future, legions and legions of victims, blood like rivers, tears like rain, muffled screams breaking the night.

And when I close my eyes, I see Cas. Cas, who had his mortality and humanity and everything else stolen from him. By me.

I see Esther, facing down death, asking for nothing from the two immortals she's fallen in love with.

If God is real, if these saints really speak to him and intercede for us sinners here on Earth, will they intercede for me? If I atone?

Because there is something I can do, something I can give Cas and Esther both, and even as fear moves cold and slippery in my veins, my thoughts freeze into one certainty.

I can save Esther.

And maybe, just maybe, I can save myself.

"I've never skipped class before," Esther says excitedly as we park my car in front of Bonaventure Cemetery.

"There's a first time for everything." I get out of the car, and then cross around to help Esther out. She leans on me quite a bit as we walk down a path leading to the river.

"Where's Cas?" she asks.

"Cas can't skip Latin," I respond, keeping my voice uninflected with everything I'm feeling right now. "He can barely even count to ten in it. And I left him a note in his room to come find us after class."

By which time, of course, it will be too late, but that was the point. I can only be brave for myself; I wouldn't be able to be brave for him too. Wouldn't have been able to bear his pain along with my own, because I feel everything of his more strongly than I feel my own.

Even now I won't pretend it's noble. My love for him is selfish, and it always has been.

It's the first of May today, beautiful beyond measure. The leaves above the path have unfurled into a thick green canopy, and the sunlight that reaches us is dappled and green-gold. I stop when we reach a clearing by the river, and I take a moment just to breathe the air, to listen to the water rushing and the breeze rustling and the birds chirping far off in the distance. Just to watch Esther be happy and at peace, her eyes clear and alive despite the shadows beneath them, despite the hollows in her cheeks.

I wish Cas was here, just so I could see him happy and at peace too. But I have last night, and even if I were to die a thousand times, last night would still be enough to hold on to.

"Are you afraid of dying?" I ask after a few moments.

Her eyes are so sublimely pained, so honest and golden when she answers. "Yes."

"Me too," I say.

"Afraid of me dying or of you dying?"

"Both."

She nods. She could accuse me of being selfish or paranoid or morbid, but she doesn't. Instead she says, "There are times when I'm not scared. When I remember that it will probably happen so gradually that I won't be that aware of it. There are times when I believe that God will take care of me. And then there are times when I feel like the only thing separating me from death is a flimsy veil. A handful of painful, tiring weeks. And those are the times when I know there's nothing on the other side of the veil. No new life, no white light, *nothing*. Just—the end."

And I hear the void in her voice, the bleak despair, and it's like a thumb against my already-bruised heart. It hurts to hear the end of Esther's curiosity, to see the bounds of her readiness to learn and explore and live.

"You've never asked us to change you," I say quietly.

Esther looks at me.

"You ask about everything else. You have a burning curiosity that seems insatiable. So why not ask about this? It would be natural to."

She opens her mouth and then closes it. She only speaks after she turns away from my gaze, which is unusual for her. She's never shied away from me before, even when she should. "It didn't seem like a question I could ask. Everything else—well, I knew you would forgive me for wanting to know. Especially when I wouldn't be alive to know your secrets for very long." Her voice nearly breaks under the strain of keeping it free of emotion. "But asking for what you have . . . I guess it didn't feel like the kind of thing that could be asked for. It felt like it had to be given. Offered freely."

She's facing the river now, and she hasn't heard me walk up behind her. She startles a little as I sweep her hair off her neck and over her shoulder, and then she relaxes back into me. The posture is disarmingly trusting, and I feel a tight pain in my chest.

"I'm offering now," I say, my mouth near her ear. "I can make you like us. You wouldn't die from the leukemia, you wouldn't have to die for hundreds and hundreds of years. You could live."

She doesn't speak, but I can smell the cocktail of emotions running through her blood—adrenaline, dopamine, oxytocin.

Caution laces her voice when she speaks. "What would happen to me? My family?"

Respect for her overwhelms me. Casimir—so deeply unhappy in his life and so unloved by whatever family he had left—had jumped at the chance when I offered. Had practically flung himself into my teeth. But not Esther. She's too intellectual, too perceptive, to take any step when she can't see where her foot would land. Even in the face of certain death.

That takes a strength that even I don't have.

"You wouldn't physically age. Your parents would notice, eventually, but probably not for another decade or two would they realize it's something more than good genetics."

"And I would have to *feed* . . . like you and Cas?"

I run a fingertip along her throat, finding the yielding thrum of her jugular vein. "Yes."

She shivers. "I don't know if I can do that. Hurt people. Kill them."

"You don't have to hurt them when you bite. There are ways to do it gently. And you never have to kill a victim if you don't want to. Many vampires give themselves over to a feeding frenzy and drain all their victim's blood. But it's not necessary. Cas has never killed, for example."

"But you have."

"Yes."

"Did you enjoy it?"

"You know that I did," I say heavily. "I'm not a good person anymore, Esther. But that doesn't mean that you wouldn't be. That Cas isn't."

Still leaning back against me, she turns her head so she can look up into my face. "I think you are a good person," she says quietly. "If you weren't, you wouldn't have left Rome. You'd still be killing."

I don't have an answer for that. Maybe she's right, but I doubt it. Good people don't bite their boyfriend until he bleeds. Good people don't enjoy the feeling of having people they love at their feet, humbled and marked.

Esther looks back at the river, and we spend a long time like that, with the water rushing past and the breeze waving the green branches above us and the cemetery silent at our backs.

"Okay," she says finally. "Yes."

"Yes?"

"I want to be like you. Change me."

This was the answer I wanted. This was why we came here. But I still can't help the flash of deep anger I feel. Not even anger, really, but anguish.

Pure anguish.

I keep it all inside. "It won't take long," I explain to her. "I'm going to bite you, and I will feed from you. A lot. You will probably feel light-headed. You may even lose consciousness. I will help you wake up enough to drink my blood."

"How much will I have to drink?"

"Not much. You probably won't want much. Enjoy that feeling, because it will be the last time you will feel it."

I say it with a smile, but she doesn't smile back. She's shivering again, covered in goose bumps.

"Are you ready?"

She nods, suddenly determined. "Yes."

I put my hands on her shoulders and turn her around so she faces me. And then I cradle her face with my hands.

She blinks up at me, her long eyelashes casting shadows in the May sunlight.

"There's one more thing," I say, swallowing past the tightness in my throat. "When I change you—the process will take a lot out of me. I'll almost certainly lose consciousness after a while. So don't be alarmed."

The lie comes out easily, too easily maybe, because part of me bitterly rebels at the idea that she won't know what I'm doing, what I'm giving up for her and Cas. But if she knew, she wouldn't allow it to happen, and so it has to be this way.

But I don't bother to hide the pain and fear in my voice when I ask her, plead with her, "Will you . . . will you hold me as I fall asleep? Promise not to let me go or leave?"

Her brow furrows. "Of course." She reaches up to touch the tears clinging to my own long eyelashes, and worry clouds her expression. "Enoch?"

I bring my mouth crashing down onto hers before she can say another word. I kiss her with everything I have, every angry, scared feeling. I kiss her for all the kisses she and I will never share, and I even kiss her for all the kisses I'll never share with Cas. I kiss her with all the hope I have for the two of them, for the forever that they'll have. And then when her body is arching against mine and her heart is pounding with something other than fear, I kiss a line of hot kisses down to her neck, whisper a prayer to a God I don't believe in, and sink my teeth into her flesh.

She cries out, and her blood spills into my mouth, hot and metallic, delicious even with the poison it carries. I thought I would have to force myself to drink, that my body would resist the tainted blood, but it turns out that's not the case. Biting her was the hardest part—now that I'm here, drinking my own execution is as easy as drinking wine on a Miami beach. As easy as falling in love.

Her cry, which echoed through the trees, is replaced now

by a soft sigh, half surrender, half sweet sensation, and I wish I could freeze time and live in this moment forever, my face in her neck, her body warm against mine, the sun gentle above us.

But of course, the moment must end, and I reluctantly pull away. She stands, dazed and delirious in my arms, and as I bite my own wrist to offer my blood to her, I feel the first swell of death radiate out from my stomach. It won't be long before her blood is absorbed into my own, and so we have to move fast.

"Drink quickly," I urge her, and she slowly lowers her mouth to my wrist, her eyes glassy. I cup the back of her head, and then she's drinking. Her mouth twists against her first sip, the hot copper taste new and unpleasant, but she still drinks. One swallow, two swallows, three swallows.

It's enough. I pull my wrist away, and for a moment we both sway on our feet, our mouths dripping with blood. And then I fall to my knees.

She takes in a deep breath, and another one and another— her breathing ragged and her eyes wild—and then she also drops to her hands and her knees, gasping and retching as her body slowly transforms itself.

I watch with drooping eyes, wishing I could be there to hold her and comfort her as I did with Cas. I transformed Cas under a full moon, as chilled November winds blew around us, a proper vampire transformation, but it feels fitting that Esther should get the warm spring and the sunlight, the splashing river and the chattering birds.

And if I'm honest with myself—and why not be, at this point?—I prefer this May afternoon for my death too. It feels less lonely to die during the daylight, somehow.

Next to me, Esther lifts her head, her body finally still and her breathing even.

And then she's there to hold me. As I slump to the side, and she's cradling me in her arms, and I feel dizzy dizzy dizzy, the forest ceiling spinning above me, even the steady beat of her heart seeming to come from all distances at once, far and near, near and far.

I want to tell her I love her, want her to tell Cas that I love him, that I love him so much that it hurts me, that when I met him it had felt as if I'd always loved him, always known him somehow.

I want them to be happy.

I don't want to die in vain.

But I can't seem to make my mouth work. I can't seem to order my thoughts. Esther is speaking to me, and I hear the fear in her voice as she realizes that something is wrong, that something is happening that shouldn't, and then I hear pounding footfalls on the path and I know that Cas has found my note and has come racing here.

I force my eyes open, and pure joy flits through me as I see my Casimir's face one last time. They are both touching me, and Cas's face is pressed against my neck as he sobs, and it is like I imagined that night alone with him in chapel.

Death is sharp.

Death is sweet.

And finally, as my last breaths rattle erratically in and out and my senses dim—as I feel the boy I love crying against me and the girl I've just begun to love kissing my face—death becomes more than sweet sharpness.

Welcoming.

Dizzying.

Enough.

ABOUT THE AUTHORS

RENÉE AHDIEH is the author of the #1 *New York Times* best-selling *The Wrath and the Dawn* and *The Rose and the Dagger*. In her spare time, she likes to dance salsa and collect shoes. She is passionate about all kinds of curry, rescue dogs, and college basketball. The first few years of her life were spent in a high-rise in South Korea; consequently, Renée enjoys having her head in the clouds. She lives in Charlotte, North Carolina, with her husband and their tiny overlord of a dog.

RAE CARSON is the *New York Times* bestselling author of fantasy and historical fiction, including the Girl of Fire and Thorns series and the Gold Seer trilogy, which have won multiple awards and honors. Her books tend to contain adventure, magic, and smart girls who make (mostly) smart choices. Rae lives in Arizona with her husband and cats and the occasional scorpion.

BRANDY COLBERT is the author of the critically acclaimed debut novel *Pointe* and *Little & Lion*. She lives and writes in Los Angeles.

KATIE COTUGNO is the *New York Times* bestselling author of *99 Days*, *How to Love*, and *Fireworks*. She studied writing, literature, and publishing at Emerson College and received her MFA in fiction at Lesley University. Katie is a Pushcart Prize nominee whose work has appeared in *Iowa Review*, *Mississippi Review*, and *Argestes*, among others. She lives in Boston with her husband.

LAMAR GILES writes novels and short stories for teens and adults. He is the author of the Edgar Award–nominated novels *Fake ID* and *Endangered*, and of *Overturned*. He is a founding member of We Need Diverse Books and resides in Virginia with his wife.

TESSA GRATTON has wanted to be a paleontologist or a wizard since she was seven. After traveling the world with her military family, she acquired a BA (and the important parts of an MA) in gender studies, then settled down in Kansas to tell stories about monsters, magic, and kissing. She's the author of the Blood Journals series and Gods of New Asgard series, co-author of YA writing books *The Curiosities* and *The Anatomy of Curiosity*, as well as dozens of short stories available in anthologies and on merryfates.com. Her current projects include full-time writer for *Tremontaine* at Serial Box Publishing, a new YA fantasy from McElderry Books in 2018, and her debut adult fantasy, *The Queens of Innis Lear* from Tor, also in 2018.

BETHANY HAGEN is the author of *Landry Park* and *Jubilee Manor*. A former librarian, she lives with her spouse and two children in Kansas City.

JUSTINA IRELAND enjoys dark chocolate, dark humor, and is not too proud to admit that she's still afraid of the dark. She lives with her husband, kid, and dog in Pennsylvania. She is the author of *Vengeance Bound* and *Promise of Shadows*. Her essay "Me, Some Random Guy, and the Army of Darkness" appears in *The V-Word*, an anthology of personal essays by women about having sex for the first time. And her forthcoming book *Dread Nation* will be available in 2018.

ALAYA DAWN JOHNSON is the author of six novels for adults and young adults. Her novel *The Summer Prince* was longlisted for the National Book Award for Young People's Literature. Her most recent, *Love Is the Drug*, won the Andre Norton Award. Her short stories have appeared in many magazines and anthologies, including *Best American Science Fiction and Fantasy 2015*, *Zombies vs. Unicorns*, and *Welcome to Bordertown*. She lives in Mexico City, where she is getting her master's in Mesoamerican studies.

E. K. JOHNSTON had several jobs and one vocation before she became a published writer. If she's learned anything, it's that things turn out weird sometimes, and there's not a lot you can do about it. Well, that and how to muscle through awkward fanfic because it's about a pairing she likes. Her books range from contemporary fantasy (*The Story of Owen*, *Prairie Fire*), to fairy-tale reimaginings (*A Thousand Nights*, *Spindle*), and from small-town Ontario (*Exit, Pursued by a Bear*) to a galaxy far, far away (*New York Times* #1 bestseller *Star Wars: Ahsoka*). She has no plans to rein anything in.

JULIE MURPHY is the #1 *New York Times* bestselling and award-winning author of *Ramona Blue*, *Dumplin'*, and *Side Effects May Vary*. She lives in North Texas with her husband who loves her, her dog who adores her, and her cats who tolerate her. When she's not writing, she can be found reading, traveling, watching movies so bad they're good, or hunting down the perfect slice of pizza. Before writing full-time, she held numerous jobs, such as wedding dress consultant, failed barista, and ultimately, librarian. Learn more about her at www.juliemurphywrites.com.

GARTH NIX has worked as a literary agent, marketing consultant, book editor, book publicist, book sales representative, bookseller, and as a part-time soldier in the Australian Army Reserve. He has been a full-time writer since 2001, and his books include the award-winning and bestselling Old Kingdom series: *Sabriel*, *Lirael*, *Abhorsen*, *Clariel*, and *Goldenhand*; the science fiction novels *Shade's Children* and *A Confusion of Princes*; and many fantasy novels for children, including *The Ragwitch*; the six books of *The Seventh Tower* sequence; *The Keys to the Kingdom* series; and the forthcoming *Frogkisser!* He is also the author of *Newt's Emerald*, a "Regency romance with magic"; and with Sean Williams has cowritten the Troubletwisters series and *Spirit Animals: Blood Ties*.

More than five million copies of Garth's books have been sold around the world, his books have appeared on the bestseller lists of the *New York Times*, *Publishers Weekly*, *USA Today*, the *Sunday Times*, and the *Australian*, and his work has been translated into forty-one languages. He lives in Sydney, Australia.

NATALIE C. PARKER wears many hats: author, editor, organizer. She is the author of the Southern Gothic duology *Beware the Wild* (a Junior Library Guild Selection) and *Behold the Bones*. She is also the founder of Madcap Retreats, an organization offering a yearly calendar of workshops and retreats for aspiring and established writers. Though she earned her BA in English literature from the University of Southern Mississippi and her MA in gender studies from the University of Cincinnati, she now lives on the Kansas prairie with her partner. *Three Sides of a Heart* is her first anthology.

VERONICA ROTH is the author of the bestselling Divergent series, including *Divergent*, *Insurgent*, *Allegiant*, and *Four: A Divergent Collection*, and the science fiction/fantasy novel *Carve the Mark*. She lives in Chicago with her husband and dog.

SABAA TAHIR is the #1 *New York Times* bestselling author of the young adult fantasies *An Ember in the Ashes* and *A Torch Against the Night*. She grew up in California's Mojave Desert at her family's eighteen-room motel. There, she spent her time devouring fantasy novels, raiding her brother's comic book stash, and playing guitar badly. She began writing while working nights as a newspaper editor. She likes thunderous indie rock, garish socks, and all things nerd. Her books have been published in thirty-four languages. Visit her website at www.SabaaTahir.com and follow her on Twitter @SabaaTahir.

BRENNA YOVANOFF was raised in a barn, a tent, and a tepee and was homeschooled until high school. She spent her formative years in Arkansas, in a town heavily populated by snakes, where sometimes they would drop turkeys out of the sky. When she was five, she moved to Colorado, where it snows on a regular basis but never snows turkeys. She holds an MFA in fiction from Colorado State University and is the author of *New York Times* bestseller *The Replacement*, *The Space Between*, *Paper Valentine*, and *Fiendish*. Her most recent novel, *Places No One Knows*, is out now. She currently lives in Denver.